I0831780

CAVEAT
Fuzzy

By Wolfgang Diehr

Pequod Press

CAVEAT FUZZY

A Pequod Press Science Fiction Novel

Manufactured in the United States of America
First Printing 2012

V 10 9 8 7 6 5 4 3 2 1

ISBN: 978-0-937912-22-5

On the cover: Alan Gutierrez, Caveat Fuzzy
2012 (*www.alangutierrez.com*)

Pequod Press
P.O. Box 80
Boalsburg, PA 16827

www.PequodPress.com

H. Beam Piper Continuations Presented by Pequod Press

Paratime Novels

Gunpowder God

The Fireseed Wars

Siege of Tarr-Hostigos

Kalvan Kingmaker

Great Kings' War

Time Crime

Terro-Human Future History

Fuzzy Ergo Sum

Caveat Fuzzy

Space Viking

The Last Space Viking

Space Viking's Throne

Dedication

To Doctor James Farrow:
Who started me on this road.

To Professor Christopher Leland:
Who showed me the potholes.

To Leila E. Smith:
Who came back for me when she
realized I was still at the last rest stop.

PROLOGUE

Bradley, never 'Brad,' Small was a minor felon, as his name would suggest. In his youth on Terra he had engaged in petty theft, aircar theft and even burglary, earning him time in juvenile hall and later prison. On Freya he ran afoul of a minor noble over the attention he had shown a young woman, while on Gimli he barely escaped the authorities on charges of fraud.

On Zarathustra Bradley decided to turn over a new leaf. He started out by trying to get a job with the Chartered Zarathustra Company. Unfortunately, the discovery of the Fuzzies resulted in the Company losing its charter and changing its hiring policies. Personnel with a quasi-legal background were no longer welcome. His attempt to gain employment at The Bitter End bar met with similar results. The owner, Raul Laporte, preferred to not hire men with a known criminal history. Criminals were okay, but known criminals might bring unwanted attention to Laporte's extralegal activities. Bradley even lost out on any land grab schemes after the new colonial government leased the unseated lands back to the now Charterless Zarathustra Company.

No job, no land, no cash. With no other ready options, Bradley returned to what he knew—crime. But he decided to be smarter about it. First, he strong-armed a prospector who was reputed to carry a stash of sunstones acquired illegally from the res. This provided working capital since his victim dared not report the theft as he would be arrested as well. Though the sunstones had a market value of thirty thousand sols, the pawnshop only paid fifteen thousand. That was enough for the enterprising thief. Bradley then studied prospecting and acquired mining equipment. Next, he acquired a used aircar and altered the serial number and

VIN plate, a skill he'd developed on Terra in his youth.

His preparations complete, Bradley flew over to Beta Continent where he was quickly spotted by the Zarathustra Native Protection Force and arrested. He was fined fifty sols and released. Bradley made several such forays and was caught each time, only to be released after another, though higher, fine. He became something of a joke to the ZNPF officers, which was part of his plan, a plan that was about to pay off.

He had expected to be caught at least three more times before finding a hole in the protective grid around the Fuzzy Reservation. However with the discovery of the alien rocket ship on The Reservation, the Zarathustra Native Protection Force was stretched thin enough to finally allow Bradley Small access to Beta Continent undetected. He flew low to the ground to avoid any surveillance devices and set up camp under a fibroid weave canopy, one formerly used by the military to block detectable transmissions, near a vein of black flint. It had taken months of research and study of satellite cartography to decide which vein of flint was both likely to yield a good load of sunstones and be safe from ZNPF notice. Now, Small was ready to start digging up sunstones and getting rich enough to retire, provided his luck held.

Of course, Bradley Small would have to take his treasure to an underworld dealer where he would make far less money than the Charterless Zarathustra Company would pay. Sources indicated that Raul Laporte still bought illicit gems, though at two-thirds the CZC rate. Or, Bradley could simply cache his stones until he was ready go off-world and sell them at much higher prices on Fenris, Marduk, Loki or some other planet he had never been to, but that meant travel and customs inspections and the chance of being caught smuggling. Still, no risk, no reward.

Bradley turned his attention to the business at hand. Traditional blasting was out of the question as it could draw attention from the ZNPF. Instead, he set up a heavy-duty sonic drill. It would pulverize the flint to dust a quarter cubic meter at a time, which in turn would be sucked up by a construction-grade vacuum hose that would gather and separate the flint dust from any small gravel. An evacuation hose would blow the flint dust into a nearby stream. Bradley idly observed that sunstone flint was almost always found near a body of water.

It was an efficient method of surface mining and did little damage to the environment, although it was much slower than blasting and scanning. It would take a couple of days to get as much work done with the sonic drill as blasting could do in a few hours, but Bradley was patient. He had provisions enough to last a month, and could do a little hunting with a sono-rifle when he needed fresh meat.

Bradley Small had been mining for two weeks when he discovered he had visitors. It was a small band of Fuzzies, possibly attracted by the noise from the sonic drill. Bradley had anticipated this possibility and had come prepared. He slipped under the canopy and came back out with a case of Terran Federation Armed Forces Emergency Ration, Extraterrestrial Type Three. Fuzzies were supposed to love the stuff, though Bradley wouldn't eat it on a bet, as was the case for most Terrans.

Opening a couple of tins, Bradley tossed the cakes to the Fuzzies where it landed at their feet. One Fuzzy, possibly the leader, took a piece and sniffed, and then nibbled some and promptly spit it back out in disgust. Bradley had never heard of such a thing. He considered the possibility that he bought a defective batch and tried a bit. It took all of his willpower not to spit it out. It wouldn't do to have the Fuzzies thinking he purposely offered them something bad. The extee-three tasted terrible, but it was the normal terrible that it was supposed to taste like. So, nothing was wrong with it, yet the Fuzzies didn't like it. Maybe this was a new species of Fuzzy?

The Fuzzy leader started yeeking something at him and he quickly put in his ultra-sonic hearing aid. Bradley knew very little about the Fuzzy language; nevertheless anything was better than nothing.

"Ota eleh! Shiru!" The Fuzzy pointed at the human, then made a sweeping gesture and pointed away.

Bradley had no idea what any of the words being barked at him meant, but the message was coming through loud and clear; the Fuzzies wanted him off their land. Apparently, they didn't like trespassers in these here parts, Bradley thought with a grin. He pondered for a moment over what else he might bribe them with. The extee-three was out and he didn't think to bring any toys. Well, if he couldn't bribe them, he would just scare them off. Fuzzies were supposed to be pretty timid in the wild, although Bradley doubted he could just chase them off by yelling at them. Story was that the Fuzzies discovered humans, not the other way around.

Slowly, he reached down to his sono-stunner and drew it. He considered shooting a Fuzzy, but then he would have an unconscious Fuzzy to deal with while the others ran away. Instead, Bradley aimed into the open sky and fired a short burst. The Fuzzies yeeked in alarm and covered their ears. The feedback from the stunner overloaded his hearing aid, creating a loud white noise that hurt Bradley's ears and left him disoriented for a moment. By the time he was able to compose himself the Fuzzies were aiming some sort of spears at him. These were short even by Fuzzy standards and seated on some sort of launching rods.

Bradley realized that the spears would be just as deadly as a rifle at this range, even thrown by a Fuzzy. Reconsidering his earlier position on unconscious Fuzzies, he aimed the sono-stunner at the little band and started to pull the trigger. It was an action he would never complete.

The first spear caught him in the chest, followed by one to his throat and another in the right leg. Bradley Small was dead before he hit the ground. The Fuzzies inspected the corpse to make sure he was no longer a threat, policed their spears, and then went through the campsite. Most of what they found was strange and incomprehensible to them, except for a small leather bag filled with stones that glowed when held in their hands. The Fuzzies took the bag of stones and left the body where it fell.

After a few hours, the local scavengers went to work on the late Bradley Small. Soon, nothing was left save bones scattered around the camp. Two weeks later, an NPF officer discovered the bones along with the camp, reported the find and an investigation was launched. While many theories as to the cause of death were bandied about, none included the possibility of death by Fuzzy.

I

"On the sixty-first count of enslavement, how do you find?"

"We find the defendants guilty."

The courtroom no longer reacted to the verdict. After all, they had heard it sixty times before, as well as the sixty-one recitations of guilty for illegal imprisonment, the sixty-one recitations of reckless endangerment of a sapient being, and the litany of other charges. The Fuzzies in attendance had long since fallen asleep. The reading of the verdict was taking nearly as long as the trial itself, but Chief Colonial Prosecutor Gustavus Adolphus Brannhard wanted every single count preserved on the record. The police were already lining up at the station to pull their names out of a hat for the privilege of shooting the defendants in the head, which was the mandatory punishment for most of the listed crimes.

With the reading of the verdict completed, the gallery breathed a sigh of relief. It was exciting at first; a guilty verdict on a capital charge was always exciting. However, the long drone of the same verdict over and over quickly lost its luster. Even Judge Janiver looked relieved.

"Having been found guilty on all charges, this court has no choice other than to sentence all defendants to death. Time, date, and manner of execution will be determined…" Judge Janiver looked at the screen embedded in his bench-top,"…Tuesday of next week. Bailiff, escort the prisoners back to their cells. Court is adjourned."

The gavel came down and a few people came over to congratulate

Gus on a job well done. Little Fuzzy, awakened by the sudden burst of activity, saw that everybody was crowding around the prosecuting attorney. Gus waved it all off, saying that a first-year paralegal could have gotten the same verdict. After all, with sixty-one Fuzzies, several members of the local constabulary, Chief Harry Steefer and some TFN marines, not to mention the Holloways, all testifying under veridication to what they saw at the warehouse in Mortgageville and the reservation on Beta Continent, it was like shooting fish in a barrel with a shotgun.

Jack and Morgan Holloway and Little Fuzzy stepped up to add their congratulations. Jack was still in a hover-chair as he was recovering from major surgery, and Little Fuzzy was sitting on his lap.

"Good job, Gus," Jack said. "After this, people will think more than twice about hurting a Fuzzy."

"Hell, Jack, the Fuzzies did the heavy lifting. Have three humans witness a crime and you'll get three different stories. Have three Fuzzies witness a crime and it's the same story three times. Or in this case, sixty-one times. And it is known far and wide that Fuzzies don't lie as a rule. Oh, and thanks for letting Little Fuzzy be the test subject for the veridicator." Gus ruffled the Fuzzy's fur and Little Fuzzy smiled. "Leslie was a little concerned that Jeff Rand might start telling not-so things at the wrong time if he acted as test subject too many times."

Jack had to remind himself that Jeff Rand used to be Wise One of the forest fire Fuzzies. At least Coombes hadn't named his family after a bunch of legal terms. There was an attorney in Mallorysport who named his two Fuzzies Felony and Misdemeanor. The names people would hang on a Fuzzy!

"You weh'come, Unka Gus."

"You are one clever little Fuzzy," Gus said, again ruffling his fur. "The clincher, as if this case even needed one, was your testimony, Jack. Fuzzies make great witnesses, but human juries still need to hear human testimony to remove any reasonable doubt."

"It was either testify or shoot them myself, Gus. I very nearly saved you the trouble of prosecuting those bastards Morgan and I caught. If Morgan hadn't pickpocketed my pistol, well, I'm not sure what I would have done."

"Too bad you have to be a cop to execute those Khooghras. I wouldn't mind putting my name in the hat," Morgan added. "To be fair, though, I did kill the one that tried to sneak up on Jack."

"Who told you that you had to be a cop?" Gus quickly explained that colonial law differed from planet to planet and that on Zarathustra any civic-minded person was welcome to participate, provided they took the orientation course and passed the psych exam. "Ben pushed that little gem through the legislature last month. Partly to get the fees from the orientation but mostly to give the people a greater sense of community. However, Ben is considering the possibility of using a good old-fashioned firing squad on this crowd."

Gus jerked a thumb in the direction of the defendants being escorted out in chains. The shackles were extremely heavy due to the light collapsium lamination treatment so the prisoners had to struggle to keep step with the bailiff. "He and Grego are discussing a deal to televise the execution as a warning to anybody else that might get the idea to harm a Fuzzy. The firing squad would be more dramatic than some cop shooting a man in the back of the head."

The trio moved out of the courtroom and passed several policemen. Colonial Marshal Max Fane wanted total security for the trial in case of a riot. Everybody wanted a piece of the defendants, it seemed. Even the cops were handpicked by Max based on their psych profiles. The Marshal took a dim view of vigilante justice.

"Ah, so that's why Judge Janiver didn't automatically impose sentence," Jack observed. "The firing squad is too good for these mutts.

We should hang them, instead. Or maybe bring back the electric chair."

"Electric chair?" Morgan mulled it over. On Freya executions were varied and considered barbaric by the more civilized Federation planets, yet the idea of electrocution had never occurred to the Freyan populace. "That sounds interesting. Personally, I would just have them drawn and quartered, but this electric chair sounds equally entertaining."

"Entertaining, he says! Well, I'll suggest that to Ben," Gus said with a smile. Not for the first time he thought that Freyans were a little too murderous as a people, though Terrans were pretty execution happy themselves back in the pre-atomic days. "Hell, we should set up a gallows in the Grand Platz and sell tickets."

"Actually, that is what we often do on Freya," Morgan said. "All executions are public events. We used to draw and quarter the more vile criminals on a regular basis, but we've become a bit more civilized since joining the Federation. We still make exceptions from time to time, though."

"Seemed like a good deterrent," Jack noted. "I attended a number of executions on Freya while I was there. I saw hangings, beheadings, a quartering or two and one catapulting."

"Catapulting?" This was a new one on Gus who had also been to Freya, though briefly.

"That one is reserved for noblemen who offend the ruling class," Morgan supplied. "The offender is bound to a boulder and catapulted into a mountainside. It is a rather spectacular event that shows the overclass and underclass alike that none are above the law."

Gus imagined what it would be like to hurdle through the air helplessly as the rock face of a mountain rushed up to meet him. He suppressed a shudder. "Great Ghu on a goat!" he whispered. "What does a nobleman have to do to rate that kind of treatment?"

"Oh, the usual," Morgan said. "Abuse of office, failure to pay the proper tribute to the king…there are a couple of warnings first, of course...one princedom tried to reinstall the marital night prerogative...."

"What's that?" Gus asked.

"That's where a landholding nobleman gets to have intimate relations with a common woman on her wedding night," Jack explained.

"So?"

"The common woman isn't *his* wife," clarified Morgan. "The king at that time was something of a prude and decided to call it rape. The execution was attended by all the land-bearing nobles of that princedom by royal decree."

Jack noted the chief prosecutor's reaction and added, "What they do to common rapists is even more extreme, and the offender usually lives to regret it...at least for a little while. Well, time for me to take care of a few things, and then get back to the res. I'll bet my desk is buried under a ton of paperwork by now."

"Hasn't Gerd been picking up the slack in your absence?"

"I'm afraid not, Gus. Gerd is working with the CZC to pick apart that rocket found in Northern Beta. I think I'll have to ask for a temporary assistant or two until he gets back. George Lunt has been running things the last month or so, and Ruth pitches in when she can, but George has his own work to attend to so I don't imagine he did more than the bare minimum necessary to keep things running. Even that would be a lot to expect considering all he's had to deal with lately. I've heard that NPF has run up quite a bit of overtime in the last six weeks."

"Somehow word got out that those illegal prospectors who got themselves blown up found a super-rich deposit of sunstones or diamonds or some other mineral wealth as well as the rocket. The place is crawling with people trying to get rich overnight," Morgan explained. "Victor sent over some of his own security men to help the Native

Protection Force keep a lid on the excavation site."

"That just shows how smart Grego is," Gus observed. "If there are sunstones and they get snatched up by the wrong people, they could damage the market prices."

"On top of that, every amateur archaeologist on the planet is trying to find another rocket or anything else that might prove that Fuzzies came from outer space," Jack added. "Most have sense enough to apply for a permit, but lack the patience to wait for the approval. Ben had the trespassing fines doubled twice over to discourage that sort of thing. Too bad a lot of people have more money than sense."

"Well, look at the upside," Gus said. "The treasury will be getting fat on fines and maybe confiscated assets used in furtherance of the crime."

"At the cost of disturbing a lot of Fuzzies," finished Jack irritably.

* * * * * * * * *

"…and the verdict is in; guilty on all counts!"

The man on the screen, 'Spin' Wheeler, was a local celebrity and the talk show host of *Spinning Zarathustra* until coming to work one day in a state of inebriation. Miguel Kourland fired Spin and replaced his segment with *Tuning in with Tuning*. Spin quickly found work at B.I.N. with his new show *Spinning Wheels*, where he made a new reputation attacking the Charterless Zarathustra Company and the colonial government.

"Next Tuesday, Judge Janiver will impose the death penalty on the convicted brain donors, and well he should. Slavery is a nasty business to say the least. But how should the punishment be administered? Back in the bad old days, convicts were put down by lethal injection, like a stray dog. This was less of a deterrent than hoped for. Today, on colony planets, a bullet in the back of the head is the preferred method of execution. But why not give these vile villains a more spectacular, and dare I say, entertaining demise? My sources tell me that the Colonial Governor is considering a televised firing squad. Now, as you know, I hate to agree with anybody in the government about anything, but I have to admit that he has something, here. But why not…?"

Ben Rainsford pressed a button on his desk and the screen went dark. "Spin Wheeler agrees with me. Clearly, I've been in this job for too long when a Khooghra like that agrees with me."

Colonial Marshal Max Fane shrugged and said, "Why not hold a lottery?"

Ben stubbed out his cigarette, then turned to Max. "Victor suggested that to shore up some funds against future expenses," started the Colonial Governor, thinking that Max was changing the subject. The last several weeks had been hard on Ben and his brain wasn't packing a full clip at times.

"No, sir, I mean for the privilege of being on the firing squad," explained Colonial Marshal Max Fane. "People buy a ticket for, oh, say, a sol apiece, and the winners get to be on the line to shoot the Fuzzy slavers. They can buy as many tickets as they want. Then we have a big drawing and select our shooters. It will be a real feast day in Mallorysport, I think."

Ben Rainsford mulled that over. "Not a bad idea, really, if a bit old-fashioned."

Max rolled his eyes. "Old-fashioned? Well, you should hear about executions on other worlds. On Uller they take a criminal, cut off his forelimbs, crack open his silicon shell and tie him down over a *k'gakk-ma* nest. Think of it as being fed to army ants the size of cockroaches. On Yggdrasil the Khooghras tie the offender onto a spit over a fire pit and slow cook the poor bastard."

This was a new one on Ben. He tried to imagine what a Khooghra would consider a crime and failed. "What do they do with the body afterwards?"

"Eat it, of course."

I should have seen that one coming, thought Ben. "All right, say we do this: do we shoot them one at a time, or in groups, or all at once? Does one lottery ticket get you a go at the first firing order, or all of them?"

"Hmm...I would go one at a time, one ticket per firing order, five shooters per order," Max said. "We would sell more tickets that way and more people would get a shot, in a manner of speaking, at the firing line. The show will last longer, too. Mr. Grego should like that."

Ben nodded. "Plus we have to go to him for the lottery print run. Is there an independent printer we could use? I've been criticized in the media for giving too much business to the CZC."

Max shook his head. "I'm sure Mr. Grego's crew could do the job faster and cheaper than any Mom & Pop operation in Mallorysport..."

"They could, but that's not the point," Ben said. "On any other world a government contract would be bid on, and the lowest bidder with quality merchandise would get the contract. On Zarathustra nobody can compete with the CZC for anything. So, I'll have to make some concessions to the situation and let some non-company contracts go out here and there. Like the paper works for the lottery tickets. We have to spread the wealth a bit or people will keep thinking that the colonial government is in bed with the CZC."

Ben's desk screen activated and his secretary, Francine M'bata, informed him that the Holloways were asking to see him. "Send them in, Fran."

Jack and Morgan entered and shook hands with Ben and Max. "You two must have come here straight from the trial." Ben waved his head in the direction of his wall-mounted viewscreen. "I just got the word; guilty on all charges."

"Gus made it sound like it was the easiest trial he ever won," Jack said with a smile.

Max Fane snorted. "No disrespect to Mr. Brannhard or his competence as an attorney, but I would have to say that a brain-damaged Khooghra couldn't have failed to secure a guilty verdict."

Jack laughed, then clutched his chest. While in no real danger, he was still sore where the surgeons installed his new heart and lung. The other men pretended not to notice since Jack 'didn't want to be fussed over like a damned invalid child.' When the pain subsided, Jack said, "Gus would agree, Max. So, Ben, I hear you're thinking about setting up a firing squad for these bastards."

"Max and I were just discussing that." Ben explained Max's idea for the lottery.

"Put me down for 1,000 tickets per firing order," Morgan said. "I want another piece of these *kleetook'na*."

Jack explained that a *kleetook* was a small bloodsucking mammal, roughly half the size of a Terran field mouse that survived by attaching itself to a larger animal and drinking its blood like a giant tick. Unchecked, the afflicted animal would grow weak and die within a Freyan month, depending on its size. *Kleetook'na* was the pluralized form in Freyan.

Jack changed the topic of discussion to that of assistants; namely, he wanted a couple. "I'll be a few weeks just getting out of this damned chair. I'll need somebody who can reach the top drawers of the file cabinet." The fact that the hover-chair could float up and down was tactfully ignored.

"Actually, Jack, I already discussed this with Gerd," Ben said. "He said Ruth is sending out somebody tomorrow, but you will need a second assistant given the amount of paperwork that has piled up in your absence. I'll put an ad in the *Zarathustra Times* for a temp."

Now who would Ruth have thought to send over? Jack asked himself. "Well, that's great, Ben. Tell you what; I have to check in with the doc, then buy a new power cartridge for my aircar before I fly back to Beta. I've had it with the recharger and that antique solar unit. How about we get together at cocktail time before I head back? Relax, Morgan, I promise to behave and stick to that tea you've been pouring into me."

Morgan assumed a look of innocence and winked at Little Fuzzy, who smiled and winked back. "I didn't say anything."

"You didn't have to. I know how much stock a Freyan of character puts on a Blood Oath." Jack ruffled Little Fuzzy's fur. "Especially with the oath-ee watching." Jack turned back to Ben. "Look, I know you and Morgan have some business to discuss, so I'll mosey on over to the hospital while you two talk. See you for cocktails, Ben?"

"How is 1700 for you?"

"Perfect. See you then." Jack and Ben shook hands, and then he turned his chair around and headed for the door.

"I'll walk you out, Commissioner," Max Fane said, as he nodded to the governor.

As soon as the door closed behind the two men, Morgan wasted no time getting down to brass tacks. "Governor, I am prepared to pay fifty million sols for Epsilon Continent, plus cover the leaseback fees owed to the Charterless Zarathustra Company. I've cleared it with Victor and he has no objection to the sale."

Fifty million sols was a lot of money by anybody's definition, but Epsilon was just over eight million square kilometers. "What exactly do you need an entire continent for? That's a bit extravagant even if you do have more money than Ghu."

"For a new settlement. I have about two thousand people and some…exotic animals that need a home and I want them set up out of the way of any interference. And for the record, it's not just me paying for this."

"Have you discovered a new alien species?" As a xenonaturalist, Ben was very interested in any new life-forms. As the governor of Zarathustra he was concerned about the legality of transplanting those life-forms into the local ecosystem. "Is the Federation aware of what you are doing?"

"Aware of and in support. In fact, you'll earn some good will from the Federation if you help me with this."

Ben leaned back in his seat to think for a moment. "Good will isn't something I worry about, really. It was the Federation that stuck me with this job in the first place. Ah, hell, I'll talk this over with Victor and Commodore Napier and see what they think. However, I will want the full story on who these people are and why they need to be relocated before I give the final okay. When will they be here?"

"In nine days, give or take. Everything was prearranged before I left Magni on my way here."

Magni? Ben had heard of it: a planet with 1.21 gravity and no indigenous sapient life-forms. It was originally discovered by two separate exploration companies based on Thor and now owned by the Chartered Magni Cooperative. Their primary source of income was derived from iron and nickel mining and collapsium production. The descendants of the original colonists were said to be built like brick walls on steroids.

"These people are from Magni?"

Morgan was evasive. "Yes and no. I'll have to explain after they arrive or you won't believe me. I'll also have to ask that you keep this quiet. Jack, Gus, Victor, the Commodore and maybe Marshal Fane will be the only people in the loop…at least initially. Do we have a deal?"

Ben thought hard before answering. The possibility of meeting a new race of aliens made for a pretty big carrot to the governor. "After I meet these new settlers and hear their story. If it all washes, then you have a deal. If not, I may have to send them packing."

Morgan smiled. "I very much doubt it will come to that."

"Do these…people…have any marketable skills? This government doesn't need a bunch of welfare cases."

"These are all trained farmers and miners. They can fend for themselves well enough. And they will be quite comfortable in the cooler climate of Epsilon Continent."

Miners? Well, that made sense coming from Magni, but Magni orbited a B2 sun making its mean temperature somewhat higher than Zarathustra's even though its orbit was forty percent further from its primary. Ben said as much.

"It gets pretty chilly underground, actually. The core temperature of Magni is much lower than most inhabitable planets. Oh, and you won't need to place that ad for Jack. I think I know somebody who will make a great assistant…."

II

Federation medicine had made tremendous leaps in the last several hundred years. Devices that were inexpensive and readily available for home use could identify almost any ailment or condition a person could be suffering from, although one thing hadn't changed significantly since the days before the discovery of penicillin—blood still needed to be drawn.

Akira Hsu O'Barre stared at the tiny medical device she had picked up from the apothecary. All she had to do was prick her finger on the almost invisible needle and the miniature machine would do the rest. Akira wasn't squeamish about seeing her own blood, or afraid of the needle which was virtually painless to use. It was the potential results that she feared…results that could change her life.

She quickly jammed the needle into her index finger and pulled it out. There was no pain or even any blood where she had stuck herself. Akira thought she might have missed until she noticed the countdown on the small readout. It took five seconds to get the results. Some models worked faster, but this brand boasted greater accuracy.

Positive.

Akira dropped the device on her night stand and sat on the edge of her bed almost in shock. Tears welled up in her eyes as she said softly to herself, "Oh, Ghu, what am I going to do now?"

* * * * * * * * *

Victor Grego sat back and mentally processed the request, no, *demand* he was just given. John Morgan Holloway had just marched in and stated that he would like one of the CZC employees to take an extended leave of absence to go to work for Jack Holloway.

"Morgan, surely there are many qualified people who don't work for the company...."

Morgan waved that away. "It has to be Akira, Victor."

Grego stubbed out his cigarette and stared levelly at Morgan. He knew that the young man was involved with Miss O'Barre, and in all likelihood would marry her before too long. The rumor mill had gone into overdrive on that subject and there was even an office pool about when the nuptials would take place. So why the rush to yank her away from the company to put her to work for his father?

"Have you cleared this with Miss O'Barre, Morgan?"

"Out of respect, I felt I should clear it with you, first, Victor."

Out of respect? Well, Morgan was definitely respectful. "Hmm...I'll tell you what; explain what Freyan custom this will satisfy and she's all yours. Provided she chooses to go, of course. I'm not running an escort service, here."

Morgan smiled broadly. "I must be pretty transparent."

"Well, only to me and Jack, I think. Almost everything you do appears to be motivated by Freyan rules of conduct. Which isn't a bad thing by the way, since you tend to behave yourself better than most Terrans I have known—if we discount your shooting one of my best friends."

Morgan winced, then nodded. "Tell you what, take a wild guess and I'll let you know if you are warm or cold."

Grego thought for a moment: Akira working for Jack must satisfy some Freyan rule that would allow them to marry. He said as much.

"Good call, Victor. For Freyan nobility to marry below their station, the woman has to prove herself to the noble's family. Oddly, even to me, the family isn't supposed to know that she is proving anything. I have a Tri-D disk of a theatrical production where that is the central plot. The gist is this; Jack has to see Akira as a woman of value without knowing that I intend to take her as a wife."

Grego made a mental note to get in on the pool. "What does Akira think about this? For that matter, why would Jack have a problem with her? He doesn't stick his nose into other people's business, as a rule."

"Akira doesn't know. If Jack rejects her I don't want her to know that I was going to ask her, um, for her hand."

Grego nodded. "That is the correct, if old-fashioned, idiom."

"There is also the possibility that Akira won't like Jack, either."

Not like good old lovable, peaceable Jack Holloway? Grego thought. He suppressed the urge to laugh. Almost everybody who didn't like Jack was either dead or skipped planet. Jack was an honest, plain-spoken man who didn't screw people over. People less honest tended to get on his bad side rather quickly, though. "I very much doubt that will be a problem, though I do see your point. Fine. I'll approve the leave of absence as long as you don't twist her arm too hard. She still has a couple of years left on her contract with the CZC, I think, unless she plans to pay off the balance."

"I offered to do that for her," Morgan said as he shook his head. "She refused. 'A contract is a contract' she said. The Company held up to its end, so she intends to hold up hers."

I knew there was something I liked about that girl, Grego thought. He also considered pumping Morgan for a possible wedding date, then decided to play fair. It wasn't like he needed the pool money, after all. "Would you like me to *suggest* she take the time off to work for Jack? I can make it sound like it was all my idea."

Morgan looked sheepish, a rare thing for the Freyan. "I...well... would you?"

"Absolutely. But it will cost you a case of Freyan ale."

Morgan smiled and shook Grego's hand. "Done and done."

* * * * * * * * *

The Two Moons Tavern was the preferred watering hole for the Mallorysport police. Unlike most bars, the Two Moons was a single level establishment with a huge skylight in the ceiling that could be adjusted for desired opacity. During the day, it was typically kept dark, but at night it was set for the clearest setting so as to catch the light of Zarathustra's moons, Darius and Xerxes. As a well-known cop bar, one where people not in uniform were required to check their guns and knives at the door, it was also the safest place for Ben to meet people for cocktails outside of Government House or Company House.

Even though Ben Rainsford was a popular governor with high approval ratings, mostly due to his working a deal with the Charterless Zarathustra Company that floated the government and planetary services without resorting to taxation, there was always the possibility of an assassination attempt. In fact, during the last election a Juan Takagashi supporter tried to shoot Ben after a public debate. Fortunately, for Ben, the would-be assassin made his attempt at the Two Moons Tavern, with the predictable outcome.

Jack floated in ahead of Morgan and Gus and met up with Ben at his usual table. The governor already had a drink, so Gus bought a round for the rest. Ben never accepted a drink that somebody else paid for to avoid the appearance of accepting special favors. He also declined buying others a drink to avoid the appearance of currying favor. Gus privately thought that Ben needed to relax a bit.

Jack noticed that Gus had a water glass filled to the brim with bourbon. "I thought you were cutting down."

"I am," Gus said. "I only have two of these a day. Except on Sunday.

Then I have a third."

Morgan cringed inwardly. How Brannhard was able to consume that much hard liquor defied imagination. Even by Freyan standards that was an impressive amount to consume on a daily basis. "I'll have a Freyan ale for me and an Earl Grey Green with honey for Jack."

Gus stifled a laugh and downed half his glass. He considered lighting his cigar, then remembered Jack's forbearance when he was on the mend. But one doesn't suggest cocktails in a bar unless one expects people to drink them in his presence, so he downed the rest of his drink and ordered a refill. "I feel your pain, Jack. Allan and Natty rode herd on me for two months after that liver transplant. I still have to do my drinking on the sly or I get a lecture in pidgin Fuzzy about liver damage. They seem to think it's a lifetime deal."

"Good luck explaining the benefits of Federation medicine to them. At least Morgan here understands that this is a temporary situation." Jack glanced meaningfully at his son. "At least he'd better."

"Once the doctors and Little Fuzzy are satisfied that you are in the clear, I will be happy to buy the first round, father."

Gus snorted. "A little formal, aren't you? I always called my old man 'dad'."

"Actually," Jack said, "on Freya he would be required to address me as 'sire,' Gus. Little though I'd deserve it."

"No blame is attached to you, father," Morgan said as he received his ale. "Uncle Orphtheor carries that burden, and he is much too dead to be held accountable."

"So, once Jack is all better, are you planning on sticking around or heading back to Freya?" Ben asked.

Morgan drained his stein and signaled for a refill. "Actually, I am not as welcome back on my home planet as I would like. Were I not a wealthy land-owning nobleman I wouldn't be able to set foot there."

Gus, having followed Morgan's example, contemplated another refill, then thought better of it. Natty and Allan might smell it on him. "With your family name established won't you be considered legitimate?"

"Absolutely. Unfortunately, I burned a few other bridges there. I'll explain some other time."

"Sounds like your son, all right," Gus quipped. "How many planets have you worn out your welcome on, Jack?"

"A few, but none I would care to return to." Jack turned to Morgan. "Are you exiled? Oh, maybe you would rather not discuss it…"

"It's nothing like that. Let's just say I managed to embarrass some very important people. It's tied into my reason for wanting to buy Epsilon."

Ben took notice of that and became confused but said nothing. How Magni and Freya were connected should make an interesting story. "Just remember, Jack, that I have to push the sale through the legislature, if I decide to approve it. Tell you what, though, I'll have to tell them you offered half of what you told me so that they'll think they buffaloed me into jacking up the price. They would never accept your first offer, no matter what it was."

Gus snorted. "Damned straight. You've been doing a good job of keeping those idiots in line, Ben. I'm especially impressed that you kept them from mangling the constitution."

Ben laughed and lit a cigarette, then remembered that Jack was on the wagon and snubbed it out. "My veto stamp is on its last legs. Last week I had to nix the no taxation amendment. If something happens to the sunstone deal, we'll need to shift to taxation in a hurry. Strangely, I had to nix another amendment to start taxation the next day." Ben shook his head. "What the hell are these people using for brains, anyway? It's a good thing this crowd can't vote on their own pay raises the way they do on some other planets. Say, Morgan, how is the government laid out on Freya?"

"Hmm…much like old Terra's feudal societies. My equivalent title would be a baron, I think. Barons used to be landowners who managed their territories for the prince. Each realm is a princedom which is under the authority of a regional king, of which there are five on Freya. These kings answer to a, um, higher ruler, a great king or, um emperor. There is only one emperor. His heir is an arch-prince."

"How do these kings support themselves?" prodded Gus.

"Well, each nobleman is a landowner of greater or lesser degree. He typically develops the land one way or another. In our pre-Federation days the barons would pay tribute to the princes, who in turn paid the kings who paid the high king. Nowadays most nobles make their money from industry and trade. The underclass can own land of their own and everybody pays taxes. The high king has a council, not unlike Parliament in England before space travel, which oversees the day-to-day administration of planetary affairs."

"There you go, Ben," Jack said with a smile. "Declare yourself Great King and run the planet like a feudal society."

"Off with their heads!" yelled Gus. "I can think of a few people I'd like to see one foot shorter from the top. Too bad the Federation frowns on Madame Guillotine." Gus relayed what he had learned of Freyan executions, assisted by Jack and Morgan. Ben shared what he had learned earlier about the Khooghra justice system.

"Speaking of public executions, what did you decide on the Fuzzy slavers," asked Jack.

"I'm going with Max's idea. We're holding a lottery, one sol per ticket per firing line. There will be six men per firing line; each will be issued one bullet apiece. Commodore Napier agreed to supply the rifles and some men for security. It seems that the military still uses firing squads and has old-style single-shot carbines for the job. He also said he will buy a round of lottery tickets for his officers and NCOs who were working with the police when the Fuzzy slavers were found."

"That'll boost morale," Jack chuckled. "I'll bet Pancho Ybarra suggested it."

Gus asked about the Marine security task force. "Don't you think the Marshal's men can handle it?"

"Of course they can, but with everybody either attending the execution or watching it on the screen, there's bound to be an increase in criminal activity. I want every cop I can muster patrolling Mallorysport and the surrounding areas. I'm even borrowing some bodies from the CZC security force that Victor offered."

"Mr. Grego has been very generous with Company assistance," Morgan noted. Before anybody could jump to Grego's defense, Morgan added, "That's good public relations."

Jack checked the time and noted it was getting late. "I'll have to collect Little Fuzzy from the Fuzzy bar and hit the sky. It'll be close to midnight on Beta by the time we get home."

"Why not just stay overnight with me. Flora and Fauna would love to see you and Little Fuzzy?" Ben suggested.

"I appreciate the offer, Ben, but I've been away too long as it is. And to tell the truth, I miss my own bed. It will be good to sleep in my own place again after all this time in the hospital."

"I second that," Gus said. "I went through the same thing after my liver transplant. Those hospital beds are designed for easy access to the patient, not patient comfort."

Jack said his good-byes and paid his tab and floated out in his hover-chair followed by Morgan. Outside the bar Morgan offered to drive and Jack accepted. He didn't want to admit it, but he was feeling his age. And then some.

III

It was morning and everybody was hungry. Little Fuzzy noticed that Pappy Jack was still snoring and made sure nobody woke him. "Pappy Jack still need much sleep after sur-ger-y to fix heart and lung." He also reminded everybody that Pappy Jack and Unka Morgan didn't get in until after big moon highest time; midnight.

The Fuzzies went out, fed and watered the dogs, inspected them for vermin and injuries, and then groomed them. While Zarathustra was unique in the fact that it had no bloodsucking parasites such as mosquitoes, fleas or ticks, it did have tunnel worms, which would enter the body, travel under the skin, and eventually lay eggs within the host. An afflicted animal, left untreated, could die in weeks from such an infestation. There was also a particularly nasty variety of insect that fed on living skin. It did relatively little damage, but the wounds could quickly become septic.

Satisfied that the dogs were worm and insect free, the Fuzzies took them out for some exercise. Pappy Jack said the dogs needed to run every day to stay strong. They were just returning from their run when Jack walked out of the cabin.

Back when the dogs were first introduced as mounts for the Fuzzies, Jack expressed concern that the Curtys might confuse their masters for prey. Larry Wolvin explained that the dogs were raised from birth being cared for by Fuzzies and trained never to attack one. Any dog that lacked the proper temperament was removed from the program and either used in security work, human pets or, in extreme cases, put down. Fortunately, the Curtys were known for their even temperament and high intelligence.

Jack saw the Fuzzies running toward him with the dogs and thought, *Uh-oh, here comes the warden. Now I'm gonna get it.*

"Pappy Jack!" yelled Little Fuzzy. "Where's floating chair? Dok'tor say you not walk, yet."

Jack let out a sigh. "Just getting a little exercise. I'll use the chair if I have to go further than this, hokay?"

Little Fuzzy discussed it with the others. "Hokay, Pappy Jack. But not go far. Dok'tor say so."

Jack agreed and walked back into the cabin. He didn't want to admit it, but his legs were feeling weak, so he planned on getting into the chair right away. It didn't seem fair for his legs to be so dodgy when he'd been shot in the chest. Maybe it was time to consider getting some physical therapy.

Little Fuzzy, satisfied that Pappy Jack was behaving, led the others away from the cabin to hunt for goofers—land-prawns were becoming scarce on the reservation—but asked Baby Fuzzy to stay behind and keep an eye on Pappy Jack. The Fuzzies were beginning to see that their Pappy Jack was old by Big One standards, and wanted to make sure he didn't hurt himself.

Later, when Jack took the hover-chair out for an inspection of the area, he noticed Baby peeking out from behind the trunk of a featherleaf tree watching him. Jack smiled and pretended he didn't spot his little hirsute watchman.

Jack couldn't help thinking about his current infirmity as he glided around in his chair. Next thing you know, I'll get fat from lack of exercise, Jack thought.

Then Jack noticed the Fuzzy called Jackie Gleason, named for a long-dead overweight comedian. The Fuzzy was so called because he had put on about five pounds after he came to the res. That was a lot of weight for a Fuzzy.

How long before all the Fuzzies became like that, Jack thought. He had seen it on other planets like Yggdrasil. The natives would start getting things handed to them in the name of diplomatic relations, and before long the natives discovered they didn't have to work as hard to get by. Next thing you know, you had a lot of fat natives lying around.

That was *not* going to happen to the Fuzzies, decided the Native Affairs Commissioner.

* * * * * * * * *

Joseph Aaron Quigley had been and done many things in his lifetime; a college student on Mars, a Terran Federation Marine, a scout on Yggdrasil and, most recently, an illegal sunstone prospector. At the moment he was a very frightened man. Worse, he was afraid of a bunch of Fuzzies.

To be fair, there were hundreds of the diminutive hirsute Zarathustran natives, each armed with a weapon of one type or another. That wasn't the problem in and of itself, though. Back in college Joe had taken a few classes in anthropology. What he was seeing now flew in the face of everything he had ever learned.

While the study of *Fuzzy sapiens zarathustra* was a very new discipline, since their existence only became known in the last few years, certain things were pretty much standard for any sapient race. Technological advancement went through certain stages at a more or less consistent pace. Even the Yggdrasil Khooghra, according to archeological evidence, advanced at a steady pace. Their advancement stages were the furthest apart of any known sapient species, but still steady.

In the wild Fuzzies were typically a nomadic species operating in family units of four to eight, according to current studies. They did not specialize; everybody did the same things to survive. Fuzzies did not create camps where some of the members would stay to care for the young while the rest went hunting and foraging. And they never, ever gathered together by the hundreds to prepare for war.

Until now.

These Fuzzies had instituted specialization. Hunting parties went out to gather food for the rest. Groups of "makers" from different tribal units gathered together to exchange ideas and develop new things. Lots of new things. Those too old or injured to engage in hunting cared for the young and guarded the prisoner; namely one Joseph Aaron Quigley. The Wise Ones of each tribe gathered to discuss things and compare ideas. But even that didn't scare Joe as much as what he saw in the social and technological development of the Fuzzies in the last two months.

Joe was the only survivor of an illegal prospecting operation. Somehow, the mass-energy converter exploded, killing everybody. Joe had only survived because he was outside of the camp collecting the surveillance cameras, and even that was a close call. The nearby Fuzzy encampment had found him and cared for him, though it was quite clear he was their prisoner. That was when things started getting scary.

The leader of the clan that captured him, *Bal-f'ke*, or Red Fur, had sent out emissaries to other clans and called them together. Within weeks several dozen clans had come in answer to that call. *Bal-f'ke* then created a council of chiefs. To give everybody a turn speaking without fighting to be heard, *Bal-f'ke* had found a sunstone, no doubt kicked up during the explosion, and stuck it on the end of a stick with tree sap. The scepter was passed from Fuzzy to Fuzzy, each speaking in turn.

The makers were also very busy. In two months Joe watched them go from chopper-diggers to atlatls. Another Fuzzy adapted the spear-thrower idea to rocks instead of spears with a design not unlike a lacrosse stick. One Fuzzy innovator had been showing the others some catgut he had taken from a zarabuck; a new accomplishment in itself as zarabucks had proven almost impossible for a Fuzzy to bring down previously. Another Fuzzy instantly recognized the advantage of the thin, strong wire for attaching a stone axe-head to a handle.

Two weeks earlier another family unit came in and shared another interesting piece of technology—the sling. A Fuzzy with a sling could launch a small rock at least three times further than a Fuzzy with the Lacrosse stick, and five times as far as a barehanded Fuzzy. Joe couldn't help wondering if bow and arrow tech was far behind.

Joe Quigley broke out in a cold sweat. In two months the Fuzzies had advanced millennia socially and technologically. They were still about ten thousand odd years behind Terran civilization, but they had an advantage nobody but Joe Quigley knew about; the Fuzzies weren't as harmless as everybody thought.

* * * * * * * * *

It was another day and Native Affairs Commissioner Jack Holloway signed his name at the bottom of a report before placing the document on top of the ever-growing pile in his outboxes. It was bad enough that he had the backlog that piled up while he was stuck in the hospital, nevertheless the workload almost tripled since the so-called 'Fuzzy Rocket' up in the northeast of the res was discovered. Jack made a mental note to shoot the owners of B.I.N. the next time he was over in Mallorysport. Thanks to that irresponsible newscast two months ago claiming that a 'Fuzzy rocket ship' had been found on Beta, every amateur scientist and lookiloo on the planet had been caught trespassing on the Fuzzy Reservation trying to get a look at the excavation site. Before long they might even start coming in from off-world. Enough was enough. Jack finally had to authorize the relocation of the rocket to a secure warehouse on Alpha. Let it be Victor Grego and the Marines' headache for a while.

Jack grabbed the next paper off the stack from the inbox. Another trespasser report from Major George Lunt. *Poor bastard has to be cranking these things out by the ream.* George had it worse than Jack; he and his crew on the Native Protection Force were out nabbing the violators and writing the reports. Maybe with all the fines they were collecting that assistant he asked Ben about could get written into the budget on a permanent basis.

Technically, Gerd van Riebeek, as Deputy Commissioner of Native Affairs, was Jack's assistant. In fact, he should have cleared up most of the paperwork while Jack was recovering in the hospital. Unfortunately, Gerd was also the resident scientist, both a xenonaturalist and an anthropologist, on staff and was working with Juan Jimenez's department on the rocket over at Science Division. Zarathustra was a small planet in terms of population and people with a background in any scientific discipline were at a premium, so even though it was a bit out of Gerd's area of expertise, he was the government's representative in the matter.

The upside was that the Charterless Zarathustra Company was picking up the tab for Gerd's pay while on the project. Jack had no idea what Victor Grego was getting out of the deal; maybe dibs on any new technology they discovered in the rocket. One thing was for sure; Grego wasn't footing the bill out of his love for new discoveries. The previous discovery, the Fuzzies themselves, had almost destroyed the CZC.

Jack grabbed the next paper from the inbox. This one was a report on the huge gathering of Fuzzies in the north near the dig site. According to the most recent estimate, there were over two hundred Fuzzies gathered in the area. Ben Rainsford suggested that it might be some sort of pre-programmed instinct in the Fuzzies to gather like that every so often, perhaps once a generation or so. If so, why weren't the local and adopted Fuzzies striking out for the big Fuzzy Family Reunion? So far none of his own family or the others in the neighborhood seemed the least bit interested in leaving the nest other than to get adopted by a Big One. Jack was no naturalist like Ben, but it didn't sit right. If it was instinct, then why was it that only the wild Fuzzies were making the trip? For that matter, only the Fuzzies in that general area were involved—for now.

Jack added the report to a file folder and moved on to the next paper; an authorization request for a prisoner work detail to clean up the excavation site. Jack smiled. Victor Grego didn't miss a trick. By having a chain gang clean up at the dig he was able to exercise total control over the area. Prisoners could be questioned under veridication at the end of each work detail whereas normal wage earners couldn't be, or at least not without some justification. Somebody had been digging up something out there before the explosion and Grego wanted to know what. Hell, so did Jack and everybody else. The smart money was on sunstones, but there were also diamonds and precious metals to be found on Zarathustra. Jack signed off and made a note to have George Lunt send a ZNPF detail to ride herd on the operation and make sure the Fuzzies weren't annoyed by the convicts.

Jack pushed away from the desk and stood to stretch his arms and legs. He was allowed out of the hover-chair for brief periods to exercise his legs. At his age he couldn't afford to get complacent and sedentary. From his office window he could see Little Fuzzy and Morgan tossing a plastic disk back and forth. What was that thing called, again? A freebie? No, a Frisbee. One of the NPF cops found the specs in an historical archive and made one with a home molding kit. The Fuzzies were crazy about it. Even the dogs enjoyed chasing and fetching the silly things.

Morgan barely had time to say hello after flying in from Alpha before the Fuzzies waylaid him to come and play.

Jack's watch started beeping. He turned off the signal and pulled a pill bottle out of his desk drawer. He took two pills and chased it with some Earl Grey Green tea. He would have preferred his usual hot coffee but the doctors were insistent that he moderate his intake until the system accommodation treatments had run their course. That also meant no tobacco or alcohol. At least he was developing a taste for the tea. It was close, but not quite as good as some of the Freyan teas he had tried when he was younger. He had developed new sympathy for what Gus Brannhard had gone through after his liver transplant. Of course, Gus didn't need the system accommodation meds, or at least not as many for as long, since he was much younger than the Native Affairs Commissioner. Being over sixty did have a few drawbacks, let alone being over seventy.

The new heart had been implanted seven weeks earlier while the new lung had only resided in his chest for the past two weeks. He would need the accommodation meds for at least another week. The doctors had agreed to release him on the grounds that he would have to behave himself and, ironically, have his son look after him. The same man that had shot him in the first place.

My son.

That still took a little getting used to. Jack had to admit that Morgan was a fine young man, even though they did damn near kill each other in that damned duel. Smart, strong—strong enough to carry the new power unit for the aircar by himself, in fact—and very responsible…and hopefully engaged to that pretty little Akira O'Barre, soon. They'd make some good-looking grandchildren for him, he'd wager. Jack couldn't help smiling at the thought of grandchildren, something he thought he'd never live to see.

Jack started for the door when the viewscreen beeped. He returned to his seat and tapped the 'picture on' button. It was the colonial governor.

"Hi, Ben," he said, moving his hands together in an approximation of shaking hands. The governor did the same. "Checking up on me? I promise I'm behaving."

Ben Rainsford returned the gesture. "Good to know, Jack. Actually, I just wanted to give you an update. George Lunt will probably call you in a while, but I wanted to be the first."

"Okay, shoot."

Ben shuffled some papers until he found the one he was looking for. "Well, that team of geologists and God only knows what all other 'ologists' Victor and the Terran Federation sent over have been carefully digging the place up looking for more bones and clues as to who was flying that rocket and who managed to blow themselves up."

"Yes, I just signed off on the prison work detail. I've been meaning to get out there, but I can't get past the warden and his guards to go anywhere." Jack jerked a thumb toward the window. Ben could just make out John Morgan and the Fuzzies in the background. "You know he swore a Freyan Blood Oath with Little Fuzzy to protect me from harm and is taking it very seriously."

Ben laughed, and then said, "Too bad he didn't do that before shooting you." When he stopped laughing his face became very serious. "Well, this is going to add to your discomfort, I'm afraid," Ben added soberly as he reached for something off-screen. It was a small leather bag, like the ones human children used for marbles. He poured the contents on the desk in front of him. It looked like gravel until Ben picked one pebble up and rolled it between his hands. It glowed bright red.

Jack knew what it was without being told. After all, he had spent years digging up and selling that very same thing. "They found sunstones up there? Any idea how many?"

Ben shook his head. "We don't know, yet. These were dug up from that pit the rocket was buried in. Initial scans show a concentration of stones in the flint easily ten times that of the ore in Yellowsand. At least forty percent of them are thermo-fluorescent."

Ben didn't look happy as he said it, nor should he. A few sunstones were valuable. A lot were still good. But the kind of concentration Ben was talking about would glut the market and destroy their value. Victor Grego had even reduced production at Yellowsand to keep the market stable. Well, at least now they knew for sure what was going on before the explosion; illegal sunstone mining.

"Found these, too." Ben held up what looked like a chunk of blue glass the size of a shotgun shell. Jack asked what it was. "Chemical analysis says it's a ruby."

"A blue ruby? I never heard of such a thing. Wait, doesn't that make it a sapphire?"

"Not this time. I don't understand how it is different from a sapphire, but Juan Jimenez tells me it is. He started giving me this whole lecture on how new technology in Second Century A.E. discovered minor differences between rubies and sapphires resulting in a reclassification of the two gems as separate entities. I stopped him before he went into agonizing detail, but he assured me that these are rubies, not sapphires."

Jack admitted that he had seen a lot of blue sapphires in his time, but none that looked quite like that.

"They're still analyzing the other rubies," Ben said. "This could open a new gem market. Azurites, maybe? They'll need some sort of name, I guess."

"Let the guy who first found them pick a name," suggested Jack. That the illegal miners were after sunstones was no surprise. That they found such a rich vein was, and the blue ruby was an unexpected bonus.

"Wait, those prospectors blew themselves to Em-See-Square. Any stones they dug up would likely be vapor, now, right?"

"Assuming they didn't haul a few loads out before the big bang."

And if they did, there had been plenty of time to smuggle them off-world before they were found out. If they made it back to Terra or Baldur or Loki or Thor, and dumped the sunstones en masse onto the market, then the damage was already done and it was just a matter of time before the repercussions hit.

The Zarathustra government was financed on royalties paid by the Charterless Zarathustra Company for the sunstones mined at Yellowsand. If the bottom fell out on sunstone prices, the colonial government would go down with it.

"I think we need to increase security at the spaceport, Ben. It's a little like closing the barn door after the horse escaped, but what else can we do?"

"Already done." Ben scooped the sunstones and blue gem back into the leather bag. "I'm having these put away in a secure location. If we get lucky, the other stones those prospectors dug up vaporized with them like you suggested. If not, and we find them before they leave planet, we'll lock them up and hold the stones against the possibility that Yellowsand becomes tapped out."

"Good idea," Jack said. "In the meanwhile, why don't you look into other sources of government revenue?"

"I've already increased the fines for trespassing on the res from fifty to two hundred sols, and Victor suggested we open a posh resort like they did on Modi." That seemed like the sort of thing a businessman would suggest, especially when he had the largest construction company on the planet. Jack said as much.

"Yeah, he also suggested running it for us, for a modest percentage of the net, of course. Well, he does have to justify his actions to the stockholders on Terra, so I can't fault him for eking out whatever profit he can."

"Especially with a whopping big stockholder right here on Zarathustra," Jack said, reminding Ben that Morgan was a major shareholder with the CZC. "Say, maybe we should ask his advice. According to Victor, Morgan is a money magnet. He increased his inheritance by about a factor of ten."

"Actually, if we accept his offer on Epsilon, we'll be able to bank a good chunk of cash and let it gain interest. Imagine, buying a whole continent!" Ben shook his head as if to clear away the cobwebs. Land on colony worlds was relatively inexpensive but fifty million sols was still a lot of money. "Has he said what he wants it for?"

"Not yet. Why not just go ahead and sell it to him? Use Zeta Continent for your game preserve." Jack leaned back and reached for his pipe, then remembered he was on the wagon for the next two weeks. "Damned doctors are all killjoys," he muttered to himself.

"What was that?"

"Just wishing I could shoot a few doctors, Ben."

Ben nodded. "Same here. Mine has me watching my cholesterol. It seems I'm allergic to the balancer drugs. Back to Zeta, the Company has a mining interest there. Not the best place to relocate endangered species, especially harpies. Well, back to work for me, but you should still be on medical leave."

"That reminds me. When do I get that personal assistant? With Gerd on leave of absence I'm getting buried in paperwork over here."

Ben looked surprised. "Oh? Didn't Morgan tell you? He went over your head and selected the new hire."

Now it was Jack's turn to be surprised. "He did? Who?"

"Beats me. But he said you'll have your new assistant by the end of the week."

Jack rubbed his chest where the neo-dermaplas was still growing to replace the scar from the laser surgery. Damned thing itched like crazy. "Now who could Morgan have…oh, Nifflheim!"

Jack laughed until the pain in his chest forced him to stop, then smiled for a good while after that.

IV

Records Division was, perhaps, one of the more important divisions of the Charterless Zarathustra Company. Every piece of information, be it about personnel, financial, historical, medical, scientific or general flowed into its massive archives, both in electronic and hard-copy formats. The people who worked in that massive repository of information often went unnoticed by the rest of the company.

Akira Hsu O'Barre had been working in Records Division for twenty-two months. On Myra Falada's recommendation, she had transferred in from the secretarial pool and found a place where she could excel. Her computer and filing skills quickly caught the attention of the division chief who then promoted her to assistant manager of the archive section. She enjoyed her work and expected to make manager within two more years, assuming her boss retired like he constantly threatened to do. Or would have had she not been asked to take an extended leave of absence.

Akira came to Zarathustra on the work exchange program. As such, she owed seven years of service to the Charterless Zarathustra Company, four years of which she'd already completed. Akira had been content to complete the remaining time and possibly stay on afterwards, until Victor Grego summoned her to his office. The last time that happened, she had been tasked with spying on John Morgan. This time she had been asked to accept a temporary position outside of the company working for Jack Holloway. It was well-known that Mr. Grego and Mr.

Holloway were friends, and even better known that Mr. Holloway was still recovering from his duel with Morgan.

Still, being asked to take time off from the company to work for the Native Affairs Commissioner took her completely by surprise. She accepted when Grego assured her that the time spent on leave would still be applied to her contract period. Actually, she would have accepted anyway. If John Morgan ever planned on proposing to her, she would need to be in his father's good graces.

She would eventually have to either complete her tour of duty or pay back the balance of her schooling costs. Akira could easily afford the pay-out with her savings but she liked working for the company and living on Zarathustra. John Morgan Holloway the Lesser had offered to pay off the debt but she had refused. Her debt, her responsibility. Besides, she suspected Morgan was testing her in some way with his payout offer.

Akira was now busy clearing her workload and bringing her temporary replacement up to speed. "If you have any questions after I leave, you can screen me at the Native Affairs office. Any questions for right now, Betty?"

"Yeah," Betty Kanazawa said. "Why are you taking this break? Word around accounting is that you're on the fast track."

Akira sighed. "Mr. Grego asked me to. He called me up to his office yesterday and hit me with the request."

Betty's eyebrows shot up. "Seriously? The big boss himself? Where does that come from?"

"I really don't know for certain, but I'd bet a hundred sols that Morgan talked him into it."

Betty sat on the edge of the desk. "Well, water-cooler talk has it that you and Morgan are gonna get engaged. There's even a pool on when the big day will be."

"Fishing for some inside information so you can win the pool?" Akira laughed. "Sorry, but he hasn't popped the question. I've been doing some research on Freyan customs and it seems that I may have to jump a few hoops before then."

"What kind of hoops? I'm betting you already jumped through the big one...." Betty paused as she watched Akira's face stiffen for a moment, then relax into its usual sunny self.

"Oh, there's some old story about a young noble who wanted to marry a common woman. As the story goes, the noble's father refused to allow any marriage below his station. So, the girl disguised herself and entered the father's household as a servant; washing dishes, scrubbing floors, doing the laundry—real Cinderella type stuff. Well, after a while the father recognized her and realized that she was a woman of quality, regardless of her station. There's more, but that's the down and dirty of it. Somehow it caught on and now all Freyan women, except those in the nobility, have to serve the groom's father for one month—that's a Freyan month—to get his blessing for the marriage."

"You're going through with this?" Betty shifted on the edge of a desk and tapped her teeth with a pen. "Sounds to me like a good way for the father to get some free labor out of a hopeful young girl."

"Nope. The girl has to be paid the going rate for her work. If she is found unacceptable, she is given her wages and goes on her way. If she wins the old man over, then she has a small dowry for the husband."

Akira turned off her computer station, turned the security key and put it in a pocket. The terminal would be locked out for all personnel until either Akira returned or security came to override her protocols with a replacement key and system wipe. "Actually, I have a pretty good dowry already, though I doubt my temp job on Beta has anything to do with Freyan tradition."

"You do!" Betty exclaimed. "How big a raise did you get when you came over from secretarial?"

"Five percent, then another ten when I was promoted to assistant manager. When I signed on with the company I took the stock option deal. Every week ten percent of my salary is set aside to buy common stock in the Company. The money that stock generated was rolled over for more stock. I even put my profit-sharing bonuses towards more shares. Two years ago when company stock dropped after the Fuzzy Trial I used my entire savings and bought up over a thousand shares for three centi-sols on the sol."

"What? You could have lost everything."

"It was a chance, but I was betting on Mr. Grego pulling a zarabunny out of a hat. I bought the shares right after I heard he was making extee-three for the Fuzzies. Besides, the CZC is the largest employer on the planet. If the Company went down, the local economy would go with it. I was banking that the new colonial government wouldn't let that happen. When the CZC signed the mining agreement with the government and got back almost all of the unseated lands, the stock rebounded and even went up an extra eighty points. If I wasn't rolling the dividends back into the company, I would be making more money from the stock than my regular paycheck."

"Really? I never signed on for the stock option. I think I'll do that today. But, wait, if you have all this money, why do that Freyan servant thing? You have the dowry already."

Akira rolled her eyes. Betty was smart in a lot of ways, but at other times she was clueless. "I just said that I don't think that this is about that. Even if it was, it isn't about the dowry, it's about getting Morgan's father to see me as a suitable prospect for his son. Anyway, Jack Holloway is still recovering from his surgeries and needs some help in the office. He is a friend of Mr. Grego's and is the father of a major stockholder. I suspect there is a company angle that the boss is working to keep things running smoothly, too. I don't mind. I'm really looking forward to it."

"I'll bet you are," Betty winked. "If things don't work out with Morgan, you can take a shot at Jack."

"Actually, I thought you might like a shot at him," Akira countered with a laugh.

Betty giggled, then became thoughtful. "You know what? I might at that. Older guys know things. I dated this one guy on Terra in his fifties. He really knew how to treat a girl. Too bad I found out about his wife."

"Wife?" Akira pretended to be shocked, though she knew Betty too well to be surprised at anything she was involved in.

"Yeah, a real old-money battle-axe who had it in for me when she found out. Now you know why I moved to Zarathustra. So, do you think I would make a good stepmother for your future husband?"

"I told you, he hasn't asked me," Akira said. Then she added, "Yet."

* * * * * * * * *

Things were coming together for Clancy Slade. His beard was back in place to reduce his resemblance to that mutt Leo Thaxter; he even had a good job with the Charterless Zarathustra Company, working security under Major Lansky. His daughter was safe at home and he was out of Prison House. He had to talk to the police about how he had been forced to take Thaxter's place whenever they thought up a new question, but he was able to keep the money Thaxter's friends paid him to do the job—not that he had a choice with his daughter kidnapped. He didn't like the way he earned it, but twenty-five thousand sols was a windfall he was only too happy to have. He was already looking into a house outside of Mallorysport where his daughter would have room to run around.

Clancy was just returning home from work. All new hires got the night shift until they proved themselves and a day slot opened up. He didn't mind. He was paid better working for the CZC security section than any job he held previously on Zarathustra or Gimli, and the other guys were easy to get along with for the most part. They did rib him a bit about his resemblance to Leo Thaxter at first, hence the return of the beard, but it was all good-natured and nobody went so far as to call him a Fuzzy fagan.

There was one co-worker who needed to be set straight, though. That was Kristoff Hoffa, the practical joker. No gag was too old or too infantile for him to pull. Whoopee cushions, joy buzzers, rubber chickens, itching powder…Hoffa used them all. Then he went too far and posted a mocked-up wanted poster with Leo Thaxter's face on Clancy's locker, then shouted, "There he is! Get him!"

Nobody twitched a muscle or cracked a grin. Clancy simply walked up to the laughing Hoffa and punched him dead in the nose. For the rest of the shift everybody walked around or over Hoffa's unconscious body until Major Lansky tripped over him. Literally. Lansky took in the black eyes and bloody nose, saw the torn wanted poster in the trash and put two and two together instantly. Hoffa was dragged off to medical with no questions asked.

Clancy checked the mail port as soon as he entered his apartment. One of the benefits of living in Mallorysport was the near instantaneous delivery of letter mail. Letters and small packages were sent through a complicated network of pneumatic tubing. It was the one planetary service not administered by the CZC, though the company had installed it during the early days of planetary development. Mail was under Federation Colonial Office jurisdiction and could not be privatized.

Clancy extracted the letter and returned the pneumatic cartridge to the portal. It was another receipt for payment for a locker rental at the spaceport. This was the third one he had received in the last two months, despite his not having rented a locker. Clancy decided to go down to the spaceport and straighten things out on his next day off. Right now he needed to get his sleep if he was going to spend any time with his daughter after school let out.

* * * * * * * * *

Leo Thaxter placed the package inside the locker, and then shut it. After locking and double checking to be sure it was secure, he inspected his face in the mirror finish of the door. Grey hair, strong jaw, dark eyes, good teeth, full beard and a slight tan. As a whole the face was pleasant, a face that could go unnoticed on any world. Until he smiled. Leo stared at his reflection; it showed a forced, unnatural smile, as though it had been brought out of a dark place and plastered on his face. Even the eyes were likely to draw attention as they had a menacing quality about them, and Thaxter knew it.

I just won't smile, then, he decided.

Leo walked out of the spaceport to his aircar. The aircar still had that new vehicle smell of freshly installed plastic and ionized metal. He flew to the outskirts of the city to a ranch cabin. The cabin was a simple four-bedroom affair with a power cartridge similar to that of the aircar, much like most dwellings outside of the city's power grid. Or so it appeared. In truth, there was a small M/E converter unit in place of a septic system. The unit was capable of sustaining several much larger buildings and was abusively expensive, making it an extravagance most residents of Zarathustra could not afford, especially when the CZC power grid was more than sufficient for their energy needs at very reasonable rates.

The cabin was purchased under the name of Clancy Slade. Leo Thaxter decided to make good use of his look-alike's identity. On most planets such a subterfuge would be caught by tax offices while collecting property taxes, but Zarathustra was a tax-free planet. As long as Leo didn't come into direct confrontation with the local police—something he planned to avoid anyway—and didn't create any red flags with the credit agencies, he could comfortably pass himself off as Clancy without anybody getting wise. He even rented the spaceport locker in Clancy's name and paid in advance. To avoid giving away his hideout, he used Clancy's real home address and checked the box that indicated he wanted paperless billing. That would keep the real Clancy from finding out his doppelganger was still on Zarathustra.

It had been a dicey maneuver. Two months earlier Leo Thaxter had taken great pains to be seen leaving the planet. He'd over-tipped the cabbie, made a fuss about getting first-class accommodations on the shuttle and even looked directly at as many surveillance cameras as he could find at the spaceport. The hard part had been sneaking back off the shuttle without anybody noticing. Fortunately for the escaped convict, security was designed to keep people from sneaking onto the shuttle, not off.

Leo had given his first-class ticket to a large man in coach and even slipped him two hundred sols to use Clancy's name until he reached Gimli. The man happily accepted the upgrade and the conditions by which he got them. Once off the shuttle, Leo had gone underground. He had money enough to live for years without resorting to robbery or, worst of all, wage earning. He'd bought the cabin outside of the city where he wouldn't have any close neighbors to bother him, and acquired his furnishings on the sly from fences he knew only by reputation, not from anybody who would know him personally.

The inside of the cabin was comfortably appointed, if a bit Spartan; the furniture, a fully stocked bar, a television screen and a state of the art computer. Everything the atomic-era colonist in hiding needed, but without any curios, knickknacks or even hunting trophies which were a decorating staple on newly colonized worlds. No zarabuck hides decorated the walls nor did damnthing-skin rugs cover the floor. It was just the bare necessities.

Leo poured himself a tall drink, then sat down and turned on the viewscreen setting the channel to B.I.N. The morning news was just ending with an editorial. The station owner, Ivan Dane, was railing against the Charterless Zarathustra Company and the Colonial Government. He didn't come right out and say that the two were in a conspiracy to keep the 'Fuzzy Rocket' away from the public, but he came close enough that people would automatically draw that conclusion. Next, he wondered why the Federation representative in the form of Commodore Napier wasn't taking an active role in the disposition of the artifact. Or was he? Dane ranted a while longer before thanking the viewing audience and signing off, with the intimation that if *he* were running things the public wouldn't be kept in the dark.

So that's it, you little bastard, Leo said to himself. *You're trying to take over the whole damned planet.* Leo smiled. *Sweet racket if you can pull it off.*

Leo sat and thought about it for a while. Running a whole planet. He would have liked to get in on the caper, but he was a known and wanted felon. He wouldn't even be able to pull the strings behind the scenes; sooner or later somebody would rat him out for the reward or just to get him out of the way. If not for the fact that Dane and Murdock had conspired to kill him, he would have simply left the planet to them. No, Dane and Murdock had to pay. Leo didn't care about the rest of their little group; they could have the planet if they could take it, but nobody plans a hit on Leo Thaxter and lives to laugh about it.

V

"...and the big bright thing in the sky is called the sun."

"Sun?"

Joseph Aaron Quigley, or just Joe, smiled at the Fuzzy, though he made an effort not to show his teeth. Baring teeth was a sign of aggression among these Fuzzies, unlike the ones on the res who understood man showed his teeth in friendship. Usually.

"You are doing very well speaking my language, Red Fur," the human said.

Bal'f'ke, or Red Fur, as Joe called him, nodded. He had been teaching the *Koo-wen*, Big One, the language of the *Jin-f'ke*.

Joe had quickly learned that the language was different from that of the Fuzzy language tapes. Fuzzies, it seemed, possessed more than one tongue. In the two months since Joe had been taken prisoner, he had managed to learn over two hundred words and communicate effectively with his captors. In return, he had taught several Fuzzies some basic Lingua Terra terms. Initially he concentrated on words like food, water, hungry, thirsty, that sort of thing. Now he was working on things that didn't immediately impact on Red Fur's comfort and survival, like the names of astral bodies.

Bal-f'ke appeared to be the most intelligent of his students, which made sense as he also appeared to be the grand marshal of the Fuzzies that had gathered together in the last two months. Of course, as any former military man could tell you, leaders aren't always the sharpest knives in the drawer. Many a lieutenant ended up the victim of a fatal accident when he proved mentally under-equipped to lead his men effectively in combat.

Joe had decided some weeks back that he would have to escape and turn himself in to the authorities the first chance he got. Anything was better than being the prisoner of a bunch of very angry Fuzzies. He laughed at the thought. Ordinarily, a Fuzzy, or even a small group of Fuzzies, would be no match for one unarmed man. However, even without the incredible numbers he was surrounded by, these Fuzzies had atlatls, slings, spears, stone axes and, worst of all, a new bunch came in the day before with bow and arrow technology. The bows were crude and the range limited as they were made from the wood of a featherleaf tree, until one Fuzzy got the idea to use zaraoak, a wood comparable to blackthorn in hardness and resilience.

While very few Fuzzies were strong enough to pull a bow that strong, the ones that did displayed surprising accuracy and the numbers were growing. Escaping became less likely all the time. It would be like an elephant trying to hide from the great white hunter. There were trees enough around him to hide behind, but two hundred plus Fuzzies could cover a lot of area in a hurry. Joe would never make it with those odds. Even considering the greater speed a healthy human could run at, he couldn't outrun spears and arrows. At least these Fuzzies didn't have dogs to ride on like the domestic ones in the south. The breed they used on the res, the Curtys, was often used to protect children and livestock on other planets. A one hundred and twenty pound Curtys could kill a two-hundred pound man with very little trouble. Yet they were gentle with children, provided they grew up with them or were well trained. No, Joe was very glad he didn't have to worry about the dogs on top of everything else.

"Why big moon called Dar-y-us and little moon called Zerk-zees?" asked one Fuzzy. Climber was her name, Joe recalled.

"Why you called Climber, and him called Red Fur? To make important things easy to understand," Joe explained.

Another Fuzzy picked up two rocks and held them up to Joe. "These rocks, yes? Not have different names?"

Joe examined the rocks. One was basalt and the other feldspar. Now how did one explain the difference to a Fuzzy? "Yes, have different names, but also called rocks. Darius and Xerxes both have different names, but both are also called moons. Understand? This rock is also called basalt, and this rock is also called feldspar."

He went on to explain that basalt was a common extrusive volcanic rock with fine grains while feldspar came in many different varieties. As Joe expected, the Fuzzies constantly interrupted him to explain what this or that meant, and why it mattered that they were different when they were just rocks. Joe tried to explain that if you knew what each thing was and how it was different from other things, you would know how to use those things better.

"Okay, look at, um, Spearsender's bow. It is made of the wood Big Ones call zaraoak. But he used to have a bow made from a weaker wood my people call featherleaf. Which throws the arrow, or little spear, farther?"

Everybody agreed that zaraoak was better.

"Good, now if I said 'go run fast and get me zaraoak to make bow with,' you would know which kind of wood I wanted, yes?"

That got the point across.

Red Fur called for a break to eat. While the other Fuzzies scampered off for some raw goofer, Red Fur turned to Joe.

"Your people very wise," he said.

Joe nodded, then shrugged. "Sometimes we are not so wise. Our world was much like yours, once, and we ruined it. Now, we go to other worlds and sometimes ruin them. The Big Ones who came to this world want to keep it safe, but there are always a few bad people who do not care about such things. They just take what they want."

"Are you bad Big One?"

Joe was taken aback by the forwardness of the question. Then he answered as honestly as he could. "I'm not sure. Maybe."

Red Fur nodded, a gesture he picked up from the human. "That why you kill Sun Fur?"

Joe expected that question to come up sooner or later, and decided to tell the truth. "I didn't kill her. That was one of the other Big Ones, and it was an accident. But I gave the order, so I am responsible."

Red Fur said nothing for several heartbeats. When he spoke, there was controlled anger in his voice. "*Jin-f'ke* not kill *Jin-f'ke*. This thing you name 'murder' new to us. You say Big Ones murder each other. When caught, they too, killed. You say to teach others not to murder. How can killing teach others not to kill? This a strange thing to us. Yet, many in tribe want make you dead, kill you for death of Sun Fur. I want you to make dead, to die when I saw her body. Now, I not know how I feel, but afraid what will happen if my people kill you. I afraid we may become like you. Do not think that a good thing."

Red Fur turned away from the human, then looked back over his shoulder. "Our People will decide what to be done with you. Most will listen to me, but not all. When I have decided what we will do, I will tell you."

As Red Fur walked away, Joe considered his possible fate. He didn't want to die, but he wasn't certain if he didn't deserve to. He would have to think hard on how he would escape, and if he still wanted to do so.

* * * * * * * * *

Bal-f'ke watched in fascination as the strange *Koo-wen* in the yellow not-fur used made-things to dig into the dirt. Unlike the previous *Koo-*

wen who had made a great burrow to live in, these Big Ones lived and worked in the open.

Did that mean that these Big Ones were different from the ones that killed Sun Fur? They acted different, and they came in all sizes and colors. One was very big compared to the others with dark skin and darker fur on head. Like the *Jin-f'ke,* the fur came in different colors though the skin varied wildly. Would these Big Ones try to hurt his people?

Joe said that killing was an accident, but how did one make an accident with a weapon he knew could bring down a *shima-kato*, what Joe called a 'damnthing.' It was a killing weapon, wasn't it? These new Big Ones…would they make friends with the *Jin-f'ke*? Not all *Jin-f'ke* were alike, so maybe the *Koo-wen* were different, too. Red Fur decided to wait and see what the new Big Ones did before passing judgment. There was still so much he didn't know.

* * * * * * * * *

The Bitter End was in full swing for the 1600 crowd. The doors had opened mere minutes earlier and the lounge was already packed. People in their late teens to early thirties filed onto the floor and started dancing. Some did the latest dance adapted from a Thoran religious rite, others were doing "the Khooghra" and the rest did various dances popular on Terra six months earlier. On the dance floor the music was nearly deafening. Directional sonics spared the people sitting at tables and the bar the brunt of the music allowing them to converse among themselves without raising their voices.

John Morgan Holloway the Lesser and Akira Hsu O'Barre sat at a table near the dance floor. Unconsciously, the couple took the same table they had occupied two months earlier. During Jack Holloway's convalescence the pair had had few opportunities to spend time together. The younger Holloway had to do some recovering as well. Morgan intended to make it up to Akira.

A cocktail waitress dressed in the archaic uniform popularized on Terra in First Century Pre-Atomic approached to take their orders. Like most of the service staff, she was hired in from Junktown.

"Kin I take yer ordahs?"

Morgan ordered a Freyan ale while Akira ordered a Three-Planets. The waitress rushed off to fill the order. While they waited the music changed to a First Century dance song.

"*Shattakk!* What is that?"

Akira concentrated on the music before answering. "It's something called 'disco music' from the era before hyperspace travel. It pops, don't you think?"

Morgan shook his head in negation. "I prefer your symphony pieces. Say, why are Terrans always referencing First Century A.E. and earlier, but very little of what came after? I've gone through the libraries and found very little by way of new music or literature after that era."

"Didn't you take history back in college? Well, I guess they wouldn't cover this very thoroughly. After the Third World War most of the Northern Hemisphere was left a radioactive wasteland. Everybody, the survivors, I mean, migrated to the Southern Hemisphere. The population of Terra was cut almost in half."

"Yes, that much was covered at university. So?"

"Well, a lot was lost during that time. Technology was set back decades in many areas, for example. Countries that had managed to accommodate the existing population suddenly found themselves inundated with refugees. These people needed to be housed, fed, their medical needs attended to. Medicine advanced faster than ever before, as did farming and artificial food production, like carniculture.

"Other areas suffered. It was a struggle just to survive for many years. The entertainment industry had all but vanished completely. Fortunately, there were archives of music, movies, television, literature and some technology in government bunkers and private collections that survived the devastation of the war. Old movies and music, all in the public domain, filled the entertainment void for the next couple of centuries. Terra stabilized and started advancing in other areas a little at a time: collapsium, contra-gravity, the hyperspace drive and even artificial gravity. But progress was slow and there were very few people interested in creating new music or movies until around the Fourth Century A.E., and the less said about most of that the better. The same was true of television programs and live theater. Did you ever see those awful western films where they used Freyan oukrey in place of horses? Gah!"

"Actually, I have. The oukrey seemed perfectly normal to me. It was the, uh, cowboys?—that seemed off to me. Why didn't they use real horses? I've seen some on Terra, very much alive."

"It took a while to get their numbers up and they were protected by the world governments. Some breeds of horses are lost forever while others flourish, now. The Shetland pony is mostly gone, though some of the toy breeds are still around."

"Hmm…maybe I should arrange to have some horses brought in to Zarathustra. Other animals, too, like Terran chickens and cattle."

"I wouldn't mind some turkey now and then," Akira mused. "You had better check with Mr. Grego before you decide to play Old McDonald, though. Alien species have to be cleared before being imported."

"They do? Hmm…I had best speak with Governor Rainsfield about something…Oh, here come our drinks."

The waitress served the drinks, accepted her tip and quickly hustled off to the next customer. The Bitter End was famous for the speed at which it filled drinking orders.

"A Three-Planets," noted Morgan. "I'm not familiar with that one."

"It's a concoction of 150 proof Terran rum, a half shot of Thoran *nildin* and a squirt of Lokian *looehlaf*," Akira explained. "I can't drink more than one or I'll be down for the count. I doubt that there are ten people on Zarathustra that could drink more than three and still walk straight."

"Really? I'll have to test that theory on Gus Brannhard. If it knocks him out, I won't even think about trying it. How does it affect you?"

Akira smiled. "It loosens me up and gives me a quick buzz, but I'll have to stick with much weaker stuff afterwards. I don't want to get too loose, especially before going to work for your dad."

Morgan feigned surprise. "You are starting work for my sire—er, father?"

"Yes," Akira nodded. She started to take a sip, then stopped and sniffed it instead, then nodded approvingly. "This is the only place on Zarathustra to get the mix just right. You can tell by the aroma that wafts up from it. Would you like to try it?"

Morgan set down his ale, then took a careful sip of Akira's drink. It didn't seem very strong. "You said you were going to work for Jack. Are you leaving the Company?" Without thinking he took a gulp from the drink in his hand forgetting it was Akira's. It was surprisingly good; tart from the *nildin* and the *looehlaf* covered the more aggressive flavor of the rum. Sheepishly, he returned the drink to Akira, who set it down.

"No, just taking a leave of absence. Mr. Grego asked me to help out with Jack's back-log of paperwork while he is recovering." Akira tried to figure out whether Morgan was genuinely surprised or just putting on a façade. Try as she might, she couldn't tell. "You wouldn't have had something to do with my transfer to the res, would you?"

"Me? I would have just hired on a full staff," Morgan replied. "Say, that's not a bad idea. Maybe a few people to do the cooking and cleaning while father is stuck in that hover-chair. It is a good thing Fuzzies don't shed like dogs or it would really be a mess around there." Morgan pulled a handheld device from a jacket pocket and spoke into it. The display read: HIRE HOUSEHOLD STAFF FOR JACK. He put the personal organizer back in the pocket. "Little Fuzzy will like that, I think. His Pappy Jack will have more time to play with him."

Morgan was deflecting, Akira decided. "Where will you get the staff?"

"Hmm…can't I just take out a want ad on Beta?"

"Well, yes." Akira fumbled for her purse, knocking over her drink. The automated table opened a six-inch hole in the middle where a small suction hose came out and sucked up the liquid in seconds. This was followed by a second apparatus that sprayed a cleaning solution over the spill site that was then soaked up by an arm with a heated cloth. The cleaning arms recessed back into the hole which sealed seamlessly.

Morgan raised a hand to signal the waitress. When she arrived, Morgan tried to order a replacement for Akira's spilled drink.

"Oh, make it hot tea, instead. If I am this clumsy, already, I better not push my luck with more alcohol."

Morgan nodded to the cocktail waitress and away she went. "I didn't think you drank all that much."

"Oh, well, it doesn't take much with a Three-Planets."

Morgan accepted the explanation though he couldn't recall if she had even taken a single sip.

Akira extracted a device similar to Morgan's from her purse and scrolled down the display. "Here it is. There is a temp agency in Junktown where you can hire people at low rates. The people there are so desperate for work they'll relocate in a heartbeat to fill almost any position. I think you'll find a decent cleaning and cooking staff there."

Morgan made a note of the agency, then returned to the previous subject. "So, when do you start working for my father?"

"Tomorrow. Or at least that's when I'll be heading over."

"Tomorrow?" Morgan extracted his personal organizer a second time. He said something in Sosti that Akira took for a curse. "I'm getting my new portfolio card tomorrow, then I have to run over to Company House to have my balances transferred. If you can wait, I'll fly you over to Beta myself."

"That won't be necessary." Akira's tea arrived and she blew on it to cool it off. "Whew—that's hot. No, Betty wants to fly me over and meet Jack. I think she has a thing for older men."

Morgan raised an eyebrow. "Betty…oh! The woman you introduced me to the last time we were here. Hmm…I hope she dresses a little more conservatively before meeting him. He did just have heart surgery, you know."

"I'll make sure she behaves," Akira laughed. "Do you think she would make a good stepmother?"

Morgan almost choked on his ale.

VI

Jeffrey "Small Eyes" Manson knew why he had been 'volunteered' by the other cons to test the collar scrambler, and it had nothing to do with his below-average height. While the others made a point that his sleight frame and short stature made it easier to slip away unnoticed by the guards, that was just an excuse to use him as a guinea pig, and Small Eyes knew it. The real reason was because he was convicted of molestation of a minor.

Somehow, word had gotten out in the general population, probably a guard with kids of his own passed the word, and Small Eyes became the target of every "accident" in Prison House. Many convicts had wives and children and as such had no tolerance for those they considered a deviant. Even the name "Small Eyes" was prison lingo for a man with his proclivities. The other cons wanted him dead, and this way they wouldn't get caught taking him out. However, it was made quite clear that the alternative was even less pleasant. The average lifespan of a child molester in prison was just slightly longer than that of a tin of extee-three at a Fuzzy picnic.

Small Eyes approached the border of the pole array that kept the cons from trying to make a break for it. Going outside of the containment area meant sudden and violent death for anybody wearing the explosive collar. But Small Eyes had the scrambler that one of the others had cobbled together in the prison workshop. With the scrambler in place, the collar would, or rather, *should*, stop receiving the signal from the array of poles and instead accept a false signal that would keep the explosive mechanism dormant. At least, that was what he was told. Small Eyes more than half expected the collar to go off, removing his head in the process, as soon as he cleared the border. The only reason he was prepared to go through with it was the outside chance that the other cons were telling the truth; that, and the fact he knew what would happen to him if he went back without testing the scrambler. At least the collar would kill him quickly.

It was decided that the best time to test the scrambler would be while the rocket was being hauled out on the barge. Everybody, inmates and guards, would be watching the rocket as it was lifted out of the crater and hauled away. It would also keep anyone from hearing the collar explode, thought Small Eyes wryly. Before stepping through, Small Eyes considered praying, though he suspected that any deity familiar with his past would not look kindly upon him.

The convict stood at the border, indicated by a series of red beams that stretched from pole to pole, took a deep breath and started through the warning barrier. One step. Two steps. Three. He had cleared the poles and was still breathing. The scrambler worked! At this point Small Eyes was supposed to report back to the others about the success of the test, but the lure of freedom was too strong; he was out and planned on staying out. Small Eyes started running south in the hopes of crossing the res and getting to a settlement where he could steal some clothes.

Fifty meters past the perimeter was a ten-meter high cliff face. He elected to go around instead of over the ridge that bordered the dig site as it would make him too visible. Besides, he wasn't a good climber. When he saw that there were a few bushes with ripe berries, Small Eyes quickly plucked the fruit and smeared it on his yellow jumpsuit in the hopes of making himself less conspicuous. Several minutes of rubbing revealed that the treated fabric resisted discoloration. When that didn't work, he tasted a few then spit them out. Not ripe, yet. Swearing blasphemously, he threw the berries onto the ground. Small Eyes was always hungry thanks to the giant Samoan, who often took most of his food. Forgetting the berries he proceeded through the bushes crouching low to stay hidden. After several long minutes Small Eyes worked his way to a path that allowed him to walk up to the top of the ridge without being seen from the dig site.

While not an outdoorsman, Small Eyes had read about the native wildlife; bush goblins, goofers, harpies, zarabucks, veldbeests, zarawulves, tunnel worms and, worst of all, damnthings. It was several hundred miles to the nearest settlement off the res, and once he was discovered missing there would be a major search. He considered discarding the jumpsuit as the color made him too visible, then changed his mind since it was the only protection from the elements he had. The fabric was even resistant to tunnel worms that burrowed under the skin. Damnthings, being colorblind, were attracted by movement, not color, so the bright yellow wasn't a problem there. He didn't know what the zarawulves sensory apparatus was designed for, but they were on the endangered species list and unlikely to be a problem, while harpies were all but extinct on Beta Continent.

At the top of the ridge were enough trees and brush to conceal his movements without hunching down, so Small Eyes picked up his pace. The goal was to get as far from the dig site as possible before evening headcount. Or it was, until Small Eyes spotted the Fuzzy.

The common story was that Fuzzies were childlike, friendly and trusting. Their size and primitive weaponry made them almost completely harmless to adult humans.

Childlike.

They are not really children, thought Small Eyes, just *like* children, but it had been such a long time....

* * * * * * * * *

Runs Fast watched as the *hat-zu'ka* chewed the bark off of the tree trunk. He was almost close enough to use his spear thrower and kill the animal. Actually, he could launch the spear from a much farther distance, but his accuracy was not as good as the others in his clan, so he wanted to be close enough to ensure a clean kill.

Finally, he was ready. He drew back his arm and took careful aim, then launched his spear. The spear caught the *hat-zu'ka* in the side just below its foreleg, killing it almost instantly. Runs Fast lived up to his name and quickly recovered his spear. Grabbing the dead *hat-zu'ka* by a hind leg, he started dragging it back to the others when he heard a scream. It was the voice of one of the people, he could tell. Runs Fast released his kill and ran towards the sound.

A *Koo-wen* had seized Watches Clouds and was running away. It was the first *Koo-wen* Runs Fast had seen other than the one Red Fur kept as a prisoner. This Big One was not as tall as the other *Koo-wen*, and with less fur on top of the head. Though the *Koo-wen* was much larger, Runs Fast was quicker on his feet and ran ahead of it. Runs Fast was unsure if it was a male or female, though it did look different from the one back at the gathering place. Perhaps the females were shorter with less fur. But why take one of the People? Did it lose a child and want a replacement?

A *hat-zu'ka* would sometimes do that, taking one of the young of another to replace one that had made dead. Or maybe the *Koo-wen* was going to eat Watches Clouds? No, that was a never done thing. Only *gouru* ate their own kind, not people, and the Big One was clearly some sort of people, though strange.

Runs Fast stood in front of the *Koo-wen* and aimed his spear. "Stop! Let Watches Clouds go or I will use my spear," he shouted in his ultrasonic voice.

The *Koo-wen* stopped and looked at the Fuzzy but didn't release his captive. Runs Fast was unsure what to do next when the Big One lunged forward and tried to grab him. Runs Fast was too close to actually throw his spear, so he used it to stab the *Koo-wen* in its middle. The point failed to penetrate the strange not-fur of the Big One, but the surprise of the impact caused the *Koo-wen* to lose its grip on the squirming Watches Clouds. The Fuzzy ran as fast as she could, screaming for help while Runs Fast menaced the *Koo-wen* with his weapon.

The *Koo-wen* saw his captive escape and turned his attention to his attacker. Runs Fast noticed that the Big One's face became red as it showed its teeth and roared. Backing up to stay out of reach, he loaded his spear thrower. He doubted he could throw his spear hard enough to get through the strange not-fur, so he aimed higher and launched with all his strength. The spear caught the *Koo-wen* on the strange shiny thing around its neck. Though the spear bounced off harmlessly, it jarred a piece of the shiny thing off. Runs Fast was horrified at what happened next.

The *Koo-wen* grabbed at his neck with a look of terror even the Fuzzy could understand, then the shiny thing made a bright flash of light and a sound like thunder when a storm is overhead.

Runs Fast leaped back as blood and bone and brains sprayed all about. The Big One, now minus a head and hands, fell to the ground and thrashed silently for a moment, then became still. By that time Watches Clouds had returned with several other *Jin-f'ke*. There was a long discussion about what to do with the body. Red Fur arrived shortly after and made a calculated decision.

* * * * * * * * *

From the air-yacht, Victor Grego and Gerd van Riebeek watched as the barge slowly rose into the air taking the artifact with it. With all the attention the rocket was getting from the general public, it was time to relocate the artifact to a more secure location. For extra security, Commodore Napier loaned the colonial government a squadron of Terran Federation Naval air craft, each loaded with heavily armed and armored Marines. In addition, a contingent of Charterless Zarathustra Company security personnel under the command of Major Lansky surrounded the rocket on the barge itself. Victor Grego was taking no chances with the artifact, although he'd had to smooth a few ruffled feathers among the Marines.

"Is all this necessary?" Gerd inquired. "I think either of the forces is sufficient. No disrespect to your security personnel, but your average space marine is worth three good civilians in a fight."

"Oh, I agree, up to a point. Don't forget who trained my security force, and Chief Steefer is a retired army major. Still," nodded Grego, "this is overkill in the extreme, which is just how I like it. To quote an actor from one of those old 2-D westerns that Diamond likes so much, 'with this ostentatious display we might be saving some poor miscreant's life'." Grego did a passable impression of the actor he was referencing.

Diamond, hearing his name, looked over from the portal he was using, then seeing that Pappy Vic and Pappy Gerd were not speaking to him, returned his attention to the aerial display outside.

Gerd laughed. "*Big Jake*, right? My mother was hopelessly in love with John Wayne when I was a child. We couldn't afford a Tri-D set, so we watched all those old Hollywood films."

"Hollywood in New Zealand?"

"No, the original in, um, California, before World War Three. We were able to download the films from a public domain data stream."

Grego nodded again. "Yeah, for my mother it was Clark Gable and Mickey Failer…"

"Failer?"

"Second Century A.E. heartthrob. Even my daughter liked him."

Gerd nodded, then something struck him. "Wait...your daughter?"

"By my first wife." Grego noted the surprise on Gerd's face. "Gerd, a man of my position and affluence could hardly be expected to live like a monk. I've been married three times. My first wife died in an accident, the other two divorced me. The consensus was that I am too married to my work to properly maintain a stable home-life. Thank Ghu I had the sense to get a pre-nup each time."

"Mr. Grego?" It was the yacht pilot. "Major Lansky and Lieutenant Commander Taylor want to know if you are ready to proceed to Alpha Continent, sir."

Taking one last glance out the portal, Grego took in the dig site with the prisoner work detail, the barge holding the rocket secured with fibroid straps and magna-clamps, and the sky full of navy craft. "The word is given. Second star on the right and straight on 'til morning."

"Sir?" Anga looked back, confused.

"Tell them to proceed, Mr. Anga," Grego said as he wondered if anybody read the classics, anymore. He quickly grabbed up Diamond and set him in his specially designed seat and harness. "Gerd, we need to strap in."

"We do?"

"We most definitely do. Mr. Anga is an excellent pilot, the best, in fact, but I question his sanity when he's at the controls. Trust me; you'll want a harness on for this trip."

Later, Gerd said the flight back to Alpha Continent wasn't so bad, though he white-knuckled his armrests the entire trip.

* * * * * * * * *

Jack had just finished his lunch and was about to return to his office when two aircars landed outside his cabin. He mentally flipped a coin and decided to follow doctor's orders, for a change, and use the contra-gravity chair instead of walking out to meet his guests. Morgan was off surveying Epsilon Continent and Major Lunt was up to his badge dealing with trespassers, so Jack assumed it had to be his new assistants.

From the first vehicle stepped out two attractive young women; Akira O'Barre and a young lady Jack had never met. From the second came Ruth van Riebeek and a girl in her early teens who looked familiar but Jack couldn't place her.

"Hi, Jack," Ruth said. "I have a summer assistant for you."

Akira looked over at Ruth with a look of surprise on her face. "What? I thought I was the assistant."

"You are," Ruth replied. She went on to explain that Ben had told her and Gerd that Jack needed some help while recovering, and two assistants, one experienced and one in training, might be better than one. "I'll admit I twisted the Governor's arm, a little."

Jack knew Akira worked for Victor Grego at the Charterless Zarathustra Company and would be highly qualified in her field. He suspected they would be doing more baby-sitting for the little blonde girl than getting any useful work out of her. He tactfully refrained from saying as much. "Well, I think a few introductions are in order. I am Jack Holloway, Chief Commissioner of Native Affairs." Jack extended a hand to the woman with Akira as she was closest.

"Betty Kanazawa, Mr. Holloway. I just gave Akira a lift over." Betty took the hand and shook it warmly. "I hope you don't mind if I stay the night and return home tomorrow."

"Uh…not at all. You two can take the guest room." Jack was a little flustered by the young woman. *Was she hitting on me? I must be old enough to be her grandfather.* Jack turned to the blonde girl who introduced herself as Lolita. "Lolita? Wait—Lolita Lurkin?"

"Yeah. Dat was me onna TV when dose Fuzzies got loose," said Lolita. "I'm rilly sorry if dat wuz a prob'lem, Mistah Holloway."

Back when Jack was being tried for the murder of Kurt Borch, a few crooked cops on the CZC payroll tried to smear the Fuzzies as vicious brutes by claiming that they had attacked Lolita Lurkin. The truth that her own father had beaten her while drunk soon came out, exonerating the Fuzzies and putting the girl's father in lockup.

"Lolita has been in the foster system for the last two years and I thought a little work experience would be good for her," Ruth explained. She added that Lolita's mother had passed away five years earlier and that she had no other family on planet to stay with.

"Why not? I had my first job at thirteen passing out flyers for the local stores. As long as Akira doesn't mind training her." Jack nodded to Akira, who smiled. In a near whisper he added to Ruth, "I suggest you butter her up but good since that isn't what she signed on for."

Jack looked around at his cabin, the office building in the distance and the barracks a little further down. "But where will she stay? I only have so much room in the cabin, and the barracks is no fit place for a young lady—"

"Oh, that's not a problem," Ruth interrupted. "She'll stay with Gerd and me. Id, Syndrome, Complex and Superego will love having another Big One around."

Jack noticed a group of Fuzzies running over. "You like Fuzzies, Lolita?" She nodded. "Well, here's a chance to introduce yourself to a whole mob of them."

The Fuzzies, Jack's family and a large group of un-adopteds from the res, swarmed the newcomers. They were especially interested in Lolita as she was the smallest Big One most of them had ever seen.

"Akira, maybe you would like to take a look at the office while I have a chat with Ruth. I'll be along in a moment to help you get settled."

"Sure, Mr. Holloway. C'mon, Betty."

Jack turned to Lolita Lurkin who was still being mobbed by the Fuzzies. "Little Fuzzy, show Lolita around, and then bring her to the office, okay?"

"Hokay, Pappy Jack. Lolita, come." Lolita followed along as the Fuzzies led the way. Jack idly recalled a time when all the domestic Fuzzies spoke a mish-mash of Fuzzy and Terran. Now many of them spoke Lingua Terra almost as well as humans.

Jack turned to Ruth. "Now tell me the real reason for the kid."

Ruth sighed. "Gerd said you would see through my story. Well, since Ivan Bowlby died there have been a lot of new prostitution rackets popping up to fill the void he left behind. Junktown girls Lolita's age are especially preyed upon. I've been trying to find legitimate employment for all the foster girls who were thirteen, hoping to keep them off the streets. I've just about run out of workplaces in Mallorysport and at the CZC, so I was hoping you wouldn't mind an extra hand. I cleared it with Ben. He says the budget can handle a few extra bodies on the payroll…."

Jack held up a hand and Ruth stopped talking. "I would have liked a little heads up," he admitted. "Oh, Nifflheim, the more the merrier. The kid can do gofer work and help around the office. The Fuzzies seem to like her, so I guess she'll be okay. I'll even take one or two more if it will keep them away from the predators...provided they are prepared to earn their keep. Ghu knows where I'll put them, though. Hey, if you have any teen boys in foster care, I could use one or two for the heavy lifting.

"They can be put in the barracks with the NPF police. Spending time with a bunch of cops might steer them towards the right path. Plus, it might get Morgan off my back about letting him hire a household staff." Privately, Jack thought Ben would pass kittens when he got the bill for the extra bodies. “But no more surprises, Ruth. We old folks don’t adapt to sudden changes all that fast.”

“Well, I do have one more surprise,” Ruth said with a smile, “but I’ll have to wait awhile before letting you in on it.”

Jack rolled his eyes and turned his chair towards the office building. *If it’s what I think it is, I hope they don’t name it after me. Too many Jacks and Johns as it is, already.*

VII

Ivan Dane winced as he reviewed his earlier live editorial. He had been trying to appear fatherly, but instead looked a bit like the eccentric uncle that kids like and parents try to avoid. He would have to work on that. Dane scribbled a note as Brandon Murdock swaggered in.

Dane looked up and said, "Is there something wrong with your hands, Mr. Murdock?"

Murdock quickly glanced at the aforementioned appendages. "Naw. They're fine. Why?"

Dane nodded towards the door. "Because you failed to use one of them to knock before entering."

Murdock took a step back and rapped on the door three times with his knuckles. It sounded like he used a hammer. "Happy?"

Dane exhaled, then asked, "Was there something you wanted?"

"Nope. But Doc Quigley does. Says he's got somethin' ya should come see."

"Tell him I'll be right there." Murdock turned on a heel and left the office. Dane scribbled another note, then followed. On the way out he noticed the fresh indentations in the hardwood door where Murdock had knocked. Shaking his head, he went down the hall a ways, then adjusted a picture frame. A partition in the wall opened and Dane went down a set of stairs.

Back when Ivan Bowlby was still alive, he'd operated a number of illicit enterprises. Among them was a drug operation that he ran out of a lab in the secret basement. The drug-producing gear had since been gathered up and stored and replaced with different equipment. There, a dark, bald man was adjusting something on a large device.

Dane took in the lab before addressing its lone occupant. "Dr. Quigley, Mr. Murdock informs me that you have something to show us."

"Yes. Yes, I do." Dr. Quigley indicated an apparatus to his left.

To the layman it looked like a giant ray-gun from a low budget space opera aimed at a glass box. In reality it was a gamma ray projector typically used to sterilize lab equipment. Similar models were used to irradiate foodstuffs for sale, since they destroyed harmful bacteria, as gamma radiation dispelled instantly and left no harmful residue. This model had been slightly modified to serve a different purpose. Dr. Quigley opened the glass case and dropped in some pebbles as Professor Darloss, Dr. Rankin and Mr. Lundgren entered the lab.

"Gentlemen, observe what happens when I subject these jellyfish fossils to a five-second burst of gamma radiation."

Before he could activate the device, Murdock shouted in protest. "Hey! Shouldn't we get behind some lead shieldin' or somethin'? I wanna have kids someday. An' I don't want them with two heads or flippers."

Quigley shook his head and chuckled. "Mr. Murdock, this is not one of those clumsy and inaccurate X-ray machines from the dark ages," the scientist said. "The gamma beam will strike only what it is aimed at. Nothing more. I could stand right next to the target and not receive a single milli-rad. Now, if I may continue…?"

"Please, proceed, doctor," Dane said.

Quigley nodded, then set a dial on the projector and flipped a switch. For five seconds the invisible gamma rays bathed the pebbles, and then the machine shut down automatically. The pebbles inside the glass case appeared unchanged.

"Nothing happened," Lundgren observed.

Quigley extracted a handful of stones from the case and said, "Wait for it."

As the three men watched, the pebbles developed a dim glow. Within seconds the brightness doubled, then tripled until the stones glowed like tiny little stars.

"Hey, ya made sunstones!" Murdock exclaimed. "For real?"

"These are not true sunstones, Mr. Murdock," Dr. Quigley explained. "Unlike the real gems, which are thermofluorescent due to some quirk in the chemical composition, these stones possess a slightly different character in their chemical make-up that can be activated by gamma bombardment. As such, they will glow for an indeterminate amount of time and then revert to their normal state. I do not know how long that will be, as yet. I will have to measure the luminescent decay for several days to get a solid estimate of their half-life. This batch, I would hazard to guess, will remain active for about two weeks, but we'll need a number of trials to be sure. I will also need to use alternative forms of radiation, possibly in various combinations, to see what gives the stones the longest active periods…."

"Are you saying these stones are radioactive," Dr. Rankin asked, taking a step back.

"Oh, no more so than that antique wristwatch you are wearing. I wouldn't advise sitting in a room with, say, several tons of radiated stones, but these are certainly safe enough to handle." Dr. Quigley held out a large blue gem easily two centimeters in diameter and tossed it to Murdock who jumped back and let it fall to the floor.

Dane picked up the stone and inspected it. "We could get quite a price for this if we market it right." Dane thought about the possibilities and a slow smile spread across his face.

Quigley shrugged. "I still have to analyze more true sunstones and determine what chemical interactions cause the thermo-fluorescence. We are a step closer, I think, than we were before. I believe that the jellyfish who were exposed to radioactive deposits in the oceans while still alive were the only ones that fossilized into sunstones, while the unexposed did not. That might explain why deposits in the flint are varied instead of uniform." Quigley noticed the confused look on Murdock's face and clarified. "Some are sunstones and some are just pebbles, Mr. Murdock. That gives me a starting point for my analysis."

Quigley moved to a cabinet and extracted something from a drawer. "These stones were given a longer burst of gamma radiation combined with beta particles. Notice that they glow without being exposed to a heat source. I daresay that there could be a market for these, as well."

"We could undercut the legit stone sales…at least here on Zarathustra," Murdock observed. "Ya figure we could get maybe two hundred sols a karat for these things?"

"I was thinking of giving them to the CZC, actually."

Murdock, Darloss, Rankin, Lundgren and Quigley stared at Dane quizzically.

"Not these, the heat activated ones. Doctor, we will need many more of these faux sunstones, but only the ones with the very limited lifespan. You can still work on making true sunstones from the fossils, but these here will do nicely for our immediate plans."

Dr. Quigley looked confused for a moment, and then his expression cleared. "Limited…oh, I see—"

Dr. Rankin interrupted Quigley. "Gamma rays leave no residual radiation. So where is it coming from?"

Quigley started as he realized Rankin was correct. "Hmm…that is a very good question. We should check the true sunstones and see if they emit anything. It might be endemic to the thermo-fluorescent make-up of the stones themselves…."

"Or the gamma emitter is faulty," cut in Rankin. "This model also projects alpha rays and X-rays, yes?"

Quigley nodded.

"I suggest we have this machine serviced. The shielding may be damaged. This is a less expensive model, as I recall, so it might use lead instead of collapsium shielding. Normally sufficient to the need, but there have been cases where the lead would crack or even degrade from constant exposure."

"I'll have it sent out for servicing as soon as I can think of a way to do it on the sly," Dane interjected. "An entertainment company has no valid reason for owning such a device. We'll need to arrange for a cut-out to take it in. A few hundred sols in the right hands should take care of that, well enough. In the meantime, since the radiation levels are safe enough, we'll need to make some more *faux* sunstones…."

* * * * * * * * *

Red Fur carefully examined the dead *Koo-wen*. The body still rested on the zarabuck hide used to drag him closer to camp. Red Fur had ordered the strange not-fur removed, then wrapped the headless body in grass and vines just as they would for one of their own who had made dead. Now came the hard part.

"What we do with dead *Koo-wen, Bal-f'ke*," Makes-Things asked.

"We give to *Koo-wen* who dig in the dirt and see what they make do," Red Fur replied.

"What? *Koo-wen* might be angry," Climber argued. "Come with noise things and make us dead."

"When *Koo-wen* killed Sun Fur, they wrapped her like this," Red Fur pointed out. "We do same, see what they make do."

"And if they come to make dead?" Climber demanded.

It was a fair question. As leader, Red Fur had to be willing to take risks for the benefit of all. Red Fur looked very serious as he said, "We hide. If we have to, we fight."

* * * * * * * * *

Ismet Runako knew there was going to be hell to pay. He and Niyol Fintan had searched the camp from hell to breakfast and failed to produce one Jeffery "Small Eyes" Manson. There was no way the child molester could have gotten out past the perimeter with the explosive collar around his neck, yet he was gone just the same. It was possible the other cons executed their own brand of justice since many of them had children of their own and didn't like the idea of Small Eyes being released after his prison term was up, but if so, where was the body?

Ismet considered stuffing every convict on the work detail into the veridicator and asking what they knew. Unfortunately, it was impossible to compel them to speak. The con would just sit there and accept whatever punishment came his way for not cooperating.

The only other possibility was that the collar malfunctioned, somehow, and Small Eyes either found out, or just didn't care and got lucky. That meant a ground search outside of the perimeter. That shouldn't be too hard, thought Ismet. Every prisoner had a tracking device implanted in his brain when he was processed into the prison system. Finding Small Eyes should be easy enough. However, the simple fact that he got out in the first place would result in a reprimand and even docked pay.

Ismet muttered to himself as he pulled the tracking device from equipment storage. "If only these things worked within the perimeter," he groused. "Come on, Niyol. Let's go bag us an escaped convict."

Niyol selected a sono-stunner for the escapee and a Thorco .375 H&H rifle in case they came across a damnthing. The three-hundred grain round would put a Terran rhinoceros down, so it should be good against the deadly damnthing. Niyol tossed another .375 to Ismet. Ismet used his radio to explain the situation to the guard captain before starting out.

The two prison guards walked through the perimeter without harm. Also, without getting a signal from the tracking device.

"You think the chip in his head malfunctioned, too?"

Ismet considered the possibility and dismissed it. "Two malfunctions on the same con? Let alone the only con to walk out of here since we set up? No; either he had help, which I very much doubt, or he found a way to disable both the collar and chip. I can't imagine how, though."

"Or, he never left the perimeter."

"We went over the entire area with a fine-toothed comb. No Manson. He got out, somehow."

"I guess we'll have to do this the old-fashioned way." Niyol chambered a round and flipped off the safety on the rifle. He wanted to make sure he was ready if something big and dangerous showed up. There was also the possibility of bagging a zarabuck for dinner. It would be a nice break from the processed food they had been living on.

Ismet and Niyol watched the ground for signs that Small Eyes had come through. It took the better part of an hour to find the escapee's trail as neither man was an experienced tracker. They followed the trail up to the ridge and briefly lost it. Ismet doubted that Small Eyes could have climbed the steep rock wall and searched for another way up. This time it only took a minute to find the path previously used by the escapee. After a short jog up the slope and they were at the top where they found the escapee's tracks again. From there, they walked for about ten minutes until they spotted a zarawulf tearing at a mass of vegetation.

The common zarawulf was Zarathustra's answer to the extinct Tasmanian tiger. Almost two hundred pounds, a meter high at the shoulder and shaped like a pit bull, but with a muzzle closer to a thylacine with brown and black striping similar to a Bengal tiger and five-inch fangs, it was regarded as the third most dangerous animal on Beta Continent, after the damnthing and harpy. Their only saving grace being that zarawulves were rare and avoided human settlements as a result of being hunted by humans, almost to extinction, when the planet was first settled. A few lived in captivity at the Mallorysport Zoo, and one brave individual of questionable intelligence was attempting to domesticate a few down in Southern Beta.

"Rifle or stunner," whispered Niyol as he leveled his .375 at the predator.

"Stunner. The damned things are on the protected species list, now." Ismet, who had failed to arm himself with a sono-stunner, took his rifle and held it at the ready in case Niyol's stunner failed to work effectively.

Niyol cautiously lowered his rifle, drew the sono-stunner, took aim and fired. It took a steady thirty second blast before the zarawulf dropped and lay still. Ismet kept his rifle at the ready in case the beast recovered too quickly while Niyol inspected the green mass. Carefully, as Zarathustra had proven to have unpleasant surprises in the past, the guard inspected the green bundle.

It was a naked and headless body. Discounting for the missing head, the two men agreed it was the right height and build for the missing Jeffery Manson.

Ismet pointed at the body where the head should have been. "Did Cujo here eat the head?"

"I don't think so." Niyol examined the body more closely. "I can smell cordite, or rather cataclysmite, and there are burns all around the neck and shoulders. The collar went off, I would say."

Ismet thought for a second, then asked, "Why didn't we hear the explosion? That would have been at least as loud as a gunshot from the .375."

"The rocket being loaded onto the barge would have drowned that out pretty easily, I think," Niyol said after a moment's thought.

"Yeah, that makes sense," Ismet agreed. "How did he get all wrapped up like that? Was he trying to hide?"

"Nope. He was wrapped after he lost his head. See? No burns on the foliage. I've seen the footage of the Fuzzy funeral that was introduced at trial two years ago. This looks like a Fuzzy burial wrap."

"Huh. Better call this in and have a unit come collect what's left of Small Eyes, here," Ismet said. "Hey, let's let the word spread that he died a couple of steps outside of the perimeter. That'll discourage any of the other cons from trying to make a break for it." The guard turned his attention back to the zarawulf, which was still unconscious, and spotted something on the ground. "Niyol, grab that piece of metal. It might have something to do with the escape attempt."

* * * * * * * * *

In the bushes Red Fur, Makes-Things, Climber and Runs Fast watched as the two *Koo-wen* did incomprehensible things around the body of the Big One who made dead. Makes-Things' ears had started bleeding when the Big Ones made the *hagg-tullu* fall down and stop moving. They could see it was still alive by the faint cloud of dust kicked up in front of the muzzle. Not dead, just asleep.

Why not kill hagg-tullu*?* Red Fur wondered. Was noisy made-thing not for killing, or was *hagg-tullu* too strong to be killed? He noticed Makes-Things was injured and ordered the others to take him to the healers. As the others complied, he watched the *Koo-wen* take the dead one away. Two more Big Ones came in one of the melon-seed shaped made-things that flew like a bird and threw the body on board. They acted like they had no respect for the dead one.

Koo-wen like that with all of their dead, or they not like this one? Red Fur had much to think about.

The *Koo-wen* called Joe said that Sun Fur was killed by accident. The noisy made-thing didn't kill the *hagg-tullu,* just made sleep. But wasn't *shima-kato* killed by noisy made-thing, the *stunner*, as the Big Ones called it? When Joe Quigley's Big Ones made big burrow, they used same weapon to kill the *shima-kato*. Or did it go sleep, then killed inside big flying made-thing? If *stunner* made-things fall asleep, why Sun Fur made dead, and Makes-Things' ears bleed?

Red Fur thought hard and realized he would need to talk more with Joe Quigley.

VIII

Colonial Marshal Max Fane was at a loss as to what he could do. The two men who had abducted Gus Brannhard were still as tight-lipped now as they were two months ago when they were apprehended by the Charterless Zarathustra Company security team. The problem was that they were likely facing a death sentence, scratch that, they were *definitely* facing a death sentence, so they had nothing to gain by giving up their confederates. Only a pardon from the governor would get them off-world alive. Since Gus and Ben were good friends, there was no chance of that. Max had tried to talk the Governor into accepting a plea deal for a twenty to life sentence, but Ben wouldn't go for that, either. He wanted to make it very clear what happens to people who interfered with government officials. Max didn't blame the Governor for his position, although a little flexibility would have been helpful.

That the two men would likely be executed shortly after their trial didn't bother Max Fane one little bit. Given the chance, he'd shoot the sons-of-Khooghras himself. The thought that their most likely accomplice, Raul Laporte, would get away scot-free did bother him. A great deal, in fact. Laporte had been a thorn in his paw since the day he made planet-fall. Moreover, Laporte was the most likely person to know where Leo Thaxter had skipped off to. Not being able to get Laporte was bad enough, but to lose Thaxter on his watch was beyond endurance.

In the reflection of the glass Max saw that Leslie Coombes and another man had come to join him. Behind the two-way mirror sat

Anthony Nicholovich Anderson and Duncan Rippolone. Against procedure, the two men had been left alone in the interrogation room on the off chance they would get to talking and give something away. Instead, the two men just sat mute.

"Anything new, Marshal?"

Max shook his head. "Nothing, Mr. Coombes. These mutts are serious pros. They'll go straight to Nifflheim without a peep. We need some kind of leverage to use against them. The problem with that is they know they'll end up getting a bullet in the head, so there isn't much we can threaten them with."

"They need hope," Coombes' companion said. Max turned and saw that it was John Morgan, the man who shot Jack Holloway in that duel two months ago. "They need to think they have something to gain if they cooperate, and something to lose if they don't."

Max refrained from pointing out that he knew that. *What was this kid doing here, anyway? Wasn't he supposed to be on Beta with Jack?* "Unfortunately, they don't either way," he said. "They're already as good as dead and damned well know it."

"When is the trial?" Morgan asked.

"Next week," Coombes said. "I held off for as long as I could hoping that the Marshal could get something useful, but I am all out of excuses, now. The defense wants to get this show on the road."

"I hate giving apologies, Mr. Coombes, but you have mine, anyway," Max said. "You have no idea how much I wish I could have come through for you with this one."

"You can't squeeze blood from a stone, Marshal. I can't imagine who could have done better."

"Maybe something will come to us," Morgan added. He turned to look at the two men through the glass. They looked familiar, somehow, but he couldn't place them.

* * * * * * * * *

Raul Laporte flipped through the stations on the viewscreen, then turned it off in disgust. Nothing but re-runs, talk about the upcoming executions for the Fuzzy Slavers and more conjecture on the so-called Fuzzy Rocket. Laporte had to admit that he was looking forward to the executions. The governor had resurrected the good old firing squad and held a lottery for civic-minded citizens to get in on the fun. The mobster had even bought some tickets for himself. He probably wouldn't win, he knew, though it might have been nice to kill somebody legally for a change.

What he had been looking for was any indication that Tony and Ripper had ratted him out. Of course, it was unlikely that the cops would let that slip to the media if they had. Still it never hurt to check and be sure. The few cops on his payroll hadn't been able to get at the two men and help them out of lock-up, or even arrange an accident for them. Security was tighter than an old maid's virtue.

Still, he did learn that the trial would begin in a week. Lots of things could happen between the holding cells and the courthouse, even though they were all in the same building. It was simply a matter of arranging them. Just in case, it was time to be ready to disappear at a moment's notice.

* * * * * * * * *

"Here you are, Mr. Mo—, um, Mr. Holloway. Your new portfolio card."

Morgan accepted the embossed plastic with his picture, thumb print, retinal scan and DNA sample. Like all such cards, it would not be accessible to anyone but him. It would become inert if more than ten feet from the designated holder.

"You will still have to transfer your balances at the CZC finance center, sir," added the young woman from behind the bulletproof glass. She appraised the young man through the security window.

"Thank you. That will be my next stop." Morgan was so preoccupied thinking about the two men in custody and where he had seen them before that he didn't even notice that the clerk was trying to flirt with him.

After six weeks of waiting, the new portfolio card with John Morgan's new legal name was ready. On Terra it would have taken six days, but Zarathustra was still a colonial planet and operated under some limitations. Granted, the Charterless Zarathustra Company could have produced the card quickly, but the colonial government couldn't let something as sensitive as a personal identification and portfolio card be produced by a private company. As soon as Morgan received the word that it was ready for pick-up, he raced over from Epsilon Continent to collect it.

"Well, there you go, Morgan. It is now official," Leslie Coombes said. "I noticed that you left off 'the Lesser' from the name."

"That is only important to me and other Freyans," Morgan said. "The Federation prefers terms like junior and senior. Besides, one day I will likely become the Greater Holloway and would have to get the card remade again."

Leslie nodded absently. "True. Say, if you are heading straight to Company House, I wouldn't mind a ride."

"Certainly. I can show off my new aircar."

The two men left Police House and flew off in Morgan's aircar. It was the CZC Zebralope 700, a sporty model that boasted its speed and comfort. It would do until his hyperspace yacht arrived with his personal air-yacht for local travel.

"I hope Marshal Fane didn't mind my tagging along with you," Morgan said conversationally.

Coombes waved it away. "Max is used to that sort of thing. At least you weren't another lawyer. He hates that."

"Those men seemed a little familiar, somehow." Morgan adjusted his flight path to avoid another aircar. The Darius-Mallorysport spaceport briefly appeared in the windshield, then vanished as Morgan readjusted his flight path.

"From this planet?"

"I think so. I haven't seen or met all that many people since I made planet-fall. I was a bit preoccupied as you may recall."

Coombes mused that while Morgan was like his father in a lot of ways, he shared Victor Grego's gift for understatement. "Maybe you came across them at the spaceport?"

"No— Wait! They came in on the same ship I did. We were even in the same shuttle from Darius." Morgan pulled a one-eighty, narrowly missing another aircraft as he raced back to Police House. Coombes, flustered by the aerial acrobatics, took a moment to ask what the devil was going on.

"I have an idea I want to bounce off the Marshal." Morgan didn't say another word until he was alone with Max Fane and Leslie Coombes, where he quickly outlined his plan.

"I'll need to talk this over with Mr. Brannhard," Max said. "I'll call him right now."

* * * * * * * * *

Affanita Goncalo drank her third brandy slowly. She had to. She was nearly broke. Affanita was a sunstone prospector. Like many in her profession, she used to work a claim over on Beta Continent until the discovery of the Fuzzies. The new Colonial Government created a reservation for the newly discovered natives and booted all of the prospectors out. Except for Jack Holloway, according to rumor, but he donated a large chunk of his land grant to the Fuzzy Reservation, so he might have gotten special dispensation to work his old properties. While sunstone deposits were planet-wide, the best diggings were on Beta; at least thus far nobody had found a better one.

Affanita and the other displaced prospectors were allowed to find new diggings elsewhere and given a land grant to replace the properties they lost, but the digs were never as good. With the Charterless Zarathustra Company granted a thousand-year lease on the unseated lands, the pickings for new dig sites were thin. In fact the Company managed to wrangle a special deal that allowed them to work the single largest deposit known on the planet, Yellowsand.

It was time to pack it in, she had decided. She could either uproot and move to a different planet, or take a job with the Company like every other person on Zarathustra. Affanita checked her wallet and decided she could afford one more drink before calling it a night. She was about to order when the bartender brought her a fresh drink. A double, in fact.

She stared at the drink, then said, "Um, not that I'm complaining, but I didn't order this…."

"It is from the gentleman at the end of the bar, miss," explained the bartender.

Affanita looked over at the indicated man and quickly sized him up. A geek. He was tall, skinny, pale and looked like he could have been stood up for the prom. Not her type at all. What he was doing in a dive like the Xerxes Tavern was anybody's guess. Then again, he was buying. That rated a thank you at the minimum. She stood up and walked to the end of the bar.

"What's your name, Tiger?"

"Would you believe that it is 'Tiger'?" The man smiled. "Actually, it is Richard."

"Okay, Richard. Thanks for the brandy, but I'm not the type of girl who goes home with whomever buys me a drink."

"I didn't think you were, though I'll admit I harbored some hopes. Actually, I wanted to help you out."

"Really? With what? You got some new lotion for my dry hands? Prospecting is murder on the skin." Affanita took a long drink from the double. It was a better brand of swill than what she had been drinking. Stronger, too. It had to be something off-planet. "Seriously, Tiger, what's the deal? I'm not the cutest broad in this dive."

Richard looked around the bar, and then took a sip from his drink. It looked like a soda pop. "Actually, at the moment you are the only, uh, broad in this dive. However, I want to retain your services as a prospector, not a prospective date."

Affanita stared levelly at Richard. He seemed to be serious. "Doing what? You have a big dig you need help with?"

Richard extracted a small leather pouch and handed it to her. Affanita opened the bag and looked inside; it was full of sunstones. At least fifty thousand sols worth, if she was any judge.

"This is…I…what do you want me to do?" Affanita grew suspicious. Nobody tossed around this kind of loot in a bar, especially in a hole like the Xerxes. Or anywhere else, for that matter.

"Sell these for me." Richard took another hit from his drink. "I don't have a prospector's license."

She took another drink. "You can get a PL for twenty sols, Tiger. I'll bet that's less than what this drink you bought me costs. Now, what's the scam?"

Richard shrugged. "Okay, my acquisition of these stones was less than completely on the up-and-up. I need to sell them through a third party to avoid unwanted attention. I haven't been on planet long enough to explain hitting such a rich deposit."

"Forget it." Affanita handed the pouch back and started to back away, leaving her drink behind on the bar. "I won't have any truck with somebody who robbed another prospector...."

"I did no such thing," interrupted Richard. "I can't tell you where I got these, but you may be assured I robbed nobody in your profession."

She stopped, held onto the rail to get her balance, then returned to her seat next to her drink. Despite herself, she was very curious. "Then where...?"

"I know people with vast connections. Trust me; these stones are unregistered and untraceable."

Affanita looked at the bag. If she even got five percent of their value, she would be set for a couple of months, maybe more. Still—"I don't know...?"

Richard tossed the bag next to Affanita's drink. "Tell you what. I'll just let you take these, free and clear. Inspect them, test them, sell them, do whatever you like. They're yours. Later we can talk about a percentages on future stones."

"What? Wait. What?" Affanita was starting to feel the effects of the brandy and doubted what she was hearing. "You're just givin' me these, um, these stones? How do you know I won't just run off with 'em?"

"You are perfectly free to do so if you wish, Affanita. But I think you will be back for more. And I will be back with more. Much more." Richard sized up the woman and realized the Thoran brandy he bought for her hit her a bit too hard. Since he needed her, he decided to make sure she stayed healthy. A place like the Xerxes Tavern was not the place where that could be counted on. There was a serial rapist on the loose and he needed the woman safe and healthy for his plans. "I think we should call you a cab and get you home before somebody takes advantage of you."

"I'm not a cab, 'm a woman." Affanita giggled. She was barely conscious at this point.

"Hey!" the bartender called out. "You better not have slipped her anything."

"Nah, nothing like that," Richard said. "I think she may have been a little too primed to deal with a good Thoran brandy. That's all. I'll just call her a taxi."

"I'm not a tazi, ei'der," mumbled the woman.

"I better not find out different, pal," the barman warned. Under the bar he tapped a command on a keyboard and a screen lit up showing the exterior of the bar. If the geek did anything other than put Affanita in a cab, he would be out there with a sawed-off pool cue in a heartbeat. For all he knew the skinny geek could be that rapist he read about on the data stream. The Xerxes might be a dive, but it was a dive where women weren't molested.

Richard dropped fifty sols on the bar, collected the tipsy woman and eased her out to the street, where he pressed the taxi call button. Thirty seconds later a cab floated down and Richard deposited Affanita in the back.

"Where to, Bubba?" the cabbie asked.

Richard started when he saw the cabbie, then quickly recovered. "Take the young lady to…" Richard took out the woman's wallet and opened it. "…8486 Featherleaf Lane. Here's ten to cover the fare and an extra fifty to make sure she makes it there in one piece. And get her into her place. No funny business or…."

"Hey, Bubba, I do this sort of thing all the time. The lady'll be safe with me. Besides, what my wife would do to me beats any threat you have on tap."

"That's good for both of us. There's an overprotective bartender in there I would hate for either of us to upset."

"You mean, Antonio? Yeah, he's a real mean one to cross, but a good guy to have at your back."

Richard smiled and tossed another fifty at the driver. The cabbie soared away with his fare and Richard called for another taxi. As he rode away, a large bearded man wearing a hat and sunglasses stepped out of the bar to watch him go.

IX

Gerd carefully applied the mildly caustic acid to the metal plate and used a specialized brush designed to withstand the acid to gently wipe away the loosened rust and grime. The metal plate had been painstakingly removed from the rocket with a combination of sonic vibrations to loosen the corroded bolts from the wall, and a magnetic extractor to gently pull and hold the plate. The belief was that it might be the ship's registry, or some alien equivalent. Unfortunately, the characters that Gerd had managed to uncover made no sense to him. A linguist would need to be brought in, and there were none on the planet as far as he knew.

With the first coat of corrosion removed, Gerd inspected his work. It would be a long time before anything useful could be gleaned from it. The rocket itself was older than any metal artifact in human history. Older than anything found on other planets, in fact. Except for Mars. Mars was lousy with artifacts a hundred thousand years old and older. Still, the rocket was a monumental find.

What they really needed were a few experienced archaeologists. Gerd was a xenonaturalist and anthropologist. He had taken a few courses in archaeology and paleontology back in his university days to fill a few electives, but had never been on a real dig before. Then again, what could an archaeologist bring to the party? Nobody had ever dug up a millennia-old rocket, before. Not even on Mars. Aside from being better suited to collecting and cleaning the artifact fragments, an archaeologist would likely be just as clueless as everybody else in this case.

"Aren't you supposed to be home with your wife, by now?"

Gerd turned and saw Victor Grego and Pancho Ybarra with Diamond trailing behind them. Everybody else was gone. "I guess I didn't hear the harpy on the pole telling me it was quitting time, Mr. Slate."

Grego looked confused.

"A reference to another old cartoon I used to watch as a child."

"Oh, right, the Flagstones or something like that, wasn't it?"

"*The Flintstones*, Mr. Grego," Pancho supplied. "Harpy. Good one, Gerd."

Grego nodded and continued, "Anyway, Ruth is here with Id, Syndrome, Superego and Complex. I didn't want too many people, Big Ones or Fuzzies, coming in here so I promised to corral you myself." Grego glanced at the plate Gerd was working on. "Getting anywhere?"

"Well, as a metal polisher, I make a good naturalist," Gerd said wryly. "I never had to clean a metal artifact before. Frankly, I should be working on those skeletons we found at the dig."

"Juan Jimenez is on top of that, and a herd of damnthings couldn't pull him away," Grego said. "This is the first real opportunity he's had to work at something other than administration since I promoted him."

"Humph. I guess I know how he feels," Gerd said. "Say, any luck finding a linguist, Mr. Grego?"

"I'm afraid not. When I selected the teams for this world it was with an eye towards exploitation and development. Since we believed this was a Class III uninhabited world, I didn't bother with linguists, archaeologists or anthropologists. Even you were hired on your primary vocation. I did send word out that we needed people in those areas as soon as the rocket was discovered, but it will take at least another two months, assuming there are any on Gimli, before we can expect anything on that front." He glanced at Lt. Commander Ybarra. "Anything the Navy could do?"

"No, sir. We fell into the same trap you did in staffing the base. We put out some feelers with the last ship, and we're hoping somebody will come in from Gimli in a couple of months."

Gerd nodded. "It could be longer than that, really, since we've known about Fuzzies for years and nobody from Gimli, expert in those disciplines, has dropped by for a chat with them. The rocket might spark some interest. Still, we might have to wait for somebody from Thor or Yggdrasil or even Freya to pop over. That means another four months, minimum. Frankly, I would have thought the Fuzzies themselves would have attracted more attention from that community."

"Good point," Grego said. "In fact, some might even be headed here, now. It takes a while for the news to travel by hyperspace and longer to get funding and relocate. We could be in for a whole flock of '-ists' and '-ologists' by year end."

"I hate to admit it, but the Space Navy dropped the ball on this one, too," Pancho added. "It's been more than two years since the discovery of the Fuzzies. They should have had some people brought in by now."

"Mummy Woof waiting, Pappy Vic," Diamond pointed out.

"So she is, Diamond. Come along, Gerd. We don't want your wife to get mad at us."

Grego walked with Gerd and Pancho to the elevator. "Um, Pancho, would you mind if Gerd and I speak privately?"

Pancho nodded once and moved to a different elevator far enough away to give Grego and Gerd some space.

"Gerd, I understand Ruth spends a lot of time going back and forth between here and Beta Continent, what with her social work and you working on the artifact." Grego refused to call it 'The Fuzzy Rocket.' "Why not just have her move in with you here in Company House?

Your old apartment is certainly roomy enough for the six of you, and I would even be willing to arrange a second suite if you feel you need the space."

Gerd rubbed his jaw thoughtfully, then said, "We talked about doing something like that, but with Lolita Lurkin staying with us while she works for Jack...well, I don't see how we can get around that."

"Doesn't Jack have an extra room?"

"I think Akira O'Barre will be staying in it, according to Ruth. She was there when Akira moved in."

Grego mentally slapped his forehead. Of course Akira was staying there. "Tell you what, I'll have a Quonset hut sent out to Jack's land grant, and the women can bunk in together. I think an old rooster like Jack will feel more comfortable with the hens out from underfoot, and Ruth can move back in with you, here." Grego omitted the fact that Jack had already ordered the hut for his guests earlier that day; plus another two, one to be filled with physical therapy and weight training equipment, some human sized, some downscaled for Fuzzy use, and the other for extra storage.

Gerd was skeptical. "What's the catch?"

Grego played innocent. He was surprisingly convincing. "Catch?"

"Mr. Grego, I worked for you long enough to know that even your most magnanimous gestures come back to profit you one way or another. Shall I list them? We can start with the extee-three you had the Company supply and ended up with the Yellowsand charter."

Juan told me Gerd was shrewd, damn-it. "Hey, that was just lucky. I had no idea that there would even be a Yellowsand mining operation at that time. Okay, I'll admit that I am hoping to win you and Ruth back to the company. You were both very good at your jobs, especially Ruth, and I hate to lose qualified people. Yes, I made some...unfortunate choices when the Fuzzies were first discovered, and Ruth did quite the hatchet job on me as a Terran Federation Naval operative. But I like to think that the past is the past. Me, Ben and the Fuzzies are all good friends, now. Right, Diamond?"

"Yes, Pappy Vic. Pappy Ben, Pappy Jack, Unka Panko…" Diamond went on at some length naming all of the Big Ones and Fuzzies who were friends.

"See, Gerd? One big happy family. If you come back it will be to an assistant Division Head position with a substantial bump to your old salary. Ruth would be working with Ernst Mallin as his chief assistant." Grego noticed that Gerd was silent on the subject as they walked. "One more thing; you two could keep an eye on us evil profiteers and keep us honest. Think about it."

"I can't promise anything, Mr. Grego. And I can't just leave Jack in the lurch, especially while he's recovering." Gerd mentally winced when he realized that he had pretty much already done that by working on the rocket.

"The job offer is open-ended. You and Ruth talk it over. Talk it over with Jack, too."

Gerd stepped into the elevator while he considered the offer. Granted, it was a good, no, a *great* opportunity, but he hated to leave Jack and the Fuzzies. Then another thought struck him. "Does Juan Jimenez know about this?"

Grego laughed. "Who do you think suggested it?"

* * * * * * * * *

Juan Jimenez looked over the arrangement of bones for the umpteenth time, then scribbled some notes on his pad. With him were Dr. Hoenveld and Dr. Mallin, plus a team of lab techs and interns.

"How does it look to you, Chris?" Juan asked Hoenveld.

"I'd say this is the correct arrangement, Dr. Jimenez." Hoenveld pointed to a left femur and a number of smaller bones set off to the side. "These do not belong to any of these fossilized skeletons. We don't have three sets of bones, but four incomplete sets. This one here," Hoenveld indicated the female skeleton on the fourth gurney, "is the closest one to completion of the bunch. Still, we have far more to work with than would typically be the case. Back on Old Terra, anthropologists would conjure up an entire hominid out of a single tooth, which made for some very embarrassing scientific *faux pas*. Still, archaeology and anthropology are outside my fields of expertise."

"Mine, as well," Dr. Mallin admitted. "Even though I took the requisite classes back at the university, which was well over thirty years ago."

"I know, doctor," Juan agreed. "We are all working outside of our fields on this. Still, you two are the best available on the planet for this job."

"Not true," Hoenveld argued. "Gerd van Riebeek is far more knowledgeable in this area than we are."

That Dr. Hoenveld would admit anybody was better at anything science related than himself was amazing. It also underscored how much they needed more qualified people to work on the project. Juan was a naturalist, like Gerd, but he lacked Gerd's background and experience. If he hadn't quit the company when the Fuzzies were first discovered, Juan had no doubt Gerd would be the division head instead of him.

"Ernst, nobody on the planet knows more about the brain and sapient mentation than you," Juan said. He wasn't just buttering Mallin up. Dr. Mallin was *the* authority in those fields on Zarathustra. "Judging by these skulls, do you think these are the fossils of sapient beings?"

Dr. Mallin screwed up his face as he considered his answer. "I just can't be sure, Dr. Jimenez. These bones look very much like oversized Fuzzy fossils. The skull cavity suggests a smaller brain-to-body ratio than that exhibited by the current existing population, but that wouldn't preclude sapience in and of itself. Fuzzies break a lot of rules in that regard. The average human brain is about three pounds. It was once believed that two pounds of brain mass was the minimum requirement to achieve functional sapience. Then we discovered the Yggdrasil Khooghra. Their brain masses are around three point nine pounds, and we all know what they are like. Neanderthal man had a larger cranial capacity than *Homo sapiens*, but I very much doubt that they were smarter than us.

"Now along come the Fuzzies with a brain mass of one pound, give or take, yet they are easily ten times smarter than a Khooghra. How the brain is arranged would account for much of that, of course. These fossilized skulls possess the capacity for a two and a half pound brain. Albert Einstein's brain was only two pounds or so. However, Einstein's neural density was far greater than average, which is also the case with Fuzzies. Khooghras, by the way, possess the lowest neural density of any sapient species."

"So you are saying," Hoenveld said, "that these skulls might have held a brain that could have rivaled that of Albert Einstein, or just that of an oversized Zarathustran primate."

"I'm afraid so, yes. It is interesting that the cranial cavity leaves very little room for the frontal lobes which, on Terra, would be an indication of low intelligence. However, Ullerans and Lokians also have small frontal lobes. A Freyan kholph possesses larger frontal lobes than a Fuzzy, yet is clearly non-sapient, though very intelligent as primates go. I just can't narrow it down from this little bit of evidence. Not yet."

Juan expected something like that. Current Fuzzy physiology allowed for larger frontal lobes, but there was no way of knowing whether or not that was the only marker for sapience on Zarathustra, yet. A lot more testing would be needed before any ruling could be justified.

Juan stood up straight and stretched. It seemed like he had been hunched over the fossils for hours. He glanced at his wrist chronometer and realized that he had been hunched over for a good long while. "Guys, let's call it a night and try this with fresh eyes in the morning. Maybe that work detail at the dig will have found something useful by then."

"A clay pot would be nice," Hoenveld observed, as they moved out the door. That brought on a lecture from Mallin about how Fuzzies only made weapons, not crockery. Crockery would suggest cooking of some sort and Fuzzies in the wild ate their food raw.

After the room was empty of all but a few of the night staff, one person looked over the bones and took a series of photographs, then left the building.

* * * * * * * * *

The sound of a heated argument filtered through the door of the visitor's room where Anderson and Rippolone sat. They couldn't catch everything being said through the door, but the gist seemed to be that Leslie Coombes didn't want the prisoners to have a visitor, while Marshal Fane said that even these sons-of-Khooghras had rights. After a few minutes the noise died down and a dark-haired man was escorted into the room by Officer Chang who inspected the prisoners' shackles before exiting and closing the door behind him.

The two prisoners eyed the newcomer for a few seconds. Finally, Rippolone broke the silence. "Who're you supposed ta be?"

"One second, gentlemen." The dark-haired man extracted a pen from a jacket pocket, depressed the end quickly five times, then set it in the middle of the table. "Now we may speak without being overheard."

"Fine. Now, who the hell are you?" demanded Rippolone.

The dark-haired man leaned forward. "Mr. Campanili sends his regards, Ripper. I was supposed to be your back-up if you ran into any problems. Well, clearly things have not gone well for you." The dark-haired man waved a hand indicating the interrogation room. "Not well at all."

Anderson spoke before Rippolone could respond. "I don't know what you are talking about, Mister—?"

"Guido will do, Tony." Guido leaned back as though at ease with his surroundings. "You did a pretty good job grabbing up Banner—, excuse me, Brannhard, but you got sloppy and got pinched. All I need to know is this: what have you told the local police?"

"We ain't said nuthin'," Rippolone said belligerently.

Guido shook his head and held up an index finger that he wagged side-to-side. "That is a double negative, Ripper, which means you said something."

"We have been steadfastly silent since our arrest, Mr. Guido," Anderson supplied. "We know better than to speak out of school."

Guido sighed dramatically. "I wish I could believe that, Tony."

"Who do you think you are, anyway? We don't know you from Adam," Rippolone argued. "I'll bet you're some cop tryin' ta sucker us."

"Ripper, look at his face," Anderson cautioned. "Don't you recognize him? He came in on the same ship from Terra that we did. He had that fancy private room in First Class."

The color drained from Rippolone's face. "Waitasec…Guido? *The* Guido?"

"You have heard of me, then." It was not a question. "I came to make sure you didn't botch the job, and to make sure you couldn't talk if you were caught. Ideally, I would try to get you off-planet. Regrettably, that is not an option as I lack the resources to extract you from these accommodations. I am very sorry, gentlemen, but I hope you understand that this is nothing personal." Guido reached a hand into his jacket.

"Nothing pers—, hey! Waitasec, we got a guy here that can help you get us out," blurted Rippolone. "Ain't that right, Tony?"

Anderson considered his options before speaking. He didn't have any. "Raul Laporte. He set us up with the hideout, aircar and weapons. He even gave us the directions to find Brannhard's home. I wouldn't be at all surprised if he had a few cops on his payroll. If anybody could get us out of here, he's the man."

Guido slowly withdrew his hand and sat quietly for several seconds before speaking. "This Laporte…where can I find him?"

"He owns The Bitter End over in Junktown," Rippolone said, then he did a double take. "Wait-a-sec, how come you don't know Laporte? Mr. Campanili gave us the lowdown on him before we left Terra…."

"I was given a different contact," Guido interrupted. "As it turns out, my information was not as good as yours. I was told to contact a Leo Thaxter, only to find that he was incarcerated long before my arrival on this world." Guido drew a breath and let it out slowly. "Gentlemen, eliminating you would be relatively easy. In fact, you wouldn't feel a thing when you suddenly expired two days from now." Guido patted his jacket where the two men suspected he had some sort of drug injection device in an inner pocket. "However, I am under orders to bring you back in one piece if at all possible. Mr. Campanili may want to deal with you personally, or simply question you. I neither know nor care which.

"I will have a talk with this Mr. Laporte. Beyond that, I can make no promises. I trust I can count on your continued discretion?" Guido picked up the pen, depressed the end five more times, and returned it to his pocket. "Good day, gentlemen."

* * * * * * * * *

"Guido? Seriously? That was the only name you could think of?" Max Fane was holding his sides as he laughed. "I can't believe these mutts fell for that! Oh, and I liked that trick with the pen."

"I saw something like that in an old spy thriller movie," Morgan admitted. "Is there something like that in reality?"

"White noise generators," supplied Max. "It sets up a static sound in the normal and hypersonic ranges. I never heard of one small enough to be disguised as a pen, though."

"These are hitmen, Max, not collapsium engineers," Gus Brannhard said. He turned to Morgan. "But still, 'Guido?' I should have prepped you better."

Morgan looked a little sheepish as he admitted that he heard the name from a gangster movie. "It sounded authentic to me. The only other name I could think of was Utgareles, a particularly nasty murderer who was executed on Freya twenty T-years ago. They seemed impressed enough. Is there an enforcer by the name of Guido working for the Campanili Family?"

"Not that I ever heard of, but they don't exactly advertise," Gus admitted. "You watch a lot of old Terran movies, don't you?"

"It helped me to learn a lot of Terran idioms and cultural details," Morgan said. "It also caused me to make a number of social *faux pas* in college since most of the movies were outdated."

"It doesn't matter," Leslie Coombes said. "We got the whole thing on tape. This will be enough to bring Laporte in and have him questioned under veridication. We'll have the warrant in about an hour and then we can go pay him a little visit."

"We?" Max asked.

"I'm prosecuting everybody involved with Gus's abduction, remember? That means I'm involved in prosecuting Laporte, too." Coombes turned to Gus. "I'm beginning to see the appeal of working your side of the street, Gus. By the way, that was a good prep job you did on Morgan, name notwithstanding. And Morgan, you missed your calling as an actor."

Morgan winked. "I couldn't fit it into my busy schedule. I did take part in some theatrical productions back in college, though."

"What really sold it, Mr. Holloway," Max Fane added, "is the fact they remembered you from the voyage in from Terra. Good thing we had these mutts in segregation with no television, radio or newspapers. That business with the duel was all over the news for quite a while."

"Call me Morgan, Marshal. Mr. Holloway is my father."

X

Gerd entered his old living quarters in Company House and plopped down into his overstuffed sofa chair. He hadn't realized how much he missed some of the things he had left behind when he quit the company.

He had made the chair himself in the employees' workshop, from featherleaf lumber and animal hides that he had hunted himself. The stuffing came from the feathers of banjo birds he had shot and eaten during some of his field trips. As a naturalist, he would never hunt for sport. Still, a man had to eat and there was no point wasting the hides and feathers.

Back when the Fuzzies were first discovered by Jack Holloway, he quit the company when it became clear that they were trying to keep the Fuzzies' sapience from being recognized. Gerd smiled when he recalled how he had told off Leonard Kellogg. Had his mother been there she would have washed his mouth out with soap.

Once out of the company, Gerd jumped at Jack's offer to become his partner as a sunstone prospector. The idea was that they had a better chance of staying alive if they worked together. After the Pendarvis Decision, Gerd stayed on with Jack as his deputy commissioner of native affairs. Then, he and Ruth got married.

Things had been going pretty well, though there were times when the money was tight. Gerd wasn't making quite as much as deputy commissioner as he had with the Company, and Ruth was no longer employed at all though she did still volunteer with Social Services. Add four active Fuzzies, Superego, Id, Syndrome and Complex, and the money barely stretched from week to week.

Ruth had talked about taking on a full-time position with Social Services, but that was on Alpha. They would only get to see each other on the weekends.

Victor Grego's offer was a damned good one. Even without Ruth getting her position back, their financial troubles would be under control. They could even start planning on having children who weren't Fuzzies.

Gerd decided he would talk to Ruth, then Jack, and see what they had to say about it. The worst of it, after leaving Jack hanging, was moving back to Alpha Continent. He liked Beta and working directly with Fuzzies.

* * * * * * * * *

Jack Holloway strolled around the homestead without the contragravity chair. Akira was getting familiar with the office and Betty had chased him out of his own cabin to cook something up for dinner. Real take charge woman that Betty. She reminded him of his mother that way. He just hoped she was as good a cook as she was attractive. Morgan's mother, Adonitia, had been.

For now Jack just wanted some exercise while Morgan was over on Alpha. His chest had stopped itching and his new lung seemed to be working well enough that he didn't feel winded while walking. He also noticed his joints were less stiff. Jack had to admit that he felt better than he had in years.

Gus confessed that Morgan flipped for the full body treatment while he was incapacitated. Jack glanced at his reflection in a window as he walked passed. At least they left his hair and crow's feet alone. He regarded his wrinkles and white hair as trophies of a life well lived. Had Morgan interfered with those, well, full-grown man or not, he would have gone over Jack's knee.

Something flew passed Jack's head and he instinctively reached for his pistol, even though he hadn't worn it around camp since the res was created. Just as well; it was that silly Frisbee. Little Fuzzy, Baby Fuzzy and two of the dogs came running after it.

"Pappy Jack! You play Friz-bee with us," Little Fuzzy asked.

Jack thought about it and decided he needed the exercise. "Hokay. Just don't make me run for it, too much.

They moved away from the house and Jack sent the disc for a long low spin towards Little Fuzzy. The Fuzzy snatched it out of the air and shot it to Baby Fuzzy, who leaped twice his height into the air to catch it. Baby spun and launched it at the nearest dog, Trigger, before he hit ground. Trigger snapped it up and took it back to Little Fuzzy, who in turn sent it back to Jack. Jack didn't have to move an inch; the disc sailed straight to him with impressive accuracy.

Jack threw the Frisbee to the other dog, Bullet, and started thinking about a Fuzzy Olympics. Almost any sport a human could do, a Fuzzy could do better, with the exception of team sports. Fuzzies had no concept of competition with each other. But running, jumping, pole vaulting, shot put, all these and more were workable. And it could be a tourist attraction. Ben was sweating bullets trying to come up with new sources of revenue in case the sunstone market collapsed. There was always taxation, but the simple fact was that Zarathustra simply didn't have the population to support a planetary government and public services through tax revenues.

After ten minutes of playing, Jack felt pleasantly tired and decided to quit before he pushed himself too hard. Tossing the Frisbee around had been more fun than he expected and the Fuzzies were dead accurate with the disc when they wanted to be. Jack barely moved a step from his initial throwing position the entire time. That started him thinking of making some throwing stars for the Fuzzies. A goofer or zarabunny would likely drop dead with a single hit. Not as deadly as a bullet or arrow, but easy to carry.

Jack's chain of thought stopped as Lolita Lurkin shouted his name.

"Mistah Holloway! There's a call for ya on da screen. Somethin' 'bout a dig site?"

That would be the crowd up where that rocket was discovered. Jack hoped there wasn't another problem up there, like somebody finding a mummified Fuzzy in a space suit. Wouldn't that play Nifflheim in the news.

"Little Fuzzy, why don't you take some of your friends out and do some hunting. We could use some fresh meat."

"Hokay, Pappy Jack," Little Fuzzy said. He and Baby scampered off, yeeking for some hunting partners.

Jack walked quickly to the office where Akira was talking to somebody in a prison guard uniform on the viewscreen.

"Here he is now, sir." Akira stood up to make room for Jack to take the seat.

Jack sat and noticed the man on the screen was agitated. "What can I do for you, son?"

"Well, we had a con break the perimeter…and um…."

"And he made a mess," finished Jack. He knew all about the collar and pole security system. "He didn't hurt any Fuzzies in the process, did he?"

"Not that we saw. Um, can I ask you keep this quiet? What I'm about to tell you, that is."

"As long as it isn't something illegal, Mr.—"

"Call me Ismet. No, sir, not illegal, just embarrassing." Ismet explained about where they found the body and the grass wrapping.

"That's standard Fuzzy procedure for preparing a body for burial," Jack replied. "No stone cairn?"

"Negative, sir. We had to stun a zarawulf that was mauling the corpse, though. Think maybe the Fuzzies were scared away before they were finished?"

That was possible. "Did you see a collection of rock nearby? Something that might have been dropped in a hurry?" Ismet admitted that he hadn't seen any. "Then the body may have been left for you to find."

Ismet accepted that, then asked why the Fuzzies hadn't come out when he and Niyol found the body. Jack explained that Fuzzies in the wild tended to avoid anything they didn't understand. "If you saw anything at all, it would likely be backsides disappearing into the brush." A thought struck Jack. "You stunned the zarawulf? Did you use sono-stunners?"

Ismet nodded.

"Fuzzies have hypersonic hearing. That sonic blast might have sent them running. Tell you what, I'll come up in a few days and see if I can get a dialogue going with your neighbors. I have a few questions of my own."

"We look forward to your visit, Commissioner."

The screen blanked out. Jack sat and considered what he knew of the Fuzzies in general. The burial wrapping was standard for every Fuzzy tribe he had ever come across, and he'd come across a lot. So the northern Fuzzies recognized that the dead convict was a person, not an animal, which was a generous conclusion given that the man was a convicted felon. Too bad the law only allowed for the shooting of people who commit crimes instead of shooting the kind of people who commit them. The odd thing was the lack of a stone cairn. The Fuzzies left the body out where it could be found.

Maybe the Fuzzies up there didn't want any direct contact with humans. The big explosion might account for that, or maybe the illegal prospectors committed a few atrocities on the locals and now the Fuzzies didn't trust Big Ones in general. Fuzzies were smart enough to stay away from anything dangerous once they knew it could hurt them. Unfortunately, they could also generalize.

Damnthings would make you dead and eat you, so all damnthings were bad. Big Ones made a big boom that maybe hurt some Fuzzies, or some other thing the humans did hurt some Fuzzies, so all Big Ones were bad. That would explain their timidity. They would also be stuck with the dead Big One whose head went boom. It would be too big to bury, too much like people to eat. So, they wrapped it up and left it for other Big Ones to find and, hopefully, take away before it made bad smells.

Jack smiled as he considered the likelihood that some Fuzzies might have hid in the brush to watch and see what the Big Ones would do when they found the body. Jack was still lost in conjecture when the viewscreen came back on. It was Victor Grego. Jack pressed the ACCEPT CALL button a second time.

"Victor," Jack shook his hands together and the image on the viewscreen reciprocated. "How is Gerd doing on that rocket?"

Grego grimaced. "About how you would expect. It isn't Gerd's area of expertise, but he's the best we got. Actually, Gerd's the reason I called."

"Oh?"

"I offered him his old job back, plus a raise and promotion. He turned me down."

"What? Why? You would pay him a damn sight more than he makes as my deputy, and the work is far less dangerous. He has a wife to think about."

Grego nodded. "I pointed that out. But he's too loyal to you and the Fuzzies to leave you in the lurch."

Now there was a little piece of irony. At the moment Gerd was over on Alpha Continent working for the Company while Jack was being buried in paperwork. He'd already left Jack in the lurch.

"Well, if you recall, he quit after Kellogg mishandled the Fuzzy situation and came to work with me as my partner prospecting sunstones, ideally so we could keep each other alive."

Grego winced. "Actually, killing you or Gerd was never an option in my book. Discrediting you both, I'm sorry to say, was."

Jack waved it away. "Water under the bridge, Victor. The thing is, Gerd should take the job…he gets his seniority back, too, right?" Grego agreed. "Then we'll just have to find a new deputy commissioner of native affairs. I'll miss having him here, but a man has to do what's right for himself and his family."

Grego looked visibly relieved. "I'm very pleased to hear that, Jack. Now we just need to convince Gerd of that."

That will be tough, Jack thought. "Well, I could always fire him."

Grego thought that would cause too many hard feelings and Jack agreed. They discussed it until another call came in. Jack made an apology and put Grego on hold to accept the other call and wondered how he got to be so popular all of a sudden.

It was Betty. "Jack, you better round up the gang and get them over here for dinner before I feed it to the river pigs."

Yup. Just like his mother in a lot of ways.

"Yes, Ma'am," he said, then switched back over to Grego. "Gotta go, Victor. Betty just rang the dinner bell. We'll discuss this later."

Grego agreed and Jack signed off and headed back to his cabin.

Back at Company House Victor Grego idly wondered who Betty was and why she was cooking dinner for Jack.

XI

As the ship flew through hyperspace, Thor Folkvar watched the gray nothingness of space-minus through a specially polarized portal. Thor forced himself to drag his attention away from the display. He was starting to feel like the abyss was staring back. He decided to check in with the bridge.

Like most private hyperspace yachts, this one was roughly half the diameter of the commercial models. Still, it was large enough for most practical purposes. The curvature of the floor, while noticeable, wasn't difficult to walk on. Down in crew quarters and around the Dillingham hyperdrive engine, the curvature was not unlike walking on a large dome, though the artificial gravity was evenly distributed so there was no sense of climbing or descending. One simply felt like they were at the apex of the dome with every step.

Thor stepped from the elevator and nearly ran into a horror the equal of anything in an H. P. Lovecraft novel. It stood erect on stumpy legs and broad, six-toed feet. There were four arms, one pair from true shoulders and the other connected to a pseudo-pelvis midway down the torso. The skin was slate-gray and rubbery looking. The narrow head bore an unpleasant saurian resemblance with small, double-lidded red eyes, slit-like nostrils, and a wide mouth filled with opalescent teeth. It was also completely naked though it bore a stencil-painted emblem of the House of Honirdite on its chest and back.

"Gaah!" Thor backed up a step and put a hand to his chest.

"Kronkeenk, I wish to Nifflheim you wouldn't do that. I could have a heart attack or something, you geek."

"Znidd suddabit, you sovt-szhelled ape. Yoo no prize, eit'er," countered the Ulleran. The two traded barbs for a moment, then pleasantries in the manner of old friends. "Vhere yoo go in sudge hurree?"

"The bridge. I'm bored and just want to do something, so I decided to bother the captain to pass the time. You?"

"Preparing vor sleep-cycle. Vas long szhivt." Kronkeenk made a gesture of polite dismissal and proceeded down the passageway.

"Sleep well, Kronkeenk." Thor turned and on his way to the bridge.

The bridge appeared to be relaxed. Personnel sat at consoles that monitored the ship's systems and controlled the hyperdrive. Two Thoran security guards sat in seats behind the captain, Terran and Freyan technicians pressed buttons and watched screens and a Sheshan steward brought a drink to the captain. Only the captain seemed agitated, which was the normal state of affairs for the Freyan native. Like the yacht's owner, the captain had been schooled on Mars. He was competent and versatile, yet young enough to still believe he had something to prove.

"Captain Zeudin, how are things going?"

"Mr. Folkvar!" The captain had been so focused on the screens and readouts that he hadn't heard Thor enter. "We will arrive ahead of schedule, sir."

"Oh? Found a shortcut through hyperspace, Captain?"

"No, sir. I am afraid the current laws of hyperspace physics remain unaltered. Maybe someday we'll break the sixty-hour per light-year barrier, but not on this trip. No, we simply left ahead of schedule and have had no difficulties that might have slowed us in our travels."

"Ah, do your travel estimates always include estimated difficulties, captain?"

"They do. As such, I have never failed to arrive on or ahead of schedule." Capt. Zeudin stood up and moved about the bridge, more to stretch his legs than to micromanage the crew. "How do our passengers fare, sir?"

"A little bored, for the most part. This is the first space voyage for some of them, after all. The menagerie seems to be managing well enough, if a bit restless."

The captain nodded. "Animals are always restless in hyperspace, and even with the time dilation effect, a journey from Freya to Gimli, then to Zarathustra is a fair stretch. Especially for this bloody lot."

"I have them on maximum sedatives, captain. Especially the larger ones." Thor chuckled. "They do grow them big on Freya."

The captain looked over Thor with an appraising eye. "Well, you have been there, so you should know. You're pretty big, too, you know."

Thor stood over two meters tall and sported impressive muscle mass, a common enough trait on the heavy gravity planet of his birth. Unlike most other Magni colonists, Thor actively worked at building up his body. For a while he had competed in the body-builder circuit until he realized he would never place above third in any show. Unlike the competitors from lower gravity planets, Thor couldn't develop the deep cut and muscle separation that the judges favored. His greater muscle density and thickness actually worked against him. Moreover, strongman contests operated on a planet-to-planet basis, blocking him from competing off Magni. Thor loved to travel too much to compete under that restriction.

Eventually, he met John Morgan and accepted a job as a bodyguard, little though the Freyan seemed to need one. Morgan traveled from world to world searching for the father who abandoned him, investing money in the local companies and playing detective. Thor, almost twice Morgan's age and already well-traveled, was able to advise the Freyan on local customs and taboos. When Morgan would get depressed over yet another failure to locate his father, the two would get roaring drunk and occasionally start a bar brawl, then stand back-to-back taking on all comers. Until that mess with the Chartered Magni Cooperative was discovered.

"You're no runt, either, Captain. When do we make planet fall?"

"If we don't bounce off the gravity well by cutting it too close, twenty-eight hours and change."

"And if we bounce?"

Captain Zeudin shrugged. "Add a couple of hours or so. Can't predict something like that."

"I'd better get the passengers ready, then." Thor hustled out of the bridge and took the lift one level down. Second level, normally used for storage, was packed wall-to-wall with cryogenic freezers on one side, and what could only be classed as a zoo on the other. The animals it contained were unlike anything currently living on Terra.

Thor walked over to a man who was pouring feed into a trough. Once full, a button was pressed and the trough smoothly entered a cage and a grate closed behind it. The animal within the cage appeared to be large, dangerous and out of sorts. Thor was very glad for the heavy barrier between himself and the Freyan *vig'nol.* The man attending to the menagerie turned and saw the visitor.

"Where is everybody?" the Magnian inquired.

"Sleeping. Old habits are hard to break, and this was always our allotted sleeping period." The caretaker spoke with a soft German accent not unlike that of one schooled in the Bavarian dialect of Southern Germany. The man's voice was a deep bass that would be the envy of any Terran singer; it sounded as though it reverberated from the deepest recesses of his barrel chest. "I worked in a different area, so my sleeping cycle is out of phase with the others. Are we almost there?"

"The captain says another twenty-eight hours, give or take."

The man nodded his large head, something a casual observer might have thought impossible given the thickness of his neck. "A new world. One with no masters. Will they accept us despite our differences?"

"This is a world where humans and the native inhabitants live together in peace. I think this is your people's best chance for a home. And John Morgan plans on purchasing a tract of land where you will be free of interference. Hopefully, he was able to swing the deal."

"And if he couldn't…?"

The Magnian shrugged, "Well, either you can try to live and work with the local population or we'll just start looking someplace else. Don't give up hope, Johann."

"Hope is all my people and I have, Herr Thor. We cannot afford to lose it."

* * * * * * * * *

Jack awoke at his usual 0700 without the need for an alarm clock. He had a strange sense that something was off. He couldn't think of anything that would cause such a feeling until he heard soft breathing next to him on the bed. That was not unusual in the least; the Fuzzies often snuck into bed with him while he slept. He had gotten so used to it that he didn't even wake up anymore when it happened.

Then came the snore. It was a well-documented fact that Fuzzies did not snore in the wild since it could attract dangerous predators. Jack sat up in the bed and turned to look at the source of the sound. It was a very attractive and very nude young woman.

Jack jerked backward with such force that he lost his balance and fell off the bed. Cursing softly, though blasphemously, he crawled up to the side of the bed to re-examine his new bunkmate. The covers had come away from the sleeping woman and hit the floor with Jack leaving her completely exposed, though undisturbed in her slumber.

It was Betty Kanazawa. Jack experienced a mixed sense of relief, since for a moment, he was afraid it might have been Akira, which would certainly be grounds for another duel with Morgan (once was quite enough, thank you very much). Then, confusion as to how Betty had ended up there.

Quietly getting to his feet, Jack noticed his usual pajama bottoms were missing. He carefully returned the blanket and sheet to the sleeping woman and dressed as quietly as he could before tiptoeing out of the bedroom. In the kitchen Jack made a pot of tea and took his medications.

The medications!

Jack read the labels of each and found that prolonged usage could create a sense of euphoria in some patients if ingested with alcohol, other drugs or highly caffeinated beverages. Like tea. Jack felt like swearing, but couldn't think of anything vile enough to cover the situation. Searching his memory, Jack recalled that after Akira and Lolita had retired, he had started feeling the side effects of his medication, which wasn't much different from a few stiff shots of bourbon.

Did I take advantage of that young woman?

Jack struggled to recover more details and finally recalled that Betty had challenged him to a few hands of poker. Jack, having spent time on Fenris where poker was the number one pastime, quickly cleaned out the seemingly less experienced Betty. That was when she started anteing articles of clothing, which she also quickly lost. After that, try as he might, the details were too hazy to remember.

Jack was no prude. Ghu knew, he had done a lot of things in his youth far more questionable than a few rounds of strip poker, though he had never forced himself on any woman. He hoped that still held true.

Jack jumped a bit as the teapot whistled. It was an old-style stove top model he had picked up on Freya. He started to pour himself a cup, then remembered the medical interaction. He rooted around in the cupboard for a caffeine free brand and found a Darjeeling tea of Morgan's that would do. Jack wasn't partial to Darjeeling and grimaced as he started a new pot. He set the tea to boil, again, and then sat down to ponder his situation further.

A soft hand caressed his shoulder and he nearly jumped out of his skin. Jack turned to find a smiling Betty wearing one of his housecoats.

"I hope you don't mind, but you won all of my clothes last night," Betty said with a little laugh.

"Ah…about that…"

"What?"

"Um…as it turns out none of those things will fit me and they clash with my gun belt, so by all means feel free to put them back on." *When in doubt, act casual.*

Betty laughed and punched Jack lightly in the shoulder. "Okay, I'll be right back. Oh, I guess I won't need this…" She pulled off the housecoat and draped it over his head before walking back into the bedroom to recover her wardrobe. Her own nudity didn't seem to bother her in the slightest. It certainly bothered Jack, though not in any bad way.

Well, I couldn't have done anything objectionable last night or Betty would be a lot less easygoing this morning. It wasn't until the teapot whistled that Jack remembered Betty had brought an overnight bag with her.

* * * * * * * * *

The zarabuck paused from his grazing and raised his head. It had caught an unfamiliar scent in the breeze and looked about for its source.

The animal could neither see nor hear anything to be concerned about. The high grass of the veldt obscured much of its view. Still, any animal large enough to be a threat would be visible. Or should have been. Several golden animals with similarly furred bipeds on their backs came out of the brush and raced towards the buck. The zarabuck had never seen anything like it before. This was understandable since dogs were somewhat new to Beta Continent, and dogs used as mounts for the indigenous natives even more so.

Little Fuzzy notched an arrow into his bow and let fly with impressive accuracy, especially considering how he made the shot from a charging Curtys, the dog breed favored as a mount for the Fuzzies. The arrow caught the zarabuck in the rear haunch. The animal jumped and ran, but its speed was greatly reduced by the injury, allowing the slower dog riders to overtake him. Several more arrows struck the buck and brought him down.

Little Fuzzy noticed that Baby Fuzzy's arrow struck the buck in the neck and praised the young hunter for his expertise with the bow, which Baby Fuzzy accepted with pride.

The Fuzzies quickly dismounted and started stripping the buck of its hide, then cut out large portions of meat. The meat was piled onto the hide and each Fuzzy took a small portion and fed it to his mount. They were careful not to feed the dogs too much. A full dog was a slow dog and prone to nausea when running long distances.

After each dog was given his treat, the Fuzzies wrapped the remaining meat in plastic bags and stuffed them in their backpacks. While Fuzzies were perfectly content to eat the meat raw, they preferred to cook it when they returned home. Cooking improved the flavor and the meat would stay good for a longer time. They also intended to share with the others back at the res.

Before remounting some of the Fuzzies noticed that their dogs had heeded the call of nature. They quickly dug holes and buried the ordure just as they would their own waste. This eliminated the bad smells that might scare away future prey. Back at the res the waste would be dumped into a tank that used the methane it produced for power. This kept the grounds clean and provided clean energy for some of the Fuzzy-operated equipment.

As the Fuzzies were preparing to remount, the dogs started growling and looking towards the west. The Fuzzies followed the dogs' line of sight and spotted the damnthing bull bearing down on them. The smell of fresh blood must have attracted it from downwind.

Rather than mount up and make a run for it, as instincts developed over millennia of surviving in a hostile environment would have them do, Little Fuzzy called the group together and had them form a wide arc. As the damnthing approached, the Fuzzies fired arrows at it. Most of the first volley of the missiles buried themselves in the beast's massive head to little effect, save for the one that pierced its left eye. The rest struck the forepart of the torso and legs.

Undaunted, at first, by the numerous arrows, the damnthing continued forward, then stumbled and fell. One of its monstrous hooves had fallen into a small hole and threw off its balance. The Fuzzies quickly seized the advantage and circled the beast, firing arrow after arrow into its leathery hide. The damnthing managed to get back on its feet and start another charge until the Fuzzy called Maid Marian chanced a close-in shot on the right eye that pierced the orb and penetrated into brain.

A more reasonable animal would have accepted the fact that an arrow in the brain would mean it was time to lie down and stay there. A damnthing, by definition, was far from a reasonable animal. Rather than quietly expire, it lunged blindly forward, narrowly missing Maid Marian with its brow horn, and thrashed about wildly. Little Fuzzy ordered everybody to back away, although too late to keep one Fuzzy, called Bird

Chaser as he had not yet received a new name from the Big Ones, from being struck by a hoof of the thrashing and kicking monster.

Bird Chaser was knocked away from his dog mount with a broken arm. The dog, well trained, gently grabbed the Fuzzy by his backpack with its powerful jaws and dragged him away from further danger.

The damnthing spent several long minutes of thrashing and kicking before it finally realized that it was dead. Then it simply crashed to the ground and laid motionless. Two Fuzzies went to Bird Chaser's aid and put a splint on his arm while two others found a couple of long sticks. Once the Fuzzies were satisfied that the damnthing wasn't playing possum they quickly stripped off the hide and as much meat as they could carry or drag behind them in the hide without over-taxing the dogs. Part of the hide was cut away and combined with the two branches to make a travois for the injured Bird Catcher. The travois was attached to his dog's saddle so he could drag it behind while another Fuzzy took the reins. This was to keep the injury from being jarred as they traveled.

Little Fuzzy and Baby Fuzzy assisted Maid Marian in hacking out the brow horn of the damnthing. Fuzzies did not typically take trophies of their kills in the wild, but association with Big Ones had started the practices among the domestic Fuzzies and a damnthing horn would impress everybody, human and Fuzzy alike.

Little Fuzzy considered doing something with the damnthing hide. The idea of using the hide for a blanket or to keep the rain off would be a good thing. In the Fuzzy villages—where Fuzzies had their own homes instead of living with Big Ones'—animal hides were used to cover the floor or block window openings like curtains. Living with Pappy Jack, there was no place to put up his own hides or lay them on the floor; Pappy Jack already had such things.

A smile grew on Little Fuzzy's face as he got an idea.

XII

Akira and Lolita were up and dressed in time for breakfast, which Betty was helping Jack prepare. Instead of Jack's usual coffee and toast, the couple fried up some eggs, Terran-introduced potatoes, river swine sausage and tea. The four ate, then Lolita went out to find some Fuzzies to play with before starting work gofering. Betty pushed Jack and Akira out of the kitchen while she cleared away the dishes and loaded the washer. Jack decided to stretch his legs a bit without the hover-chair and Akira followed him outside.

"Really, Jack," Akira said, "do you think your shenanigans last night constitute proper behavior with a young impressionable girl in the house?"

"What?" Jack was confused until he realized that Akira was referring to Lolita. "Oh, Nifflheim, I didn't even think about that…."

Akira laughed. "Relax, Jack. I'm just yanking your chain. Lolita was completely out of here before Betty put the moves on you last night."

The elder Holloway let out a long breath. "Well, that's a relief… wait, she put the moves on me?"

Akira nodded. "Let me guess, she challenged you to a game of poker, lost all her money, and switched to throwing her clothes in the kitty, which she also lost all of. Sound about right?"

Jack grimaced. "From what I can recall. Last night is more than a little hazy after that point."

"You didn't start drinking with her, did you? Your medications…."

"Nothing stronger than tea. However, I learned this morning that caffeine doesn't mix with some of the meds." The pair sat on a bench that overlooked the dog pens. "I was hoping Betty didn't think I took advantage of her last night."

"Ha! If there is a victim in this it was you. Betty likes older men because they tend to be more stable. Don't worry; she doesn't have any 'daddy issues'."

Jack admitted he was relieved to hear that. "Does she do this sort of thing often?"

"Actually, no. Oh, she plays the odd game of strip poker, usually at parties where everybody joins in, and more often than not is the last one undressed. She's actually a bit of a card sharp. And before you get the wrong idea, she only sleeps with men she is seriously interested in. Believe me, she doesn't get that interested all that often. She broke up with Frank Patel last month and hasn't been with anybody since."

"Humph." Jack reached for his pipe only to find that the pocket was empty and mentally cursed the doctors. "In that case, I hope she wasn't disappointed with my performance last night. Don't let it get around, but I don't entertain very much myself."

"Since she is currently cleaning your kitchen, I would say you did all right. She doesn't play maid for just anybody, either." Akira leaned back on the bench and stretched her arms over her head. "So, Mr. John Morgan Holloway the Greater, what are your intentions towards my friend?"

"Now don't you start that Greater nonsense," Jack said. "Morgan is the Freyan, not me. As for Betty, well, I don't really know, Akira. She's a nice girl and if I was about thirty or forty years younger—I never robbed the cradle before."

Akira smirked. "Pretty big cradle, Jack. You like her, don't you?"

"What's not to like? Betty is a free spirit without all those pesky inhibitions most Terrans lug around and secretly hate. Don't tell anyone, especially Morgan, but she reminds me a bit of his mother…and mine." Akira looked surprised. "No, not like that. Betty sees what she wants and goes after it, and isn't afraid to put some effort into the project. Adonitia went after me, not the other way around. I actually resisted getting involved as I wasn't sure I would be staying on Freya. I wasn't able to hold out for long, though. She had me hooked and reeled in short of a Terran month. After I learned about her death I pretty much lost interest in dating."

"Really? But didn't you still, um…?"

"That's none of your business, young lady, or do you want me poking my nose into your doings with my son?"

Akira blushed a little at that. "Jack, about Morgan and me. Well…."

Before Akira could finish, Little Fuzzy rode up on Trigger yelling something. It took a moment before he calmed down enough to explain about the accident during the hunt. "We make splint like you teach us, and a travois to bring Bird Chaser back on."

"Good job, Little Fuzzy. We'll get him to the doctor and put a cast on that arm. Akira, can you call Lynne Andrews and let her know we have a patient?"

"On my way." Akira jumped up and hot-footed it back to the cabin to make the call.

"Where is the rest of your hunting party, Little Fuzzy," Jack asked.

"They bring damnthing meat on hide. Take many dogs and go slow. I come fast with Bird Chaser to fix bad arm."

Bird Chaser had to have taken a lot of jarring behind a fast moving dog, even on the travois. Try as he might, Jack couldn't get it across to the Fuzzies that hurrying could be a bad thing in such instances.

"Pappy Jack, we make talk about idea I have?"

"Sure, Little Fuzzy. Right after we make sure Bird Chaser is all fixed up."

* * * * * * * * *

While The Bitter End was closed until 1500 Alpha Time as a rule, the sealed hardwood doors were insufficient to prevent the horde of gate crashers that swarmed in. In the lead were officers Piet and Chang in riot gear and gas masks, armed with sono-stunners and pacification rifles, followed by twenty cops similarly equipped. A sleep-gas grenade sailed over to the middle of the dance floor and exploded, sending the powerful knockout gas spreading throughout the lounge. Two burly men who had been reaching under their jackets fell unceremoniously onto a table knocking it over. They were disarmed, cuffed and left where they were. The officers quickly spread throughout the floor. Piet took the stairs with six men while Chang secured the lower level and sent a squad to check the kitchen and behind the bar.

On the upper floor the officers methodically checked every door and hallway until they arrived at Raul Laporte's office.

Unlike the other doors, this one was made of metal that defied all attacks. Piet tapped on the door with the butt of his rifle. It was like hitting a granite mountain. Piet swore luridly.

"Collapsium-laminated," he said. "Probably over poly-steel, not that it matters. We won't be breaking through this door, damnit."

"You think the walls are collapsium, too?" Montgomery van Damme asked.

"I doubt it." Piet tapped the walls next to the door. They sounded hollow. "Good catch, Monty. Somebody go back to the transport and get a couple of vibro-hammers. We should be able to break through this in about half a minute."

The door slid open to reveal a tall, thin man with sandy hair. "I would rather you didn't do that. Is there something I can do to help you, gentlemen?"

"We have a warrant for the arrest of Raul Laporte," Piet proclaimed.

"Please step aside."

The sandy-haired man did as instructed and Piet quickly moved into the office, followed by the rest of the squad. Van Damme covered the civilian while the rest went through the room, looking for any place Laporte could be hiding in or could have exited through. Piet noticed with disgust that the inner walls were also collapsium-covered. The vibro-hammers would never have gotten through.

"Mr. Laporte no longer owns this establishment, gentlemen. I do."

Piet turned to the man. "And you are?"

"Ricardo La Rue, officer."

"When did you acquire this business?" van Damme asked.

"About an hour ago," La Rue said. He pointed at some papers on the desk. "I have the documents here to back my claim."

"When did he leave? Where was he going?" Piet demanded.

La Rue glanced at his wrist chronometer. "About thirty minutes ago, and I am sure I have no idea where he was going."

Piet swore under his breath as he pulled out his radio. "Dispatch, we need to send a team to the spaceport. Alert the management there not to sell anybody even close to matching Laporte's description an off-world ticket. Have them swab for DNA for anybody who even vaguely matches his description trying to leave." Piet returned his attention to Ricardo La Rue. "Now just where did you come from?"

La Rue took the seat behind the desk, and then said, "If I am to be subjected to a battery of questions, I think I will need to contact my attorney."

Piet had expected something to that effect. "You do that. Have him meet you at the station."

* * * * * * * * *

Ruth walked into the office and made a beeline toward Jack. Jack hadn't heard the aircar come in over the barking and howling of the dogs but knew it had to be a visitor. The hypersonic noise generated by the contragravity tended to hurt the dogs' ears.

"Ruth, got more young bodies for me?"

"Actually, yes. Three boys and two more girls."

"All in their early teens with raging hormones," Jack said as he rubbed his forehead. "I'll have to start carrying a shotgun to keep them apart."

"Jack, can I talk to you about something?" Jack indicated a chair and Ruth sat down. "It's about Gerd…."

"The job offer?"

"He told you about it?"

"Not yet," Jack said as his chronometer started beeping. "One sec." Jack took out his pill box and washed a few pills down with his tea. Decaffeinated. "Victor gave me a call. He felt it wasn't kosher to poach my deputy without a heads up."

Ruth nodded thoughtfully. "Jack, what do you think?"

"About the job? Sounds like a great opportunity, and he'd be crazy to pass it up. Especially if that thing you hinted at the other day is what I think."

Ruth looked confused, then her face brightened. "Oh! That. Um… what did you think it was?"

Jack rolled his eyes. "Ruth, you two are young and healthy and have been married for two years. I'm a bit surprised you don't already have any rug-rats underfoot."

Ruth nodded and said, "Gerd doesn't know, yet."

Nothing good was ever preceded by a statement like that, thought Jack. "Why not?"

"I'm not sure if I should…"

"Money troubles."

"What? How…?"

"You wouldn't be here to talk me into letting Gerd go, otherwise." Jack leaned forward and placed a fatherly hand on Ruth's shoulder. "Look, you two are like family and I want things to go well for you. I think Gerd should take the job. I can get a new deputy." Jack smiled and added, "One who would actually be here instead of working on Alpha Continent."

"I've also been offered my old job back, too."

"*Et tu*, Ruth-ay?"

"We don't want to leave, Jack." Ruth pointed out the window at some Fuzzies who were bathing their dogs. "They're like family."

"Well, there are Fuzzies on Alpha, too, you know."

Ruth shook her head. "All adopted and civilized. Well, as civilized as Fuzzies get, anyway. This is where the action is, Jack."

"I'm confused. Do you want me to talk him into taking the job, or talk him out of it?"

Ruth sighed. "I don't know, really. Things were so much easier when I was spying for the TFN."

"Easier!" Jack laughed. "Tell you what; I'll think about it and see what I can come up with. I'll try to squeeze Ben for a raise. Maybe he can match Victor's offer?"

"I doubt that. If Gerd takes the job he'll make more than you do."

"Really? Is Victor looking for more people? Just kidding. Now let's go meet these walking hormones you just brought in and get them settled."

* * * * * * * * *

Gus Brannhard swore in every language he knew, which covered a great deal of territory. "We had him! We had that goddamned illegitimate son of a diseased Khooghra but good. How did he find out?"

Max Fane gritted his teeth in frustration. "He had an inside man. There's no other explanation. I'm having everybody, cop, civilian, lawyer, and even judge in the damned building questioned under veridication."

"Forget about the judges and shysters, Max. You'll never get them in the seat. The rest are fair game. Keep your questions limited to Laporte, though. We trample too many civil liberties and we'll be next on the hot seat." Gus shook his head. "Ben's gonna give birth to a damnthing when he hears about this."

"As long as we control the spaceport, Laporte is trapped on-planet," Coombes pointed out.

"Don't you believe it, Leslie. A little cosmetic surgery and we wouldn't know him from a bush goblin," Max said. "Remember that little conversation we had with Thaxter in the interrogation room two months ago?'

"Cosmetic surgery…" Coombes chewed on that for a moment. "How do we know this Ricardo La Rue isn't Raul Laporte with a facelift? Hell, he even has the same initials, more or less."

Max Fane shook his head. "It would take weeks for the surgical scars to heal, even with neo-dermaplas." Naturally a cop would be up on that sort of thing. "The face takes the longest to heal from cosmetic reconstruction. Laporte vanished today."

"What is to stop him from getting the surgery months ago and wearing a synth-mask until today?" Coombes looked around the room. "For that matter, he might be wearing one now waiting for those scars to heal."

Gus and Max silently considered that. "How would we prove it?" Max asked. "We can't just walk up and tweak his nose just to see if it falls off."

"DNA?" posited Gus.

Max shook his head. "Laporte's DNA was never on file. We never had enough on him to compel a sample. Believe me, I tried. There might be something on Terra, but it would take a year to get it. As it is, we had to stop taking samples at the spaceport. Without something to compare it to, it was just a waste of time."

"And a potential civil rights violation. It was a long shot, anyway. I mean, come on, he had surgery done months ago based on the possibility that two guys would show up to kidnap me?" Gus snorted and lit a cigar. "Not to mention putting up with the discomfort of a synthmask for several months. And why walk around with a synthmask now? It would be safer and easier to just go to ground until the scars healed, then step up and claim ownership of The Bitter End. No, we're barking up the wrong tree, there."

Coombes lit a cigarette. "Then where did this Ricardo La Rue come from?"

"Maybe came in with the last rush of immigrants," Gus said. "Maybe he was here all along but stayed off the radar. Who knows? We'll just have to keep an eye on him while we tear the planet apart looking for Laporte."

"First Thaxter, now Laporte," Max Fane growled. "This job is gonna be the death of me. I may yet have to tender my resignation."

"Don't start typing, yet, Marshal," Gus said. "There are still a lot of people to interview, and something may shake loose." Gus looked through the two-way mirror at Ricardo La Rue sitting in the interrogation room. "I'll get a court order for a medical exam on Mr. La Rue under the assumption that he is, in fact, Laporte. We'll look for signs of cosmetic surgery. I doubt we'll be able to get his DNA, but we don't have Raul's either, so it doesn't really matter. Still, I want to know where this guy came from."

Max drummed his fingers on the wall next to the glass. "DNA we can get. There's more than one way to get a sample."

XIII

"Have you thought about opening a satellite division on Beta Continent, Victor?" Jack asked. "This is where the action is, after all."

Through the viewscreen Victor Grego looked thoughtful. "Actually, that was part of my long-term plans back when the Company owned the planet outright. I scrapped it after the Pendarvis Decision and never got back to it."

"Well, hell, with that millennium-long lease you have, you pretty much own the planet, again." Jack took a drink of his tea, then set it down, wishing he could smoke his pipe. "Here's what I think: you want Gerd and Ruth back, they don't want to leave the Fuzzies. Fine. Just set up the Beta Division and let Gerd run it. Wait, what did you want him for, anyway?"

"It was a suggestion Juan Jimenez made. Gerd knows more about Fuzzies than any man on Zarathustra. Sorry, Jack, but he has training that you don't."

Jack shrugged. "You think I don't know that? I got old by recognizing my limitations. I'm a generalist, Gerd is a specialist. And if my ego needed boosting, I figure I'm still a better shot, pistol or rifle."

Grego smiled his toothy grin. He should have known Jack wouldn't be offended by a statement of fact. "Well, the future of Zarathustra is tied to the Fuzzies. I know it, you know it and Ben knows it. They won't be incompetent aborigines forever. Fuzzies learn fast; faster than any other species we've found to date. It won't be tomorrow or the day after, but the time is coming when we'll have to sign treaties with them. I want a man, and a woman, for that matter, whom I can trust to study the growth and changes in the Fuzzies. It has to be somebody not saddled with a lot of preconceptions. Juan thinks Gerd is that man. Ernst supports Ruth for the job. So, I want them both if I can get them. If I have to set up Beta Division to get them, it's a done deal. Now, how do we talk them into it?"

Jack laughed. "I think it's, how did Gus put it at my trial...oh, yes; it's all over except shooting the cripples."

* * * * * * * * *

Affanita sat on her cot and stared at the glowing stones in her hands. She had looked them over thoroughly, even under her portable microscope. They were sunstones, all right. So where did that Richard guy get them from, and why ask her to sell them? If they were fake, that she could understand. She would get arrested for fraud and Richard would find another sucker. But these were real, and he just gave them to her. No strings.

She was almost broke and the diggings had been poor. She had a fistful of sunstones and nobody to tell her what to do with them. Affanita poured the stones back into the leather pouch, strapped on her pistol belt and headed for the door. It was time to improve her fortunes.

Affanita left her apartment and waited at the taxi stand after pressing the call button. A few minutes later, a cab swooped down and opened the hatch.

"Where to, Bubbette?" the driver asked.

"Bub—, have we met before?"

"I dropped you off last night," the cabbie explained. "I left a note with dispatch to route me to any calls in this area. I had planned on checking in to see if you were all right. I didn't expect you to call for a cab, so you saved me a trip to your apartment."

"Wait, you dropped me off? How did you get into my apartment?"

"The landlord. We just set you on your bed and left. I just wanted to be sure you were okay. No funny business, I promise. The landlord seemed decent enough, but you can't judge a book by its cover, y'know."

This is one very solicitous cabbie, Affanita thought. "You always go to so much trouble for a fare?"

"Not always," the cabbie admitted. "But when a guy tips me a C-sol to get somebody home safe, I make good and damned sure they get home safe. Ah…well, I do tend to be extra careful with the ladies when they've had too much to drink. So, anyway, where to?"

Affanita considered what the cabbie said. Richard paid him a hundred sols to get her home and didn't try to take advantage of the situation? She wondered if she should feel a little insulted. Well, maybe he wasn't into older women. "To the nearest CZC gem buyer's outlet. Wait for me and there's another fifty-sol tip in it for you. Assuming my transaction goes smoothly."

The cab lurched into the air like it was shot from a cannon. Affanita swore in a very unlady-like fashion as she struggled into the safety harness, something she normally didn't bother with. *This is one motivated cabbie*, she thought. She said as much.

"Bubbette, for that kind of money I'd take you to Beta and back. The wife has been on my backside to take her out and coat the town crimson for the last three weeks. Maybe tonight we'll hit The Bitter End. She's always wanted to go there, but I heard it was too pricey."

"It is, but the food is excellent. Avoid the house brews, though. Try the Freyan ale. Hell, I might even see you there. I may feel like doing a little celebrating, myself."

Affanita patted the damnthing-hide purse she carried the sunstones in. Yes, some celebration would definitely be in order tonight.

* * * * * * * * *

Ricardo La Rue pressed the call button and a taxi floated down. Once inside, he extracted a silk handkerchief from inside his jacket and mopped his brow. The interview room had been ridiculously hot, he reflected.

"Where to, sir?" the cabbie asked.

"Take me to The Bitter End on the eastside of Junktown."

The cabbie rolled his eyes. "I'm familiar with it, sir," he said as he flipped on the meter. *Stupid tourists*, he thought.

La Rue nodded. Of course the driver knew where The Bitter End was located. Everybody knew that The Bitter End was the hottest lounge on Zarathustra. This was why he gave the directions. It made him seem new to the planet, and that fit in with his plans.

* * * * * * * * *

The forensic tech carefully swabbed the table as Marshal Fane watched. Once he was finished, a second tech went over the chair and surrounding carpet with a mini-vacuum designed to collect skin flakes and hair follicles. A third tech used a handheld device that scanned for prints. After a quick sweep, he checked the display and turned to the Marshal. He shrugged, "Nothing."

"I didn't think so, but it was worth a shot. You boys let me know if you find anything else. I want anything and everything we can get on this guy."

On his way out Max called maintenance and had the room temperature lowered back to its standard setting.

* * * * * * * * *

"I wish I could go, Morgan."

Jack took a pill and washed it down with the decaffeinated Darjeeling tea, grimacing at the aftertaste.

"Surely Akira has helped you catch up on enough of the paperwork to allow you a break…?"

Jack smiled at that. "Akira could run this place without me. Not only is the backlog cleaned out, she rearranged the files, updated the computer logs and adjusted the delivery schedules for food and supplies to be more efficient. That isn't the problem."

"No?"

"I can't go into space for at least two more weeks." Jack tapped his chest where the new lung was installed. "The docs say I'm still too sensitive to pressure changes. We don't want my new organs trying to make a break for it."

"*Schattakk*!" Morgan swore in Freyan. "My apologies. I neglected to consider your health. You appear to be so well recovered…."

"Relax. Personally, I think I'm good to go. Damned doctors are all overly cautious. It's my fault for staying alive for so long, I guess. Still, can't take any chances with that Blood Oath you swore." Jack made a note to pick up some decaffeinated Earl Grey in town. The Darjeeling decaf was not agreeing with him. "When are you going to tell me what this whole continent business is all about, anyway?"

"As soon as I get the governor to okay the sale. I have other promises to honor, too."

Jack decided not to push the issue. When Morgan could tell him, he would. "I need to stretch my legs a bit. Fancy a walk with your old man?"

"Certainly." Morgan put on his gun belt and hat while Jack just grabbed his headgear. Once they cleared the door, Morgan asked, "So what is this I hear about you and Betty Kanazawa? Should I plan for a new stepmother?"

"Gawd, don't start that!" Jack wondered how much Morgan had heard. Probably everything, he decided. "Betty is a sweet kid and I certainly don't object to having her around, but she's a third my age. If that."

"So?" Morgan explained that elder Freyan men often took much younger wives, especially if they lacked for any male heirs and sought to correct that. "Besides, I've certainly seen enough examples in the Federation to know that it is a common enough practice in Terran culture as well."

Jack snorted in derision. "Trophy wives. Most of those women are gold diggers looking for a payday. Or the husband decides he can afford to 'trade up' so he divorces the woman who stood by him when they had nothing and gets a young pretty one that likely has no brains or loyalty."

Morgan looked concerned. "Do you think Betty is like that? Somebody looking for a payday?"

"Oh, Nifflheim, no. She seems like a nice girl. Make that 'woman.' I just don't see why she would be interested in me. At least not for the long haul. She seems to be smart, certainly attractive, and she could land a good man her own age easily. Juan Jimenez would be a good catch for her, for example."

"Juan has a girlfriend. He just doesn't discuss his personal life at work."

"Now how did you find that out? Wait, don't tell me. It's none of my business."

The two men came upon Lolita sitting on the grass with a squad of young Fuzzies surrounding her. She waved at the two men, then resumed singing to the Fuzzy youths.

Great green gobs of greasy grimy goofer guts
Mutilated meeteek meat
Little dirty harpy feet

All wrapped up in all-purpose pluirrel pus
And me without a spoon.

The Fuzzies yeeked excitedly as one produced a straw. Morgan looked confused and Jack explained that it was an ancient folk song for children back on old Terra. Only the animals were changed to reflect the local zoology.

"I know what goofers and harpies are, but what are a meeteek and a pluirrel?"

Jack explained that a meeteek was a sort of feathered lizard found on Gamma Continent that was named by a surveyor's six year old son.

The pluirrel, another fine example of colonial taxonomy, was Zarathustra's equivalent to the platypus and roughly the size of a Terran Bonobo chimpanzee. Like its Terran equivalent, the pluirrel possessed a reptilian skeletal structure, or rather the Zarathustran equivalent of one, a furry hide and a bird-like beak. It also laid eggs, produced milk and carried its young in a pouch. Unlike the platypus, the pluirrel was arboreal, living in the trees of Epsilon Continent. It had a hairless prehensile tail, the beak was designed for tearing and shredding, and could glide from tree to tree in the same manner as the Terran flying squirrel. It was also a carnivorous omnivore and considered dangerous. Since it looked like a combination of multiple species with a giant squirrel as the base, the name 'pluirrel' was deemed to fit.

"I just love the zoology of this world," Morgan said. "We need to get a zoo set up near Mallorysport."

Jack nodded and the men continued walking.

"I could arrange for the meeting to take place here, or over in Mallorysport," Morgan suggested. "That way you could be in attendance with the rest."

"I don't know what you are doing, but it sounds big. Would you have to move a lot of equipment or personnel to make the meeting?"

Morgan thought about it, then nodded.

"Look," Jack said, "if it's that important, and it sounds like it is, then don't worry about me. Worry about the project or whatever it is you are pitching. Ben is the one you need to impress, not me."

Jack and Morgan came upon another group of Fuzzies who appeared to be fighting. Morgan stepped forward to break it up only to be restrained by Jack's arm blocking his progress. "It's not what it looks like."

The two men observed for a moment as two Fuzzies darted back and forth with their chopper-diggers swinging wildly. The blades clashed and the Fuzzies almost seemed to dance as they fought. After a minute a third Fuzzy blew a whistle and the combatants stepped away from each other.

A light went on in Morgan's head. "This is like a fencing class."

"Correct," nodded Jack. "One of Commodore Napier's men is an instructor in fencing and pugil stick and adapted the two disciplines into something usable for the Fuzzies."

Morgan took in the scene. The Fuzzies were using the metal chopper-diggers that Jack had designed when he first met Little Fuzzy. "Isn't it dangerous for them to battle like that?"

"Now don't you start!" Jack walked over and asked one of the Fuzzies for his weapon, then showed it to Morgan. "I had this duraplas strip put over the edge to keep the Fuzzies from doing serious harm to each other. I drew the line at padding the counterbalancing knob, though. A Fuzzy can take a helluva pounding for their size and shake it off. Coddling them will make them soft like those pencil pushers on Terra. I refuse to allow that to happen." Jack returned the weapon to the Fuzzy and ruffled his fur.

"Are all the Fuzzies getting this kind of training?"

Jack shrugged. "All who want it, which is most of them. Some prefer the newer weapons we Big Ones have given them: bow and arrow, rifle, crossbow. I am trying to encourage the chopper-digger training to keep them in touch with their roots. However, when you get an archer like Maid Marian who can put an arrow in the eye of a bird fifty feet over her head, well—what can you do?"

Morgan grunted in agreement. "Sure, dropping dinner from far away is better than chasing it first, then hacking away at it with a hand weapon. How were you able to get them interested in this fencing in the first place?"

"Oh, Fuzzies have always had a fencing style."

"Wait, they fight among themselves?" Morgan was surprised. Like many, he had assumed that the Zarathustran natives tended to get along better than the variety from Terra or Freya.

"Sure they do. It just doesn't go to the death, as a rule. They fight over things like 'who saw the berry bush first' and 'who is the best wise one' and occasionally come to blows over it. In the end, everybody either makes friends or the opposing sides split off and start their own tribes. It is a rare thing for a Fuzzy to fight to the death, and I have never seen it happen personally."

"That just shows how much smarter they are than us Big Ones, I guess." Morgan grew thoughtful.

"Oh, don't start agonizing over that duel, again," Jack chided. "Every culture has its rules of conduct, and they usually make sense within the cultural framework. You acted properly within the rules of Freyan society. I could have just refused the challenge, you know."

"And you would have suffered the repercussions of your own societal framework," Morgan countered. "Okay, I'll let it go. In a few weeks you'll be back to your old self and it will be like it never happened."

"Oh, no you don't," Jack said. "It happened, and for a good reason as far as you knew at the time. If getting shot is the price of learning I have a son, then I got off light. I missed all the things that made you the man you are today. There's nothing I can do about that, so I plan on sticking around long enough to spoil my grandchildren rotten…when you get around to making some for me."

Morgan felt like he was caught with his hand in the cookie jar, but kept his face neutral. "Oh, I'll get to that when the time is right and I meet the right woman…."

"You saying you haven't met her already? What about Akira? Please tell me she isn't just a fling!"

"Oh, you like her?"

"Don't play coy with me, boy. I've been around the block too many times on too many planets. I've seen how you two look at each other. Why haven't you traded bracelets, yet?"

Morgan suppressed a smile. "You don't want me to rush into anything, do you? Besides, Akira isn't Freyan; she would expect a ring."

A thought hit Jack. "Yes, a ring. Like the one I gave your mother. We traded bracelets, too. I still have mine in the safe back at the cabin."

Morgan decided it was time to change the topic of conversation. "Since you can't make the meeting personally, maybe I could set up a video feed from the yacht to the cabin."

Jack caught what Morgan was doing and decided to let it slide. "No need. You might do better without daddy looking over your shoulder. Besides, since I don't know what you are up to, there is always the possibility that I won't approve. Better I stay out of it and let Ben make the decision without my two centi-sols worth. Now, let's get back to the office so you can spend some time with your girl before you take off again."

XIV

Murdock raged like a damnthing while Dane sat back in his office chair and waited him out. The thug didn't like what Lundgren had just told him and had no difficulty in expressing his displeasure. Richard Lundgren sat quietly in a chair next to the desk, following Dane's example, and waited for the storm to pass.

"Why the Nifflheim did ya give over five hundred thousand sols worth of *real* stones ta a bunch of prospectors?" Murdock finished.

Actually, he had demanded that same thing several times in his oration, but didn't allow anybody to get in a word edgewise to explain. Now that he had wound down, mostly to catch his breath, Dane was able to cut in. "Credibility," Dane said.

"What?" Murdock stared at Dane, then selected a chair and plopped down into it. "Whaddya mean by that?"

Dane let out a breath before continuing. "We need to establish our credibility with the sunstone miners before we pull anything cute. The prospectors in turn also need to be credible to the Company gem buyers. Slipping in the ersatz gems too soon is dangerous, both to our plans and us personally. Prospectors have been known to exact their own brand of justice when cheated or played for saps. We also still need to get an idea of the *faux* sunstones shelf-life. Having a few gems go dud in the middle of a transaction wrecks the whole scam."

"But ya just had nerd boy there give away a fortune in real stones!" Murdock yelled, pointing his large hairy finger at Lundgren.

Dane found himself getting annoyed with Murdock's short-sightedness. He thought for a moment, then came up with a way to explain things. "Think of this as a counterfeiting ring, only instead of sols we are using sunstones. Tell me, have you ever worked a counterfeit scam?"

Murdock shook his head. "Naw. Knew some guys that did. They ended up doin' time."

Dane smiled. Murdock had just underlined the point he was going to make. "Ah, good. How were they caught?"

Murdock's face went blank as he thought for a moment. "They got too greedy too quick. An' were sloppy with the distribution of the bogus bucks. They mixed in too much of the phonies with the real stuff at one time."

"And there it is," Dane said with a smile. "Right now we have an easy fifty million sols worth of real sunstones, and maybe a third that in the potential counterfeits for the moment. We can get duds by the ton once we decide we can use them. That's not counting the revenues we are currently bringing in from the late Mr. Bowlby's estate or our other quasi-legal activities. We have money to burn, Mr. Murdock."

"Then why mess with fakes at all? I like money as much as the next guy, but why risk getting caught with the bogus rocks for such a small return? An' how does giving away the real stones do us any good?"

Dane shook his head. Seventeen million sols a small return? And that was just the tip of the iceberg. "The real sunstones that Lundgren passed around will eventually be sold to the CZC, the largest gem buyer on the planet. Oh, a few will go to the new independents that have popped up since the Company lost its charter, but they won't be able to handle anything like the bulk we just put on the street. That means the CZC will be the only game in town for buying any serious quantities of gems. With me so far?"

Murdock nodded.

"Good. Now, the CZC gem buyers are not stupid. Victor Grego does not typically employ stupid people. They will wonder where all these new stones are coming from, and they will look very closely at their potential purchases. While Dr. Quigley has assured me that the fakes are completely indistinguishable from the real gems, we have to be damned sure that the CZC doesn't have some clever devices we never heard of that could prove our own bright scientist wrong. That means we have to make them blasé about large amounts of stones coming in. So, we flood the streets with real stones, then after a while, we slip in a few ersatz gems with each load. We pay the prospectors a percentage, of say five to ten percent to act as front men, and the counterfeit stones find their way into the CZC stock."

"It still sounds like we lose money, ta me," Murdock growled.

"This isn't about making money," Dane said with a smile. "It is about bringing down the CZC, and with it the colonial government."

That caught Murdock's attention but good. "What? How do a few fake gems do that?"

Lundgren spoke up as Dane rolled his eyes. "When the fakes start fizzing out, hopefully in some rich dowager's jewelry box, there will be a lot of accusations of fraud directed at the CZC. The Federation will start an investigation and all of their holdings will be frozen or seized. At the minimum their stock will fall faster than a hammer on Magni. Any or all of those are good. No more sunstones coming out of Yellowsand. No more money for the colonial government. No money for planetary services or government employees. People will be out to lynch Grego and Rainsford. At the very least there will be a recall vote. That's when we set up our own candidate for colonial governor."

Murdock looked impressed. There was no bigger racket than politics, except, maybe, religion. "Who we gonna get to run?"

"That would be me," Dane said with a wide smile.

The light went on in Murdock's head. "'Kay, I got it. We take over the government and the planet. But this's still a Class IV planet with a million rules and regs that can't be ignored."

"Ah! That is where divine providence came in," Dane said. "That rocket ship we found on Beta was a godsend. With it we can argue that Fuzzies are aliens to this world and not subject to Class IV protected status. They'll still need some protection, of course, but they lose the reservation and the sunstone prospecting sites it contains."

Murdock nodded, then a thought hit him. "What about the Native Affairs Bureau? That, watzizname, the guy in that duel a few months back..."

"Holloway," Lundgren supplied.

"Yeah, him, the Native Affairs Commissioner. He won't just let us stroll over to Beta and take over."

Dane shook his head and sighed. "If the Fuzzies are not native to this world, then there will be no bureau or commissioner. Holloway can bark at the moons for all he'll be able to do. Frankly, I would like to see him, Rainsford, Grego, and especially Brannhard and Mallin all dead, but murder is a messy business and can easily come back to bite one in the ass. I prefer my ass unbitten, thank you very much."

Murdock took it all in, then said, "Well, accidents happen, ya know."

Dane slammed a fist down onto his desktop rattling his coffee cup. "Don't get cute, Murdock. Accident or not, anybody important on this planet dies, there will be a major investigation that could lead back to us. We can't afford that kind of attention. So far we've been lucky, but by now the cops know that there was an illegal prospecting ring on the reservation. That's why we have to use a string of cutouts, and established prospectors raise the fewest flags. I also saw Clancy Slade walking around as a free man, so the Thaxter switch has also been discovered. Important people dropping dead or disappearing is a risk we can't afford."

Murdock glared at Dane for a moment, then threw up his hands in a dramatic gesture that seemed out of place on the man. "Fine. Just try not to bankrupt us while ya take over the planet." Murdock turned and stormed out of the office.

Lundgren waited for Murdock to get out of earshot before he asked Dane who Mallin was. Dane simply grimaced and turned on the news.

* * * * * * * * *

Piet Dumont had been the police chief of Mallorysport until he was demoted for his part in the Lolita Lurkin Fuzzy attack fiasco. While he hadn't taken an active role in framing the Fuzzies, he had failed to stop what he knew was a setup by one of his own men, Detective Lieutenant Luther Woller. Woller was now serving time in Prison House for evidence tampering as well as other infractions and was due for release in two weeks, at which time he would be issued an off-world ticket and a metaphoric boot to the backside to use it. Colonial Marshal Max Fane had read Piet the riot act, then demoted him down to patrol officer.

Piet could have fought the demotion. Even on a backwater world like Zarathustra the Police Union was a force to be reckoned with. Piet considered it as he looked at himself in the mirror when he got home. That was when he saw what he had become; a sagging flabby useless excuse for a human being. He remembered a time when he had been a good, no, great cop. He had a stack of citations and a drawer full of awards and decorations from when he had been a patrol cop. A brave cop. A good cop. And he could be again. It was his moment of clarity.

The next day, Piet signed up with a gym, went on a diet and made an appointment with the police counselor. In the next several months he trimmed down his waistline, improved his muscle tone and signed up for psych services where he worked through issues he didn't even realize he had. He recognized the fact that his awards and citations stopped shortly after his last promotion. Riding a desk clearly didn't agree with him and he was glad to be rid of it. Piet was determined to work his way back up to something other than a chair-bound Police Chief, and without calling in any favors.

Piet knew it would be a long road and accepted that. He congratulated younger offers who were promoted over him, and gave them advice on how to avoid his mistakes. The new and improved Piet Dumont did not escape the notice of the new Police Chief, Frank Carr. Carr had been hesitant to promote Piet given his recent background, but he also remembered when he had been a young cop out to serve the people. After Piet had been instrumental in breaking up a chuckleweed distribution ring, Carr had to admit that the old Piet was back.

"Are you bucking to get your old office back, Piet?" Carr asked during a peer review.

"Hell, no," Piet replied. "Look what it did to me and what it's doing to you. You've put on, what, twenty pounds since you were promoted? Don't make my mistake, Frank. Get out and do something, anything, just don't get too comfortable with that seat and go to seed like I almost did."

Chief Carr joined the gym and Piet made corporal a week later.

People started to take notice of the new Piet Dumont. Over the next several months he gained a reputation as a man who could be counted on. As far as Piet was concerned, he no longer cared if he ever made chief again. He was happy to be a good cop and for people to know it. As such, when he invited the Colonial Marshal, Chief Colonial Prosecutor and the Temporary Acting Prosecutor to see something in the computer room, they took him seriously and accepted the invitation.

Piet backed up the video feed at high speed, then inched it forward slowly until he got it just right. Gus Brannhard, Max Fane and Leslie Coombes stood behind his seat and waited while Piet explained.

"When the Marshal here told me about Thaxter's escape, everybody assumed that he had left planet for Gimli. Well, I remembered that his sister and brother-in-law were still locked up and asked myself if I could just skip planet and leave them there if I was Thaxter. At first I thought, hell yes! Then I remembered that he had made a deal with the Acting Chief Colonial Prosecutor," Piet nodded at Leslie Coombes, "to get Rose Evins off the hot seat when her twenty years were up. That made me think even Thaxter had a heart somewhere in that chest of his since he didn't try to cadge the same deal for himself. So I downloaded and reviewed the spaceport security footage on my personal computer over and over trying to see if I could find something wrong with it, like, maybe that wasn't Thaxter on the feed. At one point I'll admit I got sleepy and went for a coffee, forgetting to pause the feed. When I got back I spotted this...."

Piet hit the play button on the computer console. There was the usual back and forth of people; some arriving on-planet, some preparing to leave and a few refugees from Junktown trying to panhandle some spare change. Max was getting impatient and was about to say something when Piet jabbed a finger at the screen. "There! Watch this guy with the hat and dark glasses."

The four men watched intently as the figure on the screen opened a locker and placed his duffle bag into it. He closed the door, then turned to go just as another man, a panhandler, slammed into him, knocking his hat off. Piet froze the image and scanned in for a close-up.

"Well?"

Max, Gus and Coombes looked closely at the image on the screen.

Gus was first to speak up. "Yeah, that looks like the son of a Khooghra, but it's hard to be sure with that beard and those cheaters on. Hey, the other guy is picking his pocket. See that, there?"

"Yeah, and so did Thaxter, or whomever that might be. In a few frames you'll see him punch the other guy and take his wallet back." Piet advanced the feed thirty seconds and they watched the figure drop the pickpocket with one punch. Piet froze the feed after the man stood back up with his wallet in hand. "Say what you will about the man, he throws a mean punch."

"Did you run facial recognition?" Max asked. He peered at the screen trying to tell if it was their man, but the angle made it difficult.

"Only a forty percent match, Marshal," Piet said. "The angle, beard and shades obscure too much for a positive match. There are about 213 people who fall into that range, after I removed the ones with the wrong height and hair color. If not for the shades, we could have nailed him on the retina scan."

"Which is, no doubt, why he wears them. He also changed his clothes," Coombes noted. "It'll be hard to prove that it really is him, especially since he was seen boarding the shuttle earlier in the tape."

"Did you get the name of the renter for that locker?" asked Gus. "It might tell us what name he is using for an alias."

"First thing I did, sir." Piet tapped a few more keys and the locker registration form replaced the video feed on the screen. "It's made out to a Clancy Slade. I looked up Mr. Slade and found that he arrived on-planet about ten months ago from Gimli with a wife, Marie and daughter, Annabelle." More keyboard tapping and Slade's immigration form appeared on the screen. "I couldn't help noticing that there was an incredibly strong resemblance between this Clancy Slade guy and Leo Thaxter. It occurred to me that this Slade might be a ringer brought in by Thaxter's cronies, but I couldn't come up with a reason for it. Still, this seemed like something I should show you."

Gus, Max and Coombes looked at each other uncomfortably for a moment before Max explained how Clancy had been forced to take Thaxter's place in prison. "He has no known ties to any criminal organization that we could find and we verified it under veridication. He was just unfortunate enough to have that particular face." Max went on to explain that the governor wanted Thaxter's escape kept quiet, and only a few select officers knew the full details of that escape. Also, at the time of the shuttle departure, Clancy was cooling his heels in Prison House under Thaxter's name.

Piet accepted the explanation gracefully. That he had not been included in the full story at the beginning didn't bother him. He understood the value of keeping a secret and his past left something to be desired. "In that case, I don't know if this is of any value, but I ran a check on Mr. Slade and found that he rents an apartment in Mallorysport on the bare edge of Junktown—"

"All he could afford," Max said, "from what I learned in interrogation."

"Really?" Piet looked puzzled. "Then how does he manage to pay for a cabin on the outskirts of Mallorysport, as well?"

"He what?" Max looked intently at the screen as Piet opened the file showing the title of ownership for the cabin. According to the title there was no mortgage or lien on the property.

"Clancy said the people who kidnapped his daughter were going to pay him off if he didn't blow the whistle right away," Gus observed. The Chief Colonial Prosecutor hadn't been in the room during interrogation, though he had watched through the two-way mirror.

"Yes," Coombes nodded. "Classic 'carrot and stick' tactic. Threaten his family and bribe him at the same time. Twenty-five thousand sols, wasn't it?"

"Yeah," Gus confirmed. "They must have made good on their deal even though the switch was discovered early."

Piet shook his head. "Uh-uh. Twenty-five thousand sols wouldn't begin to cover it. This cabin's sale price was sixty-five thousand sols, and according to the title, it's paid for, free and clear. If he is living on the edge of Junktown, then I can't believe he was sitting on the other forty thousand or more."

Max thought about it for a moment. Piet was making a lot of sense. Still…. "Maybe Clancy hedged his bets so that we wouldn't take all the money if we found out about it?"

Gus snorted. "I very much doubt that. Clancy was far too happy to be out of prison and back with his family. And we have his story under veridication. Besides, Harry Steefer hired him onto the CZC company police on Leslie's recommendation, right?"

Coombes nodded.

"And he was thrilled as all Nifflheim to get that job. If he did get that twenty-five thousand sols, he had to have gotten it after getting the security job. I'll bet he's keeping it under the mattress for a while, too, in case his new position doesn't work out.

"He's welcome to the money as far as I'm concerned, though I would like to know how the funds were transferred to him. No. I think Officer Piet here found Thaxter's little hidey-hole. Think about it: Clancy is now known to look like Thaxter, so Thaxter grows a beard like Clancy's and gets a place out of the city. If anybody comes poking around, he just introduces himself as Clancy Slade. I'll bet he uses cash for all of his purchases to stay off the grid. Unless he and Clancy bump into each other, who's going to notice?"

"Son-of-a-bitch," Max swore and nodded his head. "Good. We'll just get a couple of warrants and take a look at that cabin and spaceport locker…"

"On what grounds," Coombes asked. "All we have is a forty percent match on his face and a lot of speculation. Even Judge Wilcox won't sign off with that. And Wilcox will sign off on almost anything."

"Don't I know it!" Gus agreed.

"Ah," Piet looked sheepish and said, "And my little search of some of those documents I showed you are the subject of…less than proper procedure. I knew I couldn't get a warrant to just poke though those records willy-nilly, so I…."

"What records?" Max asked. "I don't recall seeing any records and neither do you. Understood?"

Piet nodded. Playing fast and loose with the rules was a chance he was prepared to take, but he wasn't about to drag the Marshal or the shysters into it.

The room fell silent until Piet spoke up again. "This Clancy Slade, is he a stand-up guy?" Everybody agreed that he seemed to be. "Well, legally, that cabin and the contents of that locker are his, then, right?" Again, everybody agreed. "Then why don't we just go and ask him pretty please if we can take a look at his cabin? We won't need a warrant if he gives his consent. And titles and deeds are a matter of public record, so our knowing about it won't be a problem. I don't know about the locker, though. Still, why not make this identity theft work for us?"

The three men stared at Piet, then Coombes smiled and Gus roared in laughter.

Max thought to himself that Piet Dumont had come a long way from the flabby waste of space he was two years ago and made a decision.

"Inspector Dumont is right," Max said. "Let's go ask Mr. Clancy for the five centi-sol tour."

Piet looked surprised. "Inspector?"

"I'll clear it with Frank Carr, and if he don't like it, tough. But I suspect he won't object. It's good to have the old Piet Dumont back."

"Damn straight," Gus said. "Your talents are wasted as a street cop. Come on, we ain't doing this without you."

"You bet! Hey, let me grab something first." Piet reached under the desk and pulled out a battered old briefcase. He patted it on the side and said, "Just in case."

As Gus, Coombes and Max filed out, Piet let out a long groan.

Gus turned and asked, "What's wrong?"

"Cop tradition," Piet said as he hustled out the door. "Promoted guy buys the first three rounds for his squad. I'm on the hook for one helluva bar tab next time I hit the Two Moons Tavern."

XV

Clancy Slade had pulled a double shift in order to get the next night off so he could spend some time with his family. Annabelle, his daughter, had been badly shaken by her time as a hostage and his wife, Marie, had been on pins and needles ever since. In fact, she had been pushing for them to leave the planet. Clancy's position was that they were safe enough and he had too good of a job to just walk away from.

In the interest of keeping the family peace, Clancy decided to take the family into Mallorysport to see the sights, have a fancy dinner and maybe do a little shopping. Annabelle in particular wanted to see some Fuzzies.

Clancy had intended to sleep in for one more hour before taking the family out on the town when something prodded his foot. Clancy instantly awoke and threw a punch into the air. It was a reflex he developed while in Prison House and he hadn't been able to shake it. At the foot of the bed stood Marie, looking worried.

Blearily, he asked, "'Sa-matta, babe?"

Marie dithered for a second, then said, "There are some men here who say they need to talk to you."

All trace of fatigue was replaced with fear. Clancy quickly got up, dressed and looked around for something to use as a weapon. Marie didn't like guns in the house with Annabelle around, so he had left his Company issued sidearm in his locker at work. Instead, he picked up his truncheon and tucked it into the back of his trousers where he could easily get at it if he needed to. He had no intention of getting dragged into another criminal conspiracy, not if he could avoid it.

Cautioning his wife to stay in the bedroom with Annabelle, Clancy stomped out to confront his guests. He almost fainted from relief when he saw that it was Colonial Marshal Max Fane and Acting Prosecutor Leslie Coombes with two other men he didn't immediately recognize.

"Jeezus H. friggin' Christ, guys! You nearly gave me a heart attack. Marie and Annie are hiding in the bedroom thinking you're with those guys that kidnapped Annie."

Max stepped forward and offered his hand, which Clancy shook firmly. "Sorry about the scare, Mr. Slade."

Clancy waved it off. "Hey, you guys are welcome any time. And Mr. Slade was my old man. Call me Clancy, please."

Clancy removed the truncheon from the back of his trousers and set it on an end table. Max, Coombes, Gus and Piet shared an understanding look between them.

"Glad to, Clancy. This is Gus Brannhard and Inspector Piet Dumont."

Clancy shook both men's hands. "Hey, wait! You're the guy who got grabbed up a few months back. I read about it in the news feed. Sorry, Mr. Brannhard, I really don't know anything about that...."

"That's not why we're here, Clancy." Gus leaned forward conspiratorially and said, "We need your help."

"My help? Well, sure. Anything I can do. You name it." Clancy waved a sweeping hand. "Here, everybody have a seat. Anybody want a beer, or a cuppa joe?"

Max took the end of the couch and Piet took the other end while Coombes parked in the center. Gus took the settee and Clancy flopped into his easy chair. Max noticed that the furniture all looked new, including the viewscreen console, which was currently tuned in to a

B.I.N. news program showing pictures of some alien-looking skeletons. The room was tastefully appointed while not overly lavish. Clancy's wife had been doing some shopping, Max guessed, either with Clancy's first paycheck or, more likely, the hush money from the kidnappers.

"We're on duty, but I never say no to coffee," Max said.

Clancy called his wife out of the bedroom, introduced everybody, and then asked her to make some coffee. Marie hurried back to the kitchen while Annabelle peeked around the corner. "We picked up this brand from Gimli that beats anything I ever had from Terra. It's hard-vacuum sealed so it's all still fresh."

"Sounds good," Gus said. While they waited Gus explained about the cabin and locker. "It's all in your name, so by any legal definition you are the owner. To be on the safe side, we double checked to see if there was another Clancy Slade on Zarathustra. There is not. You are currently the only one. So, we would like for you to give us permission to enter and search the cabin, and inspect the contents of the locker at the spaceport."

"I can do that? Even though these things ain't really mine?" Clancy thought it over. If everything was in his name, did he really own it? And was he on the hook if there was anything illegal in the cabin or locker?

"Legally, they are," Coombes repeated. Guessing at the thoughts going through Clancy's mind, he added, "And let me assure you that you will not be held accountable for any contraband we may find."

Marie served the coffee with a new set of cups and placed them on coasters on the new hardwood coffee table while Clancy digested the situation. Annabelle, possibly attracted to Gus's thick beard which was much like Clancy's, walked in and climbed up on his lap. She was running her fingers through the prosecutor's facial hair while Clancy reached a decision. "Marie, I'm gonna go with these guys for a couple of hours. We'll hit the town when I get back, okay?"

Marie was so relieved that their guests weren't hired killers she agreed without argument. "I'll lay out your good suit while you're gone. Don't be late or I'll trade you in for a Fuzzy."

Gus set Annabelle on the settee as he stood up with the other men. The girl reminded him a bit of the daughter he lost on Terra so long ago.

Clancy gave his wife a "Yes, Ma'am" and a kiss on the cheek and was out the door before she could change her mind. "Okay, let's go take a look at *my* cabin."

Gus grumbled to himself that the coffee really was good and he hated to leave it unfinished. He waved bye-bye to the little girl on the way out. He considered making a joke about how he might want to snatch her up himself, then realized that it would be in extremely poor taste under the circumstances and stayed silent.

"Oh, wait," exclaimed Clancy. "Spaceport locker. That explains the receipts." Clancy spun around and rushed back into the apartment, startling Marie, and then returned with some papers in his meaty fists. "I've gotten three of these in the last few months. I was gonna go down there tomorrow and straighten it out." He handed the papers over to Max.

The Marshal examined the papers. Receipts for payment on a locker rental at the spaceport. "Hey, look Piet. Clancy has a locker in Mallorysport. You must have missed that while you were looking around on the Net."

Piet smiled. "Yes, sir. Guess that one got by me. I'll be more careful in the future, Marshal."

Clancy was confused for a moment. Didn't Max just tell him about the spaceport locker? He shrugged and decided it was some sort of cop in-joke.

Five minutes later the first unmarked aircar was settling down behind a grove of featherleaf trees. A second unmarked aircar set down next to it. Everybody except Max Fane was in civilian clothes, so he had to wait in the car so as not to give anything away. He used that time to monitor the police band and watch for incoming traffic on the skycam. Gus, Clancy and Coombes intended to wait with him by the aircars until the cops in mufti gave the all clear.

Piet, in charge of the squad, elected to try the subtle approach. Grabbing a clipboard and his briefcase, he and Corporal Winslow, both in civilian suits, walked up to the door and knocked. After a polite half a minute, Piet knocked again. No response.

"So much for playing a census taker. Now we do this the hard way," Piet said. The newly christened inspector pulled a device from his briefcase called a 'skeletron key' by the cops. It was an all-purpose electronic lock-override that was illegal for anyone other than police and emergency service personnel to use. Naturally, some had found their way onto the black market, into the hands of private investigators and, of course, locksmiths.

Home burglary was a rare crime on worlds where personal surveillance equipment was widely available, especially since the advent of models that could capture the heat signature, pulse and respiratory rates of the intruders. A ski-mask was worthless to the modern criminal. While there were devices that would defeat most surveillance equipment, they were obscenely expensive and beyond the reach of simple burglars. Companies that produced the electronic locks ignored the facts of home security cameras and claimed that their locks defeated the criminals. Piet knew better.

Piet fiddled with the device until he heard the tell-tale click of the door's locking mechanism disengaging. Smiling, the inspector entered the cabin. Once inside, he and Corporal Winslow drew their side arms from shoulder holsters and went through each room systematically. Once satisfied that the cabin was empty, they signaled for the rest to come in. Clancy, as the owner of record, accompanied by several officers, went in while Gus and Coombes remained outside.

"Mr. Slade, please wait by the door and don't touch anything," instructed Piet. Then, as an afterthought, he asked permission to inspect the cabin. "Purely as a formality, sir."

"Hell, rip it apart if you gotta," said Clancy. "I want to see that bastard back in prison as much as you do."

Piet nodded and went to work.

* * * * * * * * *

Prof. Darloss took one last look in the mirror and nodded at the young woman behind him. She had done an excellent job on his hair and make-up. He stood up and walked purposefully out of the dressing room and headed for the television studio. Spin Wheeler was going to interview him on *Spinning Wheels*, giving him a chance to support his previous interview on *Tuning In With Tuning*. Even Hoenveld wouldn't be able to counter his conclusions this time.

Hoenveld, humph.

He wasn't even an anthropologist. It couldn't be denied that the man was brilliant, especially in the fields of biology, biochemistry, chemistry and a plethora of other scientific disciplines, but he was no anthropologist, physical or cultural.

Darloss fumed as he recalled how Hoenveld's counterargument in that interview with Tuning ripped him to shreds. Not this time. Darloss had access to data even Hoenveld didn't have and he was going to use it to destroy the Charterless Zarathustra Company's lead scientist.

As was the case with *Tuning In With Tuning*, *Spinning Wheels* was a live broadcast. The show would follow the evening news which, by no coincidence, was showing photographic images of the giant Fuzzy fossils currently being studied at the CZC's Science Division. The viewing audience would be primed for more information and scientific conjecture about the so-called Fuzzy Bones.

After *Spinning Wheels* would come an editorial by Ivan Dane blasting the Company and the colonial government for not making the fossils available for scrutiny by non-Company scientists. Next, there would be oblique suggestions that the two were in collusion and the intimation that they were trying to maintain the status quo at the people's expense; if the CZC and the colonial government were brought down there would be free land for all.

Darloss didn't care, really, who ran the planet. He just wanted his fifteen minutes of fame and to make Hoenveld look like an idiot. As an academician he had no interest in land or politics. Darloss was interested only in being recognized in his field, making lots of money, and occasionally dallying with a young co-ed. Just the basics.

Darloss was escorted to the edge of the studio where he could see Spin Wheeler giving his monologue to his audience. He told a few jokes about Governor Rainsfield; something to the effect that the Fuzzies were really running things. He followed up with another joke about Victor Grego being in bed with the Governor making sense since it seemed to be the only company he ever got there.

The audience members laughed, cheered and applauded. They should have; they were paid enough. Unlike the audience of the CZCN talk show, *Tuning In With Tuning*, where the audience members consisted of tourists and people taking time from their busy schedules, B.I.N. hired people in from Junktown to fill seats and look like they were having a good time while Wheeler trashed the government and the CZC on his show. Initially, the studio simply offered free admission to anyone who was interested in participating. Unfortunately, the subject matter didn't sit well with the more affluent or educated public resulting in a rapidly dwindling body count. Paying the out-of-work denizens of

Junktown to fill seats created the illusion of support for the show and the politics it promoted.

Wheeler wrapped up his monologue and announced his first guest of the evening: "With us tonight is the noted anthropologist and xenobiologist Professor Thomas Darloss." Wheeler paused while the audience applauded. Some of the applause came from a recording to make the audience sound much larger. "Professor Darloss, everybody!"

Darloss came in from the side, where he had been suffering through the monologue, waving at the audience and the cameras. The two men took their seats: Wheeler on the right, Darloss on the left.

"Professor Darloss," Wheeler said in his interview voice, "I understand you took the opportunity to examine the photographs of the Fuzzy bones shown on the B.I.N. news. What did you think?"

"Well, I did more than just look at the photographs, Mr. Wheeler."

"Please, call me Spin."

"Ah, sure. As I was saying, I did more than simply look at the photos," Darloss said. "I compared them to a full body X-ray of a Fuzzy at its current state of development." A picture of a Fuzzy X-ray went up on a screen off the studio stage. On televisions across the planet the pictures briefly replaced the image of Wheeler and Darloss. A moment later it was shown side-by-side with the fossil image of one of the skeletons at the CZC. "Notice the overall shape and structure of the two skeletons. Aside from the additional thickness of the bones associated with supporting greater mass, they are almost identical."

Wheeler made a show of looking at the screen and nodding thoughtfully. "Except for the skulls they are almost exactly alike."

"Ah, most people are fixated on the skulls, operating on the assumption that the brainpan explains all. It does not." Darloss explained about brain size and shape as demonstrated by the Yggdrasil Khooghra, Neanderthal Man and even trotted out the Einstein example.

"No, the thing to watch for is the development of the hands and feet. Notice that the lower limbs are designed purely for locomotion and the upper limbs for manipulation. It takes intelligence to manipulate one's environment."

"Interesting, Prof," Wheeler said, not sounding very interested. "I have to admit I wasn't much of a student back at university, but I seem to recall a rule about advancing sapient species that said they tended to grow larger, not shrink, as they developed. Current representatives of *fuzzy sapiens zarathustra* are roughly half the size of their ancient equivalents. What would cause them to shrink like that?"

"Many things, Spin. Primarily, nutrition. Insufficient food sources would limit the growth of the Fuzzies. The larger ones would die of starvation, likely before reaching reproductive maturity, while the smaller Fuzzies could thrive on the limited food supplies. It could also be environmental. There is an island off the coast of Beta where indigenous animals are about one-fourth the size of their continental cousins. This adaptation has also occurred in Terra's primordial past.

"The animals require a certain population density to survive as a species but are limited in space, so they simply adapted by becoming smaller over generations. Then, of course, there is the NFMp hormone that severely limits their viable reproduction unless neutralized. It could have a secondary effect of stunting physical development in the offspring when removed from their native habitat."

"Native habitat." Wheeler seized on the phrase. "Isn't Northern Beta their native habitat."

Darloss had a sly look on his face. "I wouldn't be at all sure about that. Setting aside the discovery of the rocket ship, consider the culture of the Fuzzies. Firstly, they have no religion, or even legends or folk tales. Everything is either new or on an 'everybody knows thing' basis." Darloss made air quotes with his forefingers to accent the point.

"Primitive people create myths to explain the world around them. Thor, Shesha, Gimli, Uller, Yggdrasil, and even the Freyan natives possess numerous religions, myths and legends. The more primitive the society the less sophisticated the religions, but they do exist. On Terra, home of the most advanced species in the known universe, the inhabitants have had thousands of religions and myths.

"Yet the Fuzzies have none. They are logical and analytical in the extreme…"

* * * * * * * * *

Victor Grego watched the broadcast and grew angrier with each minute. Ordinarily, nothing could have forced him to watch a B.I.N. program, let alone *Spinning Wheels*. However, he'd heard that Professor Darloss would be appearing on the show, which had prompted him to watch, just to see what idiotic and dangerous nonsense the professor would be spouting.

Grego rushed over to his viewscreen and punched out Miguel Kourland's code. After getting past a secretary, Kourland's face appeared on the screen.

"Miguel, I want you to set up another interview with Hoenveld on Tuning's show."

"Already in the works, Victor." Kourland routinely looked in on rival networks' programming and had caught the interview. Anticipating Grego's reaction, he called Tuning and told him to be ready to bring Hoenveld back on the show. "If you can talk to Juan and have him arrange things with—"

"One second, Miguel. I have another call." Grego placed Kourland on hold and his image shrank to the upper left of the screen. Juan Jimenez appeared in the main screen. "Juan! Speak of the devil."

"Victor, Hoenveld is going nuts over that Darloss interview on

B.I.N. and is demanding air time…."

Sometimes the universe works in mysterious ways, Grego thought.

"He's got it. Let me switch to conference mode." Grego tapped a few buttons, allowing Kourland and Jimenez to appear side-by-side on the viewscreen. "Okay, we all want the same thing. Juan, tell Chris to show up at the studio…"

"Tomorrow at 1900," Kourland said.

"Good," Jimenez said. "He'll be there."

"Great. Put him in a new suit and let him wear his lab coat over it if he wants, just make sure it's clean."

The three men discussed the details for a couple of minutes, then screened-off. Diamond, who had been watching the interview and Grego's reaction, spoke up.

"Funny man talked about Fuzzies?"

"Yes, Diamond. He says you all came from space."

Diamond understood space in the way most human children did and laughed. Big Ones had such strange ideas, sometimes.

That gave Grego an idea. He quickly called Kourland and Jimenez back.

XVI

"Why did Piet go in with just one man and Clancy?" Coombes asked.

Gus reminded himself that Coombes was a corporate attorney, though he had the chops for a criminal prosecutor. "Same reason the cops are in mufti. We're trying to keep this all hush-hush. Granted, the nearest neighbor is about a mile away, but you never know who might stroll by or fly over. Besides, Piet and Winslow can call for help if they need it."

"Clancy could invite us in, you know," Coombes said as he stood with Gus near the aircars. He knew better but wanted to see what Gus would say about it.

Gus shook his head. "We're on pretty thin ice as it is, Leslie. If we catch Thaxter and haul his ass back into court, I don't want to give whatever shyster he digs up any more ammunition than necessary."

This time it was Coombes who shook his head. "I really don't see what difference it makes. In eighteen years he will be duly executed by the State for crimes he has practically been convicted for already. And get to sit in prison while he waits for that sentence to be carried out, assuming he gets caught and not killed in the process. Prison. Death. That's all Thaxter has to look forward to."

"You've been working the corporate system for too long, Leslie. I can't think of a precedent at the moment, but I'll bet there's one for getting an escaped convict's conviction overturned. Mental anguish, maybe. You can find a precedent for almost anything in colonial law. So we wait out here while Piet does his job without any interference or advice,"—Gus put two fingers in the air and made quotations around "advice,"—"from us. More cases have been tossed due to prosecutorial misconduct and evidence tampering than actual innocence."

Coombes nodded. He was more than lawyer enough to understand that. In fact, he even got a client or two off on that basis in his early days as a defense attorney. "I'll have to admit that I hadn't been in an actual courtroom for about fifteen years before *The Friends of Little Fuzzy vs. the Chartered Zarathustra Company.*"

Gus stifled a chuckle. "So you're calling it that now, too?"

Coombes shrugged. "It's less of a mouthful than *the People of the Colony of Zarathustra versus Holloway and Kellogg.* Sort of. Even Victor calls it that, now."

"Speaking of the great Victor Grego, how did you two meet?" Gus asked.

Coombes considered the question before answering, then shrugged. "I was working for Page-Nicholson-Hautmann and Lee at the time. I was one of a team of lawyers trying to block a Terra-Baldur-Marduk Spacelines takeover of Preston-Lane, Inc. Well, the lead attorney came down with the flu and I got handed the job of presenting our case to the judges. I tossed out the argument my boss had written and winged it."

Gus grimaced. "Got your head handed to you, eh?"

Coombes shook his head. "Nope. Nailed it. Won the argument, blocked the takeover and was fired."

"Fired? You won!"

"Page-Nicholson-Hautmann and Lee doesn't care for showboaters. But before the ink on my pink slip was dry, I got a call from Victor Grego offering me a job. He was in the courtroom when I won the case and liked my style."

"Wait, didn't he work for Terra-Baldur-Marduk Spacelines at the time? You beat him and he wanted to hire you?"

Coombes smiled. "Victor doesn't waste energy holding grudges or plotting revenge. If he wins, he's magnanimous to the losers. If he loses, he picks up his marbles and starts a new game." Coombes looked Gus straight in the eye and said, "He never blamed the Fuzzies or you or Jack for the loss of the charter. He was rather embarrassed about his actions up to that point, though. When Victor is wrong, he owns up to it and respects others for doing the same. Mostly, he respects ability and talent, even when they're used against him. *Especially* when they're used against him."

Gus was about to ask another question when one of the plain-clothes cops ran up to him and Coombes. "Piet says that there is nobody home, but there is a computer with a lot of research data on it. He also found a secret storage space under the bar. Its empty, but he wants to know if you want to come in and take a look."

"Hell-fire and damnation, absolutely not! Just ask him to download as much as he can to a mini-backup, if he has one, and get the Nifflheim out of there."

"Have Mr. Slade give a recorded verbal consent, first," Coombes added. He glanced at Gus and added, "It couldn't hurt."

"Yes, sir!" The cop spun around and practically ran back into the house.

A tapping sound behind Gus drew his attention. Max waved them back into the aircar.

"Should we wait for Thaxter to come back and try to nab him, or what?" the Marshal asked.

"What do you suggest, Max," Gus questioned.

"Set up some discreet live cameras around the perimeter and have two man-teams keep an eye on the place a few miles from here. I think we could find an empty cabin to use as an observation post. We don't want our pigeon spotting the unmarked car and slipping away."

Gus nodded. It sounded like a solid plan to him.

"Why not just post a couple of men inside with sono-stunners and bag him when he comes home?" Coombes asked, though he again knew the answer.

"Because we're walking a fine line, legally, as it is," the Marshal explained. "If it turns out that this isn't Thaxter's place, and to be honest, I don't believe that for a Freyan second, then massive quantities of damnthing droppings will hit a very large fan. I would rather not be standing in front of that fan when it hits."

Coombes nodded. "Agreed. Can we chance at least one camera inside the cabin?"

Gus shook his head. "Definitely need a warrant for that, even if Clancy allowed it. It isn't really his place and we all know it. A legal fiction will only stretch so far. If it is Thaxter's place, even as an escaped con, he still has certain rights."

"And sometimes I'd like to strangle the left-wing libertarians who instituted those rights," Max growled, "but these are the cards we have to play."

"Well, I'll be glad to get back to my day job once I finish prosecuting your kidnappers, Gus. All this police work is too complicated. Give me a good tort any day."

* * * * * * * * *

Ivan Dane watched the replay of the news with a look that could only be described as unholy glee. The photos he bought from the CZC employee were worth every centi-sol of the five thousand sols he had paid for them. Those photos had been the center of the news report on Fuzzy Astronauts B.I.N. ran at 1800 hours, followed by another editorial on the incompetence of the Colonial Governor and possibly even criminal collusion between the Governor himself and the Charterless Zarathustra Company. The editorial ended with a demand for a recall vote. Dane couldn't help enjoying the broadcast. Even the storming entrance of Brandon Murdock wouldn't shake his moment of triumph.

"Five thousand sols?" Murdock said without preamble. "When do we start seein' a return on this—what did ya call it—investment?"

Dane pointed at the screen. "Right there. The public will see these photographs and automatically jump to the conclusion that those are the pilots of that rocket. And since those appear to be the oversized skeletal remains of a trio of Fuzzies…." He let the sentence dangle waiting for Murdock to finish it.

"Then Fuzzies are from another planet an' this ain't a Class IV inhabited world," finished Murdock. "Yah, I get it. An' why didn't ya just use pictures of the bones we got downstairs instead of payin' someone else?"

Dane resisted the temptation to pound his head on his desk. "How have you survived so long with such minimal mental resources?"

"Ya want I should show ya?" Murdock raised a hairy fist and took a step towards Dane.

Dane held up one of his hands in a placating gesture while the other surreptitiously reached for the gun he kept in a holster under the desk. "I'll explain. If we used the photos of our own skeleton in the basement, we would have to be able to account for its existence and our access to it. We can't do that without ending up in jail. Are you with me so far? Good. Three sets of Fuzzy bones are more convincing than just one set, anyway."

"'Kay." Murdock dropped the fist and took a seat.

Dane took his hand off the gun with an inward sigh of relief. "Now we have, as far as the viewing public is concerned, proof positive that Fuzzies are from another planet. We are one very large step closer to running this world. Stop counting five and ten centi-sols and keep your eye on the big picture."

Murdock thought about the situation. "'Kay, your smarter than me. I wouldn't be following you if ya wasn't, but watch the insults. Ya can't stop my fist with your brains."

Actually, I just did, Dane thought.

"So what's next?"

Dane smiled. "We hire a local law firm with a certain, ah, flexible morality, and start them working on proving that the current government is illegal and should be disbanded, then hire a political machine to set up the reformation party. I already have petitions on the street demanding a recall vote for the governorship. That requires twenty thousand signatures, but we can get a fair chunk of that in Junktown alone. We'll also have to make sure that the Company doesn't get its old charter back, but that should be simple enough."

"More cash out the air lock," Murdock growled. "I thought ya was some hot-shot shyster. Why don't ya do all the legal stuff?"

"Oh, I will be involved, of that you may rest assured, but no one man could possibly manage all that paperwork and research, not to mention typing up and filing motions, presenting briefs and bribing clerks. Besides, I have B.I.N. to run, and the greater plan to keep on track. Now, just for variety, did you have something else to talk about besides money well spent?"

Murdock glared for a second, then relaxed and shifted in his seat. "Yah, I do. Laporte has vanished an' the cops are tearin' Mallorysport apart lookin' for him."

Dane leaned forward. "Indeed? Any word on why?"

"Word on the street is he got mixed up in the Brannhard kidnappin'."

And Rainsford was out for blood. The Colonial Governor had enacted some rather bloodthirsty laws to protect the Fuzzies. Imagine what could happen to anybody involved with hurting one of his friends.

"This is both a problem and an opportunity for us, Murdock."

The thug raised an eyebrow. "How so?"

"If the police manage to capture Raul Laporte, he could be encouraged to explain how we extracted Leo Thaxter from Prison House, even though we managed to do so without his direct assistance. That would be unfortunate. On the other hand, his sudden disappearance creates a vacuum, one we could fill."

"How so?" Murdock repeated.

Not for the first time Dane wondered how Murdock had escaped incarceration for so long. "Think about it. Thaxter is gone off-planet somewhere. Bowlby is dead and gone. Laporte is now out of the picture. That leaves Spike Heenan as the last remaining crime boss on Zarathustra. And Spike is a pushover compared to Laporte or Thaxter."

"How do ya know so much about Spike?" Murdock asked. "In fact, ya seem to know a helluva lot about this planet an' the people we deal with for somebody who just got here two months ago."

"Research, Murdock," Dane said. "Now, you go and have a talk with Spike. Take some of your people with you. You've had two months to work with them, so you should know who you can rely on. Let Spike know who is running things, now. Oh, and while you are at it, I understand a number of new prostitution rings have opened up. Find out who is running them and bring them to heel." Dane thought for a second, then added, "And have a few samples of their wares sent over for…inspection."

Murdock nodded and left the office. Whatever his faults, he knew how to find things out and get things done in the underworld. Dane was confident that Murdock would handle things discreetly and effectively.

Granted, a few people might come up missing—more fuel for the M/E converter—but that was all omelets and eggs.

Dane leaned back in his chair and wondered how he might get control of The Bitter End now that the owner of record had vanished. He would have to look into that.

XVII

The five men stepped out of the egg-shaped shuttle and were welcomed by Captain Zeudin and Thor Folkvar. John Morgan, Ben Rainsford, Gerd van Riebeek, Victor Grego and Gus Brannhard shook each man's hand in turn.

"Nice little ship you have here," Gus said.

"Thanks. I won it in a poker game."

Grego, Rainsford and Gus looked surprised.

Morgan laughed. "That was a joke. Actually, I had it custom-ordered on Terra after I hit the ten billion sol mark in my liquid assets about twelve years ago. I put it to work as a luxury liner until it paid for itself, then remodeled it for cargo transport and exploration."

"You haul a lot of cargo," asked Grego. "Like what?"

"Well, the big money was in hauling foodstuffs from Freya and Terra to Yggdrasil, but I also moved furs, precious metals, manufactured goods, fissionables...pretty much everything at one point or another. One time I was paid an obscene amount of money to transport some convicted criminals from Fenris to Terra. I can't say any more about that, though. It was very hush-hush. I never even found out what they were convicted of."

Grego noted that Morgan wasn't speaking as a man bragging about his accomplishments; he was simply relaying the facts.

"Sir, if I may interrupt," the Captain spoke up, "Johann and the others are very anxious to know what you've accomplished here."

"Quite right, Captain. Gentlemen, if you will follow me."

Rainsford dropped back a bit to walk with Grego. "Victor, you said the man was rich, but you didn't say he was this well off. His own spaceship? How much does a craft like this go for?"

"More than you'll make in your lifetime, Ben, if you stay honest," Grego said. "Actually, I could afford a model like this if I cashed out some of my own Company stock, but it would be an unnecessary extravagance. No point since I am quite content to stay on Zarathustra and not go gadding about the universe."

The group piled into the cargo elevator as the standard lift would not accommodate seven people comfortably, especially with Gus Brannhard and Thor Folkvar in the party. They stepped off a moment later on second level. Ben Rainsford was immediately drawn to the live animal pens and cages. He recognized the various species by reputation alone. One pen held two oukrey, a male and female. A glass-enclosed cage next to the oukrey held at least a dozen kholphs; it was impossible to get an exact count as the quasi-primates were leaping and moving all about.

Every cage and pen held a representative of Freyan fauna save one. The last pen held three Terran horses, one stallion and two mares. Rainsford was especially fascinated by the animals from his home planet. Like most humans, he had never seen a live horse before.

Gerd, having looked at all of the living specimens, was then drawn to the cryogenic units. Each was labeled as holding the frozen embryos of this or that species. One was marked as containing horse embryos.

"Are you planning on duplicating Freya's ecosystem on Zarathustra?" Grego asked. "Pretty big project, Morgan. You'll need a fairly large crew to run something like that."

"If ever I heard a cue, that was it." Morgan turned to Thor and nodded. Thor crossed the hold and went through a door. "Gentlemen, what you are about to see may seem a bit startling. Let me assure you that the people you are about to meet are intelligent, not dangerous, and very much in need of our help."

Gerd, Gus, Grego and Rainsford steeled themselves for what they might see. Thoughts of a new sapient species, horribly disfigured refugees, illegal cloning subjects or even unrecorded mutations went through their minds. Those possibilities were still going through their minds when several, for lack of a better term, creatures entered the room with Thor Folkvar.

The beings were short by Terran standards. The tallest could not have been more than five feet six inches tall, barely reaching Thor's chest. The shortest, a female, stood around five feet. The height didn't even register on the four men.

The first things to catch their attention were the faces and the heads in general. The heads were large in proportion to the bodies. Rainsford took in the entire picture and thought he was looking at recreated Neanderthal men and women until he realized the foreheads were too pronounced, not sloping backwards as Neanderthal skull fossils indicated. The lantern-like jaws, while large, were within the human norm.

Gerd was impressed with the extreme musculature of the creatures. Even standing next to Thor, an impressive specimen of human muscular development, they looked incredibly overdeveloped. These were people who had spent uncounted years at hard physical labor. The large one in the forefront looked as though he could beat any three men at arm wrestling and not break a sweat.

Gus was rather taken by the fact that every one of the creatures was as hairy as he. Even the females. Hair running the spectrum from strawberry blonde to platinum covered almost every visible inch of skin. The group was dressed in shorts and short-sleeved shirts displaying the hirsute arms and legs of each member.

Grego, after a cursory examination of the creatures, locked onto the CMC logo stenciled on the left breast pocket of each of their shirts. The Chartered Magni Cooperative was best known for its mining interests and ore processing. Grego, as a businessman, kept abreast of news on competing companies as well as those he personally invested in.

"These are miners from Magni, yes?" Grego asked.

"*Jawohl, mein Herr,*" said the largest one next to Thor. "I apologize, I meant to say, 'yes, sir.'"

Gerd was visibly surprised. "You speak German? *Woher kommen Sie?*"

"*Wir sind auf Magni geboren, aber wir stammen von Freya,*" replied the large male.

"Wait, my German is a little rusty but I caught Magni and Freya in that exchange," Rainsford said.

"Gerd, how about a translation for the German-impaired?" Gus asked.

"*Verzeihung,*" That is, my apologies," the large male said. "I was explaining that my clan is from Magni, but our *Großväter*, ehh, grandfathers came from Freya. Ach, my manners. I am Johann Torsseus. I understand one of you is the *Gouverneur*…eh, what is the word…?"

"Governor," Gerd supplied.

"*Ja, danke,*" Johann nodded. "Der…eh, the Governor of this world."

"That would be me." Rainsford stepped forward and extended a hand. "Welcome to Zarathustra, Mr…*Herr* Torsseus. Please, call me Ben."

Johann accepted the hand and shook it with a firm grip. Rainsford got the impression that Johann was being very careful not to crush his hand.

"*Danke*. Call me Johann, *bitte*."

Taking their cue from Rainsford, Gerd, Gus and Grego moved forward and introduced themselves and also offered their hands. Morgan noticed that Gus winced a bit as one of the males shook his hand. Introductions were made all around.

"So your family came from Freya?" Rainsford said. "I didn't know they had two sapient species…."

"They don't," Gus interrupted. He looked about at the newcomers and shook his head. "Don't you get it?"

Rainsford looked puzzled for a moment, then his face cleared in shock. "Wait! Somebody did this to you? Great Ghu, how could anybody…?"

"Ben," Grego interrupted. "A little tact, please."

"It is not offensive to us, *Herr* Grego," Johann said. "We know what was done to us. Or rather, to our ancestors. We were changed to be more effective workers in the mines."

Gus was too nauseated to speak for several minutes. The idea that anybody could do something like that to the most beautiful humanoids in the known galaxy was beyond endurance.

"Gentlemen, let's adjourn to the lounge where we can discuss this in a more comfortable setting," John Morgan suggested.

He led the pack back to the cargo lift and escorted them to First level. Once off the lift, the group moved down a hallway where they passed two Thorans and an Ulleran.

Morgan, noticing the furtive glances at the alien crewmembers, said, "I hire for ability, not appearance or planet of origin."

"Sound practice," Grego replied.

Once in the lounge, everybody took a seat: the Zarathustran crowd on one side, the Freyans on the other, and Morgan, Thor and the captain in the middle where they could comfortably address both parties. Gus noticed that the room was decorated in High Freyan. Instead of form-fitting chairs and sofas, it was done up with fur-covered bench seats with down cushions. Wood, animal hides and native Freyan tapestries dominated the room. The only concessions to Terran technology were the viewscreen, an automated wet bar in the corner and a service robot that stood near the bar. Once everybody was seated, the robot became animated and moved from person-to-person taking drink orders.

Morgan waited patiently as the drinks were brought to everybody. The robot also laid out a selection of pretzels and mixed nuts, of Terran and Freyan origin, on the tables in front of the bench seats.

Gus accepted a tall glass of bourbon, which evaporated almost instantly and was quickly refilled.

The Freyans, Gerd noticed, avoided alcohol and accepted fruit drinks and snacks that looked like tiny sausages.

"Okay," Ben Rainsford said, "Since my tact has already been called into question, I'll address the damnthing in the room. Johann, how did this happen to you and your people? And why do you speak German?"

Johann smiled showing an impressive array of very large white teeth. "I appreciate your directness, *Herr* Governor. You would fit in well with my brethren. Our *Gross—*, eh, grandfathers were originally from Freya, *ja*, but they were criminals and outcasts. When the Chartered Magni Cooperative came to Freya looking for miners, several princedoms struck a bargain that allowed them to empty out their dungeons and cull the more destitute members of their provinces. The princes were paid handsomely, I have learned, but wanted to keep this thing quiet. *Der Grosskönig*, eh, the Great King would not have approved at that time. This suited the CMC as the Federation would also have objected. So, our…grandfathers were taken to Magni and made into slaves."

"Not everybody in the CMC knew where the workforce came from," Morgan interrupted. "This plan was hatched by the then head of Labor Division and kept quiet. His successors were handpicked for their, oh, let's call it moral flexibility."

"How could the CEO not know about this?" Rainsford asked.

"There is a great deal a CEO doesn't know, Ben," Grego answered. "I hate to admit it, but I rarely look into any division's activities until a problem comes to light. I depend on the division heads to run their sections and report to me their progress."

"Like you depend on me and Marshal Fane to keep you up on things, Ben," Gus added.

"I see," Ben said thoughtfully. "Johann, please continue."

"*Danke schön.* As you may know, Magni is a heavy gravity world while Freya has slightly lower gravity than your Terra. Many of the slaves died from the hard work under such conditions. After almost a thousand deaths, an outside genetics company was contacted and they began experimenting on the survivors. Many more died as a result, but eventually, well, you see the success before you."

Success, thought Rainsford with disgust. "How many of you are there, now?"

"A little over two thousand, *Herr* Governor."

"That's all?" Gus asked without thinking. "How many did they start with?"

"Over five thousand men and women," answered Morgan. "The genetic manipulation caused a lot of non-viable births, lethal mutations and just outright deaths on the table. Only the strongest…and luckiest, survived."

The room fell silent for several minutes. Grego and Gerd downed what was left of their drinks and gratefully accepted a refill that quickly vanished. Gus forgot he even had a drink and didn't notice when it was topped off. Rainsford lifted his glass as if to take a drink, and then put it back down untouched.

"How…how did you…?"

"Ah! How did we escape?" Johann chuckled. It sounded like a damnthing was choking. "The geneticists did not do such a good job on us. The changes they created within us held true for two generations. Then a baby was born that looked like one of you. Then another. Every year fewer of the children born look as we do." Johann waved a hand in a sweeping motion that indicated the altered Freyans. "In a few more generations, we may all look as our ancestors did.

"When the first one was born, we hid him from our masters. This was easy since they rarely involved themselves in our private quarters near the mines. And no, there weren't any attempted rapes of our women. A female who can easily lift an aircar power cartridge with a single arm is not to be trifled with, I think."

Gerd considered the weight of a power cartridge in Zarathustran gravity, then accounted for the weight difference on Magni and was suitably impressed.

"We raised the boy and taught him as much of Lingua Terra as we could glean from the masters—"

"I'm sorry to interrupt, but why do you all speak German?" Gus asked. "I assume that you all do."

"*Ja.* This German is an uncommon language among your people. The masters taught us that so we could not be able to speak with any who might discover us. They even gave us all German names and demanded that we do so for our children. But we still taught Sosti to our young, and that proved our salvation. We also kept our Freyan surnames, though the masters didn't know this.

"When Rheiner, the human-looking boy, was old enough to pass for an adult man, we selected the overseer that looked the most like him. We killed the overseer, then gave his clothes and papers to Rheiner. Rheiner simply walked out and nobody noticed."

"Where is this Rheiner?" Grego asked.

"He is with the others waiting to see if this world will have us. They all wait on Gimli, now. Where was I…ah, *ja*. Rheiner spoke very little of your Lingua Terra, but he could read the signs that showed the way out of the mines. From there he went in search of weapons. We had no idea that other humans might be willing to help us, so he had planned on avoiding them. Until he heard two men speaking Sosti, that is."

"That was Captain Zeudin and myself," Morgan said. "We had been on Magni for about a month at that time. I, of course, was looking for a lead on my father, so I invested enough money in the Chartered Magni Company to get access to their files. That's when I noticed Rheiner watching us. At first I thought he was a company spy. I was going to have strong words with the CEO about such sloppy surveillance."

Rainsford interrupted, "Wait. You were mad about how sloppy the spy was, but not that he was spying?"

"Of course not. I didn't mind when Akira spied on me for Victor, either. It is all part of the game." Morgan winked at Grego, who winked back. "So, I motioned for Rheiner to come over to me and he turned and ran. Right into Thor Folkvar, here, who also thought he was spying and was going to have a word with him about it."

"He knocked the wind out of me, but I managed to grab him before he could get away," Thor said. "He looked mainline human, but his muscle density was that of his father's people."

Gus sized up Thor Folkvar and figured anybody who could knock the wind out of *that* mountain of muscle was someone to be respected.

"Thor brought him over to me and we tried to question him, but he wouldn't speak. That is, until the captain spoke to him in Sosti. Then he just gushed out everything. He figured he was busted and headed back to the mines, so he went for broke. Once I had the whole story, I sent Capt. Zeudin to the nearest planet with a Terran Federation

Naval outpost. I stayed on Magni until he got back with the cavalry six months later. During that time I made Rheiner my personal aide and taught him Lingua Terra. Since we both spoke Sosti, everybody thought I brought him with me from Freya and didn't give him a second glance. Once the TFN arrived, they arrested everybody and his kid sister, put them all under veridication, tried the guilty parties and shot the lot of them.

"Most of the scandal was kept quiet, but the stock still dropped like a lead balloon. Stockholders were bailing out left and right, which drove the stock value down even lower. That's when I stepped in and bought up every share I could lay my hands on. I now control enough stock that I can have my way at every vote. I browbeat the remaining stockholders into passing a restitution program for the freed slaves. Every last one of them got about one hundred and fifty years of backpay plus a hefty relocation bonus." Morgan looked at Rainsford. "That's where most of the five hundred million sols for Epsilon Continent are coming from."

"I think you should buy Zeta, instead," Grego said. "Tell me, Johann, what will your people do to support themselves once they make a home here on Zarathustra?"

"We have much money from the backpay. We know that will not last forever, so we will work," Johann said. Grego asked what kind of work. "The men are all trained miners, of course, and the women used to grow the crops and raise the meat that fed us. Much of the food we grew was taken by the Company, but we still ate well."

Grego nodded. "A well-fed worker performs better. At least those bastards understood that much. If you are still willing to work as miners, then Zeta Continent is the better choice. The CZC already has a mining operation there and I would be willing to sell it to you for two hundred million sols. Zeta is big enough for your people to settle on, raise cattle and crops and build a sizable community. Much larger than your current population. I am sure Ben could come down on the price for the land since it is much smaller than Epsilon, and I'll even forgo the leaseback fees."

"You're willing to sell the mine on Zeta Continent?" Gerd asked. "What do you get out of it? It is certainly worth a lot more than two hundred million sols."

"Yes and no. The mine on Zeta is peanuts to the company and we lost a lot of the workers when they flew off in company cars to stake out some free land. Some of them are in Prison House for aircar theft, while others took the next spaceship out when the wanted posters were posted. The mines have been barely worked since then. Even the influx of new colonists hasn't offset the personnel loss. Trained miners are hard to get on a planet with this small a population. So, we sell it to Johann's people, buy the output from them and actually make more money than keeping it with a skeleton crew. I'm sure I can sell that to the stockholders."

"This one is sold," Morgan said.

"Wait," Rainsford said. "I am in favor of Victor's suggestion, but why don't you all just go back to Freya?"

"Looking as we do?" said Johann. "Freyans are somewhat…um…?"

"Xenophobic," Morgan supplied.

"*Ja*, xenophobic. Humans are acceptable, barely to some, but we would be seen as monsters."

"Plus there is the embarrassment to the princedoms who sold their people into slavery," Morgan added. "Family honor means a great deal to Freyans in general and to the nobility in particular. So much so that they also paid a significant amount of money to keep the matter quiet."

"You blackmailed them?" Gus asked. His already high opinion of Morgan went up a notch.

"I demanded reparations," Morgan countered, smiling, "both

monetarily and in chattels. That's where the menagerie downstairs came from. There are another few loads of that coming, also. Not just animals, but seeds for Freyan plants as well."

"So you plan on recreating Freya on Zarathustra," Gerd observed. "That's why you need the whole continent. Otherwise there could be damage to the planet-wide ecosystem."

"*Herr* Grego, I think you have a good plan," Johann said. "My people do not object to hard work, only to being slaves."

Ben Rainsford, Colonial Governor of Zarathustra, sat quietly for several minutes. He whispered something into Gerd van Riebeek's ear, then Gerd whispered something back.

Finally, he announced, "*Willkommen auf Zarathustra, meine Freunde.*"

XVIII

The synth-mask was uncomfortable. Leo Thaxter's beard itched like crazy and he sweated profusely. He could have shaved the beard and bought the higher grade air-permeable mask, but he didn't want to wait and he would need the beard afterwards to maintain his cover identity. He also had to get a new gun on the black market to avoid even the remote possibility that his old one could be traced back to him. People believed he was off-planet and he wanted to keep it that way.

Thaxter stood across the walkway from the B.I.N. waiting for the chance to enter the building unnoticed when Brandon Murdock and several men came out through the front door. Thaxter recognized a couple of them as his own former employees. That might be useful, Thaxter thought. A good general always earned the loyalty of his men by treating them well and keeping his own expectations realistic. Thaxter always thought of himself as a good general and acted accordingly. If, for some reason, he couldn't count on their loyalty to their former boss, he could always count on their fear. He had enough on every one of his old crew to send them to Prison House until Fuzzies developed nuclear fission.

Thaxter decided to approach one of the men later and remind him where his loyalties lay. A spy inside Dane's operation would be very useful. First he had business in the B.I.N. building.

Back when Ivan Bowlby first came to Zarathustra, Thaxter had helped him get set up in the entertainment business, mostly because

Thaxter didn't want to run the prostitution rackets. He had no moral objections to securing the services of a professional, just no interest in being a glorified pimp.

Bowlby had previous experience in this area before he was run off of Odin, so he was the perfect man for the job. After he got the prostitution rings established, he branched out into illicit drugs, and then the semi-legitimate arena of adult films and magazines—then television and movies.

Thaxter, while not involved with the day-to-day activities of Bowlby's enterprises, was still a silent partner and knew almost every secret Bowlby had: like the hidden cameras spread all over the building, the covert passages that allowed him to slip in and out of any room unseen, and especially the hidden safe in the basement where Bowlby stashed his cash.

When the new colonial government was established, Bowlby became concerned that taxes, particularly income taxes, would be close behind. Zarathustra was too small a planet for any decent money-laundering schemes to be installed, so instead he made a point of keeping the legal enterprises separate from the illegal ones. Occasionally, he would pump up the profits of magazine and film sales with the drug and prostitution money, but for the most part, he would just stash any cash he couldn't account for. Like most less than attractive men with poor social skills, Bowlby planned to get as rich as possible, then retire to Freya in the hopes of finding a beautiful woman to settle down with.

Thaxter had always laughed about that. Freyan women were the target of losers the galaxy over. Nobody ever considered the possibility that they might have somewhat higher standards for marriage than some punk with a few bucks.

Thaxter entered the B.I.N. building through the front door. There was at least one secret entrance going in, but Thaxter had never learned where it was. He'd had no need to go back when he was still a free man. On the way he was asked to sign a petition for the recall of Colonial Governor Bennett Rainsford. Thaxter ignored the woman with the clipboard and kept going. While he wouldn't mind seeing Rainsford kicked out of office, any petition would be computer-scanned for authenticity, meaning his handwriting could give away the fact that he was still on-planet. He took enough of a chance signing for the cabin and the spaceport locker in Clancy's name.

Once inside the building, Thaxter took the first hallway to the left, then into the first men's room on the right. Looking about quickly to be certain nobody else was using the facilities, he ducked into the last stall and locked the door behind him.

Feeling around on the graffiti covered wall, Thaxter found the faint round depression under a legend that proclaimed KILROY WAS HERE and pressed hard. A six foot by three foot section of the wall opened to reveal a dark passageway. Thaxter had to duck down a bit to get in. Once through the entryway, he pressed a glowing blue button and the wall sealed itself up and a series of lights came on. Thaxter followed the lights to a set of stairs that went down. The bottom was at least two floors below the ground floor and became a hallway. He idly wondered if the same guy who made the passage from the CZC building to the 'Last Chance Bar' in Mallorysport had built the secret passages for Bowlby.

At the end of the hall was a blank wall. Thaxter cursed softly as he felt around. The new wall had to have been installed after he went to prison. After a few minutes of rubbing his hand over the wall, he found a faint depression like the one from the men's room. Instead of opening a section of wall, a panel slid sideways to reveal a viewscreen and several nozzles.

The viewscreen came on to reveal Ivan Bowlby's pudgy face with the pencil thin mustache and goatee. Bowlby thought the facial hair made him look like a movie producer though Thaxter thought it made the man just look stupid. The image on the screen spoke.

"Only two people know of this secret passage," he said. "Myself and Leo Thaxter. Leo is in jail. However, if it is you, Leo, then I assume you have escaped and I am either helping you get off-planet, or I am dead or incapacitated. Place your hand on the scanner"—another panel slid over and a scanner plate dropped down. Behind the plate was a small globe, similar to the ones used on poly-encephalographic veridicators—"and answer each question truthfully. If you lie, this passageway will fill up with toxic gas, killing you before you can escape. Attempting to leave before answering the questions will trigger the same result."

Ivan watched too many of his own spy shows, Thaxter decided. He placed his hand on the scanner.

"State your name," the viewscreen said.

Thaxter said quickly, "Leo Thaxter."

The globe in the wall glowed blue. Damn, thought Thaxter, it *is* a veridicator.

The screen flickered, then Bowlby's face returned. "Good for you! If you were a cop or Raul Laporte, Spike Heenan or, worst of all, Hugo Ingermann back on-planet, you would be dead, now. Am I dead?"

Bowlby always was a little paranoid, Thaxter thought. "Yes." Blue, again.

Again the screen flickered. "Ever since you got busted and Ingermann skipped planet I have been expecting something like that. Either the cops would get me or one of the others would move on me with you out of the way. Did you kill me or put out a hit on me?"

"Hell, no!" Thaxter started to sweat. He admitted to himself that he thought about it a time or two, but never carried it out. The globe flickered slightly, then remained blue.

The nozzles retracted into the wall. "Thank you for playing, Leo.

You are no longer in danger of being gassed. Please keep your hand on the scanner, though."

Thaxter put his hand back. In his relief he hadn't even been aware that he had moved it.

"Do you know who killed me?"

Thaxter had a pretty good idea. "Maybe. I'm not certain, though." The globe turned a dark shade of purple before it settled back to blue. The veridicator had trouble with guesses and conjectures.

Again the flicker. "Will you attempt to kill this person?"

"Yes." Thaxter had planned on doing that anyway. The globe remained blue.

"Then the money is yours. Thank you, Leo, and good luck."

The screen went dark and the wall slid open to reveal a vault door. As Thaxter wondered how to open it, the vault flew open to reveal numerous stacks of cash and twenty safety deposit boxes. Thaxter poked around a bit and found something else that would be useful; the plans for the building with all the secret passages marked in red. The hidden room with the surveillance recorder was behind Bowlby's old office. The feed was good for a solid year, and then the older data would be replaced with the newer stuff. Thaxter had no idea if Bowlby archived the older feed before it automatically erased. Thaxter followed the secret passages on the building layout and saw he could get to the hidden room without having to go through the office itself.

Good, thought Thaxter. He pulled a device out of his pocket. *I'll be able to set up the relay and get the money out of the building without anybody seeing me.*

Thaxter took another glance at the stacks of cash and wondered how he would do on Freya.

"Ivan Bowlby, you had an overdeveloped sense of drama, and you were way too spy crazy, but you were all right with me."

* * * * * * * * *

Miguel Kourland took great pains to explain to Tuning that he was not to trip up his guest for the evening. That didn't sit well with Tuning as he liked to get the better of his guests on the show. Kourland explained that the orders came straight from the top and Tuning agreed to play nice.

"You better, or I'll replace you with a Fuzzy," Kourland warned.

Tuning remembered how Kourland had replaced Spin Wheeler and nodded before taking his seat behind the interviewer's desk. Unlike his predecessor, Tuning didn't do a monologue. He preferred to present his lineup as a news program, not a variety show.

The lights came up and the audience applauded politely. There was none of the yelling and screaming associated with the *Spinning Wheels* show. Tuning stood up from behind the desk and came around to address the audience.

"Good evening and thank you for tuning in," Tuning said, with his signature welcome. "Tonight we have Miss Darla Cross who will be telling us about her new family, a pair of adopted Fuzzies, and her upcoming role as Lady Macbeth in the new stage production of *Macbeth* that opens next week at the McGuire Theater."

Tuning waited for the polite applause to die down before continuing. "We also have Dr. Hoenveld with us to discuss the newly discovered fossils of giant Fuzzies." More applause, this time more enthusiastic. "And we have a special guest with Dr. Hoenveld. Stay tuned to see who it is."

* * * * * * * * *

Up in his penthouse apartment, Victor Grego and Diamond watched the show with interest. It seemed to take forever to get through the Darla Cross interview. The woman was a great actress, but about as interesting to watch in an interview as drying paint. Scarlett O'Hara and Rhett Butler, her newly adopted Fuzzies, were far more entertaining. When her interview was finally over, she moved over to the next chair as Dr. Hoenveld was introduced. With him was a Fuzzy.

* * * * * * * * *

"And who is this fine furry fellow?" Tuning asked.

The Fuzzy, sitting on Hoenveld's lap, spoke up. "Zorro, Unka Tuning."

Tuning was mildly surprised at being addressed as '*unka*'. "Welcome to the show, Zorro. Is Dr. Hoenveld your pappy?"

"Oh, no," Hoenveld said. "We're just friends. Zorro here is a fairly unique representative of *Fuzzy sapiens zarathustra*, which I will elaborate on shortly."

Darla Cross reached out a hand and ruffled the Fuzzy's head fur. "He's so cute I could just eat him up!"

Zorro became alarmed until Hoenveld assured him that he was in no danger of being consumed. Still, he watched the actress carefully and was on his guard every time she tried to pet him. Finally, her own two Fuzzies climbed onto her lap and she satisfied herself with petting them.

"Doctor, I understand that you are in disagreement with an anthropologist who was recently interviewed on another network about those Fuzzy bones discovered in Northern Beta."

"Yes and no," Hoenveld said. "I do agree that the fossils represent either the precursors or even another branch of the Fuzzy family tree. The skeletal structure and overall design suggests that they are closely related. However, if we assume Fuzzies follow the same evolutionary path as sapient mammals of other worlds, then I simply can't support the hypothesis that these remains belonged to a species possessing a high order of intelligence. Notice the shape of the brainpan…."

A screen lowered and the image of a skull appeared side-by-side with a cutaway diagram of the fossil.

"Notice the relatively small region where the frontal lobes would be seated. There is shockingly little space there. Yet, Zorro here possesses frontal lobes that are, to be honest, larger in proportion to his body than that of *Homo sapiens terra*."

"Really!" Darla Cross exclaimed. "Does that mean Fuzzies are smarter than humans?"

"It is much too soon to make any assumption of that nature, Miss Cross," Hoenveld said in, for him, an only slightly condescending tone. "Fuzzies have existed in a primitive culture struggling against an extremely hostile environment for thousands of years. Until they discovered us they had no time to truly develop their intellectual potential. I would say the next generation will give us a better indication of that."

"They discovered us?" Tuning asked.

"Oh, certainly. Jack Holloway found Little Fuzzy, the first recorded meeting of the two species, in his shower stall. That means Little Fuzzy found Mr. Holloway's home and investigated it. No doubt he watched from afar before hazarding to enter the cabin. As I see it, Little Fuzzy made the discovery, not Mr. Holloway."

Tuning conceded the point, then returned to the original topic. "What about the NFMp hormone, Doctor? Doesn't that suggest the Fuzzies were adapted to conditions on another world? That is what Professor—"

Back in the wings Miguel Kourland swore under his breath. Tuning was supposed to treat Hoenveld with kid gloves and here he was trying to trip him up.

"Oh, please," the Doctor interrupted. "His absurd conclusions make me doubt his credentials."

"But he is an anthropologist and paleontologist of some note, Doctor. Are you suggesting he is trying to perpetuate a scientific hoax?"

"You mean like Piltdown Man or the Martian Cave Paintings? No, of course not. I think this is more like the case of Nebraska Man where one thing was mistaken for another. Granted, these fossils are far more suggestive than a mere pig's tooth; still, he would not be the first scientist to jerk the trigger with a half-baked theory. First of all, there is no way to determine if the fossil Fuzzies possessed the NFMp since there is no DNA available, and secondly, it wouldn't prove anything even if they did.

"The production of the hormone could be the result of a negative mutation, like diabetes or lupus in humans. The mutation bred true, unfortunately, entering the genome of the species. The Fuzzies that ate land-prawns were, in fact, self-medicating the condition and therefore able to reproduce, while those that did not simply died out. The surviving Fuzzies would have taught their young the same dietary habits until it became the racial norm. Again, it neither proves nor disproves anything."

"Excuse me, Doctor, but if the dead Fuzzies in the picture were so big, why are our Fuzzies so small?" Darla Cross asked.

Hoenveld explained that diet and environment could have had a significant effect on Fuzzy development. He then followed-up with the possibility that the fossils may have belonged to a species similar to Terra's *Gigantopithecus*, in which case while distantly related, they were not the ancestors of modern Fuzzies.

"Doctor, may I ask why you elected to bring Mr. Zorro in with you?" Tuning asked. Zorro, who had been watching the audience with some fascination, turned at the mention of his name.

Hoenveld smiled. It didn't seem natural on his face. "I am glad you asked. Zorro here is the first Fuzzy I have ever examined that does not possess the NFMp hormone. He is not dependent on humans or land-prawns to provide him with the titanium based molecule I discovered to help him generate progeny."

"What does that mean?" the actress asked.

"The mutation giveth and the mutation taketh away," Tuning suggested.

"Very good, sir," Hoenveld said. He even tried to smile again, though it still didn't look right on his face. "I think I will put that on a plaque in my office."

The interview concluded on a high note and Kourland decided not to hang Tuning by his thumbs. As the guests were leaving he overheard Darla Cross ask Dr. Hoenveld out for dinner. Even more surprising, Hoenveld accepted. As shocking events rated, Space Fuzzies didn't even make the board in comparison.

XIX

Victor Grego turned off the viewscreen, then stretched. He didn't watch much television as a rule; he paid others to do that for him and provide him with a semantically correct and concise account when needed. This was too important to miss. Hoenveld did a great job even when it looked like Tuning was going after him. Hopefully it would sway public opinion.

Grego made a note to check-in with Gerd in the morning to see where he was at on the rocket and ask him what he thought of the interview.

"Diamond, would you like to have a late dinner with Pappy Vic?"

Diamond was all for it. "We have pizza?"

"Only if we leave off the extee-three."

* * * * * * * * *

The Bitter End was in full swing for the after-dinner rush. The dance floor, always busy at this time regardless of the day of the week, was packed with bodies dancing despite the limited room between them. Tonight was something the new owner called Disco Night. Disco was something dredged up from some dusty archive somewhere, and the music had to be dredged up from the same place.

Affanita sat at the bar thanking Ghu that the directional sonics spared her from the full brunt of what passed for music on the dance floor. Some of it sounded like somebody was strangling a drunken Khooghra while a tribe of Thorans banged away at their primitive drums. If the new owner installed a suggestion box someplace, Affanita was determined to find it and suggest that the music feed be permanently wiped. *Even First Century A.E. country music is better than this*, she decided. If the music didn't change soon, she was going to finish celebrating elsewhere.

She downed her Thoran brandy and signaled the bartender for a refill. Behind her, the music changed to something softer and easier to stomach. Affanita decided she could survive the noise long enough to take a table as far from the dance floor as possible and order veldbeest tenderloin. Tonight, hyperspace was the limit. Or, at least sixty thousand and seven hundred and fifty sols worth.

She had made out much better than she thought she would on the bag of sunstones Richard had given her. She banked fifty thousand sols, paid off all of her debts and was splurging for one night before deciding whether to stay on Zarathustra, or go to work as Richard's shill. Affanita had to admit, at least to herself, that even five to ten percent of another run like the first one would keep her in clover for a good long while. Richard had an interesting and effective sales pitch. She just couldn't figure what the game was. She checked around after selling the sunstones with other prospectors. She found three others who were given the same pitch and a bag of stones, though none got quite as much as she did.

Like her, they tested the stones and checked around to see if any other prospectors had been robbed or disappeared. None, except for somebody named Bradley Small who had robbed another prospector, so he didn't count. They all knew a phony stone when they saw one, too. No fakes. So where did the stones come from and why give away so many just to get the shills? It was enough to make her head spin, though the Thoran brandy would manage that on its own.

Affanita asked for a menu, collected her purse and drink, and took a table near the back. She scrolled through the menu on the electronic pad, found the tenderloin and a couple of side dishes, thumbed the SELECT button and set the pad down. While she waited she looked around the room. In the private booth she noticed the new owner, Ricardo La Rue, sitting there sharpening a large Bowie knife. La Rue stopped suddenly and stared at the knife, then quickly put it away. *What was that all about?*

She gave a little shrug, then looked around some more. Closer to the dance floor she spotted her cabbie from earlier that day along with a woman that had to be his wife. She thought about going over to say hello, then thought better of it. The wife might be the jealous type and jump to the wrong conclusion. Better to not take any chances.

A waiter appeared with her order. After he left Affanita lost all interest in the other patrons and attacked her meal like it could be her last. It had been a long time since she had tenderloin, and even longer since she could afford to get one this good. She tried to make it last but it practically vanished off her plate.

Ghu, that was good!

Affanita picked up the menu pad again and scrolled through the dessert options. After settling on a chocolate mousse she set the pad back on the table and nearly jumped out of her skin. Sitting in the chair across from her was Richard.

"I'm sorry if I startled you," the geek said with a smile. "I spotted you walking over from the bar and thought I would say hello. Hello."

"Hiya, Tiger," Affanita replied with a forced smile. "What's a guy like you doing in a nice place like this?"

"Oh, celebrating. Like you, I suspect." Richard waved to a waiter and ordered two drinks. A Freyan ale for him, another Thoran brandy for Affanita. "I guess you decided to take the stones to a dealer. How'd you make out?"

She told him though she shaved a few thousand off the price.

Richard let out a low whistle. "Not bad. Not bad at all. So, ready to do business on a regular basis?"

"Do I have a choice?"

"Indeed you do. I said it was up to you and it is. I don't twist arms." Richard smiled and added, "I suspect you would totally humiliate me in a fight, anyway. No, if you choose to walk away, fine. However, I would be remiss if I didn't point out that you would be missing out on a very lucrative opportunity. The next bunch would be almost twice as much, and while you would only keep five percent, that's still a fair amount of money."

"Twenty percent," Affanita countered.

"Oh, now, that's just not realistic," Richard replied. "Let's call it six percent...."

"Make it fifteen. I suspect I am taking some sort of risk, though I haven't figured out what it is, yet."

"Tell you what: we both know where this is headed so I'll take the short cut. Ten percent. Take it or leave it. Offer good until I get my drink. Ah, here comes the waiter, now."

"Done. When is the next delivery?"

Richard accepted the drinks, tipped the waiter ten sols, then turned back to Affanita and pulled a leather pouch out of his jacket. "Right now."

* * * * * * * * *

Victor Grego washed down two headache pills with a lukewarm coffee and chased it with a fresh cigarette. He mentally counted down from one hundred. By the time he got to fifty, the headache had abated enough that he thought he could deal with the current crisis. He flipped on the viewscreen and set it for the exterior security cameras. There, on the ground level in front of the Zero level entrance, was a mob of people demanding to see the so-called giant Fuzzy bones. There were also a couple of men with clipboards taking signatures.

There was talk of boycotting Company stores if they weren't allowed access to the bones and rocket. That almost made Grego laugh. Less than two percent of the Company's annual revenue came from on-planet groceries and goods. It was exports that brought in the big bucks. And the Company was the largest supplier of produce, meat and dairy on Zarathustra. A boycott would only hurt the people doing the boycotting.

Grego leaned back and just stared at the screen. It was a pack of amateur archaeologists and armchair biologists, he guessed, and the usual lookiloos who just plain had too much time on their hands. All because of that damned footage of the skeletons over in Science division. It had to be an employee who took the pictures, of course. He, she or they were probably paid a considerable amount by B.I.N. Grego hoped so, because if he ever found out who, they would need that money to support themselves after he fired their asses.

Grego had a brief thought about asking Johann and some of his gang to go out and scare the bejeezus out of the protestors. It would be in extremely poor taste, but still it was fun to think about. Some of the protestors might even think the bones came to life and grew skin. The altered Freyans might have even enjoyed scaring the hell out of people. Unfortunately, it would result in bad press. There would be enough of that when the sale of Zeta Continent hit the news.

He had hoped that the interview with Hoenveld on *Tuning In With Tuning* would have satisfied the crazies and conspiracy buffs enough to keep them off his doorstep. No such luck.

Diamond crawled up on Grego's lap to watch the screen and Grego absently started stroking the soft fur of the Fuzzy's head.

"Why Big Ones look angry, Pappy Vic?" Diamond asked.

Grego tried to think of a simple answer and gave up. Besides, he suspected after two years of associating with humans the Fuzzies understood more than they let on.

"Some unwise Big Ones showed pictures on the screen of the, um, bones we found. Now these people want to see the bones for themselves." There, simple and to the point.

"Do Big Ones want to help?" Diamond asked. "Maybe know what bones are?"

"No, Diamond," Grego said, shaking his head. "These are amateurs, um, less wise Big Ones who know a little but…"

Know a little!

Grego's mind kicked into high gear. Some amateurs accomplished some pretty amazing things in the past. Forrest Mims III was an amateur scientist and won an award for developing a miniature instrument that measured the ozone layer back in First Century A.E. 'Amateur' did not mean 'stupid.' Maybe somebody in that crowd might be good for something other than blocking the entrance. Grego decided not to fire the photo-takers after all. Just demote them. Grego put in a call down to Chief Steefer.

"Yes, sir?" As usual, the Chief's uniform was parade-perfect on the screen.

"Chief, do you have enough bodies to talk with those protestors and see if any of them know anything about paleontology?"

Steefer didn't even look away to pretend he was checking. As usual, he knew exactly who he had and what was available. "Certainly. You think some of those mutts outside might be useful?"

"It can't hurt to ask them. Hey! Also, see if there are any amateur linguists out there."

The Chief smiled and nodded. "I'll have Glazier, Matedne and Schröter bring in candidates three at a time and do background checks on them. I should have a list of potentials in a few hours. Will that be quick enough?"

"More than quick enough." Another idea struck the CEO. "I'll have Dr. Mallin sit in on the interviews. Maybe he can weed out the nut-jobs while your men do their thing. And see if they will consent to veridication."

The chief nodded and screened off. Grego turned to his Fuzzy.

"Diamond, I think we need to make you a company officer. Division head of the common sense department."

Diamond didn't ask if it was good to eat; he had been around the corporate world enough in the last two years to know better. "Is much fun?" the Fuzzy asked.

Grego laughed. More company heads should have a Fuzzy to help them run things.

* * * * * * * * *

Ivan Dane sat in his office watching the morning broadcast on CZCN and wondered if he was the favored son of some ancient deity. A rival network was handing him the planet on a silver platter.

"The sale of Zeta Continent, which will put three hundred million sols in the colonial treasury, will be off-limits to all civilian personnel. According to the Chartered Zarathustra Company CEO Victor Grego, the area would be dangerous for everyone except the trained and experienced miners that have also bought the mining rights to Zeta for a paltry two hundred million sols."

The broadcast went on with an interview of Ben Rainsford endorsing the sale; however, Dane was not paying any more attention. He was dancing around his desk humming a tune. He was still dancing when Murdock and Lundgren entered the office.

"Havin' a party?" Murdock asked.

Dane stopped dancing to catch his breath. "Soon, Brandon, soon!" He quickly outlined the high points of the broadcast.

"So?"

"Ghu, how can you be so dense?" Dane yelled at the ceiling.

Murdock clenched his fists and Lundgren quickly stepped between them. "Brandon, let Dane explain. Then you can beat him up."

Murdock glared at Dane over Lundgren's shoulder, and then backed away. "This better be real good."

Dane, too excited to realize how close he'd come to being beaten half to death, pointed at the viewscreen with a look of unholy glee. "Rainsford just sold an entire continent to a bunch of outsiders from Ghu-knows-where. Moreover, Grego sold these same outsiders the mining interests on Zeta for a pittance."

Murdock was unimpressed. "Again, so what?"

Dane mentally counted to ten as he reminded himself that Murdock was brought in for his brawn and knowledge of underworld management, not for his questionable intelligence. "Since the day this planet became reclassified as a Type IV Inhabited world, people have been hoping to get rich on the unseated lands, and would have done so had Rainsford and Grego not brokered a deal that gave all those unseated lands back to the CZC for the next millennium. People don't like to have money dangled in front of them and then snatched away just as they reach out to grab it. Now, out of the blue, an off-world consortium buys up an entire continent. An. Entire. Continent. Hundreds of thousands of acres of land denied to the existing population and handed over to a bunch of mysterious foreigners. I couldn't have come up with a better scenario if I tried.

"My editorial tonight on B.I.N. will crucify both Rainsford and Grego. Darloss being trashed by Hoenveld doesn't matter, now. It's all over except drowning the kittens. By the end of the week even the legislature will be signing the petitions for a recall vote."

Murdock nodded, then said, "That's no guarantee u're gonna be elected gov'ner. I know enough politics to know ya can't depend on the public to do what ya want. There'll be a new crop of candidates ten minutes after the recall's passed."

There must be a brain inside that thick skull after all, Dane thought. "True enough, but we have an edge on all of them. First of all, I've been campaigning for the job with every editorial I broadcast for the last two months. I'm already in everybody's mind as a candidate. Secondly, I have all of Bowlby's files and tapes. He had quite the little blackmail operation going on as a sideline to his entertainment business. Every person who engaged the services of one of his prostitutes or bought his drugs ended up on a video feed. Lundgren here identified no less than twenty-three members of the legislature as having used such services. They will back me to the hilt…or else."

"There are a lot more people besides those in the legislature on those feeds," Lundgren added. "People in positions of influence that can be made to work for us."

"The only thing missing are shots of Rainsford, Brannhard or Grego doing something illegal or immoral," Dane said. "That kind of publicity would bury them. Either they're monks or they chase their secretaries around the desk. Well, not Grego. I've seen his secretary."

"Dummy up some shots?" Murdock said. "Maybe even have them doin' somethin' really weird."

"Oh, I could do that, easily enough, but Grego surely has people in his employ who would catch the fakery and prove it," Lundgren explained. "We couldn't air it on B.I.N. without being sued later, either."

"So what? Once the feeds are out there most yucks will believe what they see an' ignore any evidence that they're fake." Murdock took a seat. "An' ya could dump it on the data stream where every basement-dweller on-planet will find it while lookin' for porn."

Dane sat on the edge of his desk and considered the idea. "That's not bad. Not bad at all. We'll keep it in reserve until the night before the election. That way they won't have time to refute the evidence. Timing is everything. Lundgren."

"I'm on it." Lundgren left the office whistling an archaic tune the other two men couldn't identify.

"I'll finally have them all," Dane said. "Oh, Murdock, was there something you needed when you came in?"

Murdock stood and stretched for a moment and then said, "Naw, just this."

He backhanded Dane across his left cheek nearly knocking him to the floor.

"Next time ya mouth off at me, it won't be a little love tap. Got it?" Without waiting for a reply, Murdock turned on a heel and strolled out of the room.

"Wait."

Murdock stopped and half turned to look at Dane. "What?"

He paused to waggle his jaw, just to make sure it wasn't unhinged. "I have a small job for you. Something I think you might enjoy." Dane told him what he wanted. As he expected, Murdock liked the idea.

After Murdock left Dane rubbed his cheek and made a mental note to do something unpleasant and permanent to his associate the second he ceased to be of value.

* * * * * * * * *

Murdock left the B.I.N. building from the rear and collected a few men along the way. There could be trouble at The Bitter End and he wanted backup just in case. His hand felt warm from the slap he had given Dane. It was a very satisfying sensation. He had been wanting to hit Dane for the last few weeks but held back. Dane was the boss and one didn't go around beating up their boss if they wanted to stay healthy, as a rule.

Dane was smart Murdock had to admit that to himself. Getting Thaxter out of jail the way they did was pure genius. Too bad Thaxter got away before Murdock could kill him. That was a loose end and he hated loose ends. Still, odds were Thaxter caught the next hyperspace ship off-planet and headed to parts unknown. That was almost as good as killing him.

One thing that didn't seem on the level was the explosion that killed the mining team over on Beta. All of the sunstones and medical data they had collected had been shipped off maybe an hour before the M/E converter, or something, blew the whole operation to Em-See-Square. That was just a little too convenient. Murdock suspected that Dane somehow arranged the accident to get out of paying the miners their cut. Murdock didn't care much about that, or wouldn't if Joe Quigley hadn't been one of the victims. He had liked Joe.

Dane would have to be dealt with, sooner or later, Murdock decided. If he did kill the Beta team, then there was no way of knowing who could be next. Murdock had no intention of it being him.

XX

Ricardo La Rue was not expecting visitors at this time. There had been a few over the last couple of days who needed to have it explained to them that he was now the man in charge, that Laporte had signed over all of his business interests over to him and that he expected the same level of respect and deference originally attributed to his predecessor. A few mild examples had to be made to bring the more reluctant ones into line, but that was to be expected. Once La Rue "explained" that the new boss was the same as the old boss, people quickly fell into line.

La Rue had just finished counting the previous night's receipts when his desk intercom buzzed. It was Rico, one of his personal bodyguards and assistants.

"Mr. La Rue, there's a man here to see you," came Rico's voice from the speaker. "He says it is about an opportunity you might be interested in."

Another opportunity. People like that came in all too frequently, usually with some half-assed caper they needed bank-rolled. "What is his name?"

"He didn't say, but he said the previous owner and his boss worked on a project together."

That piqued La Rue's interest. "Very well, send him in."

La Rue pressed a button that disengaged the deadbolt on the door and it instantly opened. The gentleman who entered had the look of a man familiar with the workings of the underworld. It wasn't anything he was wearing or any distinguishing features or tattoos; it was the way he moved, the way he took in the room as he entered.

After the door closed, La Rue relocked it and offered his guest a seat.

"I'd rather stand," the man said. "I've been sittin' all day and need to stretch my legs."

"I see." La Rue started getting a bad feeling about his guest. "What can I do for you, Mr.—"

"Murdock. I'm here for Mr. Dane. He wants that I should tell ya to sell this joint."

"Oh?" La Rue reached under the desk and grasped the hilt of a knife. "I have only recently acquired this establishment. I very much doubt you could make it worth my while to part with it so soon."

"Yeah," Murdock said menacingly, "we kinda thought that would be your attitude. So, we had a back-up plan ready to go in case ya refused to work with us."

* * * * * * * * *

Marshal Fane was just getting ready to leave his office to have lunch when his viewscreen signaled that he had a call. Muttering a profanity he picked up on Shesha, he went back to his desk and flipped on the screen. Piet Dumont stared out at him.

"Inspector Dumont, how may I be of service?"

"Marshal, I think I found something on our Mr. La Rue," Piet said. That got the Marshal's attention. "I did some data stream scanning on the name and came across an article about a B-movie actor from Baldur by the name of Ricardo La Rue. He was a real Lon Chaney type—"

"Who?"

"Lon Chaney," Piet explained, "The Man of a Thousand Faces back in pre-atomic silent films, and later the talkies."

"Oh, right." Max nodded. "He was the Wolfman, right?"

"That was his son, Lon Chaney, Jr., sir."

To Nifflheim with the history lesson, thought Max. "How does this apply to our Mr. La Rue?"

Piet continued, "La Rue got semi-famous doing B-movie police dramas and gangster films on Baldur. One time he played four parts in the same movie by altering his appearance with stage make-up. He was so good at it that he even fooled the director during most of the film. He was about to break into the big time when he was caught fooling around with a major producer's wife. That killed his career. The producer got him blackballed with every movie studio on the planet. Probably throughout the Federation."

"Okay…?"

"Here's the thing that caught my attention, though; one of the parts he played was that of a crime boss by the name of…get this…Raul Laporte. I don't think this is a coincidence, Marshal."

Max stared at the screen for several seconds without moving a muscle or saying a word. Piet couldn't even tell if he was breathing through the video feed.

"Raul Laporte," Max finally said. "Did this article have any pictures?"

"You bet, Marshal." Piet disappeared from the screen to be replaced by two side-by-side photos. The left one was the spitting image of the missing Raul Laporte, complete with handlebar mustache and reddish scar on the left side of his face. On the right was the face of the man they had sitting in the interview room just a few days earlier.

"My god, man!" the Marshal screamed, "Why aren't you over there arresting him, already?"

"And leave you out of it? I figured you would hang me by my thumbs if I denied you the pleasure of being in on the arrest."

Max admitted to himself that Piet was probably right. Instead, he said, "Hang you? If you weren't so damned ugly I'd kiss your ass! Get a team together and meet me on the roof right away."

"On it, Marshal!"

Forget getting a sandwich from the commissary, I'm going to have Raul Laporte for lunch.

* * * * * * * * *

For the second time that week Piet led a team into The Bitter End. Unlike the first time they met with no resistance. Once Piet was satisfied the lounge was secure, he allowed the Marshal to come into the building.

"Where is everybody?" asked the Marshal.

"The restaurant opens around 1600, I think," Piet said. "They never did any lunch business, as far as I know."

"Not legal business, you mean." Max looked around the empty room. "Still, according to your report there were armed men in the lounge when you stormed in last time."

"They might be upstairs in a meeting," Piet said thoughtfully. "That collapsium-lined office of Laporte's would keep anybody from hearing us bust in."

"He would still have vid surveillance, though," the Marshal said. "They might be making a break for it."

Piet swore. "Damn. Chang, Matedne. Check the other exits. Van Damme, York: you're with me. The rest of you go through this entire building and bring anybody or anything you find back here to the lounge. Let's go."

Piet led the charge up the stairs to Laporte's office with Max, breathing heavily from the exertion of moving his considerable bulk to keep up, bringing up the rear.

"I gotta join a gym," muttered the Marshal between gasps.

"I can recommend a good one, Marshal," Piet shot back. The inspector had no trouble running up the stairs.

Unlike their previous visit, the collapsium-laminated door to Laporte's office was ajar. York took one side while Piet took the other and van Damme pushed the door open and jumped back out of the line of fire. Kicking the door open the way it was done in the Tri-Ds would have resulted in serious injury; collapsium was a very unforgiving mistress.

Piet counted three on his left hand, then he and York rushed into the room with their assault rifles at the ready. They need not have bothered. On the floor were five men lying in a spreading pool of blood. Across the table was Ricardo La Rue. Piet pressed two fingers to La Rue's carotid artery, then shook his head in negation.

"You can come in, Marshal, but mind where you step," Piet called out.

Max entered the room and his eyes went immediately to the body on the desk. "Dead?" Piet nodded. "The son-of-a-bitch got away from me again."

"You could say that," Piet agreed. "He's holding a bowie knife with some blood on it."

"He got a piece of the citizen that killed him, eh?" Max gingerly walked around the bodies on the floor and carefully avoided the spreading pool of blood. "The ones on the floor look like they were shot, but I don't see any holes in La Rue, Laporte, whatever his real name is. Hmm…no blood trail, either. Wound is either small or just soaking into the clothes, or the killer had some sort of wrap or binding on it."

Piet examined La Rue's body more closely. "From the angle of his head and bruising on the neck I would hazard to say his neck was broken…by somebody who knew how. Ex-military would be my guess."

Max swore some more. "All right, everybody out, don't touch anything, mind where you step and call for the forensic team. I'll give Gus Brannhard a buzz and let him know what's going on, here. I imagine this news will be like watching your mother-in-law fly into a mountain in your brand new aircar. He won't know exactly how to feel about it."

The cops cleared the room and returned to the lounge. After Max brought the colonial prosecutor up to speed over the police radio he took a seat at the bar. His stomach started rumbling, again.

"Hungry, Marshal?" Piet asked.

"That and other things."

"Um, at the risk of getting busted down to patrolman, again, may I point out that we are in a fully stocked restaurant that is now a crime scene? The owner is dead and has no known relatives or business partners on-planet. Even if he did, The Bitter End will not be able to reopen until our investigation has cleared the place, probably in a few weeks, possibly months, and even then it's likely to be seized as assets used in the perpetuation of a crime…hundreds of crimes, most likely… and either sold at the next police auction or taken over by the Colonial Government."

"If we find any proof of said criminal activity." The Marshal looked up at Piet and added, "Your point?"

"Well, it would be a shame to let all of this food just spoil in the meantime."

"Piet, while you make a very good point, that is still borderline looting and as the Colonial Marshal I can hardly condone—" Max's stomach rumbled again. "Ah, what the hell. How are you at making a club sandwich?"

* * * * * * * * *

Dr. Emil Patrick Rankin started his medical career on Loki doing reconstructive surgery and providing general medical care, mostly for the Terran miners and, occasionally, for the indigenous inhabitants. It was a comfortable life if not a luxurious one. Rankin might even have gone on until retirement age in that capacity had he not been offered an obscene amount of money to perform a face-changing operation on a wanted felon.

The felon was caught with a random DNA check while attempting to leave planet and gave up Rankin's name during interrogation under veridication. Rankin lost his license to practice medicine on Loki and narrowly avoided a prison term. He tried to restart his practice on Baldur where he met Ivan Dane. Dane went under a different name at the time and was in need of Rankin's skills to alter his appearance.

It had been a substantial procedure. Dane had a great deal of body fat removed, facial reconstruction, implants in the arms and legs to increase height and reach, and even his larynx adjusted to deepen his voice. Next came the hair transplants and melanin injections to darken the skin. Steroids were used to speed-up the recovery and increase muscle mass. Rankin never learned Ivan Dane's real name, but it didn't matter; Dane was born on the operating table.

Rankin accepted Dane's offer to work with him knowing that he would be performing illegal surgery on known and wanted criminals. He no longer cared; the money was too good to pass up. Even Dane's outrageous plan to take over an entire planet didn't give him pause. He simply continued to collect his share of any monies that came in and did his job.

When Brandon Murdock walked in with a deep knife wound on his left arm, Rankin didn't bat an eye. The wound was wrapped in a neck cloth that was soaked in blood. Murdock still wore his own neck cloth which meant the blood-soaked one likely came from whomever inflicted the wound.

"Cut yourself shaving, Brandon?"

Rankin asked the question with such a deadpan delivery that it took Murdock a moment to realize the doctor was making a joke.

"Yah. It was full moons last night," Murdock quipped back with irritation. "Less comedy and more medicine, 'kay, Doc?"

Rankin took it in stride. Patients in pain were often irritable and Murdock was no joy to be around under the best of circumstances. He quickly cleaned the wound, inspected the injury for particulate matter, sprayed it with a derma-bond that closed the wound and created a temporary seal, then covered the cut with neo-derma-plas. It would take at least three days for the flesh to completely knit back together. During that time the derma-plas would protect and even hide the wound from all but an experienced eye.

Dr. Rankin was just finishing up when Ivan Dane came storming in red-faced.

"What happened?" Dane demanded.

Murdock held up his forearm and inspected the doctor's work. After making a fist and flexing the muscle he nodded approvingly to Rankin and then turned to Dane.

"La Rue wasn't goin' for it," Murdock said. "Pulled a knife, instead."

"So you killed him?" Dane yelled. "You were supposed to just… lean on him a little, let him know who was running things. I told you before that killing high profile citizens could bring the heat down on us. The police are probably dissecting every square millimeter of The Bitter End looking for evidence. There may be recordings of you being there. Witnesses."

Dane pointed at Murdock's arm. "At the very least you left your DNA at the scene."

Murdock calmly extracted a small aerosol can from his jacket. It was a high-powered antiseptic used in hospitals. "I sprayed the room with this stuff. Degrades the DNA of anythin' it comes in contact with like bleach. An' my crew took care of La Rue's men before we left. This ain't my first rodeo, ya know."

"I am very familiar with the effects of that aerosol if you recall. Still, you might have missed something," Dane snarled. "At the very least they'll have your blood type—"

"O Positive," said Dr. Rankin. "The most common blood type there is."

"Haw!" Murdock sneered at Dane. "What'll the cops do? Arrest, half the population on suspicion?"

"Thirty-eight percent," Rankin supplied. "I could change his blood type with a bone marrow transplant and accommodation drugs. I would have to use chemo to destroy the existing bone marrow, of course, and it would take a few weeks…."

"You'll have to change his face, also," Dane said. "Maybe even his fingerprints."

"Hey, I ain't no amateur," Murdock said. "I wore gloves."

"Thank Ghu for that," Dane said throwing his hands up in the air. "You'll have to burn the gloves in case they left any traceable fibers."

"I could have altered the fingerprints, anyway," Rankin said. "As you already know."

"Yes, Dr. Rankin," Dane said irritably. "You are a Ghu-damned medical genius and I am intimately aware of your expertise. Now, what happens when the man who had been shaking down and breaking into the local rackets suddenly disappears and is replaced by another man? They'll either assume he was killed, or a new gang has entered the scene. That means we would have to re-establish ourselves with most of them."

"Nah," interrupted Murdock. "Guys get promoted or replaced all the time. All the mooks need to know is that I represent the same organization an' they'll stay in line. They don't care who collects the dough from them as long as it's only one weekly pay-off."

"Might I suggest we wait and see what, if anything, the police have before we take extreme measures?" Rankin said. "I think Brandon could just lay low for a few days while Richard does a little hacking into police files to see what they have."

"If he can hack into the police computers," Dane said.

Rankin pointed out that Lundgren had his way with the TFN system without excessive difficulty.

"Fine. Murdock, go to ground in Junktown until we know what we're up against. Your men, too." Dane turned as if to leave, then stopped and took a closer look at Murdock's arm. "How did that happen?"

"La Rue pulled this big knife on me. If it weren't for my fibroid vest, he woulda gutted me like a fish. As for layin' low…."

Dane's eyes went wide. "A knife? Was it a bowie knife about ten inches long?"

Murdock nodded.

"And he used it like he knew what he was doing?"

Murdock simply held out his arm to show the derma-plas repair.

"Son-of-a-bitch! You didn't just kill La Rue…you killed Raul Laporte."

Murdock's eyebrows came together. "How d'ya figure that?"

"Trust me; I know what I'm talking about. Lay low until this all blows over."

"Nah. If I suddenly disappeared, I'd become the obvious suspect. Instead, I keep doin' like I've been doin.' No change to my routine. I doubt this La Rue, Laporte, whatever, had any cameras in his office. It coulda been used against him if he ever got busted."

"Fine. It's your neck." Dane spun around and rushed out of the room.

Murdock and Rankin stared at Dane's retreating back for a moment then Rankin extracted a pill bottle from his bag. "Take one every six hours with food or milk. No alcohol until at least a day after you finish the bottle."

"I don't need no pain killers, Doc," Murdock argued.

"This is more than just a pain killer," explained Rankin. "These are accommodation and antibiotic pills. Just a precaution against your body rejecting the derma-plas and removing the possibility of an infection. You can't play fast and loose with the bacteria of an alien planet. There was a case on Thor, where a germ that the indigenous life-forms casually dismissed, destroyed every square millimeter of skin on the body of a human in less than forty-eight hours."

Murdock accepted the pill bottle and promised to behave. After he left, Rankin sat down behind his desk and pulled a fifth of Old Atom Bomb Bourbon from a drawer. He poured a stiff shot into his coffee.

XXI

Colonial Prosecutor Gustavus Adolphus Brannhard received the message with his usual grace. “Damn. I wanted to prosecute the bastard. Well, somebody saved me the trouble, so we’ll just have to prosecute him or them, instead.”

Marshal Fane’s image nodded in the viewscreen. “We’re still waiting for forensics to finish processing the crime scene, but York found a hidden button in La Rue’s, or Laporte’s, desk that opened a section of wall. There was a hidden room behind the office loaded with file cabinets and what looks like a make-up table and mirror. There were also a bunch of wigs, make-up kits, various colored contact lenses—you name it. Real Larry Chaney stuff.”

Gus stifled a chuckle. “You mean Lon Chaney. Hey, do we know if this La Rue was wearing his real face, yet?”

“Yes. The coroner said there were some traces of make-up on the skin, but it was the real Ricardo La Rue underneath. He took a big chance disguising himself as one of his movie characters.”

“Maybe that is why he chose a colony planet,” Gus observed. “B-movies don’t make the circuit the way the topflight films do, and colony planets are the last to get even those.” Gus smiled as he lit a cigar. “Once this gets out don’t be surprised if some enterprising citizen holds a Ricardo La Rue film festival, though. What have you found in the files?”

“Oh, the usual; records of illegal sunstone purchases back when the Company held the monopoly, a couple of blackmail scams against CZC division heads, lots of information he brokered between the CZC and the TFN through cut-outs…the usual. We did dig up records of his running muscle for Bowlby, Heenan and Thaxter. That'll allow us to bring ol' Spike in and question him under veridication."

"Humph. La Rue gets points for his disguise and keeping paper records instead of encrypted computer files that we could have broken over time, but he didn't seem to think much of security beyond that. No secret codes." Gus was almost disappointed in the late gangster.

"Don't be too sure about that." Max held up a file on the screen. "We found the records where he assisted in your kidnapping, but he identified the nabbers as A.A. and D.R."

"Anthony Anderson and Duncan Rippolone," Gus said. "Not exactly a first class encryption."

"True, but we have another file detailing the assistance he intended to supply to a 'Weasel and the Geek' to bust Thaxter out of Prison House. It doesn't look like he followed through, though. This Weasel and Geek may have found other assistance."

Gus slammed his fist down on his desk, which was a mistake as it was made of solid zaraoak. He grunted in pain, then said, "Damn! If we had gotten to La Rue sooner…"

"That's not all. La Rue provided Thaxter with money and some sunstones to get off-planet. It looks like he bought out Thaxter's loan sharking business."

Now that was odd. Why buy out an underworld enterprise from a man on the run? Why not just stuff him into an M/E converter and take over? Thaxter must have had something on Laporte, La Rue, whatever. Well, that was moot, now.

"Thaxter is still on-planet, though," Gus said. "Why stick around? He could be getting facial reconstruction to avoid detection, though he could have done that just as easily on Gimli where nobody knows him."

"Maybe he wants to get his sister, Rose Evins, out of prison," Max suggested. "Even Khooghras look out for their families." An idea struck Max. "You think Thaxter offed La Rue? He may have thought he was doing Laporte a favor not knowing they were the same person."

"To what end? Thaxter is scum, but he doesn't kill without a good reason."

"That I don't know. Or…nah, it doesn't wash. It took at least three men to kill Laporte-La Rue and his men without taking any casualties. I doubt Thaxter has access to that kind of back-up. He's too hot."

Gus nodded. "True. I think we have a new player in town, Marshal. And he's trying a takeover."

"If that's so, he'll be trying to muscle in on the existing rackets." Max was thoughtful, which on his face made him look angry until surprise took over. "Bowlby's overdose! The new crew came in, tried to get him to knuckle under and ended up killing him instead, I'll bet."

"You could be right about that. We'll have to check the body again. Do we still have it in cold storage?"

"Unless somebody claimed it or it was recycled," Max said. Recycled meant stuffed into a mass-energy converter, in which case it was gone for good. "I'll head down to the morgue now and make sure we still have it."

"Thanks, Marshal," Gus said. "Give me a holler when you know."

Gus blanked the screen and leaned back in the chair. He never drank while in the office, though sometimes he was very tempted. He gave some thought to Bowlby. Bowlby had died while he was absent from his position as Colonial Prosecutor. Even though he was kidnapped from his home shortly before Bowlby's demise it still rankled him.

Gus had read the reports on the investigation. Everybody was so busy tearing the planet apart looking for him, Bowlby's overdose was practically rubber stamped. While Leslie Coombes did a good job of running the office of the Colonial Prosecutor, he lacked experience in dealing with the police and coroner. Frankly, even they couldn't be faulted; Ben Rainsford had been riding everybody mercilessly to find Gus. Nobody could fault the Governor for pushing to find the Chief Colonial Prosecutor that he personally appointed. It would set a very bad precedent not to.

Nobody could be faulted, yet police work had suffered as a result. Something would have to be done about that!

* * * * * * * * *

Roger Shijabuyenzikumligwanagwashi, or just Shija, former Terran Army Sergeant, accompanied by what he privately called the Junktown Irregulars, led the way through the brush. Shija had retired from service with a twenty-year pension and found that he couldn't live on the retirement money. This was partly due to the child support on his son in the custody of his ex-wife, but mostly because of his gambling debts. Shija had run-up a sizeable tab at The Bitter End. He knew better than to try to leave Zarathustra with the marker unpaid, so he sought out ways to make money on the sly.

Everybody knew that the best sunstone deposits were on Beta Continent, and the best of the best were on the Fuzzy Reservation. So, Shija gathered up a team of like-minded individuals from Junktown who were also down on their luck—easy to do since everybody in Junktown was down on their luck—stole an aircar and headed out for Beta.

Unlike many of the other opportunists taking advantage of the confusion created by the Fuzzy Rocket, Shija did his research. The best deposits were invariably near rivers and streams in a black flint. As such, as coincidence would have it, they came upon the stretch of land formerly occupied by one Bradley Small. The campsite had long since been cleaned out by the NPF, but signs of previous activity were still evident.

Shija checked his electronic map pad and nodded. "We'll start in here. Get the camou weave up and the sonic hammers out. We start right away. Mason, M'benga, you have first watch. If any cops or dangerous animals come around, activate the beepers."

The two men nodded and took up positions at opposite ends of the camp. The scanning equipment was outdated and bought at a pawn shop, but would still identify any man-sized bio-signatures within two kilometers. It was useless against anything as small as a goofer or a Fuzzy, but they were not considered a threat to Shija or his men.

Everybody accepted Shija as the leader due to his military background. What they didn't know was that his time in the Army was spent flipping burgers and washing tables. Shija was a cook, and not a very good one, which is why he was typically relegated to doing the short-order food preparation.

While all military personnel were expected to qualify on the weapons range, of the three qualifying levels, Marksman, Sharpshooter and Expert, Shija typically qualified as a sharpshooter, which was purely average. However, he knew how to bark orders and sounded like he knew what he was doing. Shija also knew how to cultivate the right friends and work the system. That talent more than anything else allowed him to make the rank of Staff Sergeant, but no higher.

Among the men currently working the illegal prospecting, only one had any experience in that field, Naruto Mazzola. Mazzola was one of the prospectors who was displaced when the Fuzzies were discovered and declared sapient. Rather than start a new dig with a replacement land grant, Mazzola took a job at Yellowsand working the sunstone mining operation, until it was noticed that quotas on his shift started coming up short. He quietly resigned before an investigation could start. He left with twelve thousand sols worth of unpolished sunstones hidden in the bottom of his duffle bag. Shija and Mazzola met up in a bar one night, got to talking and hatched the plan.

"Make sure to spray the working and sleeping areas," Mazzola said. "You really don't want to wake up with a tunnel worm working its way under your skin."

Shija walked over and called Mazzolla's attention to the disturbed area near the stream. "What do you make of that, Nar?"

"Sonic mining." Mazzolla pointed to the large hole in the flint. "See how round that is? That doesn't happen in nature. Somebody used a sonic drill on that site. I would wager if we look around, we might find a few more impressions like that."

"A sonic drill?"

"Yep. The sonic vibrations would turn the flint to dust and an industrial vacuum would suck up the dust and spit it out into the water. A filter would catch anything bigger than a marble, which is how the sunstones would be collected. Well, that and a lot of useless pebbles. It's a smart way to work if you are trying to keep from being noticed."

"Then why did you have us bring vibro-hammers?" demanded Shija.

"Money. Vibro-hammers are cheap. Sonic drills cost about five thousand sols each, and that's without the vacuum attachment. Maybe after we make some progress we'll be able to afford one, but we didn't have anywhere near that kind of cash to spare when we were getting outfitted."

Shija considered Mazzolla's words, then nodded. If he had that kind of money, he could have paid off Raul Laporte, in which case he wouldn't have needed to try his hand at illegal prospecting. "What do you think happened to the last guy who was here? Did he get busted or decide there wasn't anything here and moved on?"

“No way of knowing. We’ll just have to see what we find and try to keep from getting spotted.” Mazzola looked out at the surrounding countryside. “A fibroid weave canopy would have been nice.”

“Those cost even more than that drill you were talking about,” said Shija. “Back in my army days I knew a supply sergeant who did a lot of scrounging and black market stuff. You name it, he could get it. For the right price. A fibroid canopy large enough to cover this operation would have run about eight thousand sols. He never got caught, either. Or if he did, he had enough generals on his customer list to make it go away.”

“Generals?”

“Yeah. Most of them were rock-solid soldiers out to do the job, but about one in ten was out for himself and liked to live it up. Rare wines, creature comforts, off-world foodstuffs, that sort of thing. A good scrounger was also good for morale as he could get things that helped keep the rank and file’s spirits high. One time he cadged a shipment of veldbeest steaks—a good trick on Yggdrasil—for a company party. Don’t know where he got them, don’t want to know.”

“Too bad your friend isn’t here,” observed Mazzola. “We could have used a few things.”

“For all I know he’s retired, or even stationed on Xerxes. Well, let’s get busy. The sooner we get the stones, the sooner we get the Nifflheim out of here.”

* * * * * * * * *

Deep in the brush several Fuzzies were startled by the sudden strange sounds coming from the sun’s left hand. After some discussion, Strong One decided to investigate. The Fuzzies who were hunting with him argued with him, but Strong One was the lead hunter so his orders were to be followed. Unfortunately, many of them now called him by the strange name the Big One used, and the more he demanded they stop, the more they used it. It would help if he knew what it meant, but the Big One used words that made no sense, even when he spoke in *Jin-f'ke*.

Having a lead hunter was one of the new things that Red Fur had established to keep the peace. Hunting parties were led by the best hunter, and everybody was expected to obey him when on a hunt. Strong One resisted the idea at first, believing that everybody should work with their own clans and follow their own leaders. Red Fur pointed out that a team of hunters would work better than a team of hunters, makers and caregivers. Strong One had to admit there was wisdom in that, and as one of the best hunters, he was delegated as leader of an eight *Jin-f'ke* hunting troop.

Strong One and the others quietly approached the source of the strange sounds. Peering through the tall grass, they could see a band of Big Ones using strange made-things to make a lot of dust. There was a new sound, like rocks smashing together, then the other strange sound that hurt his ears stopped.

A Big One bent down and pulled some chunks of black rock out of the hole they worked in. The Fuzzies murmured among themselves that the Big Ones were very strong to lift such big rocks from the ground. Strong One thought he could lift such a rock, but not as easily as the Big Ones did.

"Thor," Fruitfinder said, using the annoying name the Big One had taught her, "this bad place. Runner come here and find bad Big One with noisy made-thing. He say to Big One 'stop make noise and leave.' Big One used other noisy thing that make his ears and head hurt."

Strong One remembered that story. Runner had told it at big-big gathering of *Jin-f'ke*. The Big One tried to attack them, so Runner and his hunting band killed the Big One and took the pretty rocks that made light when hold-in-hand. Now new Big Ones come. Maybe looking for pretty bright things. Strong One wondered if the Big Ones would go away if they gave them the pretty bright things. No, they might want more and keep digging with the noisy made-things.

Strong One hefted his stone hammer and stepped out to face the Big Ones. One of the Big Ones saw him and pointed, making the strange words. Strong One knew a few of the words from the Big One called Joe. Not a lot, but some. He decided to use the Big Ones' words, and the name Joe called him, since it had meaning for his people.

"You go," Strong One said. "I Thor. You go. Now."

* * * * * * * * *

Shija watched with interest as Tekestah Sabahatu employed the vibro-hammer. Every time he would hand up a chunk of flint, Shija would turn it over to Mazzola who would use the micro-ray scanner on it. If there was something inside, Mazzola would crack it open with his specialized tools. If not, it was tossed into the stream. So far they had found three stones; two duds and one small sunstone worth maybe 600 sols.

Mazzola received a positive reading on the next piece of flint when he noticed the largest Fuzzy he had ever seen step out of the tall grass. The average Fuzzy stood at two feet in height and fifteen to twenty pounds in weight. This one looked about two and a half feet tall and a good thirty pounds if he was any judge. Mazzola tapped Shija's arm and pointed.

"You go," the Fuzzy said. "I Thor. You go. Now."

"Oh, shit," Shija said. "This must be one of those Reservation Fuzzies. He could identify us to the NPF."

"What do we do?" Mazzola eyed the Fuzzy and wondered if there were more in the brush. He read that Fuzzies typically traveled in groups of four to eight.

"No witnesses." Shija drew his sidearm, screwed on the silencer and aimed at the Fuzzy. "Sorry, Thor. Nothing personal."

Shija's shot grazed Strong One in the shoulder and spun him around. Before Shija could take another shot, a small spear sailed through the air and caught him in the throat. The spear was followed by more spears. A *lot* more spears.

Mazzola swore and picked up Shija's fallen pistol and fired blindly into the foliage. By this time the others noticed what was happening and joined in the battle. That was when arrows started flying in.

Though small compared to anything used on Old Terra or Freya, the arrows were very sharp and penetrated deep into human flesh. With enough time and sufficient ammunition, the arrow barrage could have killed the humans. This wasn't necessary. Each arrowhead had been treated with the venom of a *net-zeetha*, a poisonous lizard endemic to Northern Beta. The toxin worked in much the same way as curare on Terra. First the infected humans became paralyzed, then their breathing became labored until they were unable to breathe at all and quietly expired.

* * * * * * * * *

When the shooting was over, the humans lay dead or dying, as were several Fuzzies. Strong One stood up holding a hand to his shoulder. He noticed that the one who had hurt him with the strange made-thing was still alive, though bleeding badly from his neck wound. He walked over and saw that the Big One would not survive such a wound. Out of mercy rather than malice, he raised his stone hammer and brought it down on Roger Shijabuyenzikumligwanagwashi's head.

"We tell Red Fur what happened here," Strong One said. He looked over the dead and injured among the *Jin-f'ke*. Some were not from his hunting party. They had to have heard the sounds of fighting and came to help. He turned to Runner. "Bring healers, too. I stay here while you make run fast."

* * * * * * * * *

Red Fur was shocked, angry, and worried. He was shocked that his people were forced to defend themselves from more Big Ones, angry that more than a hand of his hunters were dead, and worried about what he would have to do. There were so many new things since the Big Ones first arrived: the strange food that some of the people loved, the need to gather more of the People than had ever been in one place before, the sharing of knowledge and new made-things. Now there was a terrible new-thing he would have to bring to his people, and he did not want to, but saw no other choice.

Red Fur stomped over to the Big One called 'Joe.' He stared at him for many-many heartbeats before he could speak, then he had to remember to talk in the strange way that would allow the Big One to hear him. It had been hard to learn, but when Joe's made-thing in ear stopped working, it was the only way they could communicate.

"Big Ones killed more *Jin-f'ke*," he stated in the strange language Joe had taught him. "Why? Why do Big Ones kill people?"

"Not all Big Ones kill, Red Fur."

"Not so!" Red Fur yelled. "You make Sun Fur dead. Big One come many days ago and tried to use noise thing to hurt more of my people. Big One in yellow not-fur attacked two of my people. Now more of my people dead while hunting!"

The Big One looked sad, but said nothing. What could he say?

"We not let Big Ones hurt any more *Jin-f'ke!*" Red Fur shouted. "Now we make dead all Big Ones we find."

"Red Fur, if you kill any more humans, Big Ones that don't attack you first, more Big Ones will come to stop you," Joe warned.

"Then we make dead!" Red Fur cried out. "We make dead all Big Ones who come here!"

Joe shook his head. "My people have weapons that could destroy… kill you without even getting close to you. You would all die and never even see who killed you."

"*Jin-f'ke* small, yes, and not as wise with made-things, but *Jin-f'ke* know the forest and animals and places to hide. We know that you think we are like young ones. That make Big Ones slow to see we can kill them, as we killed the other bad Big Ones who come here. Tomorrow, we show you."

Joe started to protest as Red Fur turned and stomped away.

XXII

Penrosa P. Penrosa, a particularly large and strong man, worked the vibro-hammer with an ease other cons couldn't help but envy. Penrosa, or Pen as the others called him, was one of the exceedingly rare specimens of humanity that still had a pure bloodline. Born and raised on Terran Samoa, he could trace his ancestry back almost seven hundred years, all native Samoan. Like the majority of his people, he was large, strong and didn't mind hard work. Unfortunately, Pen suffered from a very bad temper, which resulted in his being convicted of manslaughter and receiving an eight-year sentence.

In Prison House, Pen was a model prisoner. He was attacked only once by three other cons, resulting in three beds being filled in the infirmary. Even Leo Thaxter didn't push too hard where Pen was concerned. Thaxter had tried to recruit Pen, but the big Samoan wasn't really criminally inclined. He intended to finish his time and get back to his life, hopefully with a better control of his temperament. Thaxter accepted that and left Pen alone.

When the opportunity to work in the open air came up, Penrosa P. Penrosa was first in line, at least after he shoved three other men out of his way. Once on the dig site, Pen was put to work loading rocks and debris onto contra-gravity platforms. The platforms would carry the load to an area outside of the perimeter where it would be inspected by CZC professionals. Once the blast crater and surrounding area were cleared, Pen was put to work with the vibro-hammer to break small sections of rock loose from the crater walls. The sonics were adjusted to shatter flint while leaving any fossils or other substances undamaged. Pen had only nine months left to his sentence so he was trusted with the heavy equipment that could otherwise be used as a weapon. One guard objected and it was pointed out that Pen didn't need any weapons to be dangerous.

Pen shut off the hammer and set it down. There was something poking out of the side of the crater where he had been working. It looked like a bone. Pen took out a small archaeologist's sonic hammer and carefully subjected the wall to a series of harmonics designed to loosen dirt around fossils. After several minutes he managed to work the bone free. While he knew very little about fossils or anatomy he knew a humanoid femur when he saw one. It was one of the biological curiosities of the universe that almost every sapient species, save for the Ullerans, had similar upper leg construction. Knees, shins, feet and even pelvises could differ significantly from species to species while the femur seemed to be nearly universal. Only size truly differed.

Penrosa smiled as he wiped the bone with a rag. This might be worth an extra ration at dinner, he thought. While the prison system met the normal dietary needs of the inmates, large, powerful men like Penrosa tended to be hungry most of the time. He was the only person in Prison House who missed Small Eyes, if only because he often took most of the molester's food.

Penrosa yelled for the platform operator to give him a lift up. The operator, an inmate trustee, lowered the platform and Pen stepped on. The lift started up, passed the lip of the crater and kept going up. Pen, worried about going above the safe altitude at which point his collar would explode, yelled down to the trustee to quit fooling around. When the trustee failed to respond, Pen looked over the edge of the platform and saw that the man was slumped over in his seat.

"Oh, Nifflheim," Penrosa said under his breath. The lift was ten feet above ground and still rising up. For lack of a better alternative, Pen jumped to the ground where he landed on something that yeeked once and went silent. Bruised, but not broken, Penrosa rolled over and saw that he had crushed a Fuzzy as he'd landed. Penrosa liked Fuzzies, at least in the abstract as he had never adopted one, and felt bad about it. Then he became worried that he could be charged for manslaughter, again.

As Pen stood up, he noticed that the Fuzzy had been armed with a bow instead of the usual killing club they favored. Then he noticed the arrow sticking out of the lift operator's neck. Penrosa, while not the sharpest pencil in the drawer, quickly put two and two together. Looking around, he noticed other Fuzzies, similarly armed, firing arrows in every direction.

The guards, armed with sono-stunners and zap-sticks, fired at random at the attackers while trying to herd the inmates towards the Quonset huts that acted as their barracks. Penrosa made a snap decision and dived back into the crater. There were too many Fuzzies between himself and the barracks and he knew that he presented a very large target.

Scrambling as fast as his considerable bulk would allow, he made for the far end of the crater and hid behind the laser drill machine. The drill was powered down and could only be activated with the magnetic key held by one of the guards. This was a security measure in case one of the inmates wanted to try something cute. That was fine with Penrosa as he was looking for a place to hide, not a weapon to use.

Peeking around the side of the drill housing Pen could see three Fuzzies at the far edge of the crater's rim. One was pointing at him. Well, Pen thought, this is it. The three Fuzzies notched arrows and let fly, all of which missed and either bounced off the drill housing or skewered the ground. Before they could try again, the trio was downed by sono-stunners.

It was several minutes before Pen felt safe enough to leave the protection of the laser drill. By the time he climbed out of the crater, the fighting was over. Bodies in yellow jumpsuits with arrows protruding from them littered the ground side-by-side next to Fuzzy bodies with blood coming from their ears. Penrosa took a moment to be glad he was alive before he lost his lunch.

* * * * * * * * *

Anthony Nicholovich Anderson and Duncan "Ripper" Rippolone sat down at the table across from Leslie Coombes and Douglas Toyoshi, the defense attorney of record. Toyoshi, who had been appointed to defend Leo Thaxter, Conrad and Rose Evins and Phil Novaes two years earlier, had been tapped again to defend Anderson and Rippolone.

"Gentlemen, I strongly urge you to cooperate," Coombes said. He had been singing the same tune over and over for the last two months. "Mr. Toyoshi has offered a plea bargain that would keep you from facing the death penalty. Given that you were caught red-handed with your victim you will not do well at trial."

"I can get you twenty years, no hard labor and a ticket off-planet when your time is up. There is simply no better deal to be had, here or on any other planet," Toyoshi explained. "But you will have to name names."

"We name anybody we'll be dead in a year, tops," Rippolone growled.

"That is a year longer than you will have if this goes to trial," Coombes said calmly. "Personally, I would like to go to court, win the conviction and add your executions to my resume. It gives me a strong bargaining position the next time I request a raise. Still, getting your higher-ups would look almost as good for me. We can put you in protective lock-down during your stay at Prison House, if you like."

"That would be little better than solitary confinement for twenty years, Mr. Coombes," Anderson said.

"I believe it was Leo Thaxter who once said, 'you're dead a whole lot longer.'" Coombes leaned back and shook his head. "Gentleman, from your own point of view, you are damned if you do and damned if you don't. Why not take the route that preserves your life for the longest amount of time?"

"And maybe a few privileges while they are incarcerated?" Toyoshi asked. "Twenty years in protected custody is a very long time."

Coombes rubbed his chin. "Like what?"

"Personal video feed, they get to be housed together, conjugal visits...."

"The justice system of Zarathustra does not provide...certain services."

"Prisoners often become the target of the amorous attentions of certain women," countered Toyoshi casually. "Should such persons choose my clients...." He let the sentence hang unfinished.

"I would have to check with the chief prosecutor, but I think we can accommodate you."

Anderson nodded. "In that case, I think we can work with you."

Rippolone sputtered and shouted at his partner. "Tony, we can't sell out the...you know."

"Or they'll kill us? The line starts behind Mr. Coombes, Ripper. We very literally have nothing to lose and possibly our lives to gain. However, I will add one more proviso for our testimonies."

Coombes leaned forward. "And that is?"

"The possibility of parole."

Coombes drummed his fingers on the table as he thought it over.

"There is a problem with that. A parolee cannot leave the planet. You would be trapped here until you completed your sentence. One slip-up, no matter how minor and you would be back in Prison House."

"As opposed to staying there the entire twenty?"

Toyoshi nodded. "Good point. Do you think you could sell it, Mr. Coombes?"

Coombes stood up and said he would be back in a few minutes. Outside the secure room he met up with Gus Brannhard. "You heard?"

"Yes. Do it."

"Really? I would have thought...."

"I don't blame the gun when it shoots me. I blame the son-of-a-Khooghra who pulled the trigger. These two are the gun. I want the bastard who pulled their trigger." Gus looked through the one-way glass at the defendants. "Get everything you can out of them. Give them what they asked for and throw in an extra-large pizza every Saturday night, if you have to."

Coombes nodded and returned to the room.

* * * * * * * * *

Ask any cop what the worst part of the job is, they will tell you it is not the shoot-outs, which are extremely infrequent despite what is portrayed in police dramas, nor is it the occasional physical altercation that is also an uncommon occurrence. Any cop, anywhere, on any planet will say the same thing—stakeouts.

It was officers Gilbert and Sullivan's shift to watch the cabin in the hopes that Leo Thaxter would show up. Prior to landing on Zarathustra the two men had never met. Ray Gilbert was from Agni, and had the dark skin to prove it, while Thomas Sullivan came in from Odin. When the two men joined the Mallorysport police force the chief, Piet Dumont at that time, took one look at their names and proclaimed them partners.

Fortunately, the two men worked well together and made a good team. Each was the other's best man at their weddings and both worked to keep each other out of trouble. They went hunting together, bought neighboring houses and their families vacationed together on occasion. They even adopted Fuzzies at the same time.

The two men had been on shift for forty-three minutes when Gilbert noticed camera three showed an aircar landing in front of the suspect cabin. He adjusted the camera settings to pan in on the vehicle operator as he stepped out.

"Does that look like Thaxter to you, Thom?"

Sullivan scrutinized the man's face and sighed. "Not even a little bit. Hair color is wrong, face is wrong…" He twisted a knob and the next screen showed a read-out on it. "…and according to this he's two inches taller than Thaxter."

Gilbert grunted in affirmation then said, "He could be wearing a synthmask, wig and shoe lifts."

Sullivan agreed. "Let's call the Marshal and see what he thinks we should do. Personally, I'd like to roust this guy just to break the monotony."

"Brother, you said it!" Gilbert opened a secure channel and called Marshal Fane. Fane wasn't at his office, but his receiver was programmed to automatically forward any secure calls. The Marshal's face appeared on the small screen on the control column. "Marshal, we have an unidentified male approaching the suspect residence."

"Did you run a check on the computer to see if he has a record?"

Gilbert inwardly winced. He should have done that before calling the boss. He glanced at Sullivan who gave the thumbs down signal. "None, sir. You want us to go have a friendly chat with this guy and see what he knows?"

"No, better not. If it is Thaxter in a synthmask, we need a warrant to yank it off of him, which means we need proof first. If it isn't ol' Leo, then this guy might be working for him, and since we have nothing on him to detain him with, he would just toddle off and warn his boss. Sorry, boys, you'll just have to sit still for a while longer. Make sure to make a visual recording of everything this guy does, though."

"Roger, Marshal."

Max screened off and Gilbert reached for the self-heating thermos for more coffee. "Guess we're still stuck here, Thom."

Sullivan shrugged. "At least now we have something to watch besides an empty cabin. Oh, Nifflheim. We forgot to run the aircar. Maybe we can get a name on who sold it to whom."

"Can we get the registration plate from this angle?"

Sullivan flipped through the different camera feeds on the screen. "Damn. I can only get a partial. Z972—that's all I can get."

"Z972." Gilbert ran the partial. "The 972 range of numbers just started about three months ago. I see a couple dozen maybes here. Eric Shepherd, John Holloway, Brandon Murdock, Samuel Hitoshi, Ricardo La Rue—"

"Wait. John Holloway? Isn't that Jack Holloway's kid? The one he had a duel with?"

"Yup. Cost me a C-note in the betting pool. I thought Jack was going to drop him before the kid cleared his holster."

"Never count on a man killing his own son, even in a duel," Sullivan grunted. "We can rule him out, at least. Who else we got?"

Gilbert ran through several more names until one stuck out like a damnthing in a veldbeest herd. "Clancy Slade."

Sullivan leaned over to double-check the name. "Oh, we gotta call the Marshal back."

* * * * * * * * *

Leo Thaxter emptied the contents of his aircar onto a small contragravity platform and hauled it into the cabin. It had taken several trips to get everything out of the vault and into the aircar at the B.I.N. building, and the deposit boxes were in a single unit. A very heavy single unit. Thaxter had been forced to sneak back into the B.I.N. hallways in search of a maintenance closet where he found, and appropriated, the contragravity platform.

While Ivan Bowlby had been generous enough to give Thaxter access to the vault, he failed to provide the keys to the safety boxes. Thaxter didn't mind so much. He bought a portable laser drill and a few other tools on the way home.

Once inside the cabin, he peeled off the synthmask and dropped it on the bar along with the wig. He wiped his face with a napkin from the bar before sitting down and removing his shoes. The lifts inside of them made his arches hurt as though he were walking on his toes. After he rubbed his feet for a few minutes, Thaxter got up, poured himself a tall whiskey, neat, and drained half of it in a single gulp. Next, he tapped a hidden button at the base of the bar with the side of his foot. The bar slid back to reveal a hollowed-out section of the floor. Thaxter discovered the hidey-hole shortly after purchasing the cabin while doing a sweep for bugs or cameras. He wondered who had put it there and why, but not enough to find out.

Thaxter tossed in the stacks of cash he collected from Bowlby's vault before he went to work on the safety boxes with the laser drill. The drill made short work of the locks and Thaxter inspected each one in turn. A few held sunstones, which came as no surprise to Thaxter. The next held diamonds, some had single-ounce medallions of gold and silver. The rest held various illicit drugs; cocaine, opium, heroin, Thoran *klinscha*, a powerful aphrodisiac and finally dried zarashrooms, a local fungoid that, when ingested, acted like a hallucinogenic.

Thaxter shook his head. Bowlby used way to much of his own product, he thought. Thaxter collected the drugs and threw them into the M/C converter along with the now empty safety boxes. The gems and precious metals he placed in a small duffle bag and stuffed it into the hiding place.

After the bar slid back into place, Thaxter went to his computer and checked the security footage. The primary files showed that the cabin was undisturbed while he was out, except for a 0.5 second glitch in the time code. Suspicious, Thaxter went into the hidden back-up security archive. He set the back-up in case somebody did get in and Khooghra with the primary file. This time he saw a bunch of men going through his home and computer.

Thaxter broke out in a cold sweat. *They know I'm here on Zarathustra*, he thought. His first impulse was to get the Nifflheim out of the cabin and run. He checked the impulse. Thaxter spent a lot of years as a free man by thinking things through before acting. That the men in the security feed were cops was not in doubt; he could spot a plainclothes cop a light-year away. The feed showed no cameras being planted inside the cabin. No doubt some were planted outside, but when he came home he was still wearing his disguise, so even if the cops did see him enter, they had no cause to come busting in. The fact that nobody had come in already since he came home supported his theory. From now on every time he went out, he would have to wear the synthmask, at least until he could be sure he gave the police the slip.

Now how did they find out I was still on-planet, and locate this cabin? He put that aside. It was time to move things forward. First, kill Dane and Murdock. Second, get facial reconstruction. Third, get the Nifflheim out of Dodge.

Thaxter was distracted by a beeping sound from his computer. The relay he planted back at B.I.N. had finished performing its function of transmitting all of Bowlby's security footage to Thaxter's computer. Thaxter knew there were cops outside, somewhere, looking for an excuse to come in and that made him want to get out. Instead, he sat down and sped through the video file to the day Bowlby died in his office.

Thaxter was mildly surprised that Bowlby would keep a recording of his own activities. Then again, he did run a prostitution ring and was known for sampling his own products. No doubt he kept a library of his 'conquests' somewhere. Plus, a record of his dealings with others made for pretty good insurance should they decide to double-cross him and rat him out later.

The feed ran through the events of Bowlby's day. As Thaxter suspected, he entertained a few of his call girls in the office. Thaxter sped through that part. Adult films were one thing; Bowlby's chubby self in his birthday suit was quite another.

Thaxter stopped the forward motion when he caught a glimpse of something. He backed the feed up until he found what he was looking for. Ivan Dane and Brandon Murdock entered Bowlby's office.

The feed had a soundtrack, but Thaxter didn't need it to know what was going on. The two men were telling Bowlby that they were taking over and Bowlby wouldn't play ball. There was some back and forth until finally Murdock grabbed Bowlby and forced him back against the wall. Dane walked over to the helpless man, pushed up a sleeve and jammed a needle into his arm. Murdock released his burden and Bowlby fell forward onto his desk.

When Bowlby stopped moving, Murdock set the body into the chair while Dane staged the scene to look like an overdose. Dane rolled up Bowlby's sleeve, tied it off and placed the needle carefully into the same puncture hole he made before. Since Bowlby was known for using his own merchandise nobody would bat an eye when they found his corpse.

"Oh, Christ! Bowlby, you poor dumb bastard." Thaxter sighed, then put on a sad smile when he thought about Bowlby's earlier *guests*. "At least you had a last roll in the hay, pal."

On the screen Dane and Murdock went through Bowlby's desk and file cabinet looking for something, which they apparently failed to find, then they wiped down everything they had touched and sprayed the room with some sort of aerosol. *A DNA degrading agent, most likely*, Thaxter surmised.

Thaxter planned on looking over some more of the video-feed later. For now he had to make plans. A new hideout, a little premeditated murder, a new face, a ticket off-planet: It was going to be a Nifflheim of a good-bye party.

* * * * * * * * *

"Marshal Fane, with all due respect," said the incredulous Officer Gilbert, "Are you out of your freakin' mind?"

Ordinarily, Colonial Marshal Max Fane would not take that kind of insubordination. Neither in person nor over the viewscreen. In this case, however, he understood the sentiments behind it.

"I wish I was, Ray, because then I would be able to disregard orders and go with my gut, which is telling me the same thing yours is telling you. I was even ready to go so far as to ask the real Clancy Slade to file a missing vehicle report so that we would have probable cause to roust the driver."

Max lowered his head and shook it. "Mr. Brannhard said the risk of it blowing up in our faces was too big. We can only stretch a legal fiction so far. Sorry, guys, but you'll just have to keep watching the cabin through the cameras. But if that guy comes out and goes for a joyride, I want you tail-grabbing his ass wherever he goes. Get him on a moving violation if you can."

"Yes, sir, Marshal," Gilbert said. The screen went dark.

"You know," Sullivan said, "people shouldn't leave their aircars outside like that. Something might happen to it. Graffiti, bird droppings, vandalism...."

"...tracking devices," finished Gilbert, catching on. "Whose turn is it to violate some suspect's civil rights?"

"Flip you for it," said Sullivan, holding up a quarter-sol coin.

It came up tails.

XXIII

"Is that everything?"

Rippolone shot back, "What? Ya want the juvie records, too?"

Anderson put a restraining hand on Rippolone's shoulder. "That is everything we know, Mr. Coombes."

"Very good." Coombes opened his briefcase and extracted some papers, which he gave to Toyoshi. "This is the plea agreement signed by the Chief Colonial Prosecutor and approved by Chief Justice Pendarvis. Please look them over and sign at the bottom. You will be transferred to Prison House and placed into protective custody first thing in the morning. Your adjoining cells have been equipped with the agreed-upon equipment; vidscreen that will only receive feeds, not call out, mini-fridge and—"

Coombes let out a small sigh as he glanced at Rippoloni, 'the pizza maker.' "You'll have to use Prison House-approved ingredients."

"Beats none at all." Rippolone accepted the proffered documents from Toyoshi and signed where the lawyer pointed. He then passed the papers to Anderson, who also signed with his free hand. The other was strapped down to a veridicator seat.

"Do you have any statements to add before we shut off the vid-feed?"

"Yeah," Rippolone said. "I want it on record that this is our last will and testament. We're dead men. You might as well put us in good suits and save the undertaker some trouble."

"Every precaution will be taken to assure your safety," Coombes said. "We might need you down the line for additional testimony."

"Fine. Now can I please get out of this damned veridicator?" Anderson asked.

Coombes nodded and an officer unstrapped the prisoner and reshackled him to the table.

"Ripper's right, you know," Anderson said. "I'll be amazed if we live past the first week."

"In general population, I would agree. But nobody has ever been murdered in protective lockdown."

The video-feed was cut off and the tech extracted the data spool and turned it over to Coombes. Coombes placed the spool into his briefcase and locked it. Before he left the building, the spool would be copied ten times and placed in as many different secure locations.

"Nobody murdered, you said," Rippolone said. "What about suicides?"

"I don't have those numbers at the moment, though I imagine there have been a few," Coombes admitted.

"Hah!" Rippolone snorted. "How do you know they weren't just staged to look that way?"

Coombes shrugged as he collected the documents. He quickly checked to make sure Anderson, Rippolone and Toyoshi all signed in the correct locations. They did. "Even security guards can be placed under veridication in the event of a suspicious death."

"Well, tell the warden to keep his veridicator dusted off," Rippolone said. "He'll be needin' it soon enough."

* * * * * * * * *

Gerd landed the aircar in his usual spot on the compound. Grego had all but chased him away from the "Fuzzy Rocket" with a shotgun declaring that the naturalist needed a break.

"Go spend some time with your family, then come back in a couple of days and tackle the job with fresher eyes," Grego had ordered.

Technically, Grego wasn't his boss, even though he was signing the checks for the duration; Ben Rainsford was. Still, Gerd decided it was a good idea and flew back to the reservation. He stepped out of his aircar and took in the scene; a sizable extension was being added to chez Holloway. Gerd noticed Jack coming out to meet him and said, "Is Morgan moving in?"

Jack took a moment to make the mental connection, then shook his head. "That's not for my son. He's building himself a small castle a little south of here. This"—Jack waved a hand at the construction—"is for my Fuzzies."

"Ah, starting to feel a little crowded." Gerd nodded. "Yeah, with my gang, I know what you mean."

"Wrong again, Gerd. This wasn't my idea. And no, Morgan isn't doing it either. Little Fuzzy came up with the idea all on his own."

Gerd started, then smiled. "Oh? So he talked you into the addition for more room?"

Jack smiled. "Not just that, he's footing most of the bill." Gerd looked confused and Jack elaborated. "Remember that lawsuit Gus filed when the Fuzzies went missing after being seized and taken to Company House?"

Gerd's face brightened. "Yeah. Gus settled out of court for, what was it, two hundred thousand sols each?"

"Plus ten thousand shares of common stock—each. I've been teaching the Fuzzies about finances with that. They each have a debit card in their names. I haven't had to pay for extee-three since."

"Yeah, I remember you putting your foot down about the government paying for the extee-three for adopted Fuzzies. 'If people adopt Fuzzies, it becomes their responsibility to feed and care for them, not the government's. Ruth and I agreed with that, partly because the same was true of human orphans."

"Damn straight," Jack said, nodding. "But if the Fuzzies have money of their own, there's no reason they can't pay their own way. Not all of them have money like my family, of course, but they can use barter; goofer skins, crafts, that sort of thing, or even an exchange of services: Fuzzies do a great job of cleaning out land-prawns and other vermin, you know. And they can be taught some economics. Little Fuzzy has a better grasp of finances than most teenagers I've known."

"Right, I've sat in on some of the classes he teaches the other Fuzzies. He uses fruit and land-prawns for the medium of exchange so that the others can grasp the concepts. What does that have to do with the addition to your home?"

Jack pointed at the cabin. "Little Fuzzy realized that Fuzzies in the villages have their own rooms and everything, and decided he and his family should do the same. Nevertheless, he didn't want to move out. So, he came to me and asked for permission to add some rooms. When I told him I would have to check my budget, he said,"—Jack raised his voice as high as it could go, which was around a middle tenor—"Pappy Jack not need budget. Little Fuzzy pay. And Mike and Mitzi and....'" Jack trailed off and let his voice return to normal. "Well, you get the idea. I decided to let him do it, provided he go through Pappy Vic. I didn't want him being taken advantage of. I told Victor not to cut him any slack on the price, either. They have to understand the cost of things in the Federation."

Gerd eyed the framework of the addition. "It seems a bit large for just the Fuzzies."

Jack nodded. "It is. I kicked in for a couple more guest rooms and to have the living room expanded. When I built the cabin after I first acquired the land grant it was with an eye towards my personal comfort. I never expected to be swarmed with guests and live-ins. Gus or Ben would occasionally come out and crash in the spare room, which I had originally planned on making into a storage area, or some of the local cops and prospectors would get together for a floating card game here, but I'd never needed any more room than I already had. Now I have a whole tribe of Fuzzies living with me, Akira and Lolita staying here, and a lot more overnight guests than I ever expected. Time to upgrade the habitat. Besides, I'll need a place to put the maid and cook for a while."

"Maid? And cook?"

"Blame Morgan for that. He figures his Blood Oath requires somebody do the domestic chores while I recuperate. Once I get a clean bill of health, though, out they go."

Gerd shifted the topic back to the construction work. "Why are you going with dura-plas instead of wood?"

"Actually, the frame and interior of the entire cabin is dura-plas. The wood exterior is just a façade. I expect this place to last long after I am gone." Jack chuckled. "Maybe it'll become the ancestral home of Little Fuzzy's descendants."

Gerd nodded. Dura-plas was cheap as building materials went, but strong and long-lasting. The wood exterior would rot away and be replaced oomphty-dozen times before the D-P would start to deteriorate, and for insulation it had almost everything short of solid collapsium beat. The Company made Quonset huts out of the same material. "What are you going to do with the Quonset huts you just bought?"

"Storage for one." Jack jerked a thumb at his workshed. "I'll finally be able to clear out the shed and use it for my other projects as it was intended for. The second is a permanent gym for the staff and the Fuzzies. I'll use that to get myself back into shape, too. The other I'll keep for emergencies, like guest overflow." Jack shook his head. "I never expected to play host to so many people, though I don't mind as much as I thought I would. I spent a lot of years living alone out here. It's nice to be part of the human race, again. And the Fuzzy race, too, for that matter."

The two men fell silent for a moment as they looked over the construction. Gerd spoke first.

"Wait…Morgan is building a castle?"

"Commissioner!"

Jack and Gerd turned to the sound of Akira O'Barre's voice. She was running up to them with something in her hand.

"Commissioner?" Gerd said. "I thought you hated titles."

"I think she's an army brat," Jack said. "She refuses to call me anything but 'commissioner' or 'sir' now that she works for me. Yes, Akira?"

"You forgot your radio, sir," Akira said as she tried to catch her breath. She had run all the way from the office building. "Major Lunt needs to speak with you. He said it's urgent."

George Lunt was not prone to overstatement. Jack grabbed the radio. "George, what's up?"

"Hell's come to breakfast, Jack. The Fuzzies are revolting," George said from the radio. "They attacked the workers at the dig site."

Jack couldn't believe his ears though he trusted the major implicitly. "Are there any casualties?"

"Yes, sir." George tended to get all regulation and formal in a crisis. "Twenty-three inmates dead, six wounded, two prison guards dead, one wounded. The civilians were all safe indoors doing whatever it is they were doing at the time of the attack."

"What about the attackers? The Fuzzies?"

"Thirty dead," George replied. "No way to count their wounded as they were hauled away by the other Fuzzies. No man left behind is their philosophy, I would guess. The guards only had their sono-stunners on them; regulations forbid lethal weaponry near the inmates in case one of them makes a grab for it. But the Fuzzies couldn't survive a direct hit. It's horrible, Jack. It looks like their brains were trying to escape through their ears."

"Good God," Jack said, almost in a whisper. "Any idea what provoked the attack?"

"None. I've never heard of any Fuzzy attacking a human outside of Goldilocks cutting Leonard Kellogg with her chopper-digger, and Kellogg kicked her first, I understand. For Fuzzies to attack a group of humans, well, you know much more than I do about Fuzzy behavior."

True, but not that much. Fuzzies typically ran away from threats if they could. Not much other choice given their small stature and limited defenses. These Northern Fuzzies were somehow different; they didn't just run away. They fought back. Maybe the attack had something to do with the explosion in that area two months earlier.

"What kind of weapons did they use?" Gerd asked. It was a damned good question. Jack relayed it to George.

"According to the survivors, bows, arrows, atlatl spears and slings. All ranged weapons. These Fuzzies knew better than to get in close with a human. I think they've had unpleasant encounters with our kind before. Nothing else would explain this unprovoked hostility. As for the arrows and spears, they must have some sort of toxin on them. Several cons were hit in places not immediately fatal, but died anyway. These are some very smart, very dangerous Fuzzies. Bigger than our crowd, too."

"Bigger?" Gerd asked for elaboration.

"Nothing outrageous like Gus Brannhard." The weak attempt at a joke fell flat. "I've been looking over the dead ones. They run two to four inches taller than what we've seen up until now, and heavier, too. I haven't weighed them, of course…."

But a cop is good at estimating the height and weight of a suspect, Jack thought. "I'm coming up there, George. Expect me tomorrow around noon."

The Major made a halfhearted attempt to talk Jack out of it, but knew better. Nobody ever got anywhere trying to talk Jack Holloway out of doing something he thought he needed to do. George signed off and Jack headed straight for the workshed. Gerd and Akira followed.

Jack rooted around in the shed until he found a six foot length of pipe. "Damn, I don't have anything long enough."

"What do you need?" Gerd asked.

Jack went back to looking around and said, "I need to make a human sized chopper-digger."

"What? What for…?"

"Maybe I can get one for you," Akira said.

Jack turned to the woman. "Does Victor Grego keep those around, now?"

"Oh, not that I know of, but I know a guy who dresses up as a giant Fuzzy for the Fuzzycons…."

A year or so back Gus Brannhard had made an offhand remark that Zarathustra should host a Fuzzy Convention. While he may have meant it as a joke, Victor Grego ran with it. He invited non-company vendors and used an empty warehouse to throw it in. Jack and Little Fuzzy were paid to give speeches and show movies from the earliest days of the Fuzzy discovery. Many of the humans dressed up like giant Fuzzies, except for Gus who was pretty fuzzy already, and brought homemade chopper-diggers to scale. One enterprising young man made a contra-gravity surfboard into a giant mechanical land-prawn and stuffed it with various cooked meats. He made quite a show of killing and eating it. The real Fuzzies were very excited about the whole thing and only a little disappointed to learn that under all the fur was just another normal Big One.

"Can you get him out here by tonight?" Jack asked.

"Oh, sure, I think he's a little sweet on me, but you'll have to contact his boss and let him know that you need him. Terrence works in Fabrications on third level. Terrence Vlosopolos is his full name."

Jack started towards his cabin. "It'll be quicker and easier to talk to his boss's boss. That way there won't be any arguments. I'll call Victor from the cabin; you call your friend from the office." Jack had a sudden inspiration. "In fact, tell Mr. Vloa—, Mr. Vlosa—, tell Terrence to bring his Fuzzy costume, too. More than one if he can."

Akira hotfooted it back to the office building as Jack trotted over to his cabin. Gerd was left standing scratching his head. Fuzzy costumes?

XXIV

"Mr. Grego, could I take a moment of your time?"

Grego turned and found himself facing an empty hallway, until he adjusted his vision downward. There stood Dr. Ang Ling Geronimo. Dr. Geronimo stood a scant four feet six inches, making him rather easy to overlook, but his martial arts skills were near-legendary on Zarathustra. In competitions sponsored by the Company, Dr. Geronimo held the world championship five years running; defeating opponents almost three times his size. Current rumor had it that if Geronimo entered in the next competition, everybody else would just bow out. Fortunately, he was as good at his job as he was on the mat.

"Dr. Geronimo." Grego correctly pronounced the name with the 'H' sound rather than the 'J' sound most people used. He firmly believed that taking the time to learn an employee's proper name showed he respected them as people and not just as corporate drones. "What can I do for you?"

"Sir, I have found an anomaly with recent sunstone purchases," the doctor explained. Dr. Geronimo was in charge of inspecting new sunstones from Yellowsand and independent prospectors as well as geological samples.

"Counterfeits?" Fake sunstones were a common problem, though none had escaped detection, as yet. Some were duds coated in fluorescent dye or hollowed out with a mini-light inserted; the schemes were as varied as they were numerous.

"If so, these are the best I have ever seen. I can't be sure, yet." Dr. Geronimo extracted a handful of glowing pebbles from his lab coat pocket. "See for yourself, sir."

Grego accepted the stones and inspected them closely. He shook one, sniffed another and even took out an old-fashioned Boy Scout knife from his pocket and tried to scratch it. As expected, the knife left no mark. Sunstones were at least as hard as Terran diamonds. It took a laser to cut, hollow out or remove rough edges from one.

"I'm not the expert you are, Doctor," Grego admitted. "What is wrong with these? They seem perfectly legitimate to me."

"To me, as well," Geronimo admitted. "It wasn't until I prepared to give them the gamma treatment that I noticed something was wrong."

"Gamma treatment?"

Dr. Geronimo explained that all gems and goods marked for export to other planets were typically exposed to a brief gamma bath to destroy potentially harmful bacteria. Innocuous bacteria on one planet could become a lethal plague on another world. German measles, little more than an annoyance to humans from Terra, had killed hundreds on Freya with shocking ease. The gamma rays destroyed all bacteria and microbes and left no residual radiation in food and non-edibles. When Grego thought about it, he recalled that he signed off on the procedure over a decade earlier. "Right, now I recall. So what happened?"

"Actually, these have not yet been exposed, which is even more curious given that they are mildly radioactive."

"What?" Grego almost dropped the stones, then checked himself. Dr. Geronimo would hardly have blithely toted them about in his pocket, and then handed them to his boss if the stones were dangerous. "Please elaborate in terms a simple businessman can understand."

"If I were to guess, I would say that these sunstones had been subjected to a previous radiation bath, likely dirty-gamma, before they were sold to the gem buyers."

"Dirty-gamma?"

"A gamma bath with another radioactive impurity present. This crops up every so often in defective gamma ray emitters." Geronimo noticed the blank look on his employer's face and elaborated. "A gamma ray is a packet of electromagnetic energy, a photon in layman terms. Gamma photons are the most energetic photons in the electromagnetic spectrum. Gamma photons, or gamma rays, if you prefer, are emitted from the nucleus of some unstable, that is to say radioactive, atoms. Gamma radiation emission occurs when the nucleus of a radioactive atom has too much energy. It often follows the emission of a beta particle. When a neutron transforms to a proton and a beta particle, as is the case in, say, Cesium-137, then over time the discharged protons change the atom to, in this example, Barium-137. Cobalt-60 or Technetium-99m could also be used, though Technetium-99m has a shorter half-life. It will first eject the beta particle, then the gamma photon to stabilize itself.

"Gamma rays travel at the speed of light and exist only as long as they have energy. Once their energy is spent, whether in air or in solid materials, they cease to exist, which is why it is so strange that these stones are even mildly radioactive. Whatever machine was used to irradiate these stones failed to adequately filter out, um, beta particles from the radio stream or maybe the same machine is also being used for alpha rays or X-rays, in which case it also uses either bismuth-210 or boron-11. Then it is possible the shielding in the emitter has degraded, most likely from misuse, and that would contaminate the gamma emissions. I will have to run more tests to determine which scenario is more likely."

Victor Grego, a well-educated and intelligent man, failed to understand at least half of what Dr. Geronimo was saying. Rather than admit that, he switched tracks.

"Okay, it sounds like you have a firm grasp of the potential 'how', now the question is 'why?' Say, how did you catch these anyway?"

"I have a Geiger counter near my work station. I choose to generate offspring one day and take no chances with the equipment. As for the 'why,' I can't think of any reason whatsoever to subject a perfectly good sunstone to gamma bombardment beyond killing any surface microbes," Geronimo admitted.

Grego leaned against a wall and thought about it. He couldn't come up with anything, either, as he barely understood what the doctor had already elaborated on.

Then Geronimo got an idea. "Mr. Grego, it occurs to me that somebody might have been trying to make them glow brighter."

"Brighter? What's the point?" A three-karat sunstone was as bright as an old-style LED. Any brighter and it might seem overly gaudy.

Dr. Geronimo sighed. "I can't imagine. I could see somebody trying to make the non-thermofluorescent stones, that is, the duds, into sunstones, but not..."

Geronimo stopped talking and stared into space. Grego began to worry that the doctor had a stroke or seizure when Geronimo turned to his boss with an expression that could only mean "Eureka!"

"Sir, I need to do some experiments on non-thermofluorescent stones."

Grego, no scientist, still caught on. "You think these are gamma-radiated duds?" He looked closer at the stones in his hand. They looked perfectly normal to his inexperienced eyes, which is why he hired people like Dr. Geronimo.

"Yes. But I won't be certain until I run some tests and, hopefully, duplicate the process." Geronimo held out his hand and Grego returned the stones he was holding.

Dr. Geronimo looked very excited at the possibility. Grego was considerably less so. The doctor ran off to his lab while Grego ran in the opposite direction to his office. Once there, he would call the chief gem buyer for the Company and instruct him to track down the source of every recent sunstone purchase. The possible glut on the market would be bad enough, but if any of the *faux* stones made it to the sales department, there would be Nifflheim to pay if, *when*, the fakes were discovered. There would be lawsuits, investigations, bad press and plummeting stock values. Even if the Company announced the discovery of the *faux* stones there would be finger pointing and witch hunts and a scapegoat if the actual culprits were never found. The CEO would make a prime patsy to the Home Office.

Grego returned to his office and called the gem buyers and ordered them to compile a list of sunstone outlets and track down all purchases made in the last month. It shouldn't take long to track all of the sellers; all legal purchases were rigorously logged and accounted for. Too many scams had been tried in the past for gem buyers and brokers to play fast and loose in the market.

Grego lit a cigarette and leaned back in his chair to relax for a moment. The last few months had been more than a little crazy. Morgan entering the scene, Gus Brannhard's abduction and recovery, the explosion in Northern Beta, the advent of hostilities between Fuzzies and Terrans, that damned duel between Jack and Morgan…Grego was almost nostalgic for the weeks following the Pendarvis Decision when his only worry was keeping the company afloat.

"Mr. Grego," said Myra's voice from the intercom. "Governor Rainsford on screen selection one, sir."

"Thank you, Myra." Grego turned his chair and tapped on the screen. "Ben, I hope this is a social call."

"I wish it was," Rainsford said. "I just wanted to give you heads up.

B.I.N. is hanging me in effigy over the sale of Zeta Continent. They are also going after you for selling the mining concern there."

Grego snorted. "Let me guess, the unseated lands issue, right?"

"What else? B.I.N. is harping on the lack of land to entice further colonization. They don't seem to understand that we can't maintain the tax-free status if the population grows too quickly."

"Not to mention the problems involved in expanding planetary services," Grego said. "Even the Company doesn't have unlimited resources."

"Then there's the Federation dues we would have to pay if the population exceeds twenty million human citizens," Rainsford added.

Grego sat straighter. "Wait. What is this?"

"You didn't know?" Grego admitted he didn't so Rainsford explained. "It takes a lot of money to maintain the Federation and its military. Normally, each planet kicks in a bit of its gross planetary revenues, about five to ten percent, back to the Federation to maintain it. That TFN base on Xerxes isn't cheap, you know. Well, low-population colony planets are exempt until they reach a certain population density. For Zarathustra that is twenty million people."

Grego was stunned. "How did I not know this?"

"When you owned the planet outright it didn't apply. The TFN was posted here to keep an eye on you as much as protect the planet."

"True. And when I…the Company lost the planet we weren't on the hook for the dues." Grego nodded thoughtfully. "Okay, if the population does get to that point, which of us is on the hook: you or me?"

"That would be me, Victor," Rainsford said. "Leslie made sure of that in the contract we signed. It would come out of the interest payments on the Yellowstone revenues. I am fairly certain that we would be exempted from any consideration for the planetary services since they are privatized."

How in Nifflheim did I miss that? Grego thought back and remembered that he was involved in making extee-three for the Fuzzies, developing the Fuzzy Phone with Henry Stensen, and whip-cracking Science Division to find out why the Fuzzies had such a low viable reproduction rate. His mind had been very full of Fuzzy thinking. Fortunately, Leslie Coombes watched out for the company and its CEO. Grego had left the contract work to him and just signed it when done. Of course, he trusted Leslie implicitly; still it was an unforgivable lapse on Grego's part.

"Victor? Are you all right? You spaced-out on me for a second there."

"Just thinking it was time to give Leslie a raise, Ben. Tell you what; I'll talk with Miguel Kourland and have him set something up to get that information out. We would all like to see Zarathustra grow and thrive, now we just need to get the message across that slow and steady wins the race." Grego considered letting Ben know about the possibility of counterfeit sunstones, then decided the governor had enough on his plate.

"Sounds like a plan," Rainsford agreed. "Now we need to schedule another play-date for Flora, Fauna and Diamond…."

After some more pleasantries the two men screened off, allowing Grego a moment with his thoughts. He had been wearing two hats since the CFO died in an aircar crash ten years earlier. Grego enjoyed the freedom it gave him to run the company his way without a bean counter to argue with, but maybe it was getting time to get a new chief financial officer; somebody young and sharp with a good eye for profit and a strong moral fiber. That was a rare combination. At one time Grego considered grooming his daughter back on Terra for the job, but she married her college sweetheart and took a position with the Home

Office. She had never even come to Zarathustra for a visit after college. Grego didn't blame her for that; a year out of her married life and job was a high price to pay for a not-so-quick trip to a backwater colony planet to visit her father.

A good CFO would watch out for the Company's bottom line like it was his own while keeping his hands out of the till. That meant somebody honest or at least with enough of their own money that they wouldn't be tempted. One name instantly came to mind.

* * * * * * * * *

Officers Gilbert and Sullivan, off from surveillance duty and looking for some overtime, volunteered to escort Anderson and Rippolone to Prison House. For security reasons, the collapsium-plated squad car parked inside the shielded bay at Police House remained on contra-gravity. While the reinforced flooring could easily support the tremendous weight of the vehicle, procedure required it be ready to make a quick departure should something go wrong with the prisoner transfer.

Sullivan remained at the controls while Gilbert stood outside the aircar with one hand on his weapon. The prisoners, wearing the usual shackles, also had the explosive collars used on work details. Instead of a pole, the damping signal was produced by a device in the squad car. If the prisoners were to escape, an extremely unlikely event, they would lose their heads when they moved ten meters from the vehicle. The card that would disable the collars was in the possession of Warden Redford at Prison House. Once in the prison infirmary, the two men would be scanned and X-rayed, their DNA taken and a microchip implanted into their skulls.

Anderson and Rippolone were escorted into the bay by Leslie Coombes, Douglas Toyoshi, Police Chief Frank Carr and four officers.

The prisoners were assisted into the back of the squad car behind the transparent dura-plas partition used to hold suspects while in flight.

"This squad car is completely armored and proof against anything short of a high-powered laser," Chief Carr said. "A laser big enough to do the job would be about the size of a monorail car and weigh around seven tons. Not a subtle weapon and the only one on Zarathustra is over on Zeta Continent where it is used to bore into the planet's crust for mining purposes."

"What about poisonous gas? High-ranged sonics? Atomic explosions?" Rippolone asked.

"The squad car was checked top to bottom. It has its own air supply, which has been tested. Sonics can't penetrate collapsium shielding. An atomic bomb would destroy the entire city, including the hitman. All air traffic is being diverted away from your route and nothing on the ground can get through to you. Hell, you're safer than I am."

Rippolone laughed. "I'll bet my pizza maker against your badge we never make it to Prison House."

Carr chuckled. "How would you collect? Relax, you'll be fine."

Carr gave the signal and Gilbert sealed the hatch. Sullivan lifted the vehicle and floated out the bay door. Once outside they were joined by two more squad cars. Chief Carr was taking no chances.

"Still alive back there?" Sullivan yelled. Rippolone glared through the dura-plas while Anderson ignored him.

"So far so good, guys," Gilbert said conversationally. "We'll be at Prison House in about thirty seconds. There, we'll enter a secure enclosure erected just for you. Once we sign you over to the warden you can relax in your nice new cells."

Rippolone grinned ruefully. "Ya know what, Gilbert? I like you. When they find me dead I want you to have my pizza maker. Have a thick crust double cheese with extra pepperoni on me. Really."

Anderson, who had been steadfastly silent throughout the transfer added, "You can have my vidscreen, too. No point in it going to waste."

Chief Carr's voice came over the radio. "I'll make a note of that. Now cut the chatter and let the men concentrate on their jobs."

"I can drive and listen at the same time, Chief," Sullivan replied. "These two are nervous and blowing off steam. They won't distract me for the fifteen seconds left of the trip."

"They—not or I'll—on foot—Ghu comes to Zara—"

"Chief? You're breaking up something terrible—"

"Kill the connection!" Gilbert cried out, as he scrambled for the radio controls.

He was a second too late. There was a screeching sound from the radio followed by a near-deafening explosion from the rear of the squad car. Sullivan glanced back and saw the mess through the cracked and bloody dura-plas.

"Damnit!" Sullivan added more colorful curses as he turned the radio back on.

"What just happened?" demanded Carr's voice through the speaker.

Sullivan looked over at Gilbert, then back to the front. "My partner just inherited a pizza maker, Chief."

XXV

Terrence Vlosopolos stepped out of his aircar carrying a duffle bag and three human-sized chopper-diggers. Some of the Fuzzies recognized him from the Fuzzycons and clambered about yeeking excitedly. With him were two Fuzzies he had adopted shortly after the first convention. Jack Holloway and Akira O'Barre walked out to rescue Terrence from his Fuzzy fans.

"Heyo, Pappy Jack," Terrence said in a high-pitched voice. "Hi, Akira."

"Gah! Don't you start that, now," Jack said. "Next you'll have all the humans calling me Pappy Jack. It took me forever to get them to stop calling me Fuzzy Fuzzy Holloway. I actually threatened to shoot the next person who did."

"My apologies, Commissioner," Terrence said in his normal voice, a low tenor. "I tend to get into character when surrounded by the Fuzzies. You won't need to shoot me to make your point."

"Jack will do. Relax, I was just pulling your leg." Jack looked down at the two Fuzzies with Terrence, a male and a female. "What name you?"

The male answered Flash Gordon and the female Dale Arden. Jack chuckled. "Those have got to be among the best Fuzzy names yet."

"There's a couple over in Mallorysport named John Carter and Dejah Thoris," Terrence said. "Their adoptive parents run a bookstore."

Jack nodded and pointed at the duffle bag. "Is that your costume?"

Terrence patted his bag. "You bet, Jack. I made the lining out of fibroid weave remnants I cadged from a military surplus outlet, then perma-bonded tanned goofer hides to it."

"Damn. I'm guessing it isn't 'one size fits all,' then?"

"I am afraid not. This suit will only fit me…or somebody of my height and build."

"Nifflheim! I was hoping either I or one of the NPF cops could wear it, but you're a good four inches shorter than any of them." Jack eyed Terrence up and down for a moment. "Can you fit protective armor under your suit?"

Terrence thought for a second before answering. "Only the really lightweight stuff, and then only if I strip down to my skivvies first."

"Hmm…lightweight would stop a Fuzzy-sized spear or arrow, I think. How do you feel about being taken into a hostile situation in that getup?"

Terrence was excited and nervous at the possibility. He was by no means the heroic athletic type, yet the prospect of going into a dangerous situation with Jack Holloway would do wonders for his reputation. It might also allow him a better chance with a young woman of his acquaintance.

Terrence tried to affect an attitude of nonchalance. "Sure thing, Jack. What's the gig?"

"Believe it or not, we have a small war going on up in Northern Beta between humans and Fuzzies. I am hoping you will be able to keep them from shooting at me while I get close enough to parlay with their leaders…if they have any."

Terrence considered the situation. "So I am to be your human… make that Fuzzy shield?"

The boy is smart, Jack thought. "Pretty much. I don't expect you to block any arrows, but maybe with you along the Fuzzies will be too curious or surprised to shoot any."

"And they have arrows and spears, unlike the local Fuzzies?"

Jack nodded.

"Ah, what the hell. I'll just have to hope that they will think I'm too cute to make dead."

The kid's got stones, too, thought Jack, *I hope to Ghu I don't get him killed.* "Look, your only function will be to walk out with me with your chopper-digger held up high…what's it made from, anyway?"

Terrence held one up for Jack to inspect. "This one is made of hardened aluminum. It was the prototype. The other two are poly-steel. I had to save up for a while to get them made."

"Hmm. Good job. Makes me wish I got the patent on the design. I could be making royalties. When we see the Fuzzies, put your chopper-digger down on the ground and place a foot on it. That will signal that we want to make friends."

Terrence nodded, then performed the action. "Does it matter which foot I use?"

"Not at all," Jack said. "Fuzzies are ambidextrous so they don't attach any significance to one side over the other. Good question, though. Any others?"

"Yes. Once the Fuzzies come over to talk, what do you want me to do? I am fluent in the Fuzzy language…."

"Thanks, but this crowd speaks a different language or dialect. As soon as it is safe to do so, you just get your furry backside out of there. I don't want you getting hurt. If I had a cop who could fit into your outfit, you'd be staying behind."

Terrence nodded. Getting hurt was high on his list of things to avoid. "If you don't mind my asking, why don't you just take a real Fuzzy?" Terrence made a sweeping gesture with his right hand indicating the mob running around them. "I'll bet you'd get lots of volunteers."

"First of all, I don't want any of my gang getting involved. This is an issue of human/Fuzzy relations that doesn't concern them. Next, I am trying to send the message that we are more alike than not alike. A giant Fuzzy might impress them more. Your costume was good enough to fool real Fuzzies, or at least they were too polite to say otherwise, so I am hoping it will work on the wild Fuzzies up north."

"And if it doesn't," Terrence said, "you want me to wear as much armor under the suit as I can get away with. I'm starting to wish I skipped that second veldbeest burger at lunch. Well, I brought along one other little surprise on the off-chance it would come in handy."

Terrence pulled a small device from a pocket and tapped a few buttons. Something that looked like a giant land-prawn floated out of his aircar. "I didn't fill it with meat like I did at the conventions. Still, I thought you might like to have it since I didn't know what you needed me for."

Not for the first time Jack was impressed with Terrence's ingenuity. "It might come in handy at that."

* * * * * * * * *

Ducking out on a surveillance team made for a feeling of nostalgia in Leo Thaxter. It was almost too easy. Cops were creatures of habit. Stakeout teams worked in eight hour shifts and changed shifts on a regular schedule. Thaxter waited for the usual change-over time the next morning, then slipped out in his aircar while the old team briefed the new team.

Thaxter came to a decision the night before after learning his hideout had been discovered. The odds that he would be able to make it off-world alive were about the same as learning to breathe in a vacuum. As an escaped felon odds were that there was a shoot on sight order out on him. It was standard procedure. As an escapee with a death sentence hanging over his head he would be assumed to be desperate, so no chances would be taken.

Facial reconstruction would do no good; DNA swabs would be taken of anybody buying an off-planet ticket. The synthmask would never make it past the thermal imaging scans, either. No, he would have to turn himself in and finish his time at Prison House then hope he could beat the fagany wrap when he was retried. He still had eighteen years to go on his twenty-year sentence, but death lasted a lot longer.

Fine. I'm going to have to go back in stir, but I'm going to get Dane and Murdock first. Thaxter briefly considered just handing over the vid feed files to the cops. Brannhard could certainly run with that. Still, it stuck in his craw to let the law do his work for him, and he wanted to put the bullet in the sons-of-Khooghras personally. Since there was always the possibility he might get killed first, he took a few precautions.

Once Thaxter was sure he'd lost any tail, he dropped down to a public parking zone and parked the aircar. He then peeled off the synthmask and wig, putting on dark glasses and a hat instead. The cops would be looking for the man who arrived at the cabin the night before. Some tunnel vision on their part might keep them from noticing him with his real face. The shades and hat couldn't hurt.

One good thing about a colony planet formally owned by a chartered company was the mass transit systems. The CZC liked workers to get to work on time and knew not everybody could afford an aircar, so numerous monorail systems above and below the ground allowed people to get anywhere in Mallorysport for a quarter-sol.

While possessing the same Abbot lift and drive capability that was the staple for extra-planetary transport throughout the Federation, though scaled down to the minimum possible size, the rail attachment removed any possibility of an accident through human error or any chance of theft, as well as providing the power for the craft from the city grid for its propulsion. The entire rail system was computer-operated with emergency robot support on board in the control room. It always ran on time and never missed a stop point.

Thaxter selected the aboveground transport since crime was less common there and therefore they were less likely to carry on duty cops. There were security cameras, of course, but they were easy to spot and avoid as long as one wasn't trying to accost the other passengers.

Thaxter paid his two bits and jumped on the first railcar headed for Junktown. Maybe he'd dropped his tail and maybe he hadn't. A little extra travel time and a few more quarter-sols to jump back and forth around the city was worth the peace of mind.

* * * * * * * * *

Clancy Slade had just finished his shift and was anxious to get home. He had stayed after his shift to get the weekly pep-talk from Major Lansky. It was the usual review for new hires on probation. It was a good review. Lansky didn't even say anything about his punching a co-worker the week before. Apparently he accepted the philosophy that some issues among the men were best settled by themselves.

Clancy paid his two bits and hopped on the railcar headed to Junktown. In another month he would be able to afford the down payment on a cabin outside of the city. He wanted to use his earnings from his job rather than dip into the twenty-five thousand sols he had stashed. Failing to keep a financial cushion was one of the reasons he had to leave Gimli in search of work on a new planet; he hadn't had the resources to hold out until the Chartered Gimli Company started hiring back the laid-off workers.

Clancy took his usual seat and opened his newspaper. One thing he liked about living on a young colony planet was printed news. He didn't like carrying a comp-tablet and scrolling through the feeds to find what he was looking for. Better to have the real thing in tangible form.

Clancy was flipping to the sports page when something caught his eye: a man two seats up across the aisle wearing a hat and dark glasses. It took a moment for it to click, but the man had a red beard just like his own and was roughly the same build, but it was his ears that caught Clancy's attention. Two months earlier he was forced to undergo mild cosmetic surgery to make his own ears look just like that. It was still a sensitive matter to Clancy and he had vowed to have the work reversed when he had the time.

Mixed emotions of fear and anger warred in Clancy's head. Only one man could own those ears. The hat and shades made for a thin disguise though the beard helped. It was Thaxter. It had to be. Clancy kept his paper up with one hand as he pulled out his own sunglasses and put them on. He had his own hat on and had left his uniform at work where it would be cleaned by the company launderer. He still carried his pistol, though. After the scare he and his family got when the police came to his house he decided to be ready in case somebody less friendly came by. Even his wife agreed.

Okay, he thought, maybe it was Thaxter and maybe it was somebody with the same ears. Clancy decided to follow the man until he was sure one way or the other.

* * * * * * * * *

Piet Dumont hated to admit it but in his heart he was a beat cop. He was a good one, which was how he rose to his previous position of Police Chief. Unfortunately, once he was trapped behind a desk he felt lost and foundered even though he still managed to get out into the field now and then. His new promotion to inspector reaffirmed his sense of self-worth, yet he started to feel trapped by it. Inspectors got out to investigate a crime after it had happened. Beat cops were in a position to stop a crime in progress or prevent it altogether.

To keep himself from falling into the same trap he had when he was Police Chief, Piet decided to walk to work and be on the lookout for anything amiss on the way. Local shop owners and vendors recognized him and occasionally gave him tips on what was what in the neighborhood. Depending on the tip, he would either call for a squad car or just handle it himself.

Shoplifting, while rare, still happened. Usually by kids too young or too stupid to realize that store security cameras watched their every move. Piet had rattled the cages of a couple of youths the day before. After scaring them with blood-chilling tales of life in Prison House, most of them exaggerated, he sent them home with a stern warning.

On this particular morning Piet's route took him by the B.I.N. building. He hated the B.I.N. news. It tended to go for sensationalism rather than facts. Any cop worth his badge wanted facts, not rumor and innuendo. There was a crowd of people with electronic clipboards harassing pedestrians for signatures to get the governor recalled. Piet made a mental note to track down the names on the petition should the recall initiative pass; he suspected more than a few may have come from the local cemetery. Old Chicago politics still cropped up now and then, especially on colony planets where the government was new and inexperienced with that kind of thing.

Piet shook his head as one petitioner approached him. She took the hint and backed off in search of other prey. Piet started to move on when he spotted what was known in his line of work as a suspicious character. The man was big and burly-looking, which was far from uncommon on a colony world, but there was something about him that screamed 'thug.' His hat was pulled down and he wore Agni-specs, sunglasses designed to protect the wearer from the harsh glare of the Agni sun, which were overkill on Zarathustra with its K0 class star.

Piet extracted his mini-comp tablet and acted like he was studying something on it as he angled it up enough to capture the man on the digi-cam. Once he secured the image, Piet accessed the police computer through the ether. The immigration photo of one Brandon Murdock, taken two months earlier, came up on the screen. He was currently listed as the head of security for B.I.N.

"Yeah, right," Piet said to himself. He suspected a more thorough search would dredge up a criminal record of some kind. Still, even ex-cons could get legitimate work once they served their time.

Piet was about to move on when another man came over to talk to Murdock. This time there was no need to check police records as Piet recognized him; Whitey Harkins, low-level muscle formerly in the employ of one Raul Laporte. Now this was interesting. Piet decided to take a seat on a bench and watch things for a while. He called in that he would be late and bought a newspaper. Checking the paper only to make certain it was right-side up; Piet then ignored the print and peered over the top to watch Murdock and Whitey. Making sure to flip a page now and then, Piet continued his surveillance. If something should break, he had his mini-comp ready to send a distress signal to the police.

* * * * * * * * *

Chief Carr fumed as the lab techs went over the squad car. Two prisoners were lost on his watch and he couldn't even blame the officers doing the transfer. Or rather, he could, but he didn't run things that way. No scapegoats in his jurisdiction. Just the real Khooghras responsible. He already put a team at the Mallorysport-Darius Spaceport with portable veridicators to screen everybody buying an off-world ticket.

What had happened was as unique as it was obvious. The killer managed to break into the police band and send a cancellation order to the damper field that was keeping the explosive collars dormant. Gilbert caught on almost instantly and tried to sever the connection. Good thinking, just too late to help the late Anthony Anderson and Duncan Rippolone.

"I'm sorry, Chief," Damon Lords said, one of the lab techs. "There's no way to trace the signal. According to the onboard computer, it was a wide-spectrum dispersal."

"Wide spectrum…so it was a single unit that would have affected radio signals across all the frequencies?"

"Yes, sir. I would guess that it would have covered a radius of about three hundred meters, affecting every radio in that range. No matter what frequency you were on, it would have been hit."

"Thank you, Damon. That is very useful." Carr turned away from the tech and grabbed his belt radio. "Dispatch? I want a canvass of the area around the site of the explosion for six hundred meters in every direction. Send every available man we have. We are looking for every radio subjected to interference this morning at 0942. Make a grid map of the results. Yesterday!"

Maybe the hitman wasn't as slick as he thought he was.

XXVI

As soon as he had his supplies and props loaded, Jack hustled Terrence into the aircar and took off for Northern Beta. He wanted to get away before Gerd knew what he was up to. It also meant dodging Morgan. The Blood Oath between Morgan and Little Fuzzy would require keeping Jack out of trouble. Heading into a hostile territory, even though the hostiles were Fuzzies, simply would not have been allowed.

Well, hell, thought Jack, *I didn't agree to any of it and I'll be damned if I'll let it interfere with my job.*

Jack didn't want to admit it, but he was still a little shaky if he was too long out of his hover-chair and hated to leave it behind. All the running he did the day before hadn't done his body any favors, either. He took along his medications; Jack was too old to delude himself into thinking he didn't need them and planned on getting a lot older. He also left instructions to tell Morgan and Little Fuzzy what he was up to one hour after he was gone. By the time either of them got the message, it would be too late to interfere. Jack didn't believe in lying to people, though delaying the truth was occasionally necessary.

It took just under a Z-hour to get to the dig site. There he met with Ismet Runako, whom he had spoken with via viewscreen earlier.

"You're going to what?"

Jack expected this reaction. "I am going to go down there with Terrence Vlo…Voloso…"

"Vlosopolos," Terrence provided.

"…Right, Terrence," Jack said. "The two of us will attempt to get a dialogue going with the Fuzzies. Maybe we can avoid more bloodshed and work out a peaceful arrangement with the locals."

Ismet was dubious. "Couldn't we just gas the lot of them then deal from a position of strength?"

"I see you've been to Yggdrasil," Jack said. "These aren't Khooghras, Ismet. Fuzzies can't be won over by force. They can be very accommodating, but they also have a serious vindictive streak if you give them cause. No matter what happens with me, no hostile action will be authorized. Understand?"

"Yes, Commissioner, I do," Ismet said, nodding. "I also understand that the Governor can overrule you on this if he has to. If anything happens to you, I will call my boss, who will call his boss, who in turn will contact Mr. Grego. He, I am quite certain, will call the Governor."

I must be getting old, it used to be I could intimidate the hell out of people and get my way in situations like this. "Okay, fair enough, though I suspect Mr. Grego would take your call direct in this instance. Tell you what; as long as I am alive, assume I have the situation under control. I'll keep an open com-link and if things go to Nifflheim I'll authorize the use of sleep gas. No sono-stunners! Clear?"

"Great Ghu! After that slaughter the last time we used them, you don't have to tell me." Ismet jerked a thumb at Terrence. "What about Mr. Vlosopolos, here?"

Am I the only person on Zarathustra who can't pronounce his name? "He comes with me until after we make peaceful contact. If the damnthing droppings hit the wind generator: Do what you must to get him out alive. Clear?"

"Clear. I must insist that you both be inoculated against the poison they are using on their spears and arrows. The dose is good for twelve hours, then you can take boosters in capsule form. That is the best we can do on such short notice."

"I'm all for it," Jack agreed. Then he recalled his accommodation medicines. "Is there a drug interaction problem?"

"Oh, Nifflheim. We don't know," Ismet admitted. "It hasn't been that thoroughly tested yet."

Jack suspected that would be the case. "Then give me a self-injection ampoule and I'll use it when and if I have to. Terrence, will you be good?"

Terrence waved it off. "I'll be fine. No medical problems, here."

Terrence quickly shed his clothing, received his injection, strapped on the lightweight body armor, rated for small arms below .30 caliber, then struggled into his Fuzzy costume. Ismet looked it over appraisingly.

"You know, that outfit on a full-grown man seems vaguely familiar. I think I saw an old movie with a character that looked a lot like that. *Space Wars* or something…."

"You all set, Terrence?" Jack asked.

"Yes, Commissioner. Just one more magna-seam…there."

"Call me, Jack. Okay, let's do this."

* * * * * * * * *

It took almost an hour of switching rails and shooting back and forth across the city before Leo Thaxter was confident he hadn't been followed by the police. He thought he saw another man in dark glasses making the same switches he did, but he didn't get a good look and he stopped seeing the shades two exchanges earlier.

Thaxter stepped off the railcar at the stop closest to the B.I.N. building. From there he took a moving sidewalk to the corner of the block where he could get a good look at the entrance. There was a crowd of people with electronic clipboards accosting people for signatures as they walked by. At the top of the entryway stood Brandon Murdock in a lame attempt at a disguise with what looked like Whitey from Laporte's old crew. They just stood there watching the crowd. What was that about?

Thaxter debated just shooting Murdock and running, but he really wanted that shot at Ivan Dane. It was Dane running the show and he was the one who jammed the needle into Bowlby's arm. Instead of shooting, Thaxter took a seat on one of the benches across from the building. If Murdock was just standing outside, he was there for a reason. Thaxter decided to wait and see what it was.

* * * * * * * * *

Clancy managed to keep up with Thaxter though he knew he had been spotted. Hoping to stay on the trail without being detected, Clancy depolarized the lenses of his glasses to minimum opacity. Sometimes less was more. Next he gave a fiver to a man for his hat which was a different style and color from his own.

It worked. When Thaxter looked around for anybody following him, he didn't give Clancy a second glance. When Thaxter stepped out of the rail car and onto the moving sidewalk, Clancy followed at a discrete distance.

Clancy watched as Thaxter took in the scene at the B.I.N. building and found a seat on the bench. A woman approached Clancy for a signature and was rudely rebuffed. He was tired, anxious and in no mood to be bothered. He wanted to go home and get some sleep. Instead, he took a seat on another bench. He had gotten a close enough look at the man to know for certain it was Thaxter and wasn't about to let him out of his sight.

* * * * * * * * *

Terrence Vlosopolos did his best to act calm and relaxed as he followed Jack Holloway to the ridge, or at least as calm and relaxed as a man could be in a giant Fuzzy suit walking into a potentially hazardous situation.

"Relax, Terrence," Jack said. "In all the time I have studied Fuzzies on and off the res I never heard of one Fuzzy killing another."

"Fuzzies never killed a Big One before, either," pointed out Terrence, "Yet here we are because that very thing happened. Several times over."

"I believe these Fuzzies were provoked." Jack looked up at the ridge, then down at the ground and followed the tracks, fresh Fuzzy and days-old human, to the path leading up. Ismet had said it would be easy to find, even without the tracks. "Remember what to do if you see any Fuzzies?"

"Try hard not to scream like a little girl and faint?" Terrence chuckled. The laugh was forced. He was scared and trying not to show it. "No, wait…I stop, raise my chopper-digger with both hands, then set it on the ground and place a foot on it."

"Right," Jack said, nodding. "Save the screaming and fainting for later."

"I'll do my best."

Jack knew gallows humor when he heard it. Terrence believed chances were good he wouldn't live to see the end of the day. Jack didn't try to give him a pep talk. Most people wouldn't take the situation seriously. After all, everybody knew that Fuzzies were just cute furry little children, right? Better to have somebody along who knew how dangerous the situation was. Hopefully, Terrence would have a good story to tell his grandchildren about. If he survived. So no pep talk, but a few positive facts couldn't hurt.

"Remember, that armor under your fur is rated for .30 cal and below."

"Jack, I watched a demonstration once where an arrow went through light armor like it was made of cheese," said Terrence. "I realize that Fuzzies can't pull a two-hundred pound bow…hell, I can't either… but still…."

"I'll bet that the arrow in the demonstration was steel tipped," Jack countered. "I don't think this crowd is up to mining and smelting iron ore, then smithing it into arrow heads."

"A furry."

Jack was confused. "A furry what?"

"Not crowd of Fuzzies," Terrence said. "A furry of Fuzzies. You know; a murder of ravens, a gam of whales, a congress of demons…"

"I thought a group of demons would be a bar association," Jack quipped. It was obvious to him that Terrence was trying to keep his cool. That was smart. Jack was a little nervous himself entering a dangerous situation with somebody he barely knew and had no idea what he was capable of. "Did you just make that up? The furry thing?"

"Yup. I'm trying to keep my mind active to distract me from how scared I am. I don't have any armor on my head, you know."

"Terrence, if you weren't a little scared, I would be worried. Don't let it get to you. I have a mug back at the cabin with a line from some old 2-D western that says 'courage is being scared to death but saddling up anyway.' Hell, I'm a little scared. All I have is the fibroid weave vest under my shirt and a lot of faith. I'm counting on these Fuzzies being as reasonable as my own gang. I do like that 'furry of Fuzzies' idea, though. I think it will catch on."

"I hope we're around to find out."

Jack stopped dead in his tracks when an arrow sprouted from the ground before him. He cursed under his breath then said to Terrence, "Get your game face on. It's show time."

* * * * * * * * *

Thaxter's patience was finally rewarded. A camera crew came out of the building and set up a perimeter around the crowd at the entranceway. Moments later, Ivan Dane stepped out of the front entranceway and waved at the crowd. A number of people who had signed the petition had waited around and the crowd had steadily grown. That suited Thaxter just fine; it would be harder to fire at Dane and Murdock but easier to slip away afterwards as the crowd panicked and ran in every direction. He was less thrilled about the cameras. Still, as long as he kept his back to them, they wouldn't catch his face.

Getting up from his seat on the bench, he stepped forward into the crowd and worked his way to the front. From behind another man followed him from another bench. The second man tried to work his way through the crowd to keep up with Thaxter, but his progress was somewhat slower.

At the top of the steps Ivan Dane spread both arms wide and yelled out, "My friends! We are a mere five hundred signatures away from our goal! Soon, the illegal and corrupt government that runs this world will be brought down. The Yellowstand agreement can then be broken and free land will be available to all."

* * * * * * * * *

Piet Dumont was disgusted. Free land was a myth; one way or another you paid for it. This mob clearly lacked the mental wherewithal to realize that with the Yellowsand agreement gone, taxation would have to be implemented. Taxes on food, goods, personal income and, yes, on the land itself. That wasn't 'free' by any stretch.

Piet was about to give up on his surveillance and get to work when he noticed a man with dark glasses and hat working his way into the crowd. Almost on the first man's heels came a second that looked very familiar though too far away to be sure. Something was off kilter. Piet couldn't pin it down but his gut said to stick around. A good cop always went with his gut.

Piet stood up and moved forward to the crowd. He wanted a better look at the two men. To be safe, he called in for back-up to set in at a discrete distance from the gathering; close enough to get in quick, far enough away to stay out of sight.

* * * * * * * * *

Six Fuzzies stepped out from behind trees and bushes. Each held his bow at the ready. Jack made a small gesture with his hand and Terrence stepped forward, chopper-digger held high above him. He laid it down on the ground before him, then stood up straight and placed his right foot on top of it. Jack, also carrying a chopper-digger, did the same.

The Fuzzies looked confused as they lowered their weapons. Jack wasn't sure if it was because a Big One acted like a Fuzzy, there was a giant Fuzzy with the Big One, or if these northern Fuzzies had a different way of showing they wanted to make friends. Jack hoped like hell it wasn't that last possibility.

The Fuzzies spoke amongst themselves for a moment, then one of them scampered off. Jack assumed it was to get the Fuzzy equivalent of the guard captain. The remaining Fuzzies kept a wary eye on Jack and Terrence while they waited. They were especially interested in Terrence, though whether they could tell he was wearing a costume or not remained a mystery.

"They seem impressed with you, Terrence," Jack said in a low voice.

"I'm pretty damned impressed with them, too, Jack," Terrence said nervously.

Jack could tell that Terrence was almost scared witless. Still, he didn't quake or sweat nor did he look as if he were about to turn and run. Jack respected that.

A group, or rather a furry of Fuzzies joined the other five and appraised Jack and Terrence. One, possibly the leader, with dark red fur stepped forward and said something in his ultrasonic voice. Neither of the two men understood what he said though Terrence had equipped his costume with an ultrasonic hearing aid. Jack muttered profanities under his breath, cursing himself for a fool in not bringing his own hearing aid.

"Did you get any of that?" Jack asked Terrence.

"I heard the words, but couldn't understand them. These guys have a much different language. Still sounds like old Terran Japanese, though." Terrence said something back in Fuzzy. The Fuzzies didn't seem to understand. "Nope, they don't understand our brand of Fuzzy, either."

One of the Fuzzies, the presumed leader, stepped forward and spoke in the human audible range. "Who you?"

"Hey, he speaks Terra Lingua!" Terrence exclaimed.

"I am Jack Holloway. This is Ter—, uh…" *Damn, I should have thought up a Fuzzy type name for him.* "Terrific Hunter."

The Fuzzy speaker nodded in an oddly human fashion. "I Red Fur. He not *Jin-f'ke*. He big-big, like you. Why you come here?"

"I want to make peace with Fu—, with *Jin-f'ke*. Stop the killing."

"Peace!" Red Fur shouted. "Big Ones kill Sun Fur. Make big hole in ground with big-big noise. Attack *Jin-f'ke* at moving water place… river! At river. Big Ones bad!"

One of the many things Jack liked about Fuzzies was the fact that they always went straight to the point. Big Ones would do well to follow their example.

"Big Ones have laws to deal with bad Big Ones." *Damn, that won't make sense to a Fuzzy.* "We make dead Big Ones that hurt Fu—, *Jin-*

f'ke."

"No. *Jin-f'ke* made dead Big Ones who hurt *Jin-f'ke!*" Red Fur yelled.

So, they were *provoked and now they were fighting back.* Jack reviewed the situation and came up with the only course of action he could think of that didn't involve gassing or killing more Fuzzies. "Very well. Red Fur, I, leader of the Big Ones, surrender."

* * * * * * * * *

Thaxter finally made his way to a point at which he could take aim and shoot. After a moment's deliberation, he decided to take out Murdock first, Whitey if he reached for a gun, then Ivan Dane. The idea was to remove those who would present the greatest danger first. That was definitely Brandon Murdock. Thaxter had plenty of opportunity to study the man after he was sprung from Prison House; the way he moved and carried himself made it clear he was accustomed to handling difficult situations. Soldiers and cops often had that same air about them.

Thaxter quickly raised his pistol and put two slugs into Murdock; one in the chest and one in the throat. Even a fibroid weave vest wouldn't stop the .45 round and the bullet in the throat, a lucky shot, clinched the deal. Whitey ducked behind a signboard while Ivan Dane stood too stunned to move.

As expected, the crowd was running in every direction to avoid being caught in the gunfire. In Federation history there is a certain progression that would almost seem to be a law of nature in gun ownership. When worlds are first colonized, it is expected that everybody carry a pistol or rifle of some sort to defend against the inimical wildlife and even more dangerous sapient denizens if there are any. As the world becomes tamed and civilized, the use and ownership of guns slowly becomes controlled, especially within the limits of large population centers. As the population increases, the need for protection against wildlife typically decreases. Laws are then passed restricting the use of firearms until finally only the military, constabulary and select individuals with special permits can carry guns.

As such, one of the allures of a new colony world was the freedom to carry sidearms. Unfortunately, this did not always come with proper instruction in their use, or sufficient experience to use them wisely. While gun ownership was a given on colony planets, firearms familiarity and training were far less common. As a result, when Leo Thaxter fired at Brandon Murdock, the crowd, instead of drawing their own weapons and shooting back, simply ran for cover.

That suited Thaxter just fine. He changed targets to Dane and pulled the trigger. As he did so, a bullet caught him in the shoulder, skewing his aim. He looked back and saw Piet Dumont holding his service pistol. Thaxter spun and ducked simultaneously and got off a shot at Piet, catching the inspector in the center of mass. The last thing he wanted to do was kill a cop; that was a guaranteed bullet in the head if caught. Cops usually wore bulletproof vests but a .45 could still get through. Even if the round failed to penetrate, the impact could break ribs and cause severe internal bleeding.

Thaxter watched in mild horror as Piet flew backwards and hit the ground. *Now I've done it. I'm a dead man who just needs to put on a good suit and lie down.* Thaxter decided he was going to take some more company with him and retargeted on Ivan Dane, who lay wounded at the top of the steps.

Before Thaxter pulled the trigger, three bullets ripped through his body from behind, spinning him around and knocking him down. He didn't need a doctor to know the hits were fatal; he could feel himself slipping away. The last thing he saw before the blackness took him was his own face staring down at him.

Clancy Slade took a moment to check Thaxter's body for a pulse and collect the dead man's gun before rushing over to help Piet. By this time a police squad car floated down to street level and spewed out four cops with sidearms drawn. Clancy, knowing how it looked with him kneeling over Piet with a face that was indistinguishable from Leo Thaxter's quickly set his and Thaxter's guns down and put his hands behind his head. He most definitely did not want to become the victim of mistaken identity.

Two policemen rushed over and covered Clancy and Piet while the other two checked on the dead and wounded. Officer Chang collected the dropped pistols and cuffed Clancy. Clancy didn't protest. It would take a DNA test or a fingerprint to prove who was who and he wasn't going to waste his breath in the meantime.

Piet, alive and conscious, though seriously wounded, was stripped of his shirt and protective vest and subjected to a field dressing to keep him from bleeding out before the ambulance could arrive. Before he passed out, he nodded weakly at Clancy.

"Good job, big guy."

XXVI

"That's right, Miss O'Barre," Ben Rainsford said through the viewscreen. "Jack surrendered and was taken prisoner by the Fuzzies. He made it clear that he didn't want any interference while he tried to negotiate a peaceful settlement, so we're not charging in with guns blazing."

"You wouldn't really do that, would you?" Like most humans, Akira had fallen in love with Fuzzies in general. The idea of them being mowed down in a military assault disturbed her almost as much as the idea of Jack being hurt by the Fuzzies. "Couldn't you just gas them?"

"As it turns out, no. Gus reminded me that Jack is still on the accommodation meds. I checked with a doctor and found out that there could be a fatal interaction if he is exposed to anesthezine gas." Rainsford leaned forward closer to the screen. "Is Morgan back from Zeta, yet?"

"He should be here any minute, Governor. I'll give him the news. It will be better coming from me, I think."

"Are you sure? I think this is really my job…."

"Yes, Governor. Morgan will be less likely to do something rash if I handle it."

Rainsford didn't look happy about it, but agreed. "Call me if you or Morgan need anything. I'll be speaking with Commodore Napier about possible tactics, so I might be out of touch for a while. I'll get back to you as fast as I can if you need me."

"Thank you, Governor. I'll keep that in mind."

Akira broke the connection and stared at the dark screen for several seconds before turning the screen back on. She punched in the code for Betty Kanazawa.

Little Fuzzy, Baby Fuzzy, Mama Fuzzy, Mike, Mitzy, Ko-ko and Cinderella wandered into the cabin for an extee-three snack and overheard Akira talking with Betty on the screen. The two women were definitely upset.

"But Jack could be killed in a firefight with those wild Fuzzies," wailed Betty from the screen.

"I doubt it will come to that, Betty. Those Fuzzies let Terrence go, after all."

"Sure, to tell the Big Ones not to mess with them or else."

Little Fuzzy listened quietly until he had a full picture, then shooed the rest back out of the cabin. Once outside, Little Fuzzy did some fast thinking. Pappy Jack was in trouble. Fuzzies had taken him prisoner. This was a strange concept to him as Fuzzies typically wanted to make friends, not pick fights. However, Big Ones could be as different as night and day from each other. Maybe his own people could be that way, too.

"Hokay, we need to go help Pappy Jack from bad Fuzzies," Little Fuzzy declared.

"How we make do?" Ko-ko asked. "Big boom place far-far."

That was true. It had taken almost a week for Little Fuzzy, Allan Quatermain, Natty Bumppo and a few others to ride up to the place where they had heard the explosion. Pappy Jack could be dead by then. And once they got there, what could less than two hands of Fuzzies do? There were supposed to be as many Fuzzies there as leaves on a featherleaf tree. They needed transportation and what the Big Ones called an army.

"Mike, Mitzy, Ko-ko, Cinderella, Mama Fuzzy and Baby Fuzzy, make run fast and get all Fuzzies and their dogs," Little Fuzzy ordered. "We make army for Pappy Jack."

"How we get to big boom place?" Cinderella asked.

"Heyo! What are you kids up to?"

The Fuzzies turned and saw John Morgan Holloway the Lesser walking towards them.

"Unka Morgan will know what to do," Little Fuzzy said. "Unka Morgan, we make talk fast!"

* * * * * * * * *

After Jack had surrendered, he was taken into custody and escorted to the Fuzzy equivalent of a holding center. It was little more than a small depression in the ground surrounded by needle vine bushes. While the bushes only rose to a height of four feet, the sharp needlelike thorns that covered the vine like branches were incredibly sharp and painful to remove. Jack noticed that there was some sort of discoloration on many of the thorns and suspected that they may have been treated with the same toxin used on the spear and arrow heads. To top it off Fuzzy guards with toxin-treated chopper-diggers blocked the exit. Jack was pretty impressed with the accommodations. He was even more impressed to find that he had a human cellmate.

"Hello," Jack said, offering his hand. "I am Jack Holloway, Native Affairs Commissioner."

The man accepted the hand, then introduced himself. "Joseph Aaron Quigley, the cause of all this mess."

"The cause?" Joe had Jack's undivided attention.

"Yes, Commissioner," Joe said. "Not intentionally, of course."

Joe explained about the illegal mining operation he had put together a few months earlier and the massive sunstone deposit he and his crew had discovered. Nothing was held back. Joe spoke of Sun Fur's accidental death, the discovery of the rocket, the skeletal remains that may or may not have been the pilots, the explosion and his resultant imprisonment. "I've been living on raw fruits and vegetables and stale extee-three for the last two months."

"Nifflheim! I'm almost tempted to believe you've suffered enough. Still, you'll have to be tried on manslaughter charges when we get back. I'm sure the courts will take your remorse and hardships into consideration. Stale extee-three...."

"Believe it or not, the damned stuff tastes better stale, which is just a slightly improved version of horrible." Joe chuckled at his own joke.

Jack didn't join in.

"Look, Commissioner, I will freely admit to all of my crimes under veridication if you get me out of here in one piece and maybe let me have a damned pizza and a tall cool beer."

Despite himself, Jack found himself sympathizing with Joe. "I think I can arrange that."

Joe looked Jack in the eyes. "I've heard about you. People who mess with the Fuzzies either end up dead or in jail."

Jack nodded. "If I catch them and they don't put up a fight, then it's up to the courts. If they do put up a fight, well, then it's up to me, I guess. There's an execution scheduled for this Saturday for a Fuzzy slavery ring. I didn't kill any of them though my son did. One tried to hack me up from behind." Jack looked Joe over. He was dirty, unshaven, thin and generally miserable looking. "Play ball and you might get five to ten in Prison House."

Joe snorted. "Ball, badminton, hockey, tidily-winks, you name the game and I'll play. Just get me away from these damned Fuzzies in one piece."

* * * * * * * * *

Thor Folkvar was accustomed to the eccentricities of his employer. As a rule the eccentricities took a benign turn: buying up substantial interests in companies, helping genetically engineered Freyans find a home; that sort of thing. Other times they were less benign, like challenging his father to a duel and damn near killing him and then whip-cracking the surgeons and doctors to patch the old man up.

Thor thought Morgan would settle down and be a bit less…off… after he set his sights on Akira O'Barre. Of course, the woman was a bit skinny by Magnian standards. He doubted she could even lift her own weight in the gym; still, she was attractive as far as frail off-Magni women went. Unfortunately, she wasn't keeping Morgan's eccentric nature in check.

The Magnian was on the bridge chatting with Captain Zeudin when the order came up to bring the yacht down to Beta Continent. That, in and of itself, was not particularly strange. Collecting three hundred Fuzzies with their dog mounts was. Moreover, the Fuzzies were armed to the teeth with bows, crossbows, scaled down .22s that looked like ancient military rifles and something that the hirsute natives called a *shoppo-diggo*. It took a lot to make Thor nervous. These Fuzzies made the grade.

Morgan followed the Fuzzies in along with his paramour barking orders to get the Fuzzies situated and head for the northern region of Beta Continent yesterday. The crew jumped to it escorting packs of Fuzzies with their dogs—they refused to be separated—to the various cargo bays. The animals and cryonic units from Freya and Magni had already been dropped off on Zeta Continent, or the Fuzzies would not have all fit on the yacht.

Thor carefully worked his way through the herd of Fuzzies and Curtys to Morgan and Akira. "What's the deal, boss?"

"Jack's been taken prisoner by hostile Fuzzies up north. We're going to get him back."

"With an army of Fuzzies?" Thor thought about it and realized it made sense. A demonstration of a superior force would go a long way to making Jack's captors open to negotiation. Fuzzies coming to the rescue would send the message that Jack was a friend to Fuzzy-kind. All in all, it was a good idea, provided nothing got in the way.

"It is Fuzzy land," Morgan pointed out. "According to Federation law, Fuzzies make the rules and enforce them if they want. Technically, humans are not supposed to interfere without their tribal consent."

"Unless asked," finished Thor. "I take it one of these Fuzzies requested assistance?"

"Little Fuzzy did." Morgan looked about trying to spot the Fuzzy in question to no avail. The sea of fur made each Fuzzy and dog almost impossible to tell one from another. "Since Little Fuzzy lives and works with the Native Affairs Commissioner—"

"Works?"

"He teaches some classes for the other Fuzzies," Akira supplied.

"Right," Morgan said. "I figure that makes him an authority figure, so when he asked me for help, I was happy to oblige."

"The fact that Jack is your father didn't enter into it, of course," Thor observed ironically.

"Of course not," Morgan replied airily. "Now let's go get him back."

* * * * * * * * *

"We have him."

Gus had just walked into his office after a meeting with a defense lawyer over a stolen zaragoat case. Normally, he didn't bother with the smaller infractions. The fact that the accused was a former client was the only reason he agreed to a sit-down. He had to explain that, as a prosecutor, he did not make special deals with former clients. He ended the meeting and assigned the case to Tanaka Webster. He was a little put out that Leslie Coombes was appointed interim chief prosecutor and not him, so Webster would be looking to do a good job without considering Gus's past relationship with the defendant.

Gus reached for a cigar just as his secretary, Nikita, appeared in his viewscreen informing him that Marshal Fane was waiting on line one.

"Put him through, Nikita." The secretary's face vanished in a colorful display of light and was replaced by the less pleasant, though smiling face of Max Fane. "Marshal, what can I do you for?"

"We have him," Max said without preamble.

"To which 'him' do you refer, Max?" asked Gus.

The Marshal's smile got even wider. "Leo Thaxter."

Gus put down the unlit cigar and stared at the screen. "Leo Thaxter? *The* Leo Thaxter, accept no substitutes, and by substitutes I mean Clancy Slade."

"Printed and DNA-checked." Max tried to look sober but couldn't keep the smile off his face. "In fact, it was Clancy Slade who sent Thaxter on to his final judgment." Max relayed the events that took place in front of the B.I.N. building. "Dropped Leo, went to help Piet, who had been shot by Thaxter, then calmly allowed himself to be taken into custody. I may have to make Clancy a cop after this."

"I'll bet the CZC is paying him better," observed Gus. He put the cigar away and pulled out a Thoran import. This was a special occasion, after all. "Clancy is smart, I'll give him that. He knew better than to argue with your men wearing that face. Hey, by any chance did one of your men get a sample of this Ivan Dane's blood at the scene?"

"You better believe it. Unfortunately, no matches to any known criminals."

Gus grunted his disappointment; finding something to arrest Ivan

Dane on would have been a good way to get him off his soapbox. "Well, hang on to it. We might get lucky."

"I never…hold on, I have an incoming call." Max's image froze for a minute, then jumped when he came back. "Gus, Jack is a prisoner of those Northern Fuzzies."

"Prisoner?" Gus couldn't believe his ears. "Of Fuzzies!"

"George Lunt just called in to apprise me of the situation."

After a string of colorful metaphors, Gus asked what George was doing about it.

"Nothing. Jack said not to interfere no matter what just before he surrendered to the Fuzzies."

That sounded like Jack. He didn't want a war with the Fuzzies, which would wipe them out in about ten minutes, so he'd surrendered hoping to negotiate a peace treaty. And, if anybody tried to rescue him, there was a good chance they'd undo everything Jack was trying to accomplish. Gus wanted a drink.

"There's nothing we can do about it so we'll just wait and see what happens. Have you told Ben, yet?"

Max looked horrified at the suggestion. "Great Ghu, no! After the way he tore this planet apart looking for you? Besides, between his love of Fuzzies and his loyalty to Jack, he's likely to have a stroke. I'll bring him in if and when I have to, and not a second sooner."

"I endorse and support that plan," Gus said. "Now we just need to keep it out of the news. What say we sic the reporters on Clancy. We can build him up as a hero. The media will eat it up. I'll make it up to him later."

"Ah, hero of the day and all that." Max agreed. "It's a good idea. With all the cameras around the shooting scene somebody will have either gotten footage of Thaxter shooting, or Clancy shooting back—or both. Better to let Clancy clear himself to the public before somebody takes a shot at him thinking he's Thaxter."

"Exactly. In fact, I'll talk to Ben and see if we can't pin a citizen's medal of some type on him before the press. That will give Ben a chance to look good on camera, too."

Max agreed, then his face went dark. "Want to bet this Dane fella won't try to spin the shooting into a law-and-order issue for the recall vote he is trying to get?"

"No bet. Just keep plugging away at that DNA and see if we can't get him on something before he has the chance."

"Damn," Max said. "Something just occurred to me. As far as the public knows Leo Thaxter is still in Prison House. How are we going to spin this?"

Gus thought for a second. It wouldn't do to have Ben Rainsford implicated in a cover-up, especially with the recall petition floating around. "We'll say the shooter was an immigrant with a history of mental illness. Invent a name for him. Thaxter committed suicide in solitary confinement. Warden Redford made up the solitary story when he released Clancy Slade. People who remember seeing Thaxter as the shooter shouldn't be hard to convince that they confused him with Clancy."

Max looked dubious on the screen. "You think that'll fly?"

Gus shrugged. "Well, there will be a few people who will scream conspiracy or something, but with a live Clancy and a dead Thaxter they should be ignored by the *hoi polloi*."

"Let's hope so," Max said as he screened off.

XXVII

Affanita sat in the climate-controlled office sweating bullets. She had brought in the sunstones to be sold at one of the Company outlets only to be grabbed up by two CZC security men and hauled off to Company house. Now, sitting in Victor Grego's office, she wondered if she would be turned over to the police or stuffed into an M/E converter. There were stories going around that made her think the latter was more likely than the former.

Affanita jumped when Grego entered the room and took a seat behind his desk. She looked around and saw that the security guards had left the room. Not that they were needed; there was no way out. She faced Grego and waited for what was to come.

A moment later a tiny man with Asiatic features entered the room carrying two small leather bags. He poured out one, then the other, keeping the contents separate.

"Is that all, Dr. Geronimo?" Grego asked.

"From this woman's offerings, sir." Geronimo indicated the stones at his left. "These are the mildly radioactive stones...."

"Radioactive!" Affanita blurted.

"...indicating that they are the counterfeits." Geronimo finished as though Affanita had said nothing.

Grego picked up one of the stones from the left and rolled it in his hand until it glowed brightly. "You're certain?"

"Very much so. In fact, I have succeeded in duplicating the

process and created a number of fine specimens for you to inspect." Dr. Geronimo reached into his lab coat and extracted six more sunstones. "I have measured the rate of luminescent decay in each stone and determined that it depends on the strength and duration of the dirty gamma exposure."

"Really? Is it possible to make the stones permanent? So they don't decay?"

"Possibly. I would recommend against it, though," Geronimo said. "The stronger the dose of dirty gamma, the higher the residual radiation. A stone that would glow for one hundred years or more would emit a potentially dangerous level of radiation."

Grego nodded and leaned back in his chair. "This amount is safe, though?"

Geronimo scooped up the ersatz sunstones and rolled them between his hands.

"Yes. It is a geometric progression of exposure to increase the thermoflorescent properties of the stones." Dr. Geronimo went into exhaustive detail explaining that each time unit, two weeks, required twice as much exposure as the previous time unit. If two weeks required a five-second dose of dirty-gamma rays, four weeks would require a twenty second dose and so on. The longest a stone could be made effectively thermofluorescent without harming the owner was two years.

Affanita found herself becoming more bored than frightened. She noticed that Grego didn't seem to be following the explanation any better than she was.

"In other words, aside from the radiation hazard, the cost of creating the *faux* sunstones with an eye towards permanence would exceed that of mining the real thing," the scientist concluded, "And subject whoever carried it to harmful levels of radiation."

"If he has to explain that again, I would rather you just tossed me into an M/E converter," Affanita muttered a little too loudly.

Grego had to fight to keep his expression neutral. He would lose intimidation points if he started laughing. "Thank you, Dr. Geronimo. Madam, do you understand why you are here?"

"I passed you some bad stones." Affanita saw no point in playing dumb. "I didn't know that at the time, but I should have figured something was off about them." She explained about Richard "last name unknown" and how she was hired to act as the go-between for the gem buyers. "I checked the stones out and they all seemed fine to me. I don't have any equipment for measuring radioactivity, though."

Grego nodded thoughtfully. He was inclined to believe the woman. Still….

"I am afraid you will have to be interrogated under veridication," he informed her. "If you cooperate and work with us, you will be released and even paid for the genuine sunstones. I will also expect your assistance in finding this Richard person. He and I need to have a rather long discussion. I am even prepared to pay a reward for his apprehension."

Affanita couldn't believe her luck. "You got it, Tiger. I'll even gift-wrap him if you want."

* * * * * * * * *

"Mr. Morgan, I can't…"

"Holloway."

George Lunt, Commandant of the Native Protection Force stopped at the seeming non-sequitur. "Beg pardon?"

"The name is Holloway, just like my father whom I intend to rescue," Morgan explained. Now that he successfully claimed the family name he was somewhat touchy about it being ignored.

George let out a sigh and apologized, then started again. "Mr.

Holloway, I don't care whose son you are, how much of a bigwig you may be with the CZC or even how much money you have. You are still a civilian and you are not entering a hostile environment under my jurisdiction. Hell, I would have stopped Jack, too, if he hadn't snuck in while I was rounding up my men."

Morgan started to argue, then stopped himself. Arguing would only waste more time. Major Lunt was only doing his job, which he had to be good at for Jack to have hired him in the first place. Bullying the man would be a waste of time, too. The only way in was to use the rules against him.

"One second, Major." Morgan went over to his desk and accessed the viewscreen. When he arrived in Northern Beta in his yacht, he had invited George Lunt and Ismet Runako aboard to plan how they could work together to retrieve Jack. He hadn't counted on Lunt being a stickler for regulations. "Okay, fine. Let's see what the regs say in this instance." Morgan punched in a code and a moment later Leslie Coombes appeared on screen. "Mr. Coombes, Jack Holloway is being held by some hostile Fuzzies on the Reservation. Major Lunt here says I can't go in and rescue him. Is that right?"

Coombes didn't look at all surprised at the news. He shouldn't, as Ismet had relayed the situation through his chain of command at the top of which was Victor Grego. Grego, in turn, went to Coombes with the same question. "I am afraid the Major is within his purview to prevent you from acting. Only the NPF has the right to go into Fuzzy territory to deal with hostile natives."

Morgan swore luridly. He picked up a few new phrases from Jack and used them. "What about the military?"

"Only at the NPF's request. Or the Commissioner's."

"So nobody can go in except the NPF, and they won't go because they were ordered not to."

"That would be correct. Only the Fuzzies can come and go as they please," Coombes added. "After all, it is their real estate."

Morgan smiled like a very large cat that had gotten the better of a particularly meaty canary. "Thank you, Mr. Coombes. That will do very nicely." Morgan broke the connection before Coombes could ask what he meant.

"You heard him, Major. The Fuzzies can go in and get Jack."

"What? No! This is a dangerous situation and I won't let any Fuzzies get hurt."

Morgan and George went back and forth for a few minutes while Little Fuzzy, who had been quietly observing the entire thing, slipped out of Morgan's office and back to the docks. There, Little Fuzzy wasted no time in organizing the Fuzzy teams and their mounts.

"We go save Pappy Jack," Little Fuzzy said in his hypersonic voice; partly to keep Big Ones from overhearing and interfering, and partly because the ultrasonic pitch carried better allowing all the Fuzzies to catch what was being said across the spacious bay. Little Fuzzy quickly outlined his plan and the Fuzzies formed up in ranks at the cargo-bay door.

The yacht was hovering a mere two meters above the planet's surface with a platform reaching to the ground. Morgan had planned on leading the charge to rescue his father when George Lunt demanded that he stand down. Though the Fuzzies liked and respected George and the rest of the NPF cops, Pappy Jack was too important and loved not to be helped, no matter what.

Little Fuzzy, the *de facto* boss of his people when Pappy Jack wasn't around, led the Fuzzies down the ramp. That was when they hit their first snag; they didn't know which way to go. None of them had ever seen the other Fuzzies' camp. Little Fuzzy thought hard as he looked around, then spotted Pappy Jack's aircar. He hopped off of Trigger and ran over to the vehicle and went inside. A few heartbeats later, he emerged with a handkerchief. When he returned to his dog mount, he remounted, then held the cloth to Trigger's nose.

"Trigger, find Pappy Jack," Little Fuzzy ordered.

Trigger sniffed at the ground, ran over to the aircar where he sniffed the ground some more. After a moment, the dog barked loudly and ran towards the ridge face, the other mounted Fuzzies hot on his tail.

* * * * * * * * *

"You have to trust Morgan, Betty. He's very capable and trustworthy, especially in a situation like this. Don't forget, he saved Jack's life before when that Fuzzy slaver tried to attack him from behind."

Betty, still on the viewscreen, was upset about Jack Holloway's imprisonment by the Northern Fuzzies. Akira knew that Betty was infatuated with the older man, and had even managed to get him into bed with her, but her current reaction was out of character.

"What is Morgan going to do?"

That was a good question. He left with hundreds of Fuzzies and their dogs in that ship of his. Presumably, Morgan was planning on a show of force. Akira said so to Betty.

"You'll have to excuse me if I am less inclined to trust in the man who shot Jack in the first place," Betty said, referring to the duel two months earlier.

Akira rolled her eyes at the screen. "That was a matter of Freyan honor. He had to challenge Jack to claim his name."

"Freyan honor my shapely backside," Betty said in disgust. "Freyan honor got Jack shot in the first place."

"Morgan also took a Blood Oath to protect Jack," Akira added. "If he doesn't do his best to recover Jack in one piece, his life is forfeit under the terms of the oath…if I understand it correctly."

That caught Betty's attention. "Oh, Ghu, Akira! I don't want anything to happen to Morgan, either. Uh, who would kill him, anyway?"

"Either Little Fuzzy or Gus Brannhard, I think. I have to admit that I didn't follow the details very well."

The two women were silent for a moment. Betty spoke first.

"Does Morgan know that you're pregnant?"

Akira was stunned. "What? How…what makes you say that?"

"Oh, pu-leeze. I've known you since the day you arrived on planet. In the last few weeks you've avoided alcohol, put on a few pounds and jumped at the chance to move to Beta. Either you're pregnant or you're going through a mid-life crisis thirty years ahead of schedule and in the wrong gender."

Akira decided not to bluff it out. Betty acted flighty and wild at times, but she was as sharp as they came when it mattered. "I'll tell him when and if he proposes. Not one second sooner. I don't want him to think that I am trying to trap him. Besides, if he does ask, I want it to be because he wants to, not to satisfy some rule of Freyan society."

Betty pursed her lips and nodded. She more than understood Akira's position and agreed. Betty had had several chances to land a rich husband herself and passed on them because they were after a trophy wife. Betty was nobody's status symbol. She wanted a real man who wanted her for her. Which got her thinking about Jack Holloway again and she felt a lump in her chest as she choked back her sobs.

* * * * * * * * *

"We've got something, Chief."

Those were the words that Chief Carr had been praying to hear. Two days before, he had asked Colonial Marshal Max Fane to back off and let him run the constabulary. After all, wasn't that the job of a police chief? The Marshal agreed that he had taken too much of Carr's job for himself and backed off. Then the prisoners lost their heads in a thoroughly literal way. So far the Marshal wasn't butting in on the investigation, but that wouldn't last long. Carr needed suspects and he needed them *now*.

"Tell me you have a name and I'll turn over my firstborn son to you, when I get around to having one."

"A name, yes, but it is an obvious fake," Chang said. "John Smith."

"Gah! You just lost out on getting a good kid. Description?"

"That we have, assuming this guy didn't use a synthmask."

Yeah, my luck would run that way. "Tell me what you have."

"Based on the canvass we were able to zero in on the location of the signal. It was the San Giacomo apartment building. It's a bit of a fleabag and the owner doesn't ask too many questions when he rents out the rooms, though he gave a pretty good description of the most likely tenant."

"And?" Carr prompted.

"He rented the room the same day Tony and Ripper made planet fall on *the City of Asgard*." Chang consulted his notebook. "The shuttle landed at the Mallorysport-Darius spaceport at 1000. Mr. Smith rented the apartment at 1600 the same day."

"All right, it's a little thin, but it's all we have. Put an APB out on this John Smith, double the men at the spaceport and have forensics tear his apartment apart...after we get the warrant. I'll call Gus Brannhard, you get the men in place."

Chang gave a smart "Yes, sir" and moved out. Carr stared at the screen for a moment before tapping out the Chief Prosecutor's office. It was going to be another long day.

XXVIII

Red Fur considered what to do with the two Big Ones. The one called Joe Quigley told him that the Big Ones were powerful and could destroy the *Jin-f'ke* from so far away that even those with the sharpest eyes could not see it. The Fuzzy leader did not doubt this. He had seen for himself many of the wonders the Big Ones had created: made-things that moved around and did work, melon-seed shaped flying things that they traveled in, noisy weapons that could kill *Jin-f'ke* easily from a distance. It seemed the Big Ones could do almost anything.

They could be killed, too. Poisoned arrows made Big Ones as dead as anything else. When cut, they would bleed. Big Ones were large and strong and wise; they were not impossible to kill. Yet, the warning of such weapons that could kill his people from far away worried Red Fur.

Then the new Big One, the Jack Holloway, came to the camp and made overtures of peace. He allowed himself to be taken prisoner. Why? If the Big Ones were so powerful, why make friends? *Jin-f'ke* liked to make friends. Maybe the Big Ones did, too. But if so, why the killing? Red Fur's thoughts went round and round until his head started to hurt. The Fuzzy leader decided it was time to speak with the Big Ones some more.

* * * * * * * * *

The dog cavalry of Fuzzies quickly surrounded the encampment of the Northern Fuzzies. The dogs, under their masters' guidance, took their positions quickly and silently. The riders, instead of giving commands in their normal ultrasonic voice that the opposing force might hear, whispered to the mounts and the other Fuzzies using the language of the Big Ones. Little Fuzzy had taken great pains to explain the tactical advantage involved in keeping their voices low and using a language unfamiliar to their foes. He learned about the tactic from a Big One movie where people called *Navajo* talked on the radio in a language nobody else could understand.

When the Fuzzies had all reached their appointed positions, they indicated it by raising a bow, chopper-digger or the scaled down rifles designed for them by Mart Burgess. Chances were that the dog riders had already been spotted by the Northern Fuzzies when they first rode up. Little Fuzzy anticipated that possibility and decided it wasn't important; Fuzzies did not attack other Fuzzies without provocation, and Little Fuzzy fully intended to inform them of their presence momentarily.

Looking about at the various groups in his area, Little Fuzzy could see that they were all in place by their raised weapons. After several heartbeats, he could see flashing lights from the further edges of the perimeter; that would be Mike, Ko-ko, and Cinderella signaling with their flashlights. Little Fuzzy signaled back; all was ready.

Everybody counted to five from the last signal, then yelled at the top of their hypersonic little voices. The noise permeated the entire area. Even the dogs, despite their training, howled in agony at the sudden assault of hypersonic noise. After several heartbeats, the yelling and howling stopped, almost simultaneously. Now it was time to wait and see what the other Fuzzies would do.

* * * * * * * * *

Red Fur had been on his way to speak with the new Big One called Jack Holloway (the Big Ones had the strangest names) when Climber, Runs Fast and Makes-Things all ran up to report that many-many new people on strange new animals had surrounded the camp. When he asked what the new people were doing, they did not know.

Then the yelling started. Red Fur knew what the sound was, mostly; it was the sound of many-many people all screaming at once. It was a never before done thing and it was frightening to hear, especially with the strange noises made by the new animals. All around him he could see that the *Jin-f'ke* were afraid. The strange things that the Big Ones did were no longer as frightening, they were expected. After all, it would be hard to top flying made-things and the great thunder noise that made the big-big hole in the ground.

But the people like the *Jin-f'ke* that acted strangely were different. They sat on the backs of animals never before seen by his people. They carried shiny chopper-diggers like the ones carried by the Jack Holloway and his giant furry friend. They had bows and arrows that looked different from their own, and dark made-things like the boom-sticks he had seen Big Ones carry. And there were things on their backs that Red Fur couldn't understand the purpose of.

Red Fur had trouble processing what he was seeing. Big Ones killed *Jin-f'ke*, yet here were people like him that had to be friends with the Big Ones. How else could they have such amazing made-things? Why would they be friends with the ones who killed people like them.

The yelling stopped as quickly as it started. The sudden silence was as jarring as the noise had been. Many of the *Jin-f'ke* became even more afraid. Red Fur looked around and saw the early signs of panic in some of the people's eyes. He would have to do something quickly to maintain control.

As Red Fur considered his options, one of the new people came up to the edge of his camp riding on the strange animal. The rider stopped his mount and jumped down, then placed his chopper-digger on the ground and placed one foot on it. That meant the visitor wanted to talk and, maybe, make friends.

Red Fur wasn't carrying a chopper-digger at that moment, so he borrowed one from another *Jin-f'ke* before stepping forward to meet the newcomer. When he was close enough to speak, he laid down the weapon and placed his foot on it in the manner of the new Fuzzy. That meant he would talk with the new Fuzzy.

The Fuzzy said something in a tongue Red Fur didn't understand. He placed a hand on his ear then shook his head. The newcomer spoke again in a different language, this time he used Big One words.

"You talk like Big Ones?" Red Fur asked in surprise. He should have expected that since the new people had the made-things from the Big Ones.

The Fuzzy said, "Yes. The Big Ones call me Little Fuzzy. Name means 'small person with fur all over' in their language."

"I am called Red Fur by Big Ones. In the language of my people I am called *Bal-f'ke*."

Little Fuzzy nodded. Obviously Red Fur had contact with Big Ones before, or he would not know their language. "Are you the leader of these people?"

Red Fur had to think for a moment. Leader was like Wise One to the Big Ones. He learned that from Joe Quigley. "Yes. I am leader."

"Then I am here to ask that you return Pappy Jack."

Pappy Jack? "What is a Pappy Jack?"

"A Pappy is a Big One who cares for people like us," Little Fuzzy explained. "Pappy Jack came here to make talk with you. Now he is here and we want him back."

"You mean the Jack Holloway? Yes, he here. We want to make much talk with him."

Little Fuzzy thought for a moment, then said, "Hokay, make talk with him here, with me."

"No. Big Ones kill many *Jin-f'ke,*" shouted Red Fur. "He stays with us."

"Sometimes bad Big Ones do bad things to Fuzzies, but Pappy Jack punish them. Pappy Jack make bad Big Ones dead. I have seen this." Little Fuzzy quickly recounted the events surrounding Goldilocks' murder and the subsequent killing of Kurt Borch and, later, the death of Leonard Kellogg. "Pappy Jack wise one for all Fuzzies. Makes bad Big Ones dead if they hurt us."

Red Fur soaked up the information and considered it. *Jin-f'ke* did not kill each other while Big Ones did. Would it be safe to form an alliance with such beings? Would it be safe not to? Either way, Red Fur could not simply hand over his prisoners to these new people. He would look foolish in front of his own people. He said as much to Little Fuzzy.

Little Fuzzy understood the *Jin-f'ke* leader's position. The Wise One of any clan had to look strong and decisive or the clan would argue and sometimes separate. Red Fur needed something that the Big Ones called 'a way out.' Little Fuzzy quickly developed a plan.

"Red Fur, Wise One of the *Jin-f'ke,* I have many-many more people than you. We have weapons made by the Big Ones that are greater than yours. Our dogs are also strong and good hunters. If we fight, many-many *Jin-f'ke* will make dead."

Red Fur had no doubt Little Fuzzy spoke the truth. The *Jin-f'ke* had no concept of lying. Still, he couldn't back down. People fought or ran away. Surrender was also unknown until the Big One Jack Holloway explained it to them. A Fuzzy who surrendered to his environment made dead very quickly. It was too new a concept for them to readily grasp. The closest thing they had to that was admitting defeat when they fought and lost with another of the people.

"To save many-many lives, let two of our people fight," Little Fuzzy continued. "If you win, we leave and do not come back until you ask us.

If we win, you give us Pappy Jack."

Red Fur thought quickly. It was a good idea to him. From what he could see, these new people were smaller than the *Jin-f'ke.* Still, they had wondrous weapons made by the Big Ones.

"Fight how?" Red Fur demanded. "You have Big Ones' made-things."

Little Fuzzy picked up his shiny chopper-digger and tossed it to Red Fur. Then he turned and waved for Ko-ko to come forward. "Your fighter use Big One weapon."

Little Fuzzy planned on letting whomever Red Fur picked fight Ko-ko, the second best chopper-digger fencer he knew; Mitzi was too far away to call over quickly. Red Fur had a different idea.

"You Wise One for your people…Fuhzzees? I wise one for *Jin-f'ke.* We make fight."

Little Fuzzy's stomach did a flop. While he was a good fencer, Ko-ko and Mitzi were much better and he believed either one of them could easily beat any *Jin-f'ke* they might face. Little Fuzzy didn't have the same level of confidence in his own abilities. Unfortunately, to refuse Red Fur's challenge would weaken his position and possibly cause the bloodshed he hoped to avoid. Among their own people Fuzzies would occasionally fight, then make friends afterwards. Fuzzies never intentionally fought to the death, though accidents did happen. Was the same true of the *Jin-f'ke*?

"Hokay, Red Fur." Little Fuzzy turned to Ko-ko and told him not to interfere and to honor the conditions of the duel.

"What about Pappy Jack?" Ko-ko demanded.

"When *Jin-f'ke* see that we do what we say, maybe they believe Pappy Jack is good Big One and let him go. If not, Unka Morgan will save Pappy Jack with his big-big aircar…uh…yacht."

Ko-ko looked dubious but accepted Little Fuzzy's plan. He didn't want to kill any of the people here, either. Ko-ko would explain what was happening to the others. Little Fuzzy removed his backpack and had Ko-ko take Trigger back to the other Fuzzies; if the dog sensed that Little Fuzzy was in danger, he might interfere with the duel. Back home the Fuzzies never practiced their fencing in front of the dogs.

Red Fur explained to Makes-Things what to do if he lost the duel. The maker agreed. Before the Fuzzy stepped back, Red Fur had another idea and whispered in Makes-Things' ear. The Fuzzy nodded and scampered away.

Before beginning battle, Red Fur asked that he be given a little time to familiarize himself with the shiny chopper-digger. Little Fuzzy agreed and took the time to warm-up before the duel.

Both Fuzzies covertly studied their opponent as they prepared. Red Fur was larger. Proportionately, there was as much difference in height between them as there would be between a five foot tall human and another man a full foot taller. Red Fur would have the advantages of reach and possibly strength. Little Fuzzy, however, was familiar with the metal weapons and trained in their use by Big Ones who were very wise in such things. Little Fuzzy understood the balance and use of the chopper-digger in ways that an untrained Fuzzy could not understand.

There was a disturbance among the *Jin-f'ke* that distracted Little Fuzzy. He turned and saw two Big Ones being escorted to the edge of the dueling ground. It was Pappy Jack and a strange Big One.

"Pappy Jack!" Little Fuzzy ran to meet his pappy only to be blocked by several Fuzzies.

"No," Red Fur called out in the Big One language. "He here to watch. No talk."

XXIX

The sudden absence of three hundred Fuzzies and their dogs did not go unnoticed by Morgan and George Lunt for long. Morgan was ready to follow the Fuzzies, only to be stopped by George.

"Uh-uh! Legally, the Fuzzies are fully within their rights to go anywhere they want on the reservation, even if it means getting into a fight with other Fuzzies. Federation law dictates that on native reservations the natives make and enforce their own laws. You," —George jabbed a digit in Morgan's direction— "are not a Fuzzy, nor are you an official member of the NPF or even Jack's assistant. My job is to keep non-Fuzzy people out of the res; since you are clean-shaven and too tall by double, clearly you don't pass the physical."

Morgan extracted a document from a shirt pocket. "I have a signed permit to enter the reservation." The younger Holloway had acquired the permit shortly after arriving on planet in case he needed to search on the reservation for his errant progenitor.

George took the paper, looked it over quickly, then returned it. "That is a standard research permit and does not apply in this instance. Permits are not issued to allow civilians access to hostile sites on the reservation. If you want to call the Governor, be my guest, but I'll turn in my badge before I let anybody go snooping around and getting themselves killed on my watch."

Morgan was torn between an urge to throttle the Major and admiration for his devotion to duty. It was easy to see why Jack picked him to head up the NPF. Morgan decided that the time for discussion was over. Since they were on his yacht he had the advantage.

"George, you understand that as the owner of this yacht, as long as it is not actually in full contact with the ground, my word is law, yes?"

The Major was thrown momentarily by the sudden shift in topic. "Within certain limits, yes. Why?"

"I just want that established so that nobody else aboard can be charged with any crimes for following my orders."

"What?" Realization dawned just a second too late. "Wait!"

Morgan nodded and Thor Folkvar threw a bear hug around the surprised Major from behind and lifted him off the floor. George, trained in hand-to-hand, launched a vicious kick into the Magnian's shin to no avail. Muscle and bone designed to withstand the heavy gravity of Magni easily absorbed the blow with no visible effect.

A second kick down to the larger man's arch failed to connect at all; George was held too far above the floor, and as a consequence above Thor's feet, to connect. The Major considered a reverse head butt, and decided against it. It might make Thor mad.

Realizing he was beaten for the moment, George relented and even made light of the situation. "Of course you realize, this means war."

Thor almost lost his grip as he suppressed his own laughter. He was a big fan of old Terran animated programs and Groucho Marx.

The joke was lost on Morgan, however. "Actually, I am hoping to prevent that."

* * * * * * * * *

Of the ten known sapient races, only two were documented to be completely adverse to killing their own kind, Lokians and Fuzzies. Lokians barely even comprehended the concept of violence. Fuzzies comprehended and used violence on a daily basis to survive, but rarely against each other, and even more rarely to the death.

Fuzzies had been known to fight against each other and even have duels. Unlike Terran and Freyan societies, Fuzzy duels were not declared, did not involve seconds or referees, and were never intentionally to the death. Fuzzy duels were spontaneous and often over as quickly as they began. Afterwards, they almost always made friends. Almost always.

Little Fuzzy took a few deep breaths to steady himself for the coming battle. After his long association with the Big Ones, Little Fuzzy was a bit surprised that another Fuzzy could be so intimidating. Of course, Fuzzies never fought with Big Ones in duels; that was an everybody knows thing.

As he warmed up, a concept Little Fuzzy learned from the Big Ones, with his chopper-digger, he also watched Red Fur familiarize himself with the metal weapon. Red Fur quickly became comfortable with the balance and weight of it. It was clear the *Jin-f'ke* leader had some sort of training with a similar weapon.

Looking about, Little Fuzzy could see that the *Jin-f'ke* had chopper-diggers very much like what his own tribe used to use before Pappy Jack traded them for the shiny ones. The blade end was a little longer and narrower, while the paddle end had a wide tapered point instead of the flat shovel arrangement typical of the Southern Fuzzies.

Little Fuzzy returned his attention to Red Fur just as the *Jin-f'ke* leader started over in his direction. There was no doubt he was ready to begin the duel so Little Fuzzy assumed the neutral defensive posture. In Fuzzy terms his stance said he was ready for trouble, but not initiating it. Red Fur stopped two feet away and took up the same stance.

"I am ready, Big One's Friend," Red Fur said.

Little Fuzzy took note of the fact that the *Jin-f'ke* leader did not use the name Pappy Jack gave him. Fuzzies did not typically use insults beyond calling someone foolish, nor did Little Fuzzy consider this to be one. Most likely it was some custom among the Northern Fuzzies, he decided.

Without further preamble, the two Fuzzies started moving in a slow circle, each searching for a weakness in his opponent. Red Fur jabbed at Little Fuzzy with the point of his weapon only to have it easily parried. It was not a serious attack. The Northern Fuzzy was testing Little Fuzzy's defenses. A second thrust was side-stepped and Little Fuzzy swung his own chopper-digger at Red Fur. The bare edge of the blade struck a forearm leaving a barely noticeable scratch. Both Fuzzies concluded that they had the range of the other and the attacks began in earnest.

* * * * * * * * *

Jack Holloway wanted to scream at the duelists to stop. He refrained for fear of distracting Little Fuzzy at a crucial moment. As a duelist himself Jack knew that even a mild distraction could get somebody killed; most likely the somebody you didn't want to see hurt.

What the Nifflheim were the res Fuzzies doing up here, anyway, thought Jack, especially Little Fuzzy? And what was the damned duel about anyway?

Jack suspected that Little Fuzzy was fighting to get him released. He could hardly blame the Fuzzy. Jack would, and had, done much the same when his family had been seized as evidence and incarcerated at Science Division way back in the days before Fuzzies were proven to be sapient. Clearly, Little Fuzzy had learned from his Pappy Jack's example.

If you don't want the kids to learn something, Jack thought, *don't teach it by word or deed.*

Unable to stop the fight, Jack settled in to watch with great interest. He sized up Red Fur and watched how he moved and reacted. The Fuzzy was larger, to be sure. Not much by human standards but a couple of inches made a big difference to a Fuzzy. Jack suspected Red Fur would be stronger, too. In the wild Fuzzies had to fight and work very hard to stay alive. The res Fuzzies had it easy for the last two years.

Mental Note: Strength training for Fuzzies, get more equipment and instructors.

As the duel progressed, Jack could see that it wasn't as one-sided as he feared. What Little Fuzzy lacked in size and strength, he made up for in speed, training and experience. The Fuzzy used the pugil-stick adapted skills to block and counterattack.

Jack actually laughed out loud when Little Fuzzy landed a solid blow with the balancing ball on the chopper-digger into Red Fur's abdomen. That was a move an untrained Fuzzy wouldn't think of as it wasn't a killing move.

Mitzi or Ko-ko would likely have made short work of the *Jin-f'ke* leader. They were the two best chopper-digger fencers on the res. Still, Little Fuzzy was more than holding his own. Besides, it was a very rare thing for one Fuzzy to kill another, Jack told himself. Hopefully, that applied to the Northern Fuzzies as well.

Jack was just starting to believe that everything would be okay when Little Fuzzy did a maneuver that sent Jack's heart into his throat.

XXX

Red Fur started to swing more wildly. Little Fuzzy easily dodged the attacks though he couldn't get close enough to properly retaliate. The greater reach of the *Jin-f'ke* put him at a disadvantage. The duel could go on indefinitely until one or the other became exhausted and made a crucial error. Little Fuzzy was afraid that Red Fur could outlast him, so he took a chance.

It took several more swings and parries before Little Fuzzy saw the opportunity he needed. Red Fur swung just a touch too high, allowing Little Fuzzy to dive under the blade, roll, then launch a kick into his opponent's midriff. Taken by surprise, the Fuzzy doubled over, allowing Little Fuzzy to swing the ball end of his weapon up into Red Fur's head.

Stunned, the *Jin-f'ke* leader fell back. Before he could recover, Little Fuzzy was up and holding the point of his blade at Red Fur's throat. The choice was obvious: admit defeat or die. Red Fur didn't get the chance to decide.

The *Jin-f'ke*, seeing their leader down with a point to his throat, ignored their orders and swarmed down to rescue their leader. The res Fuzzies, at first slow to act because they were completely surprised by the apparent betrayal, also swarmed forward. Much of the martial training and the newer weapons, bows, atlatls and rifles, were forgotten by both sides as the two forces clashed. It was all chopper-diggers, teeth and claws.

The Curtys, trained not to hunt or attack Fuzzies from birth, whined in confusion as their masters jumped to the ground to meet the *Jin-f'ke* forces without them. Lacking a guiding hand, the dogs barked and snapped but stayed out of the actual fighting. One *Jin-f'ke*, perhaps thinking to elevate his status as a great hunter and fighter, attacked a dog with his wooden chopper-digger, only to be pounced upon and pinned to the ground. The Curtys growled fiercely, but refrained from mauling the Fuzzy; his training wouldn't allow it.

Another dog jumped to the defense of his fallen master by moving between the injured Fuzzy and his *Jin-f'ke* attacker. While it was believed by many that Fuzzies were timid creatures that would rather run than fight, the truth was very different. Fuzzies would run to escape an animal they couldn't beat to keep from being killed. When cornered, even by a damnthing, a Fuzzy would go down swinging. Such was the case for the *Jin-f'ke*. Faced with an animal many times his size and mass, the Fuzzy chose to fight rather than run. Part of the decision was influenced by the fact that he knew he could not outrun the strange beast.

Still, he swung his wooden chopper-digger at the dog's muzzle hoping to either hurt it enough to have a chance or even frighten it off. Instead, the dog snapped the weapon up with his powerful jaws and crushed it with ease. Another thing known about Fuzzies is that they are very smart. The *Jin-f'ke* was no exception. He turned and ran. The dog, less interested in chasing the Fuzzy than protecting his master, held his ground and threatened any who came near with barks and growls.

Red Fur, allowed to stand as Little Fuzzy backed away, tried to stop the fighting. Though he yeeked with all his might, his voice was lost in the clamor about him. Never before had Fuzzies done battle among themselves on such a scale. All about him people were being wounded and killed. It was a never before seen thing that made the first appearance of the Big Ones pale in comparison.

Red Fur turned to Little Fuzzy and screamed, "We stop this!"

"How?" Little Fuzzy screamed back.

The two leaders yelled and tried to stop the fighting among those closest to them with little success. No sooner would they separate two combatants, than several more would engage them drawing them back into the fight.

The Fuzzy leaders were at a loss for what to do when a thundering sound intruded on the battle. It was a noise none of the *Jin-f'ke* had ever heard before. Even the res Fuzzies were startled. Looking up, a great round thing hovered above the battlefield. It looked like a new moon to most of the Fuzzies.

* * * * * * * * *

Jack was horrified when the fighting broke out. He wanted to rush forward and stop them. Only his Fuzzy guards with the poison-tipped arrows prevented him from running into the thick of things. He had also been in enough battles to know that, unarmed as he was, he would only get himself killed. He wouldn't be able to do anybody any good as a corpse.

Then the music started blaring overhead. Jack looked up and saw the hyperspace yacht floating down over the battlefield. That would be Morgan, Jack realized. It also explained how the army of res Fuzzies came to his rescue so quickly. *Full-grown man or not, he is going over my knee!*

The music, *Ride of the Valkyries* by Wagner, appropriately enough, was having the desired effect. Everywhere Jack looked the *Jin-f'ke* were scrambling for cover and the res Fuzzies attended to their dead and wounded. Uncountable howls filled the air as the dogs reacted to the sonic assault on their sensitive ears. Or maybe some of them were mourning the loss of their masters.

Jack, relieved of his guards as they, too, ran off in fear, walked down to the battlefield in search of Little Fuzzy. Twice before he thought Little Fuzzy had been lost to him. Three times was beyond endurance.

"Little Fuzzy! Little Fuzzy!" Jack called out over and over. He was on the verge of despair when he felt a tugging at his trouser leg. Jack looked down to find Ko-ko. There was a moment of relief combined with heartache when he saw it wasn't Little Fuzzy. "Ko-ko! Thank Ghu, you're okay. Where is Little Fuzzy?"

"Little Fuzzy this way, Pappy Jack." Ko-ko scampered off and Jack quickly followed.

* * * * * * * * *

"Seriously?" Thor Folkvar said. "*Ride of the Valkyries*?" He shook his head in disgust.

Captain Zeudin raised an eyebrow. "What would you have used?"

"Oh, *Detroit Rock City* by Kiss," replied the Magnian. Archaic heavy metal was very popular on his homeworld. "The car crash sound effect near the end would have caught a lot of attention down there."

Zeudin had never heard of it. "The what by the who?"

"Not the Who…that was an earlier group, though *Won't Get Fooled Again* would have been a good choice, too. Ah, Nifflheim. At least you didn't play any of that stuff from Freya."

Zeudin was about to protest the slight to his home world when Morgan interrupted. "Lower the ramp and get some medical assistance down there. There are a lot of injured Fuzzies. Major Lunt, if you can refrain from arresting me until we finish here, you will be welcome to come down and help me find Jack."

George agreed and joined Morgan, Thor and a number of the crewmen as they went down to the ground. Among them were the Thoran security team, the Lokian, Gimlian and Kronkeenk, the Ulleran. There were also a number of the mutated Freyans as not all of them had settled on Zeta, yet. As they scrambled down the ramp, even the rez Fuzzies were surprised at the variety of sapients as they had not seen them on the flight up.

Thor Folkvar spotted Jack at the edge of the clearing sitting on a large rock. He appeared to be talking to two Fuzzies. Thor waved to Morgan and George and pointed out the correct direction. Once there, Thor received a bit of a shock, though not as severe as the one Morgan got.

Jack stood up and punched Morgan in the jaw, sending the younger Holloway sprawling on the ground. George looked at Morgan, then Jack, and then turned to Thor.

"Is this some sort of weird Freyan greeting?" the Major asked.

"More like a spanking, I think," Thor replied.

"Damn straight it is," Jack snarled. He turned to Morgan and added, "You're just lucky they don't have hickory trees on this planet. But I'm going to start planting some real soon, so just you watch it!"

Morgan, head still reeling from the blow, managed to get back on his feet. "I came to rescue you…."

"I didn't need rescuing, damnit! I surrendered so I could get a dialogue going with *Bal-f'ke*, here." Red Fur took notice of Jack's use of his proper name. "You're just lucky Little Fuzzy wasn't hurt or I'd drag you back to Terra by the ear and find that hickory switch right now."

Morgan's face lit up with the realization that he had queered Jack's plan. Rather than defend his actions or apologize, he stood quietly. Red Fur leaned over to Little Fuzzy and asked if all Big Ones behaved like that. Little Fuzzy had to admit he saw Pappy Jack beat one other man bloody, but that was after he killed Goldilocks.

Pappy Jack returned his attention to the Fuzzy leaders. "*Bal-f'ke,* as the Wise One for the Big Ones, I want us to make friends. My people can help yours in many ways."

Little Fuzzy nodded and pulled a tin out of his backpack. "Yes. Big Ones give estee-fee. Give *shoppo-diggo* made of steel. Teach us many-many new things."

Red Fur looked at the tin of extee three in distaste. "Not want estee-fee. Big Ones and *Jin*—Fuhzzeez very different. How can be friends?"

Morgan heard the exchange and had an idea. He motioned Thor Folkvar over and whispered in his ear. The large Magnian nodded and trotted off. He returned several seconds later with select crew members and altered Freyans.

Red Fur, still arguing his position, stopped mid-word when he saw Kronkeenk approach. The Thorans, Lokians, Gimlians and altered Freyans, while interesting and unusual, were not as shocking to the Fuzzy. The Ulleran was so far beyond anything any Fuzzy had ever seen it made them doubt their senses. Red Fur fell backwards yeeking in surprise. Even Little Fuzzy was amazed.

Morgan stepped forward and spoke. "These are beings from other worlds, *Bal-f'ke*. We live and work and even play together. And we help each other. Sometimes we argue or fight; we are not perfect. We also have thosc among us who are bad. When we find them, we punish them."

"My zpezies works wit' dese hoomans on my world," Kronkeenk said.

"Bad...Big Vuns?...did bad t'ings to mine pipple. Goot Big Vuns are now helping us, Herr Red Fur," added Wolfram, one of the mutated Freyans. "My pipple owe Herr Morgan much for his help. He und his fat'er are goot Big Vuns."

Each of the alien races gave an account of their experiences with the humans—some good, some bad. They were honest and spoke to the Fuzzies as equals. They also explained about the advances in technology and standard of living. Much of what they said was incomprehensible to Red Fur.

Jack turned to Red Fur. "I have talked to the other Big One you captured. His people did bad things and they will be punished. I ask that you let us take this man to answer for his crimes."

A lot of what was said to him was difficult to understand. Red Fur got the gist, though. Big Ones want to be friends. Big Ones want to help *Jin-f'ke*. Most importantly, the Fuhzzeez wanted their Big One back.

"I make talk with my people," Red Fur said. "You take Joe Quigley, now."

"Really?" Joe couldn't believe his luck. He didn't care what happened to him as long as he was away from the Fuzzies.

"Yes. The Jack Holloway say you be punished for Sun Fur making dead and other…things I not understand. I give you to Jack Holloway for this." Red Fur turned to Little Fuzzy. "We not want Big Ones here. We only speak with you."

Little Fuzzy nodded. "Hokay. I make talk for Pappy Jack and the Big Ones." He turned to Jack. "We go, now?"

Jack nodded. "Yes. We go."

"I go, too," a Fuzzy said. "The Joe Quigley calls me Thor. I would see these things Little Fuhzzee make talk of."

"Another Thor?" Morgan said. He noticed the crude bandage on the Fuzzy's shoulder. "Okay, Thor. If Red Fur say okay, you come. And we can find others who are hurt and help them."

"Strong One…Thor want go, he go," Red Fur said. "I not say who stay or go."

XXXI

"I'm not going to take you into custody, but you will be charged," George Lunt said.

Morgan nodded. "I hope no charges will be brought against Thor Folkvar, Major."

George looked across the room at the large Magnian. Thor had acted on Morgan's orders. Failing to do so could have gotten him fired, and he didn't hurt anybody. George hated seeing people put in rock and hard place positions. "No, I see no point in that. I'll settle for your hide."

Jack and Little Fuzzy watched the by-play from the bar next to Thor, both of them drinking a decaffeinated tea. Jack considered intervening and decided against it. Morgan was a big boy and didn't need daddy to get him out of a jam.

"You're not thinking of apologizing to him, are you?"

Jack turned to Thor. "For what?"

"That punch you handed him. You didn't pull it any, either, as far as I could tell." Thor finished the mead from his ridiculously oversized stein and gestured for a refill. As the robot complied, Thor Folkvar ruffled the Fuzzy's head. "You probably understand Freyan culture better than I do, but I think if you apologize it will embarrass him far more than the punch itself."

Jack nodded. "Yeah. Fathers don't own up to their mistakes there. Hell, we usually don't on Terra, either. No, no apology. I don't do something I don't mean to do, and I don't say I'm sorry for it afterwards. Morgan's actions resulted in that little war we just saw. Some Fuzzies were killed and a helluva lot more were wounded."

"How many?"

"What? Killed? I think five or six. Wounded, I have no idea. Morgan might since his medical team treated most of them."

Thor took a long drink from his refill. "There were, what, five hundred odd Fuzzies out on that battlefield, plus three hundred dogs, right?"

Jack nodded.

"Only half a dozen were killed!"

"Yes. Mostly *Jin-f'ke*, I think," Jack said, "Fuzzies, as far as anybody knows, never had a war before. As soon as the *Jin-f'ke* attacked, everybody threw down their bows and spears and rifles and went at it with chopper-diggers. They treated it like a mass duel. As soon as one opponent went down wounded, he was ignored and the winner went on to pick a fight with somebody else. Nobody was double-teamed, and no *coup de grace* on a downed Fuzzy. It was the most civilized battle I had ever seen. And I've seen enough to know what I'm talking about."

Thor snorted in his drink, shooting froth over the bar. "Civilized battle. I don't think those two words have ever been used together like that in all of human history. Frankly, I was surprised the dogs didn't jump in and rip the Northern Fuzzies to pieces."

"Larry Wolvin trained them too well for that. A Curtys will attack anything his master tells him to except another Fuzzy. Even another human."

"What?" Thor set his stein down. "Any one of those dogs looks like they could rip a man's throat out in a heartbeat. They weigh, what, about a hundred and twenty pounds Terran Standard? Why wouldn't you train them not to attack humans?"

Jack shook his head sadly. "Because humans aren't as civilized and well-behaved as Fuzzies. If a bad Big One messes with a Fuzzy, he needs to be able to protect himself. Even those .22 rifles we gave them aren't much defense against a large human with a pistol. I'll bet it would take a full clip just to bring you down."

The four-hundred and eighty-pound, heavily-muscled Magnian nodded. "I'm not bulletproof, but I take your meaning."

"Well, if a human messes with a Fuzzy, he's going to have to deal with the dog, too. That's why I signed off on the plan." Jack finished his tea. "How long before we're back home?"

Big Thor checked his chronometer. "I suspect we're already there."

"I would like a dog," Thor said to Little Fuzzy. He and Little Fuzzy entered a discussion on the value of such beasts. It ended with Little Fuzzy taking Thor down to the cargo hold to meet some Curtys.

"Planning on adopting your namesake?" Jack asked.

"Maybe. My wife is gone and my children all grown. A Fuzzy companion might be nice to have."

Jack looked the Magnian's face over. He looked to be in his thirties. "If you don't mind, how old are you?"

"Fifty-two. If I had stayed on Magni I would probably look more my age. Lower gravity-worlds don't seem to affect my skin as much. And before you ask, no, my wife didn't die. We had a contract marriage and it termed out after three years. We renewed it, once, but after that the wanderlust got the better of me and we didn't renew again."

"Oh, well, if you decide to go back to Magni, I don't think you should take Thor with you...."

Thor Folkvar looked shocked. "Why would I return to Magni? I am a hundred pounds heavier there and suffer back pain every time I go home. Did you know that the average height for a man on Magni is five foot six? Any taller and the gravity messes with your knees and back. It also cuts ten years off your lifespan. My father, two-meter tall beanpole that he was, came from Terra and married my mother, a Magnian woman. Now, here I am too tall to be comfortable on the planet of my birth. Nah. As long as Morgan stays on Zarathustra, so will I."

Jack refilled his tea and took a sip. The Earl Grey Green was growing on him. "Good to know." Another thought struck him. "Morgan is the CEO of the Chartered Magni Cooperative. What if he makes Magni his base of operations?"

Thor looked over his stein at Jack, then set it on the bar. "Then I'll have to find other employment. Magni is a nice place to visit, but I just can't live there."

Jack nodded. It was a terrible thing when a man couldn't go home.

* * * * * * * * *

Gus Brannhard entered the office at his usual 0830, half an hour before the rest of the staff came in. This way he had time to read the newspaper and do a quick scan of the data stream. Gus turned on his desk terminal and scanned for new messages. The serial rapist of Junktown had been killed by his intended victim. Good, that would save him the trouble of prosecuting the bastard. Frankly, Gus figured the man could have been charged with felony stupid if he didn't realize that even women were armed on colony planets. Gus scanned around hoping for something on the hitman that took out his abductors. Instead, something else caught his attention immediately; it was a message from the late Leo Thaxter.

Curious, and expecting a prank, he opened the message. The face that filled the screen definitely looked like Thaxter, though it could just as easily be Clancy Slade or a digital mock-up; it would take a forensic technician to be sure. Gus listened intently as the image spoke.

"Mr. Brannhard. If you are seeing this message, than I must be either dead, off-planet or back in Prison House. I won't make odds on which one. Believe it or not, I hold no malice toward you for sending me to prison. I knew what business I was in and the likely results of my line of work. In fact, I am rather grateful that you accepted the plea bargain that kept me breathin' for another twenty years.

"That said, I have a small present for you. The following video feed was taken the night of Ivan Bowlby's death. There's a lot more, but I think you'll especially like this clip."

The video feed that followed brought a look of unholy glee to the face of the Chief Colonial Prosecutor. This was even better than catching the hitman.

* * * * * * * * *

Piet Dumont was conscious and communicative in his hospital bed when Colonial Marshal Max Fane and Gus Brannhard walked in with Officers Chang and York. He tried to sit up in his bed but Max motioned for him to stay still.

"We're here to make sure you heard the news first, Piet," Max said.

"Oh? I already know that Thaxter is dead, if that's what you are...."

"No. Not Thaxter, though he did play a part in this," Gus interrupted. "We are here to arrest Ivan Dane."

Piet searched his drug-fogged memory a moment, then recalled that Dane was one of the people Thaxter shot at the B.I.N. building. "What'd he do? Felonious bullet-catching?"

"He murdered Ivan Bowlby," Max said with a wolfish grin. "And, we have reason to believe he was involved with the illegal mining operation over on Beta. George Lunt and Ahmed Khadra are bringing over a co-conspirator right now."

"We also have Thaxter on video giving an account of how Dane orchestrated his jailbreak," Gus added. "We're going to clear a lot of cases with this."

"Son-of-a-bitch. Nurse! Get me a hover-chair, right now." Piet scrambled painfully out of the bed and shuffled over to the cabinet with his clothes.

Max tried to stop him but was afraid to restrain him. Piet had a lot of stitching on his chest from the operation to remove Thaxter's bullet and it would be a day or two before they could use the neo-derma-plas over the wound. "Piet, what are you doing? Get back in bed."

"And miss this arrest? Like Nifflheim I will. Chang, go get that damned nurse and get me a chair. York, help me with my shirt."

"Better let him come along, Max," Gus said. "The doc said the bullet didn't hit anything too vital and he's more likely to hurt himself if we try to keep him here."

Piet looked up as he zipped up the jacket. "You better believe it. Hey, where's Clancy?"

"At home with his family. Asleep most likely, since he works the night shift," Max said. "There's talk of the Colonial Medal for Bravery for his actions, yesterday."

"He earned it," Piet said. Chang entered the room with a nurse and a hover-chair. Piet sat down and let out a long breath. His chest hurt like all Nifflheim. "Now let's go arrest us a murderer."

XXXII

Gerd slammed his fist on the console in frustration. The main computer was still acting up. Joe Verganno was still trying to track the source of the glitch down in the mainframe. His best guess was that a new virus had slipped through the firewalls, which was a good trick considering the sophistication of the computer security systems.

"Careful," said a voice from behind him. "Those things are expensive as all Nifflheim."

Gerd turned to see Victor Grego accompanied by Morgan Holloway and Akira O'Barre walking around some of the worker robots. Gerd greeted each in turn, then said, "If a love tap like that can hurt a poly-steel encased computer console, then whoever you bought it from saw you coming a light-year away."

"Actually, it was built here on planet by the Company. Joe Verganno designed it himself. Still having trouble with the software, I take it."

"Yeah," Gerd said in disgust. "Without a trained linguist on planet the computer is the best we got, but it just won't scan and search the database for possible matches. It isn't programmed for it. Of course the likelihood of the alien language being in the databank is very low, anyway. We need a human, not a machine."

"Well, if you had taken a few days off like I had suggested, the bugs might have been zapped before you got back. What are you doing here, anyway?"

Gerd slumped in his seat. "For the moment I am a man without a country. I wasn't back on Beta for five minutes before Jack had to take off and tackle that Fuzzy problem up in Northern Beta. He told me that while I am on the Company payroll I shouldn't be getting involved and suggested I spend some time with Ruth."

Grego mentally winced. Jack was trying to push Gerd into taking the Company job and was showing that he could manage without him.

"Ruth, on the other hand, spends a lot of her time working with Fuzzies on the Reservation on top of her social work. We managed to spend yesterday morning together, then I got the word that Jack had been taken prisoner and tried to go help. George Lunt ever so politely reminded me that for the time being I was a civilian and had me escorted back to my cabin."

Morgan smiled and said, "If it helps, I am being charged with interfering with the NPF plus assault on an officer. Major George Lunt, by name. Leslie spoke with Gus and they think I can avoid jail time though the fine will be…what was that word he used?"

"Homeric," Akira supplied. "Ben instituted a fine table based on the offender's financial resources, according to Gus."

That sounded like Ben, Grego thought, *champion of the underdog.*

"I assume that means it will be a lot," Morgan finished.

"I think even you will feel the pinch," Grego said. "Back to you, Gerd. Why didn't you just stay home with Ruth?"

"Because Ruth isn't home. She's here in Mallorysport doing her social work. Id, Syndrome, Superego and Complex all marched off to war yesterday before I knew what they were up to, and I couldn't get through to George to find out what was going on, so I came in with Ruth. Once here, I had nothing else to do, so I came back to work."

"Aren't you worried about your Fuzzies?" Akira asked. "They could get killed fighting those other Fuzzies."

"Fuzzies don't kill each other the way humans do. And the res crowd has human weaponry and training. Was I worried? Yes. So was Ruth. But Fuzzies have been surviving oomphty-thousand years without us Big Ones, and I have to trust them to do what they think is right."

Jack has rubbed off on Gerd, Grego thought.

"And I seem to recall hearing that all the Fuzzies went off in a Big One's private spaceship," Gerd added, as he looked over at Morgan.

"Ah. Yes." Morgan actually looked a little sheepish. "If you haven't heard back yet, they are all fine. There were a few fatalities, but none of yours or Jack's family."

"Actually, I got the word last night. It saved you from being in another duel," Gerd added lightly. "I wouldn't be able to concentrate on this," Gerd tapped the metal plaque from the rocket, "if I didn't know my family was safe. At the very least I should probably pop you one."

Morgan rubbed the bruise on his jaw. "Ah, my esteemed father has already attended to that."

"Why not let Morgan take a crack at translating the plaque?" Akira suggested. "He speaks several languages."

Gerd sat up and took notice. "You do? Like what?"

"Well, aside from Lingua Terra there's Sosti, the Freyan tongue, Khooghra, Ulleran, Latin, German, ancient Martian, Barsoomian…"

Grego interrupted, "Barsoomian?"

"Yes, Victor. It was a pledge requirement in my fraternity back at Mars University. It is an artificial language comprised of words culled from a variety of fantasy books about Mars and mixed in with some ancient Martian."

"He also had to dress up as John Carter of Mars for the frat parties," Akira added, with a laugh. "You should see the pictures—"

"Which they won't," Morgan interrupted.

"I had to learn Yiddish for my frat on Terra," Grego said. "Barsoomian must have been a breeze compared to that. Well, hell,

Morgan, take a crack at it. Gerd, any objections?"

Gerd had none and produced the metal plaque from the rocket. Morgan looked at it, turned it around and traced some of the symbols with a forefinger.

"Interesting. These are the Freyan symbols for 'emptiness' or 'void'."

Grego and Gerd looked at each other in surprise. "Freyan? You think this artifact is from Freya?" Gerd asked.

Morgan shook his head in negation. "Not at all. Look hard enough at any two languages and you might find some symbols in common." Morgan looked harder at the writing on the plaque. Some of it was still obscured by corrosion. "If I didn't know better…well, I am a little rusty, but this looks like Martioform. This here, after 'void' is the Martian suffix '*hulva*', meaning 'study of.'"

"Void study," Gerd said. "Space exploration! Do the Freyans and Martians apply the same meaning to that symbol?"

"Almost," Morgan said. "In Martian it means 'space.' In fact, the symbols for dirt, fire, water and air are very similar in the two languages. That's about it, though, between Sosti and Martioform. Oddly, there are some Cyrillic symbols with equivalents in Sosti…. "

"Can you translate the rest of the plaque?" Grego prompted.

Morgan returned his attention to the artifact. "Well, with what I can make out, and assuming that this is, in fact, Martian, then it says, roughly, 'Space Exploration Craft Sooleesh One.' That's all I can get without the rest of the corrosion being cleaned off. "

"Sooleesh?"

"King of the ten gods of ancient Mars, Akira," Morgan explained. "He was a sun god, basically, like Apollo or Ra Amon on Terra or D'rhalum on Freya."

Grego's eyes went wide. "This rocket is the Martian equivalent to, what, Apollo One back in Terra's early space exploration days?"

"Apollo Seven, actually," Gerd said. "Apollo One never made it off the ground due to a disaster on the launch pad that killed the crew. This ship clearly made it off-planet."

"Then the question is: how did a spaceship with no hyperdrive travel over seventy-two light-years and crash here?" Grego looked at the rocket. It was clear even to a simple businessman that it wasn't designed for deep space flight.

"I guess we're back to the worm-hole theory," Gerd said. "This is a fantastic find! The Martianist movement will go nuts over this."

"And that's why they'll never hear about it."

Grego, Morgan, Gerd and Akira all turned to the new voice. It was Lt. Commander Pancho Ybarra accompanied by Commodore Napier.

"You just dug up the Federation's worst nightmare; something to give credence to the crackpot theories the Martianists have been spouting for the last hundred years," supplied Napier. "The Martianists have been growing in numbers and are on the verge of becoming a political power. Something like this would be just the shot in the arm they need to achieve that goal."

"So what?" Akira interjected. "How are they different from any other political group?"

"They have a lot of strange agendas, Miss O'Barre," Pancho said. "Like moving the seat of the Federation Government to Mars, terraforming Mars to be habitable again, changing all the history books to reflect the Martian Origin theory...."

"That last will raise all kinds of Nifflheim with the Religious Right, Christian and Muslim, much like the Darwin debates back in the Pre-Atomic Era," Napier added. "Wars have been started with far less provocation. The facts that a Martian spaceship landing here does little to prove Terrans originated on Mars won't even be considered. It will be a political and religious nightmare."

The room fell silent save for the background noise of the robotic crew cleaning the interior of the rocket.

After several heartbeats, Gerd spoke up. "We may have one of those here on Zarathustra if we can't provide a plausible explanation for this rocket being here. Ivan Dane is challenging the legitimacy of the current government based on a 'Fuzzies landing here from space' theory."

"Which could tie up Company assets for years while the courts decide who gets to administer the planetary holdings," Grego added. "This rocket came from somewhere, and if it can't be from Mars or the Planet of the Fuzzies, then where did it come from?"

"Any chance we can blame it on a Martianist conspiracy?" Gerd offered. "Do they have the resources to pull off a hoax this big?"

Commodore Napier considered it, then said no. "Nobody would buy it and the Martianists would demand access to the artifact to prove they had nothing to do with it, which we would have to allow for legal reasons. Five minutes in a veridicator on live television would kill that plan, anyway."

"So we need a scapegoat who isn't in a position to fight back," Grego said. "Personally, I would like to blame this all on that Ivan Dane, or even Hugo Ingermann."

"Dane would be a good choice, but right now he has too much support on Zarathustra," Pancho said. "Besides, it wouldn't be ethical to frame an innocent man."

"Innocent," Gerd snarled. "He just hasn't been caught out, yet."

"He may yet get caught with his hand in the cookie jar," Grego said. "If so, we can hang it on him. If he is pulling something, he won't dare let himself be put under veridication and prove it. Too many other crimes might come to light. And refusing to answer under veridication just makes him look guilty, anyway."

"Assuming he is, in fact, crooked and not just misguided," Pancho added. "Some people actually believe the idiotic drivel they spout. There are even psychoses for it."

"Well, we'll just brand this a hoax and let the chips fall where they may," Napier pronounced. "The rocket will be taken to a secure location and mothballed or studied. Your names will be logged as the official discoverers, then placed in a sealed file for a time when it can be safely revealed for what it truly is."

Grego shook his head. "If this rocket disappears, then we'll have even bigger problems. We need something for experts to examine and the public to tear apart or people will scream 'cover up'."

Commodore Napier, nobody's fool by any standard, caught on instantly. "Okay, Mr. Grego. What will it cost for you to build us a fake rocket? And it has to be believable, at least at first."

Grego smiled that too toothy grin of his and pulled an estimate off the top of his head. It was Homeric.

XXXIII

Ivan Dane lay in his bed under sedation. While his wounds were relatively minor, he complained so much about the pain that the doctors finally relented and put him under, much to the relief of the nursing staff. As such, he was completely oblivious when Marshal Fane, Gus Brannhard, Piet Dumont and officers Chang and York entered his room to place him under arrest.

"Now that's just plain rude," Piet said. "We go to all the trouble to arrest this mutt and he can't even bother to be awake for it."

"Well, we can still tag him," Max said. He nodded at Chang and the officer produced an electronic ankle tether. York assisted and the two men placed the tether on Dane's left ankle. No matter where Dane went, the police would be able to track his movements for as long as he remained on Zarathustra. Moreover, any attempt to leave the planet would result in a sudden explosive loss of the leg. "Chang, York, you have first watch. This Khooghra so much as hiccups, I want to know about it."

"Yes, sir!" the two officers replied in unison.

"What is going on here?" The group turned to the sound of the voice and discovered Dr. Drogan. "This man is under heavy sedation and should not be disturbed."

"This man is under arrest for murder, illegal gem trafficking, illegal mining, conspiracy to murder, and a bunch of other crimes we haven't tallied, yet," Gus said.

Drogan glanced at the patient, then back to Gus. "He's a wanted felon? Interesting; that might explain this body scan."

"What body scan?" demanded Max.

Drogan shifted uncomfortably. Doctor/patient confidentiality prevented him from giving too many details of Dane's condition. "I'll need a warrant to tell you anything more."

Max started to say something and Gus put up a restraining hand. "Dr. Drogan is correct. I'm not going to give this mutt any avenue to duck the charges, no matter how minor or unlikely. I'll be back in an hour, maybe less, with that warrant. I am sure Chief Justice Pendarvis will be happy to sign it himself."

* * * * * * * * *

"...and we'll supply them all the extee-three they want," finished Jack. He and Little Fuzzy had been discussing opening political relations with the *Jin-f'ke*, a concept unique in Zarathustran history.

"We give *shoppo-diggo*, medicine and *estee-fee* to *Jin-f'ke*," Little Fuzzy summarized.

"And?" Jack prodded.

Little Fuzzy thought for a moment, them his face brightened. "An' Big Ones not interfere with *Jin'f-ke*."

Jack ruffled the Fuzzy's head. "Very good, Ambassador. Pappy George will fly you up to meet with Red Fur, uh, *Bal-f'ke* as soon as he gets back from Alpha Continent." Jack had decided that it would improve Little Fuzzy's standing with the Northern Fuzzies if the Wise One for all Big Ones wasn't there to look over his shoulder.

"Hokay, Pappy Jack." Little Fuzzy scampered out narrowly missing Betty Kanazawa as she stormed in. The look on her face was intense.

Damn, I should have put on my gun belt. "Betty, when did you get in?"

"What were you thinking letting yourself get captured like that?" Betty demanded. She had her hands on her waist and she leaned slightly forward as she spoke. The stance reminded Jack of his mother when she argued with his father.

Jack couldn't help smiling, which was a mistake. Betty went up three octaves and railed at him for taking unnecessary chances. Jack let her wind down before he spoke.

"Betty, this is my job. It is what I do. And if being captured by Fuzzies is the most dangerous thing I ever do, I'm going to get real bored real fast."

Betty sputtered for a second, then deflated and sat on the edge of the desk. After a moment, she laughed. "I almost forgot what attracted me to you."

Jack sat on the desk next to Betty. "Ah…Betty, about the other night. I wasn't myself. It seems I suffered from a drug interaction…."

"You did seem a little loopy after you took your meds," Betty said, nodding. "Don't sweat it, Jack. I wasn't looking to trap you. I will admit that I am very interested in pursuing a relationship with you. And no, I do not have any daddy issues or a thing for white hair, though it does look good on you."

Jack let out a long breath. "I was worried, I may have taken some liberties…."

"Hah! I practically dragged you into the bedroom. You're a lot heavier than you look, by the way." Betty shifted a bit to get closer to Jack. "I'm a big girl and know how to defend myself. I strength train and take self-defense classes and could probably kick your ass even if you were fully recovered. If anything, I should apologize to you."

Jack smiled. "Oh, I think I can live with being taken advantage of."

Betty winked. "You certainly seemed to manage that night."

"Betty, I am old enough to be your father, you know. I have way more birthdays behind me than ahead of me."

Betty laughed again. "Actually, you're about the same age as my grandfather who will likely outlive us both, but I won't tell anybody if you don't."

Jack chuckled. "Deal. I'll admit that you interest me as well, Betty. That hasn't happened in a long time."

"Morgan's mother, right? I understand." Betty snorted as she tried to stifle another laugh. "What say we give Morgan a heart attack and tell him we're eloping?"

Jack laughed out loud. He pictured the look on his son's face. "I don't know. You might be a bit old for me." Jack thought about Freyan culture and remembered something. "Actually, it is not uncommon for an elderly man who has lost his wife to take a much younger bride on Freya."

"It's not all that uncommon on Terra, either," Betty remarked. "And they don't always wait for the first wife to die, first."

"Okay, here's the deal. We'll see how well things work between us and go from there. But remember, I am an old coot with a lot of hard-wired habits and I don't figure on changing any of them."

Betty nodded. "Fair enough. And back at'cha, though if anybody calls me an old anything they'll be picking their teeth up off of the floor."

Yup, a lot like mom. Jack thought about it for a moment and remembered it was that same quality that attracted him to Morgan's mother back on Freya. "So, what are you doing tonight?"

"Oh, Nifflheim! I took off after work and didn't give any thought to anything other than seeing if you were okay. Hmm…I think I am coming down with something."

"Oh? Something serious?"

"I'll say. I'll be bedridden for the next couple of days, I think. I'll have to take some sick time, of course."

Jack feigned concern over the convenient malady. "What do you think you have?"

Betty winked again. "Jack Fever. I think it could be terminal."

* * * * * * * * *

Gus Brannhard, accompanied by Victor Grego and Colonial Marshal Max Fane, pushed their way into Governor Rainsford's office unannounced. Ben Rainsford raised his head in surprise to find their three grinning faces staring back at him. Gus was almost purring with a feral look in his eyes. The last time he looked like that was when Chief Justice Pendarvis ruled that he and Leslie Coombes would be prosecuting each other's clients in the now famous Fuzzy Trial.

Gus laid a folder in front of Rainsford and tapped it with a hairy finger. "Ben, you are not going to believe what we have here."

Rainsford looked over the smiling faces. It was a little disturbing. "Okay, I'll bite. What do you have there?"

Gus opened the folder. On the first sheet was a medical file-page on one Ivan Maximilian Dane. Rainsford looked it over with a 'so what' expression on his face.

"Okay. Dane has had numerous surgeries and a recent gunshot wound. Anybody who watched the news knows about that last bit."

"Ah, but it is the kind of surgeries he has had that is so interesting," Gus said. "Notice he had leg and arm extension surgery. Plastic surgery, dental reconstruction, a larynx adjustment, hair transplants, and there are signs of significant weight loss. A lot of it. Ocular enhancement surgery, too."

Rainsford sighed. "He's vain and rich. I trust you are surrounding a point here, Gus."

"Yes, Gus, you should get to the point," Grego said.

"One shouldn't keep the Governor waiting, Mr. Brannhard," Max added.

Gus nodded dramatically. "Quite right, gentleman. Ben, when Mr. Dane was admitted, the hospital did a full body scan. Standard procedure. That is how we got all that information. Now, here is something I didn't know: a smart computer graphics artist can take that scan and do a graphic reconstruction to find out what that person looked like before all that surgery."

"As it turns out, we have some very talented graphic artists working for the Company," Grego said.

"You promised you were getting to a point," Rainsford prodded.

"Look at the next page," Gus, Grego and Max said in unison.

Rainsford suspected the three of them had practiced the presentation. It had to be truly amazing for all of them to go to that much effort. He turned the page and saw the artist's rendition of what Ivan Dane looked like prior to his cosmetic surgeries.

"Holy Mother of Ghu!"

Gus nodded once at Max and Grego. "There it is."

"Tell me he's in custody. Under guard, with lots of collapsium around his ass."

"Yes, yes and soon. He isn't skipping planet this time," Gus said. "We have him for murder and a slew of other charges. There is a list of them on the next page."

Rainsford stood up, sat down, stood up again. "Would anybody think it too odd if I did a little happy dance?"

"A little."

"Yes."

"Understandable, but not very governor-like."

Rainsford looked at the three men then said, "To Nifflheim with it. It isn't every day that Hugo Ingermann is caught red-handed." That said Bennett Rainsford, Colonial Governor of Zarathustra, danced a jig.

"He's pretty good, don't you think?" Max pointed out.

XXXIV

"Hugo Ingermann!"

"The one and only, accept no substitutes."

Jack could not believe his ears. Rainsford was smiling from the viewscreen like a Khooghra about to eat a deceased relative. He was also sweating, like he had just finished exercising.

"So, the illegal mining that started all the troubles with the *Jin-f'ke*, those anti-you and Grego editorials, the death of Ricardo La Rue, or Raul Laporte, whatever his real name was, and the Fuzzy Rocket are all part of…what, a bid to take over the planet?"

"The rocket, no, but pretty much everything else. Max is heading over to the B.I.N. building to arrest everyone in sight. Judge Pendarvis has hand cramps from signing all the writs and warrants. Once we secure a conviction on Ingermann or Dane, whatever, we'll seize the B.I.N. building and contents as assets in furtherance of a crime. Since that used to be Bowlby's little enterprise, there's no telling what all we'll find once we start tearing that place apart."

Jack leaned back and reached for his pipe, then set it down. *Damned doctors*, he thought, *how is a man supposed to celebrate without a cocktail and a pipe?* "Sounds like organized crime is wiped out on Zarathustra."

"For the next week or so. Gus assures me we'll have a new crop of criminal cartels or syndicates or what-have you to keep the police earning their pay in no time. Nature abhors a vacuum and all that."

"An unfortunate truth. Hey, when is that son of mine getting back here? I have a severe shellacking to hand him."

"Aren't you going to try to get him out of the charges George Lunt is hitting him with? He has to go to court this afternoon, Gus tells me."

"No, I am not. He got himself in trouble, he can get himself out. George asked me if I wanted him to drop the charges and I said no. I never liked nepotism and I'll be damned if I start practicing it now. Besides, Gus told me there would be no jail time involved due to the extenuating circumstances. He can handle any fine the judge throws at him."

"True. Well, I'll tell him you asked when I see him this afternoon to finalize the sale of Zeta Continent." Rainsford grabbed a sheet of paper from the desk and held it up to the screen. "I shoved this through the legislature this morning. With Ivan Dane, excuse me, Hugo Ingermann off his soapbox I am pretty much bulletproof in the media. So, the legislature is rubber-stamping things for me."

"Enjoy it while it lasts. Hey, Hugo Ingermann, if convicted, and I really don't see how he can avoid it, will be up for the death penalty. Planning on selling tickets to that one, too?"

Rainsford eyes went wide. "Oh, hell, that's a great idea. The line for that one will be clean around the planet. I'll set it up as soon as the verdict is in." The Governor looked up from the screen. "Gus just came in to remind me I have to go pin the medal on Clancy Slade. It'll be covered on CZCN."

"Okay. Talk to you later."

Jack broke the connection and leaned back in his chair. Betty came up behind him wearing something filmy from Marduk and sat down on the edge of the desk.

"Good news?"

"We got Hugo Ingermann."

Betty filled the air with some extremely unladylike metaphors. She finished with, "He should be shot from a cannon into a collapsium wall."

"No argument. By the way, when is Akira going to tell Morgan that she's pregnant?"

Betty looked stricken. "What? How did you…um…oh! You tricked me!"

"Old age and deviousness beat youth and inexperience every time. How far along is she?"

"About two months. What clued you in?"

"Nothing I can put my finger on, but I've been around a lot of pregnant women in my time and after a while you just get a sense about these things. I figured that was why she was here working for me. That Freyan tradition thing, even though I am hardly of the noble class."

Betty pulled a chair over and sat next to Jack. "What are you going to do? Will you give your approval?"

"Nifflheim, she had that ten minutes after I first met her. I also respect the fact that she isn't using the baby to trap Morgan. In fact, I'm going to speed the process up a bit and maybe have a little fun with them. Want to help?"

Betty smiled brightly. "Of course. What will we do?"

Jack explained and Betty laughed out loud.

* * * * * * * * *

The ceremony had gone well. Clancy didn't appear too nervous on camera, and Rainsford kept his speech short, which was always a crowd pleaser. Gus handed an envelope to Clancy afterwards then followed the governor back to his office. Once back, he explained what was in the envelope. It was the reissued deeds for the cabin and aircar that Thaxter had bought in Clancy's name.

"You did what?" the Colonial Governor screamed. "Gus, that

cabin, aircar and the contents of that locker were all proceeds of a crime. As such they were subject to seizure by the police."

"What crime," Gus asked in his most reasonable tone of voice.

Ben sputtered as he tried to think of an answer. "You're the lawyer. You tell me."

Gus sighed and took a seat. "Ben, the only provable crimes were committed by us, if you want to be technical. There is no law that says a convicted felon cannot buy or sell property. In fact, believe it or not, he could run for governor as there are no provisions in our constitution to prohibit it. The fact that Thaxter was an escapee is irrelevant. There is also no law that says a convicted felon cannot rent property, to wit, a spaceport locker.

"What the law does say is that police cannot enter a private residence without either a warrant or the owner's consent except in rare cases of exigent circumstances, like somebody is about to be murdered, or there is probable cause, as in a scream or gunshot coming from the dwelling. That applies to the spaceport locker as well. It is Federation law not subject to reversal by member planets. And unlike the old days before the veridicator was invented, a cop can't claim exigent circumstances if the veridicator won't bear him out. With me so far?"

Ben nodded.

"Good. So, either the police entered the cabin and took data from the computer therein with the consent of the owner, to wit Clancy Slade, or they did an illegal search and seizure of Leo Thaxter's property. Now, if Clancy was able to give that consent, then it has to be his property, in which case we have no business seizing it as we have no proof he did anything illegal. Still with me?"

"Yes, but I'm not sure I like where this is going," Ben said.

Gus shrugged. "Now, if it is not the property of Clancy Slade, then we can all be sued for violating Thaxter's civil liberties. Even though he is not alive to do so on his own initiative, there is always some ambulance chaser willing to do it on Leo's behalf for the good of the people and to get his name in the news feed." Gus put air quotes around 'good of the people.' "His sister, Rose Evins, could make a stink about it from prison, too."

Ben slumped a little in his chair. "Okay, fine, the cabin and aircar are Clancy's, but the contents of that locker…."

"The cash and sunstones in the locker were suspicious, yes, but not illegal in and of themselves," Gus continued. "There has been no reported theft of cash or sunstones in anywhere near that quantity. We have no evidence that they were stolen at all. We have no direct evidence that they came from that illegal prospecting operation on Beta, either, though I wouldn't be at all surprised.

"On a planet with income tax, we could go after either Clancy or Thaxter for tax fraud, but that would be it. Thaxter's dead and Clancy was granted blanket immunity for anything we might find even if he was a co-conspirator, which we know for a veridicated fact that he is not, so even if we *had* income tax, which, thanks to you, we don't, we still couldn't touch him.

"There is an old misquote that claims 'possession is nine-tenths of the law.' The cabin and locker were all in Clancy's name, making them his property. Trust me Ben, it isn't worth the headache to try and take it away from him, and as far as I'm concerned, he earned it when he shot Thaxter."

Ben rolled his eyes and leaned back in his seat. Gus was right, of course. He was one of the best legal minds on the planet, and if he said it wasn't legally possible, then it just plain wasn't legally possible. "You said that expression is misquoted? What is the actual quote?"

Gus looked at the ceiling and searched his memory, saying, "It's from an old Scottish expression: Possession is eleven points in the law, and they say there are but twelve."

"What the Nifflheim does that mean?"

"It means that in a property dispute, in the absence of clear and compelling testimony or documentation to the contrary, the person in actual possession of the contested property is presumed to be the rightful owner. The shirt and trousers you are currently wearing is presumed to be yours, unless someone can prove that they are not."

Gus paused to pull out a cigar and light it. "Clancy possesses such documentation, anyway, remember? Inspector Piet Dumont dug it up himself and I had it reissued so Clancy's real signature could be put on the documents. That covers our asses, too, by the way. And there are no counter documents proving otherwise; I made sure of that. It means Clancy Slade is now the proud owner of a country cabin, aircar and a lot of cash and sunstones. Good for him, I say."

Ben mulled it over, then started laughing softly. "First Thaxter's cell, now his cabin. Clancy is making a career out of sleeping in Thaxter's bed. Let's hope this is for the last time."

Gus smiled and nodded. "I'll drink to that. In fact, I'll even buy the first round."

XXXV

Richard Lundgren was very afraid. When Dane and Murdock were shot on the steps of the B.I.N. building, he had mixed feelings. Dane was a good administrator and had a long-term plan that would make all of them very rich while Murdock provided muscle and underworld know-how. However, with them out of the picture, Lundgren was prepared to take over the operation. He wasn't the least bit concerned about opposition from Dr. Quigley, Prof. Darloss or Dr. Rankin. They were all lab geeks unaccustomed to running a business. It was all set for him to just step up and take over.

Then the police stormed in with a stack of warrants to go over the building inch by inch. Warrants to search the building, rifle the files and, worst of all, seize the computers. There was a lot of very damaging evidence on those computers. A smart forensic computer cop would find the program used to hack the Terran Federation Naval communications and the virus Lundgren created to bitch up the CZC mainframe.

Taking over was out. Staying on-planet was out. Lundgren rifled the safe and stuffed all the cash and sunstones he could carry into a duffle bag. It was time to go. There was an outbound ship scheduled to leave planet the next day. Lundgren planned on being on it. With the mentality of a rat leaving a sinking ship, he left without warning the others.

* * * * * * * * *

Dr. Quigley had just finished adjusting the gamma emitter when he was swarmed by policemen. Somehow they had found the entrance to the secret passageway and followed it down to find him. The doctor was quickly handcuffed and escorted up the passage while the cops photographed and impounded everything in sight.

"I demand to speak to an attorney!" the outraged doctor yelled. "What am I being charged with?"

"Homicide, conspiracy, accomplice after the fact...we'll give you the whole long list on the ride to the station." Officer Chang recited the ancient Miranda speech then did a mental double take. "Dr. Quigley? By any chance are you related to a Joseph Quigley?"

"Yes. My son." Quigley almost mentioned that Joe died two months earlier before remembering the circumstances of his death. Instead, he asked, "Why?"

"We have a Joseph Aaron Quigley in custody. He was brought in from Beta Continent earlier today."

"He's alive?"

The officer nodded.

"Forget the lawyer. Take me to see my son!"

* * * * * * * * *

Prof. Darloss was in the middle of working on his next interview for *Spinning Wheels* by compiling a list of reasons the Fuzzies couldn't be native to Zarathustra. It wasn't going as well as he would have liked. Fuzzies being the only indigenous bipedal life-forms had already been addressed when he was on the *Tuning In With Tuning* show a few months earlier. Hoenveld, not even an anthropologist or paleontologist, had managed to refute every claim to proof with annoying ease.

Darloss considered using "McGuire's Adaptive DNA Theorem" to explain the comparative similarity in genetic make-up between the Fuzzies and the rest of Zarathustran life. The problem there was the appallingly limited intelligence of the viewing audience. Most colonials, while capable and savvy about survival, knew very little about biology beyond 'eat this and you live, eat that and you die.'

The professor's efforts were additionally frustrated by the fact that Ivan Dane had been shot the day before. Ivan—no scientist by any measure—still had a way of spinning information or suggesting avenues of research that were amazingly helpful. The loss of Brandon Murdock, while unfortunate, had no impact on Darloss's work.

There was some sort of commotion going on outside his office. After thinking about it, Darloss realized that the noise had been building up for some time. He opened the door to find a very large policeman with a raised fist standing in front of him.

"Prof. Darloss? You are under arrest for homicide, conspiracy..." Officer Akpu-nku went on at some length, then recited the Miranda as he cuffed the professor.

Outraged, Darloss screamed his innocence. His protests fell on deaf ears.

* * * * * * * * *

Dr. Rankin returned from the pharmacy in a B.I.N. aircar and spotted the squadron of police vehicles on the roof and around the building. After the shooting the day before, he quickly surmised that something of their activities had leaked to the police and now everybody was being arrested.

Rankin had no interest in participating in the dog and pony show that was to surely follow and quickly altered course toward Junktown. There, he planned to sell the medical supplies he had just acquired on the black market, then buy an off-world ticket. He could probably sell the aircar, too, if he found the right buyer in the limited time he had.

* * * * * * * * *

"Put as many more as you can spare at the spaceport, Frank," Marshal Fane barked into the viewscreen. "I'll swing the overtime somehow. It's still your baby. I don't want to step on your toes, but we have to get these clowns before they skip planet."

Mallorysport Police Chief Frank Carr nodded in the screen. Max tapped a few buttons on his desk terminal and the screen image split into three windows: Chief Carr plus photo images of Richard Lundgren and Dr. Rankin. "These are the two mutts we're still looking for."

"I'll circulate these to the men," Chief Carr said. "They might be wearing synthmasks. I'll tell the men to detain and check anybody matching their general height and build."

"Good thinking. Try not to trample too many civil liberties while you're at it, though. Ben will scream bloody murder if the media spins that the wrong way."

Carr chuckled at that. "He's a bit oversensitive, I think. Still, at least he isn't one of those micromanaging semi-dictators I could name from other worlds. Back to this…Lundgren and Rankin? How dangerous are they?"

"Damn. I should have had you in the interrogation room with that Dr. Quigley. I guess I've been doing the micromanaging, again, and for that you have my apologies. Lundgren is a computer geek and Rankin is a medico. No history of violence on either of them."

"First time for everything, Marshal. I'll have the men treat them as potentially armed and dangerous. I'll have the extra spaceport cops work in mufti with tranq-guns so as not to disturb the law-abiding citizenry."

"Good idea, but lethal force is authorized should it become necessary."

Frank raised an eyebrow. "I guess I really should have been in that interview. What all is Quigley telling us?"

"Everything about everybody. All he wants is immunity for his kid. He didn't know that Dane and Murdock killed Bowlby, not that it matters since we have the video feed to prove that, but he knows about the Thaxter jailbreak, fake sunstones, illegal mining on the Fuzzy reservation, accidental manslaughter of a Fuzzy and a litany of other crimes. Gus is going to be very busy for a good long while on all of this. Oh, and pick up Spike Heenan, too. We found some interesting documents on his activities at the B.I.N. building. Murdock was putting the screws to him."

"Huh. All this and Hugo Ingermann, too. It's a good day to be a cop on Zarathustra."

"Amen to that, brother."

* * * * * * * * *

The biology department of Science Division was crowded to overflowing. Everybody who had a legitimate reason to be there was there, along with a number of people who normally had no business there. Among those normally not in attendance were several police officers, Gus Brannhard and Ruth van Riebeek and various news reporters from CZCN and other non-company affiliates.

Officers Chase and Warlikeshire carried in a long box that had been seized at the B.I.N. building and placed on the table indicated by Juan Jimenez. The officers set the box down and stepped back. A lab tech opened the box and extracted the contents while a second tech video recorded everything.

"These were in the B.I.N. building?"

Officer Chase nodded. "They were in a hidden sub-basement through a secret corridor, Dr. Jimenez. Before your people do whatever it is you do, we need to dust these for prints and DNA. Mr. Grego insisted that we do that under your department's supervision so as not to damage anything."

Grego said nothing. It was Juan's division and he didn't want to undercut his authority in front of his people.

"Thank you, Officer. That was very accommodating of the police to agree to that." Juan inspected the items extracted from the box as they were arranged on a second table.

"These look like those bones from that B.I.N. special last week," Officer Warlikeshire observed. "'Specially that skull."

The tech set the skull down on the table. "Good eye, Officer. In fact, some of these fossils might belong to the other bones found on Beta."

"So these aren't a murder victim?" Chase asked.

"No. At least not a recent one," Juan replied. There was a short laugh among the crowd. "These are what we are calling *Fuzzy giganticus beta*. And no, we are quite convinced they didn't pilot that rocket found near their bones."

Warlikeshire smiled and said, "I never thought they did, doctor. Shall we proceed with the forensic examination?"

Juan asked for a list of chemicals that would be used and the police forensic pathologist, Dr. Laurie rattled them off. Hoenveld stated that the substances would not damage the fossils and Laurie proceeded.

In the background Victor Grego stood next to Gus Brannhard watching Dr. Laurie work. "Gus, is this at all necessary? From what I hear, the case against the B.I.N. crowd is already airtight."

Gus snorted. "There is no such thing as an airtight case, Victor. Ghu himself could testify against these Khooghras and they could get off. Legal loopholes, surprise witnesses, brain dead jury—you name it."

"Even with the veridicator?"

"The veridicator can't compel people to speak, only catch them in a lie if they do. Ingermann will know that better than anybody. Keeping his clients mum was his favorite strategy when he practiced law on Zarathustra. Plus, the prosecution can't force the defendant to take the stand where he might incriminate himself. Only the defense can do that. That means loading up on all the physical evidence we can find. Prints, DNA, fibers, witness accounts, video feeds, the works."

Grego nodded. "Ben must be all over this."

Gus shook his head. "Nope. Not even a little bit. Ingermann was using B.I.N. to attack the government. The Governor can't touch it without it looking like payback. So, he's taking a break and doing a world tour meeting people, shaking babies, kissing hands…the usual."

Grego stifled a chuckle. The mental image of Ben Rainsford picking up infants and shaking them was as strangely amusing as it was revolting. "So Juan Takagashi will run things until he gets back?"

"That's what vice-governors are for," Gus said.

"Will he be back for the execution of the Fuzzy slavers?"

"Ha! You better believe it. Front row seat."

Dr. Laurie completed his examination, recorded the results then stepped back from the table. "They're all yours, Dr. Jimenez."

Juan thanked the doctor, then nodded to Dr. Hoenveld. Hoenveld, with the aid of several biologists and lab techs, quickly rearranged the new skeleton with the previous three, swapping out bones until the four skeletons were laid out in the most likely forms.

"It looks like there are still a number of bones missing, Chris," Grego observed.

"That is to be expected after many millennia, Mr. Grego." Hoenveld was both respectful and condescending at the same time. It was an impressive trick. "When an animal or sapient creature, for that matter, dies in the wild, the bodies become targets for scavengers. These scavengers often collect choice pieces and take them back to their burrows or dens. Then there are the elements, rain, wind and storms that can blow the bones around. The very ground can even act to separate the bones through quakes and volcanic action. And, of course, if they were killed by a predator, the bones could also be scattered, gnawed or even partially digested.

"Frankly, to find four skeletons this complete is nothing less than incredible. There is also the possibility that we don't have four skeletons, but fragments from any number of remains that just seem to fit together. I daresay I could take the skeletons of many of the people gathered here and make a very convincing skeleton using the pieces of several donors."

"Still," Juan interrupted, "we have more than enough fossil remains to construct a holographic simulation of what these...creatures must have looked like. We can even simulate posture and how they walked based on the spinal alignment and pelvis. Miss Ubinger?"

A young blonde woman fiddled with some settings of a large machine then nodded at Juan.

"Ladies and gentlemen, if you will please back up? We scanned all of the fossils into the matrix as we sorted and arranged them prior to the addition of the last skeleton. Even without the recent addition, we were able to extrapolate what these creatures would look like. Miss Ubinger?"

The woman pressed a button and three quasi-hominids appeared in the newly vacated floor space. Their posture was similar to that of Terran chimpanzees. The faces, though similar to that of the Modern Fuzzy, were far burlier, with a sloping forehead, thick brow ridge and lantern jaw. The dentition was clearly designed for tearing and ripping flesh.

Several people in the crowd took video and camera pictures of the holographic display. Ubinger toggled another switch and the holographic quasi-primates simulated walking, though they remained in place.

"Our findings will be made public in case anybody wants to verify them. I think all but the most fanatical among us can conclude that these...primates would have been incapable of piloting a spacecraft."

Gus snorted under his breath and whispered to Grego, "Want to bet?"

Grego shrugged. "There will always be conspiracy theorists and crackpots among us."

XXXVI

The Mallorysport-Darius spaceport was crawling with police. Some in uniform, most in plainclothes. Richard Lundgren recognized most of them from his illegal forays into the police mainframe. At the time he was looking for cops who could be bought as per Ivan Dane's orders.

A synthmask wouldn't get through the shuttle dock security, and Lundgren knew it. Not that it mattered; he didn't have one. Instead, Lundgren tried a low-tech approach. Using a can of spray-dye he changed his hair color to red, inserted green lenses in his eyes and added a fake mole to his cheek. Glasses and false beards tended to draw more attention. Less was more.

He left the men's room intending to walk straight to the ticket counter. Instead he clashed with a woman he failed to see in his hurry.

"Hello, Richard," the woman said.

Lundgren did a double take; it was Affanita. He was too surprised to try a bluff. "What are you doing here?

"I followed you from the B.I.N. building. I was a bit surprised when I saw you come out of there, to be honest," the woman explained. "I have a bone to pick with you about those sunstones."

"What? You haven't even brought me my cut from the last batch. What are you so bent about?" Lundgren checked his chronometer. The shuttle would be leaving in fifteen minutes. "Never mind. Just keep it. I have to…make a call."

"Funny thing about those sunstones. A quarter of them were fakes.

It took me forever to get through all the questions I had to answer. Under veridication, no less. I had to cut a deal with the CZC to avoid prosecution."

"What? They spotted the fakes? How?"

"How should I know? I didn't even know that they *were* phonies. But I swung a sweetheart deal to keep out of jail. They confiscated the *faux* stones and even paid me for the real ones. All I had to do was tell them everything I knew about you." Affanita smiled. "And there's a bonus if I turn you in."

"What? No!"

"Over here, guys!"

Before Lundgren could try to run, he was seized by two plainclothes cops.

Affanita kissed Lundgren on the cheek, then said, "See you in court, Tiger."

* * * * * * * * *

Dr. Rankin, fresh from Junktown, entered the spaceport and went directly to the ticket counter. There, he bought a one-way ticket to Terra under a fake name. From there he proceeded to the waiting area.

On the way he noticed a disturbance. A man had been seized by two other men and a woman. It was Richard Lundgren. The red hair and mole didn't fool Rankin for a second. The doctor quickly turned his back on the tableau hoping that Lundgren wouldn't see him and call out. It took all his willpower to keep from breaking into a run.

At the waiting area he produced his forged documents and ticket for the clerk.

"One-way to Terra, Dr. Kildare? I hope you enjoyed your stay on Zarathustra and will visit us again."

"Yes, I think I will. I may even immigrate here one day."

The clerk stamped the ticket and returned it to Rankin. Before he could put it in a pocket, a hand seized his arm.

"Excuse me, Doctor, but could you come with us?"

Rankin turned to find a uniformed policeman accompanied by another man in civilian attire. "Is there a problem, officer?"

"Yes. Those are the worst forged papers I have ever seen," the cop said, shaking his head. "Seriously, you went with 'Dr. Kildare?' You should be shot for that alone."

Rankin was quickly cuffed and hauled away from the terminal.

* * * * * * * * *

John Smith was not his real name. In fact, use of the name had become rare since the First Century A.E. due to its overuse in the previous centuries. It was only because the name had become uncommon that the man elected to use it in the first place. It was a plausible enough name taken separately as both the patronymic and the forename were still common enough.

Smith purchased the off-world ticket and walked to the spaceport bar. Once seated, he ordered a Three-Planets and sat near a window where he could observe everything that happened in the terminal.

He carefully nursed the drink and checked his chronometer like a man nervous about taking a spaceflight. Around the third small sip there was a commotion. A woman and two men seized some guy with red hair and a pasty complexion. That was good. Anything that attracted attention anywhere but near Mr. Smith suited him just fine.

With attention on the redhead and his dancing partners, Smith decided it was time to board the shuttle. He chugged the rest of his drink and left the bar. As he expected, everybody was watching the redhead as he was hauled out of the spaceport. Except for the man who was pointedly ignoring the foursome and making straight for the shuttle dock. Smith hung back a bit. There was something off about the man and Smith didn't want to get caught up in whatever he was into. Sure enough, the man was quickly detained, cuffed and hauled away. Once the dock was clear, Smith resumed progress toward it.

At the shuttle dock security point, he produced his identification. Instead of the documents proclaiming his identity as John Smith, he produced papers in the name of Guido MacTavish. The increased police activity suggested they were looking for several people and it was possible they found out about John Smith and his likely connection to the deaths of Anthony Anderson and Duncan Rippolone.

"Did you enjoy your stay on Zarathustra, Mr. MacTavish?" asked the checkpoint attendant.

"Yes. It was a very pleasant vacation. It is a shame I have to leave before the executions of the Fuzzy Slavers. I had even bought a lottery ticket." Guido shrugged. "Can't win them all, I guess."

"Oh, and by any chance would your name also be John Smith?"

Guido, taken by surprise, stammered out, "What? No! Why would you ask me that?"

From behind Guido two plainclothes cops stepped up. "To catch you in a lie for the portable veridicator. This new model by Henry Stensen has a range of two meters. It isn't admissible in court, unfortunately, but it does give us sufficient cause to take you in and put you on the floor model." The officer looked to his partner. "Isn't that right, Officer Gilbert?"

"Oh, absolutely, Officer Sullivan."

"Now," Sullivan said as he pulled out his cuffs. "Will this be easy or hard?"

Guido MacTavish quickly sized up the situation and didn't like the odds one little bit. He was unarmed, outnumbered and on a planet where he didn't have any juice. He held out his wrists. "How can I resist such a gracious invitation?"

* * * * * * * * *

Morgan and Akira stepped out of the air-yacht and were met by a furry of Fuzzies crowding around them. By the cabin he could see Thor Folkvar and Thor the Fuzzy throwing the Frisbee back and forth. The Fuzzy's arm seemed to working well enough suggesting his wound was healing well. Thor Folkvar waved and Morgan waved back.

Little Fuzzy worked his way through the hirsute crowd and informed the two that Pappy Jack wanted to see them. Morgan looked worried, something Akira had never seen before.

Morgan let out a long breath. "Well, let's get this over with."

Akira's face screwed up in confusion. "Get what over with?"

"I defied my sire's orders by interfering up north," Morgan explained. "Now he will determine my penalty."

Akira stopped and grabbed Morgan's shoulder. "What? You're a grown man. Are you telling me Jack could, what, spank you and you'd just take it?"

"Corporal punishment goes against normal Freyan custom, at least between father and son in the nobility. No, I'll have to serve some form of penance."

That doesn't sound good, Akira thought. "Like what?"

"That is up to my father. On Freya it might include physical labor, a public admission of guilt, acting as a servant in his home…there are no hard and fast rules."

"And you'll just accept it?" Akira started getting a headache. "What kind of man are you?"

"One who owns up to his mistakes and accepts the consequences?" Morgan turned and started walking toward the cabin. Akira shrugged and followed.

Inside, Jack was sitting on the couch next to Betty. He looked angry while Betty kept her expression neutral. The elder Holloway indicated a chair and Morgan took a seat. Morgan noticed absently that the renovations were completed making the living room much larger. Somehow that made it seem more intimidating under the circumstances.

"John Morgan Holloway the Lesser," Jack said ceremoniously, "you have defied the will of your sire. Are you prepared to make amends for your transgression?"

Morgan didn't hesitate. "Yes, sire."

"Very well. It is my belief that you intend to ask this woman, Akira Hsu O'Barre, to be your wife." Jack paused dramatically. "It is my decision that this will not happen. She will be given her wages and returned to her previous employment at the CZC."

"Yes, si—what?"

"I believe that she may have influenced you into making the foolish choice of interfering in my efforts up north. No woman should have that much control over her mate, especially when he is of the nobility. A man must be strong and know his own mind. Is this understood?"

Morgan froze. He couldn't believe his own ears. Jack was forbidding his intended marriage to Akira. "You cannot be serious," he said weakly.

"What…Jack…Mr. Holloway, you can't possibly mean that…" Akira stammered out.

"The word of the family patriarch is not to be questioned," Jack said sternly. "Morgan understands this. Is this not so, Morgan?"

"Yes, but…I…" Morgan tried to find the right words. He never imagined his father could be so cruel. He was within his rights to forbid the marriage, yet…

"Do you accept your punishment, John Morgan Holloway the Lesser?" Jack demanded.

Morgan stared for a moment before he could speak. On Freya a son who went against his father could be exiled, disinherited, and even, in extreme cases, executed. To defy one's sire was almost unthinkable. He turned and looked into Akira's face and saw her disbelief and pain. He wanted to marry her, to make a family with her. Yet, he couldn't defy the will of his father. A Freyan noble accepted the will of his sire. The fact that he only recently found Jack and claimed his name was irrelevant; he accepted his name and became subservient to him as a consequence.

"Morgan?" Akira couldn't stand the suspense. "Are you going to do what he said?"

Morgan looked from Akira then back to Jack. "I…I…No."

"What did you say?" Jack demanded jumping to his feet.

"I said 'no'." Morgan stood up and glowered at his father. He had never been this angry before, not even before the duel when he and Jack shot each other. "I will accept any other penalty you choose to levy against me. I will turn over my wealth, leave the planet, or even cut off my own ears. I will even fly back to Terra and bring back the hickory tree you spoke of, but I will not give up this woman."

Tears welled up in Akira's eyes as she heard Morgan defy his father. He was prepared to give up everything for her. She couldn't let him do it.

"No. Morgan, don't. I'll go. I can't let you do that to yourself for me…."

"Woman, be silent!" Jack barked. Akira was stunned into silence. Morgan placed a protective hand on her shoulder. "Morgan, are you very certain you are prepared to defy my will for this woman? Does she mean that much to you?"

Morgan's voice was even as he answered. "All that and more."

"Very well. You are commanded to…" Again, Jack paused dramatically. "Take Akira Hsu O'Barre as your wife and accord her all the respect a woman of her quality and intelligence is entitled to, and generate heirs to carry on the family name. Oh, and meet your new stepmother. Betty, Morgan. Morgan, Betty."

Morgan was stunned. "Uh…we've met."

"Wait. Now you're ordering him to marry me?" Akira stood up and put her hands on her hips. "Was this your idea of a joke?"

"Uh…Akira…" Morgan started. He felt lightheaded from the sudden shift and had some difficulty keeping upright.

"You butt out," Akira shot at Morgan, then turned back to Jack. "Where do you get off ordering him to marry me? And when did you two get married? One romp in the sack and you're picking out floral patterns together?"

"Who said it was only one?" Betty said with a deadpan expression.

Jack looked at Betty and said, "I like her. She's feisty."

Betty nodded. "I could have told you that. She'll keep that son of yours in line, count on it."

Jack and Betty returned their gaze to Morgan and Akira. Morgan was dumbfounded and Akira was beside herself. Finally, they couldn't keep it in any longer; Jack and Betty broke out in laughter. It took several minutes for them to get control of themselves.

"That was great!" Akira said. "I almost believed it myself."

"A pretty good one, I think," Jack said. "Though if he tries another stunt like that one in Northern Beta, I will put him across my knee." Jack turned to Betty. "You said you would let Akira in on the joke. I thought she really didn't know for a moment there. I wasn't planning on scaring her, too."

"Oh, Akira can take it," Betty laughed. "I called her on the screen and brought her up to speed before they got here. I neglected to mention that we didn't really get hitched though. I wanted to see her reaction to that."

Morgan, uncharacteristically slow on the uptake, finally caught on.

"Then, you don't want me to marry Akira?"

Jack laughed some more and fell back onto the couch. He needed a second to catch his breath. "Oh…heh…I do want you two to marry, but only if that is what you want. Both of you. I did want to see if you really felt that strongly about her, though. Marriage isn't something to treat lightly the way they did back in First Century A.E. I had to know that your feelings were real."

"And Betty…"

"No, Morgan. No floral patterns for us," Betty said, giggling.

"Well, not for a while, anyway," Jack added. "We'll see how things go."

Akira laughed as she fell onto Morgan who, in turn, was knocked back into the chair eliciting a startled "oof" as they fell back. "Betty, thanks for the heads-up. I'm not sure what I would have done if I hadn't been in on the joke." Akira sobered and turned to Morgan. "I can't believe you would have given up everything for me. Not to mention cut off your own ears. Do they really do that on Freya?"

Morgan nodded. "In rare and extreme cases. Akira?"

She looked at Morgan. "Yes?"

"I do want to marry you."

"Hold it right there," Akira commanded. She stood up and turned to Morgan. "I don't care how Freyan you are! I am from Terra and expect to be given the right treatment. This will be done by Terran tradition or nothing! I want dinner, candlelight, you on your knee with a sunstone ring in your hand. Got it?"

Morgan smiled and nodded ceremoniously. "As my lady commands. And father, I know a Test of Resolve when I see one, though I was slow to catch on. I didn't think you would be so Freyan about it."

"Ring!" Jack shouted in a seeming non sequitur. "That reminds me." He jumped up from the couch and ran into his bedroom.

"I thought he was still recovering," observed Morgan.

"I don't know if I could survive it if he recovers much more," Betty joked.

Jack came back holding something in a closed hand. "Morgan, when your uncle sent me that letter telling me Adonitia had died, he also sent this back. I think you should have it."

Jack opened his hand to reveal a ring with a bright blue sunstone. "This set me back four months wages when I got it for your mother. Blue was her favorite color."

Morgan stood up and accepted the ring. "I am honored, father."

"Jack, it's lovely," Akira said breathlessly.

"Give it a dry run and try it on," Jack said. "Morgan might have to have it re-sized to fit you."

Morgan placed the ring on the third finger of the right hand. On Freya, the right hand denoted engagement, a custom normally applied to the bracelets they would exchange, and would be transferred to the left hand at the nuptials. It fit perfectly.

"I still want the candlelit dinner," Akira said softly. She turned back to Jack. "Woman, be silent? Seriously?"

"See?" Jack said as he looked back at Betty. "Feisty."

XXXVII

Gus Brannhard leaned back in his chair enjoying his imported cigar, the type he only smoked when he was celebrating. He was celebrating now. Gus had just returned from lunch when the Colonial Marshal screened-in.

"We got the hat trick, Mr. Brannhard."

"Gus," Gus said automatically. The Marshal had a bad habit of slipping into formal addresses, especially when he was excited. "What's a hat trick? Somebody pull a zarabunny out of one?"

"I'll say." Max explained that a hat trick referred to an ancient game called hockey where a player made three goals in one game. "In this case, Chief Carr is our star player."

Gus wondered when Max would get to the point. He didn't have to wait long.

"Carr's men found Lundgren, Rankin and our Mr. Smith trying to board the Darius shuttle." Max leaned back in his seat with a wolfish smile and waited.

"Smith? Wait, the elusive John Smith, our chief suspect in the murders of Anderson and Rippolone?"

"None other, accept no substitutes. By the way, his name isn't 'Smith.' It's…" Max checked a paper on his desk. "Ah, yes, his name is Guido MacTavish."

Gus couldn't believe his ears. "Guido? Really?" *I guess Morgan nailed it after all. Who would have thought?* "Alive?"

"And protesting. We have him in segregated lockdown and on suicide watch. This one isn't getting away. I understand Mr. Coombes is done in the prosecutor's office."

Gus nodded. "He was just here to cover for me while I was… missing, and he stayed on to prosecute my abductors. Conflict of interest for me to do that and my staff, while good, couldn't be expected to juggle that and their usual workload. Now he is back to work for the Company and probably glad for it."

"Good for him. I just wanted to be sure who was coming down to observe the interrogation."

Gus reached into a drawer and pulled out his cigar. "You know what? I think I'll invite him to sit in with me for old time's sake. Come to think of it, he'll have to prosecute this. It would still be a conflict of interest for me to do it."

"Going for the death penalty? On this Guido character?"

"Oh, I have to." Gus lit the cigar and took a few puffs to get it started. "He committed a capital crime. Besides, I need that on the table to get him to talk. Isn't the law wonderful?"

* * * * * * * * *

Little Fuzzy dropped the metal chopper-diggers at the feet of Red Fur. He had seen a movie where the Big Ones did the same thing with swords in front of a man wearing something called a toga. The chopper-diggers were a gift from one leader to another, or so he thought. The surrender of Vercingetorix to Julius Caesar proved too complicated a concept to explain to the Fuzzy. Instead, Pappy Jack had said that this was often how Big Ones made new friends.

Red Fur looked at the offering and selected one. He tested the balance and strength. It was far sharper than anything the *Jin-f'ke* could make. He remembered how well Little Fuzzy had used it against him when they fought.

"My people who go with the Big Ones. Where are the rest?" Red Fur demanded.

"Some come back." Little Fuzzy gestured to indicate some of the *Jin-f'ke* who came back with him and George Lunt. "The rest want to stay. Learn new things. Strong One wants to stay with Thor Folkvar, the big-big Big One."

Red Fur looked at the wounded ones who had gone with the Big Ones and came back. They looked happy and well fed and each had a shiny new chopper-digger. Red Fur nodded. "Hokay. Come. We make talk."

Little Fuzzy followed Red Fur to an open space where several *Jin-f'ke* waited.

"These are makers and wise ones from many-many clans. They want to go to the wonderful place to learn from the Big Ones. Make better bows, better arrows. Use yellow hot thing…fire. Use fire."

Little Fuzzy looked at the makers. It was a good idea. "You want *estee-fee*?"

"Some of the people want this. I do not. I want Big Ones to stay away from *Jin-f'ke*."

Little Fuzzy was confused. "You want Big Ones to stay away? Why send makers and wise ones to learn from Big Ones?"

"They want to go. I not stop them. I not…" Red Fur groped for a word but couldn't think of one. "*Jin-f'ke* not like *dawgs*. They want go, they go. I not…um…"

"Master," Little Fuzzy supplied. He had heard Big Ones call Fuzzies with dogs their masters. "You leader, not master. This is good. Big Ones not masters. Big Ones friends."

"For you. Big Ones kill Sun Fur. Kill other *Jin-f'ke*. Hurt more. No Big Ones come here." Red Fur was adamant.

Little Fuzzy understood. When the female called Goldilocks was killed by a Big One, he was angry, too. So was Pappy Jack. Pappy Jack almost killed the bad Big One with his bare hands. Little Fuzzy understood then that there were good Big Ones, like Pappy Jack and Pappy Gus and Pappy Vic, and bad Big Ones like the one who had done the killing. Red Fur had only seen the bad Big Ones. It would take time to teach him the difference.

"Hokay. I tell Pappy Jack no Big Ones come here. He and Pappy George will make it so. Pappy Jack say he make house near big boom place where police stay. Police make bad Big Ones stay away."

Red Fur didn't like any Big Ones so close. Little Fuzzy took great pains to explain that it was necessary. Red Fur didn't like it, Big Ones to protect his people from Big Ones, but eventually understood it was the only way to keep his people safe.

"Red Fur, come with me to the Wonderful Place and see good Big Ones," Little Fuzzy suggested.

Red Fur was hesitant. Big Ones were dangerous. Yet, many-many of the people from the sun's right hand had come to save the Big One called Pappy Jack. He was afraid of the Big Ones and their incredible made-things, yet he was the Wise One of his people. A Wise One should not be afraid to do anything that other people do. A Wise One could not lead through fear. Red Fur came to a decision.

"Hokay, Little Fuhzzee," Red Fur said. "I come to see good Big Ones."

* * * * * * * * *

Gerd was packing up and preparing to go back to Beta. The rocket's origins had been determined and he was no longer needed at Science Division. At least not on Alpha Continent. With Jack's blessing and Grego's offer to set up Science Division Beta, Gerd was once again an employee of the Charterless Zarathustra Company. Ruth also agreed to come back and head up her own psycho-sciences department, also on Beta. The idea was to learn everything there was about Fuzzies.

Three Galactic Standard months earlier, Gerd thought he had the Fuzzies figured out. Then that gang in Northern Beta turned everything they understood on its ear. Fuzzies were capable of war, mass organization and even specialization. They were not the furry children everybody thought they were. At least, not the *Jin-f'ke.*

"Already packed?"

Gerd spun around to find Victor Grego, his old/new boss, standing in the doorway. "Almost, Mr. Grego."

"You're a division head, Gerd. You get to call me Victor." Grego looked around at the room. "Did you collect the things you left behind last time? I can have it all shipped to your cabin on Beta."

"I would appreciate that, Victor."

Grego remembered how Juan Jimenez stumbled when using his boss's first name. Gerd, on the other hand, was used to it from his time as Deputy Commissioner.

"Gerd, in the spirit of honesty, I want to show you something." Grego walked out and Gerd followed. They took an elevator down to the Science Division Special Projects level. "Ben and I had cooked up this little project shortly after the rocket was discovered on Beta. We were concerned about the future of the planet if the Fuzzies were deemed space refugees."

Gerd followed Grego to a security door where he placed a palm on the glowing panel and the heavy doors retracted into the wall. They entered only to be faced by a second set of metal doors. Grego placed his hand on a second glowing plate. The doors behind them closed before the one in front of them opened.

Gerd had never been on the Special Projects level before and rubbernecked at everything around him, until he turned a corner and his eyes landed on something huge that was covered with a tarp. The shape was unmistakable.

"This is the ersatz rocket Commodore Napier commissioned, isn't it?"

"It is now." Grego lifted a section of tarp and the two men went under it. Sure enough, it was a duplicate of the Martian Rocket over in the warehouse. Some men were spraying the inside of the hull with a corrosive agent that would duplicate the rust and metal fatigue found on the real artifact.

"Your guys work fast in here…wait, you said you and Ben cooked this up two months ago?"

"Yes. We had the same idea Napier had. We're making as perfect a duplicate of the real artifact as we can. It will be almost impossible to distinguish the two."

"What? I thought the idea was to make an obvious fake?"

Grego shook his head. "An obvious fake would invite even more scrutiny. This has to look like a genuine attempt to defraud the public. Not to worry, no matter how good we do, there will be somebody out there good enough to spot inaccuracies. Especially as we will be adding one sure to make people sit up and take notice."

"What's that?"

"A real Martian skeleton. I have one in my private collection of Martian artifacts."

"A real…I don't get it." Gerd was confused. "Won't that make it seem even more realistic?"

"Absolutely! That's the point. Scientists will tear this thing apart atom by atom to prove it is either real or not. Sooner or later, somebody will put it together that the skeleton is twenty-thousand years older than the rocket is supposed to be."

Gerd looked over the rocket and let out a low whistle. "I can't believe Ben would go along with something like this."

"He wasn't until that Ivan Dane, excuse me, Hugo Ingermann, started using the 'Fuzzy Rocket' to declare the local government illegal. Ben doesn't want the Fuzzies to fall prey to somebody like that."

Gerd admitted he might have done the same thing in that case. "I noticed you didn't mention any of this to Commodore Napier."

"I wouldn't be surprised if he already knows. I very much doubt that Ruth was the only spy in the Company. However, even if he does, he can't admit to it; that would give away the fact that he has other spies rooting around the Company. So, I just handed him the bill for this little enterprise and he has no other choice than to pay it."

Gerd nodded. *Thank Ghu, Victor is on our side*, he thought. Another thought struck him. "You think he'll try to get Ruth to spy on you again?"

"I would be very surprised if he didn't," Grego said. "He'll think that I'll think that as a known agent she would be ineffective as a spy. And then he'll figure that makes her the perfect agent for the job. In any case, he can't waste the opportunity."

"What makes you think I'm not a spy?"

"What makes you think I think that?" Grego countered. "Okay, there's too much 'think' going on here. Look, I can count on you to do whatever is best for the Fuzzies and your friends. I respect that and I count on it. I want the Fuzzies protected, too. Even from me, if necessary."

Gerd processed that last bit. "Victor, this might be the beginning of a beautiful friendship."

XXXVIII

"I can't tell you how sorry I am to do this, Piet."

Colonial Marshal Max Fane was the kind of leader who gave the bad news in person when at all possible. In this case, it was that Inspector Piet Dumont was being forced into medical retirement from the police force. Piet took the news far more calmly than the Marshal would have expected.

"Are you sure, Marshal? The wound wasn't that bad. I didn't even need a new heart."

Max shook his head sadly. "There was significant damage near the heart and in the lung. Not bad enough to warrant new organs, but enough to make police work too dangerous for you. I know,"—Max put up a hand to forestall any protest from Piet— "you are in much better shape than I am, and as an inspector you are not expected to exert yourself physically as much as patrolmen. It doesn't matter. The regulations don't give any leeway in this."

"I see." Piet slumped in his hover-chair. "So, retirement?"

"Full pension," Max said. "We can also bring you in as a consultant from time to time."

Piet sighed. "I guess I can do private investigations like my old man did when he was forced to retire from the force back on Terra."

"You could," the Marshal agreed. An idea hit him. "You know, there is a rumor going around that Gerd van Riebeek will be leaving his post as the Deputy Commissioner of Native Affairs and taking back his old job at the CZC. If you apply for the job, I can give you a good, no, great recommendation...."

Piet took a moment before he realized what he was being offered. "Wait. What? Deputy commissioner? Do you think Jack Holloway would go for it?"

Max shrugged. "I don't see why not. You've never crossed him personally, and your record is mostly exemplary. Give it a shot. What do you have to lose?"

Piet thought about it. It would mean moving to Beta. That wasn't really a problem since he could swing back on off-days to visit with friends. He liked Fuzzies as much as the next man and his time as the former chief of police in Mallorysport had taught him to handle paperwork well enough. And he wouldn't always be stuck in a chair behind a desk. He could go out and investigate things with George Lunt. From a financial point of view it would be great. He would have his police pension plus the income from the new job.

"Okay, Max." Since he was about to become a civilian, he didn't see the need to stand on formality. "I'll go dust off my resume and take a little ride over to Beta Continent."

"That's the spirit. When will the doctors let you out?"

"Ten minutes ago." Piet threw off his blanket and stood up. Though a bit unsteady, he collected his things from the cabinet and dressed himself. "Whether they like it or not."

* * * * * * * * *

Hugo Ingermann, also known as Ivan Dane, awoke in his hospital bed. He felt like his head was stuffed with cotton and there was a bad taste in his mouth; the result of the sedatives the doctors had given him. He was still in pain from the gunshot wound though it had subsided to a dull ache.

As his mind cleared he recalled that he had been shot by somebody who looked a lot like Leo Thaxter. He also recalled that Thaxter, if it was him, was killed by somebody else.

He didn't get a good look at Thaxter's killer, but when he discovered who it was he planned on giving him a good sized reward.

Ingermann sat up in his bed and pushed the blanket aside. He had an itch on his ankle that he wanted to scratch. The itch was forgotten when he saw the explosive shackle. He had seen shackles like that on many of his past clients. He had been arrested: Now the question was on what charge? Ingermann knew the list was a long one, but that didn't mean that the police knew everything. There was still a good possibility that he could get off. He was good at that.

Ingermann buzzed for the nurse. When she entered the room she was accompanied by two policemen. "How can we help you, Mr. Ingermann?"

"I need another..." Ingermann's words froze in his throat. The nurse called him 'Ingermann.'

"Something wrong, Mr. Ingermann?" Officer Chang asked.

"I think ol' Hugo here just realized he is completely and totally screwed," York added.

Ingermann flopped back onto his pillow. He was done and he knew it.

"Would you care for some headache pills, Mr. Ingermann?" the nurse asked.

"Very much so."

XXXIX

The party was in full swing outside Jack's newly expanded cabin. All of the big names on Zarathustra were in attendance: Ben Rainsford, Victor Grego, Gus Brannhard, Leslie Coombes, Commodore Napier and Lt. Commander Pancho Ybarra, Gerd and Ruth van Riebeek and Max Fane as well as George Lunt, Ahmed and Sandra Khadra, Betty Kanazawa, Thor Folkvar, Larry Wolvin and his wife Ellaree, Peter Davis, Marcus Szymanski, Henry Stensen…the list went on and on.

Terrence Vlosopolos in his Fuzzy costume danced about and entertained the Fuzzies. He also had a following of young ladies who had heard a slightly exaggerated story of his heroism while assisting the famous Jack Holloway. Terrence was innocent of the braggadocio; Jack Holloway played up the young man's part to Akira who in turn shared it with Betty and her friends at the Company.

Amazingly, Dr. Hoenveld attended the soirée with, even more amazingly, Darla Cross. And of course, everybody brought their Fuzzies.

Ernst Mallin was enjoying an iced tea with Chris Hoenveld near the Fuzzies' playground. "It must be wonderful to be able to play like children without being judged."

Hoenveld snorted. "I never played like that. I preferred the molecule sets. Why do you suppose we were invited to this…shindig? I do not typically associate with any of these people outside of work."

Ernst Mallin took a second to adjust to the sudden topic shift, then shrugged. "Maybe it has something to do with the work we did on the so-called Fuzzy Bones."

Hoenveld snorted again. It was becoming a habit with him. "Fuzzy Bones my *gluteus maximus*. Those were an offshoot of the same species, no doubt, but I would bet any three of my degrees that they were not direct ancestors to the modern *Fuzzy sapiens zarathustra*. And that last femur we received from the dig site came from a Martian or I'm a Khooghras' uncle. The carbon dating matched that of the rocket almost exactly."

And there was the crux of Hoenveld's ire; proof of Martian space travel and he was forbidden to publish a paper on it because of Commodore Napier and Victor Grego.

"Chris, you can still document your discoveries. Oh, it won't be seen in our time, but future generations will know of your work. Your immortality is assured. And let me suggest that you lower your voice if you plan on discussing the matter further. The walls have ears, you know."

Hoenveld was quiet for a moment, then said, "What do you think this party is really about? It's not to showoff Holloway's new additions to his cabin. I've never even met the man in person."

Mallin looked about at the other attendees and spotted Morgan and Akira sitting on a bench away from the crowd. The looks they were giving each other were very telling for the psycho-scientist. "I believe we are here for an important announcement."

"Humph! Important to whom?" Hoenveld shifted his gaze to the mass of Fuzzies crowding around. "I would love to get some blood samples from the Northern Fuzzies."

Hoenveld was switching topics every other second, it seemed. "Oh? Do you think they might be a separate branch of the Fuzzy family tree?"

"Not at all. The size difference is likely due to better nutrition. The change in their culture is most likely due to the reduction of harpies in that area. The more game in one area, the fewer reasons to move about to hunt. That allowed them to develop villages and specialization. I suspect that we will see similar growth patterns in the young of the Fuzzies we associate with."

Mallin nodded. He had come to many of the same conclusions himself. "I wonder how big they will get?"

"No way of telling. Especially with the relatively new mutation that I observed in Zorro."

"Ah, yes," Mallin nodded. "Many of the Northern Fuzzies have demonstrated the same mutation. About half of them disdain land-prawn and extee-three, yet have healthy offspring."

"What? Why didn't anybody tell me this?" Hoenveld was furious. He hated being left out of new discoveries. He spotted Juan Jimenez and stomped off in his direction only to be intercepted by Darla Cross. His ire momentarily forgotten, Hoenveld escorted Darla to the buffet table.

Mallin chuckled as he watched the normally taciturn Hoenveld led around by the actress. Maybe she would add to his education in an area he had previously neglected, thought the psycho-scientist.

* * * * * * * * *

Fuzzies were practically a living carpet across the grounds surrounding the cabin. Little Fuzzy had talked Red Fur into visiting Pappy Jack's home to observe the Big Ones in their own environment. Like most Fuzzies seeing the wonders of the Big Ones for the first time, Red Fur tried to see everything at once.

"Pappy Jack lives in big made-thing?" Red Fur asked. Little Fuzzy said it was so, and that he and his clan also lived there. "Does it fly like melon-seed shaped made-things?"

Little Fuzzy laughed, then stopped himself. He remembered how amazed he had been at many of the wonders the Big Ones possessed. And if Pappy Jack wanted to, Little Fuzzy had no doubt the cabin could be made to fly.

Red Fur hefted his new *shoppo-diggo*. It was slightly larger than the one Little Fuzzy carried to accommodate his greater height.

"This good weapon, an' want many-many for the *Jin-f'ke*, but not want Big Ones around my people."

Little Fuzzy understood. "Pappy George say only one guard station near big hole place. This is so bad Big Ones not come an' make trouble. You want something, you tell Big One at guard place."

Red Fur was dubious but willing to give it a try. He had to admit that the chopper-diggers made of the—what did little Fuzzy call it? Metal. The metal chopper-diggers were truly wondrous weapons. All things the Big Ones made were better, stronger. His people could learn much from the Big Ones, as Little Fuzzy's people had. It was so tempting to just accept what the Big Ones had to offer.

Red Fur looked out at the Fuzzies all around him. Some were playing with the made-things given to them by the Big Ones. A few were bringing things to the Big Ones. To his eyes they were like children and the Big Ones their parents. The Pappy Jacks and Pappy Georges and Unka Morgans would look after them and care for them and teach them things. Red Fur had to think hard about what that all meant.

* * * * * * * * *

The official reason for the party was to celebrate the new additions to the cabin. It wasn't until things were in full swing that the real reasons were announced. Morgan had a stage constructed outside near the barbeque pit and decorated in Freyan festival style. An hour into the celebration, Thor Folkvar tapped a hammer on a metal item that looked like a cross between a bell and a scrap-metal wind chime. The sound it made, a bell-toned clang with prolonged reverberation, quickly caught everybody's attention. Once everyone was looking at the stage, Morgan and Akira entered from opposite sides and came together at stage center.

"Hear ye, hear ye, hear ye," Thor yelled. "It is my honor and pleasure to announce the betrothal of John Morgan Holloway the Lesser of Freya to Akira Hsu O'Barre of Terra. All ye in attendance here today are requested to attend the nuptials three months hence at Castle Holloway."

The band, comprised of several Terran and non-Terran members from Morgan's crew, started up playing a cheerful, if odd-sounding tune. The instruments and music were mostly of Freyan origin. As the music played, Akira removed her gloves and held up her right hand to display her engagement ring. This was an adaptation of the Freyan custom where the bride and groom typically wore long sleeves to hide their new betrothal bracelets until the official announcement.

The crowd cheered and applauded. Jack stepped onto the stage and gave a short speech about how he approved of the bride and expected many strong grandchildren to carry on the family name, also in accordance with Freyan tradition. Gus called for a toast then gave it himself inhaling a large stein of Freyan ale in the process.

"And now, I think there is another announcement to be made," Jack said after downing a stein of ale himself. *Screw the doctors and their over-cautious nature, he thought.* "Gerd? Ruth?"

The couple looked at each other; Gerd quizzically and Ruth with a smile. She grabbed her husband's arm and dragged him onto the stage.

"I don't want to upstage the soon-to-be-weds, but I do have an announcement. Gerd and I are having twins!"

Gerd, taken by surprise, stared numbly at his wife. "Twins? You're pregnant?"

"Well, one does have to follow the other," Ruth said airily.

"Twins!" Gerd picked up his stein and drained it, then yelled, "I'm going to be a father!"

The crowd cheered and raised a glass. Gus asked what gender the twins were.

"Two girls," called back Ruth.

Jack let out a sigh of relief. He had been on several planets where friends had named their children after him, usually because he saved somebody's life. Girls removed that possibility and left it open for Morgan and Akira to follow Freyan tradition and name the first son after the father without creating a surplus of Johns and Jacks. That reminded him that Akira was pregnant. Two months' worth if he was right about the timing. That announcement would have to wait until the two were properly married.

It took a while for the applause to die down, then there was more music and dancing. Red Fur watched the display and was confused. He understood the idea of the mated pair being happy about having young ones, though the concept of twins had to be explained to him as Fuzzies propagated single offspring at a time. The idea of two people making a formal agreement to mate made no sense, as Fuzzies did not typically mate for life.

After the announcements, people lined up to congratulate Morgan and Akira as well as Gerd and Ruth. Afterwards, Ruth went to the bar to get a drink for Gerd who had been waylaid by Juan Jimenez. The bar, a temporary setup operated by Morgan's robot bartender, had another person ordering a drink that Ruth knew well.

"Mr. Stensen, what a surprise," Ruth said. She hadn't seen much of the man since the Fuzzy Trial two years earlier.

Henry Stensen, designer extraordinaire and senior TFN espionage agent on Zarathustra, gently guided Ruth away from anybody who might overhear them. "Ruth, I was hoping to speak with you."

"Oh? What about?" Ruth feigned surprise though she suspected where Stensen was headed.

Stensen guided her further away from potentially curious ears. "We want to give you your old job back."

"My…" Ruth almost couldn't believe her ears even though she had expected the offer. "Have you forgotten that I was outed at the trial? The whole planet knows I was a TFN spy."

"Exactly. The assumption will be that you couldn't possibly work as a spy since everybody already knows that you were one. That means you can now hide in plain sight and nobody will suspect you."

Ruth shook her head. "That might work with Joe Sixpack but not on Mr. Grego. He's too sharp by half to be taken in twice like that. Besides, he's on the side of the angels, now. If it weren't for him, the Fuzzies would be headed for extinction. Or at least that is what we thought at the time."

"Grego is a businessman first and a philanthropist somewhere around third or fourth," Stensen countered. "He needs to be watched, and you will be in the best position to do it."

Ruth thought it over, then shook her head slowly. "Not this time. I am about to be a mother. This is no kind of work for me anymore."

Stensen shrugged. "Think it over. You might change your mind. And don't forget the extra money you will bring in as a TFN operative."

Stensen went to talk to Morgan about an invention he wanted to finance while Ruth stood thinking about the offer. She nearly jumped a foot when Grego came up behind her and said hello.

"My apologies," Grego said. "I didn't mean to startle you. I just wanted to add my congratulations on the baby. Babies, rather."

"Uh, thanks, Mr. Grego. Thank you."

"Call me Victor." Grego glanced over in the direction of Stensen and Morgan. "I noticed Henry Stensen was chatting you up. Did he offer you your old job back, yet? No, don't answer that. I just wanted to tell you that you should take it if he did. I'll likely be wary of you anyway."

"What? Then why offer me that job? I won't spy on the TFN for you if that is where you are headed."

"Great Ghu! That would be treason, I think. No, nothing like that. I want you and Gerd back because you were damned good at what you do and I value good people. I don't mind looking over my shoulder a bit if that's what it takes to get them. You just think about it. I will suspect that you are a spy whether you are or not, so you might as well get paid for it."

Grego glanced back over at Morgan and saw that Stensen had moved on. "You'll have to excuse me, Ruth. I have to go offer Morgan the CFO position at the company." As he started to turn away he flashed his toothy grin back at Ruth and said, "Maybe you can do a little surveillance on him."

Grego walked away as Ruth stood and stared. *Grego is too devious to be believed,* she thought, but he made a valid point. First, though, she would have to discuss it with Gerd.

XL

The party was over and made-things that moved about like live-things cleaned up the mess the Big Ones had left behind. Red Fur watched as the made-things, robots, did their work. Little Fuzzy brought a cup with water in it for him to drink as he sat and watched.

"T'ank-oo, Little Fuhzzee."

Little Fuzzy sat down on the log next to Red Fur. "You see everything. You still want Big Ones to stay away from *Jin-f'ke*?"

Red Fur let out a long sigh and nodded. "Yes. Here, Fuhzzees are like children. The Big Ones feed you and protect you and teach you many things."

"Yes," Little Fuzzy agreed. "Is much fun, here."

"That is why the *Jin-f'ke* must stay away from Big Ones." Red Fur could see that Little Fuzzy was confused. "Children must grow up. Here, that cannot happen. Big Ones will always see us as children to be protected. *Jin-f'ke* protect themselves and each other. You saw other Big Ones who were very different? The ones called Thorans, Ullerans, Lokians and foolish one they call a Khooghra: they like made-things, the robots that obey Big Ones like Pappy Jack.

"They not as wise, so they learn from the…Terrans? Yes, Terrans. They do not grow for themselves. They work for Terrans. I see Big Ones tell others what to do. I not see them tell Terrans what to do. Even your people, Little Fuzzy. Big Ones give names, teach things, then tell what to do and not do. And you do it! You are like made-things. Like robots."

Little Fuzzy was shocked at Red Fur's words. "Yes, Pappy Jack protects us. Teaches us. The Big Ones give us the Wonderful Food and helps our babies to be born strong. Alive. Before, only one in two hands of babies born would be alive. Now, almost all of our babies live. Without the Big Ones, we would soon be no more."

"My people also know this bad trouble. Babies not born right. But ones born right grow stronger. Many of my people have strong babies without Big Ones' help. Ones who do not like...lan'-p'awns make many strong babies. We no need Big Ones' help for this.

"Big Ones must been like us once, long time ago. Now, have many-many clever made-things. My people need learn to do these things without Big Ones. We must grow and teach our young, and they grow and learn. Maybe they learn new things even Big Ones not know. We accept Big Ones' *shoppo-diggo* to remind us what we can learn, but nothing else."

Red Fur stood up and turned to the air-yacht that brought him to the gathering of Big Ones and Fuzzies. "I go back to my people. Tell Pappy Jack we not want Big Ones on *Jin-f'ke* land. If bad Big Ones come, we will make dead. We not want to fight, but we will not let them hurt us."

Red Fur started off for the yacht. He would wait there until he returned to his people. Little Fuzzy watched as Red Fur walked away. He was sad to see the *Jin-f'ke* leader go, and sadder that he would not accept the help of the Big Ones.

* * * * * * * * *

The outside party was over: Jack, Morgan, Akira, Betty, Ben, Grego, Gus, Gerd, Ruth, Leslie, Mallin, Napier, Pancho and the rest gathered together in the cabin. Jack mixed drinks while Betty served *hors d'oeuvres* she had made earlier.

"Great party, Jack," Grego said. "Maybe I'll have you plan the next company picnic."

"Better talk to Betty about that," Jack said as he poured the drinks. "She did all of the planning."

"I'm available for reasonable rates, Mr. Grego," Betty said.

"Victor, please, when I'm at a social gathering," Grego said. "Wait, don't I know you? Betty Kanazawa from secretarial, right?" *So that is who made dinner for Jack the other day.*

"Accounting, actually. Records Division, for now, Victor. I'm covering for Akira while she is on sabbatical."

"Right, right." Grego turned to Jack. "Are you going to poach another of my valued employees, Jack?"

"Seems fair to me since you just rehired Gerd and Ruth, but I'll get back to you on that," Jack said as he winked at Betty. He delivered the last of the drinks and plopped down in his favorite chair.

"How did the negotiations with Red Fur go, Jack?" Gus asked, after he downed half of his stein of ale. He was developing a taste for the stuff.

"According to Little Fuzzy, Red Fur wants nothing to do with us." That brought a few gasps of amazement.

"Why not?" Ben demanded. "We have so much to offer them."

"Red Fur wants his people to grow up on their own without big brother looking out for them. Good for him, I say."

"Wait, you don't want the, what did he call them?" Grego said. "Right, the *Jin-f'ke*. You don't want the *Jin-f'ke* to join our Fuzzies?"

"No, Victor, I do not." Jack said firmly.

That brought a few comments out of the crowd. "Look, right now we have plenty of Fuzzies that we look out for and take care of. But do we want to do that for every Fuzzy on Zarathustra? Of course not. That would turn an entire race into welfare rats. They would never develop and evolve naturally. What happens if we Big Ones were wiped out by a war or a plague? Who would take care of the Fuzzies then?"

"The Fuzzies would have to take care of themselves," Gerd said. "Red Fur is smart enough to see that for himself."

"Exactly." Jack pulled out his pipe and stuffed it with tobacco, then lit it. "I was always against making the Fuzzies too dependent on us, but let myself be swayed by the fact that they needed us to survive as a species because they needed the, uh, *hoenveldine*." Jack used the chemical name out of respect for Hoenveld who discovered the titanium-based long-chain molecule. "Now we know that some Fuzzies, maybe more than we can guess at, don't produce the NFMp hormone that sabotages their reproduction rate. Great. That means they can get along fine without us. Especially since we reduced the harpy population to almost zero on Beta."

"What about the Fuzzies here?" Betty asked. "Are you going to round them up and dump them back in the wild?"

"Of course not," Jack said. "It would be grotesquely cruel to give them all the wonderful things we've already shown them, and then take them away. No, we'll go right on teaching them and looking out for them. Only now we will be doing it with an eye towards making them self-sufficient, something we should have done from the start. Eventually, there will be the Fuzzies we integrate into our own culture, and the Fuzzies who develop their own culture and evolve naturally. Without us."

"That might be a problem with all those sunstones to attract illegal miners up north," Grego observed.

Jack shrugged. "We'll have to keep a police presence in that area until we can clean it out, Victor. In fact, you might consider setting up your Science Division Beta on the edge of the res up there."

Gerd agreed with that plan. "I'll be in a better position to study Fuzzies in their natural habitat. Complex, Syndrome, Id and Superego could act as liaisons between the Big Ones and the *Jin-f'ke*." Gerd remembered something. "Oh, wait, I can't leave here until my replacement is hired."

"Already done," Jack said. "Piet Dumont submitted his résumé. Frankly, he's better qualified for this job than either of us were. He starts next week. George Lunt already set up a private room for him in the barracks until he can get his own place."

"Sounds like you're off the hook, here, Gerd." Grego said. "I'll expect you to start work as soon as you finish training Piet. Now, what do we do about the sunstones at the dig site? I can't drop that many extra stones onto the market and I can't afford to pay royalties to the government for stones I can't sell. Even the Company has its limits."

"Bank them in the Colonial Reserve," Morgan said. "Most planets work on the gold standard, although Thor has a platinum standard and Loki a silver standard. We'll run on the sunstone standard and then we can print our own money."

"I notice you said 'we.' Planning on making Zarathustra your new home?" Gus said.

Morgan put an arm around Akira's shoulders. "Of course. I have to stick around so Jack will have a chance to spoil his grandchildren."

Akira looked stricken, then sly. She looked at Betty and Jack who both looked just as surprised. "Are you planning on starting a family soon, Morgan?"

"The sooner the better," Morgan said. "By Freyan standards, I am running behind schedule. Most families there get started before the wedded couples enter their twenties."

"Hmm…come outside with me for a moment." Akira stood up and dragged Morgan out the door.

"I wonder what that was about?" Ben said. "Doesn't Akira want children?"

Jack chuckled and said, "Wait for it."

The room went silent. After a moment Morgan's voice could be heard saying loudly, "You are?"

Jack nodded. "There it is."

The couple returned and Morgan announced that the next heir to the Holloway name was already on its way, in direct contravention of Freyan rules of etiquette. That called for a fresh drink all around.

"Hey, what is going to happen to Hugo Ingermann, or Ivan Dane, whatever his name is now?" Gerd asked.

"He'll be tried, convicted, and put before the firing squad," Gus said. "His properties will be seized as assets to his numerous crimes and auctioned off. Along with The Bitter End."

"No doubt of getting a conviction?" Morgan asked.

"None. We have Dr. Quigley's testimony recorded under veridication. Rankin and Darloss are also cooperating. Richard Lundgren will be turned over to the TFN."

"What? Why? And who is Richard Lundgren?" Grego asked.

Commodore Napier spoke up. "Lundgren is the one who bollixed up the CZC computer."

"So that's why Joe Verganno was having so much trouble with it," Grego observed. "But that's a civil matter, not military."

"He also…what was that word…hacked into the communications feed. That's how they tricked Governor Rainsford and Marshal Fane into believing that military transport that escorted Thaxter from prison came from us. And that is a military matter. We'll also try him on the civilian charges, of course."

"So he'll likely be executed, too," Grego said.

"Actually, no." Everybody looked at Pancho Ybarra. "Talent like that is rare. We'll allow him to cut a deal that will make him work for us. We can use people with his abilities. Naval intelligence is already planning what to do with him."

"Which isn't to say that he will get a free pass," Napier added. "He'll go through boot camp to teach him better manners, then work on base without regular liberty privileges and the only computers he will have access to will be strictly monitored. If he gets cute, he goes to the stockade."

"Hmm…he might prefer a bullet in the head to that," Jack said between puffs.

"Back to the properties," Morgan said, "I would like to buy them. I'll give you a far better price than you'll get at auction. I'll also take Ingermann's B.I.N. shares since the government can't legally own stock in a private company."

"What? Why?" Ben asked.

"Damn," Grego muttered. "Beaten to it again."

"The Bitter End seems like a good investment and I could have Thor run it for me. He mentioned that he hoped he could stay on Zarathustra and with him managing the place the need for bouncers will be practically non-existent."

"I'm in," Thor announced. "I'll still need a couple of bouncers for appearances, though."

Morgan continued, "As for B.I.N., well, I think I could do something with that as well, which is why I had a man at the stock exchange ready to buy up the stocks once the news hit. Ingermann's shares were frozen, but I now have enough for a working control. The name would have to go, of course. H.I.N., maybe."

Ben looked dubious until Grego added his two centi-sols. "Auctioning it off to parties unknown might bring in the same element we just removed." That sold Ben Rainsford on the idea.

"What's going to be done with the rocket?" Jack asked. "That damned thing has been a pain in my backside since it was discovered."

"Mine, too," Ben added. "Ingermann was trying to use it to bring down the colonial government."

"We'll transport it back to Terra where a herd of scientists will go over it atom by atom and determine its origin," Napier said. Clearly Victor Grego was keeping mum about the forgery being constructed, he thought, if Jack and Ben were still in the dark. In actual fact, the phony would go to Terra and the real rocket would be mothballed in a secret facility on an out-of-the-way planet.

"Since Science Division is through working with the *fuzzy gigantus* bones, why not put them in the Fuzzy museum?" Gerd said. "We don't have any modern Fuzzy skeletons to display since the Fuzzies find it to be too morbid. They hate taxidermy, too."

"I'm for it," Grego agreed. "Juan, if you're through with them, why not send a couple of sets to Gerd?"

Juan nodded. "I'll have the two most complete skeletons delivered first thing tomorrow. The two most complete sets are of a male and a female, so you can do an Adam and Eve type display, maybe."

"I don't make those types of decisions. The staff will get together and vote on it or something. That reminds me," Gerd said. "What happened to that recall vote business?"

Gus emptied his glass and accepted a refill of Freyan ale. "I had the petitions checked. They were full of graveyard signatures. Ingermann was padding the count using Old Chicago-style tactics. It only takes one phony John Hancock and the whole thing becomes invalid. There were at least three hundred dead citizens on that petition list. The colonial government is quite safe. I'm adding election fraud to the list of charges."

"So that's it, then? Life goes back to normal," Ruth said.

"Pretty much," Gus said. "Even the criminal underworld will

eventually generate a new clutch of bosses to keep me and the police busy. Spike Heenan is going away, too."

"No," Jack said. "There's one big difference. There are Fuzzies out there that neither need nor want Big Ones to take care of them. Fuzzies that don't need extee-three to breed viable offspring. Fuzzies that have a future all their own independent of us Big Ones. That is a very big difference, don't you think?"

That's the most important thing, Jack concluded. With everything that had happened over the past few months; the duel, Gus's abduction, the Fuzzy War—all that would be forgotten over time. But the Fuzzies would be around for a long time, maybe even after Terra was lost and forgotten by the race it spawned.

* * * * * * * * *

Little Fuzzy, Mama Fuzzy, Baby Fuzzy, Mike, Mitzy, Ko-ko and Cinderella talked among themselves in their new room. They discussed what Red Fur said and their own experiences with Pappy Jack and the other Big Ones. Much of what Red Fur said had made sense to them. Since meeting the Big Ones none of them were ever hungry or lonely or in danger from wild animals. The Fuzzies hunted if they felt like it or just ate the food the Big Ones provided. They could make arrows the way they were taught or just use the ones provided by Pappy Vic.

The names they used came from the Big Ones. They didn't even use their old names with each other. In the last few years the Fuzzies had learned much, like what a Pappy really was. Pappy Jack was like their father. He was Morgan's father. Morgan grew up to become a Big One that didn't need Pappy Jack to take care of him. Would the Fuzzies ever become like the Big Ones, not needing their help?

Yet, the Big Ones also taught them much. When Little Fuzzy was lost in the wilderness, he was able to survive using what he had learned from Pappy Jack, Pappy Gerd, Pappy George and other Big Ones. And Pappy Jack came out to find him and bring him home. Little Fuzzy's people could survive on their own, true, but they could survive better with what they had learned from the Big Ones. Maybe they would one day learn to work side-by-side with the Big Ones without being like children who needed to be watched and protected.

Little Fuzzy thought on that a long time before sleep took him.

The End

Acknowledgements

Where to start? A lot of people provided help and encouragement for me to finish this and the previous book. John F. Carr pushed me (or nagged, if you prefer) to get both books out in a timely manner and was the driving force to get them both into your hands.

I have to say something about my mother, or the next family reunion will be very long and uncomfortable (kidding!). She edited, commented, nagged, and then told all of her friends that I wrote the first book. Look, Ma, no hands! (Typing with feet hurts.)

Sharon Masonis, a good friend of mine, encouraged me to start the first book. She simply couldn't get enough of the Fuzzies and was thrilled at the idea that I would try to continue H. Beam Piper's work. She must have liked the first one, because she pushed for the second one in a hurry.

I have to mention Aunt Patricia, who has been subjected to my earlier works and still wanted to read my first published novel. Besides, she's a Texan and can probably out-shoot me, so I don't want to make her mad.

I think a writer is only as good as his editing team, so I would like to mention Mike Robertson, Fred Patten, Victoria Alexander, Dennis Frank, Larry Hopkins and Jonigirl (she knows who she is.).

At the time of this writing I learned that we lost another writer from the Piperverse, Ardeth Mayhar, who authored **Golden Dream: A Fuzzy Odyssey**. Her book followed the alternative third book **Fuzzy Bones** by William Tuning, who also left us too soon. May they both rest in peace.

For anybody I failed to mention, and there are a few, my thanks for your help and support.

Wolfgang Diehr

www.ingramcontent.com/pod-product-compliance
Lightning Source LLC
Chambersburg PA
CBHW030826310726
48980CB00006B/660/J

* 9 7 8 0 9 3 7 9 1 2 2 2 5 *